HYLOZOIC

RUDY RUCKER

HYLOZOIC

A TOM DOHERTY ASSOCIATES BOOK
NEW YORK

This is a work of fiction. All of the characters, organizations, and events portrayed in this novel are either products of the author's imagination or are used fictitiously.

HYLOZOIC

A Tor Book
Published by Tom Doherty Associates, LLC
175 Fifth Avenue
New York, NY 10010

www.tor-forge.com

Tor® is a registered trademark of Tom Doherty Associates, LLC.

Library of Congress Cataloging-in-Publication Data

Rucker, Rudy v. B. (Rudy von Bitter), 1946–
    Hylozoic / Rudy Rucker. — 1st ed.
        p.   cm.
    "A Tom Doherty Associates book."
    ISBN-13: 978-0-7653-2074-2
    ISBN-10: 0-7653-2074-6
    I. Title.
    PS3568.U298H96   2009
    813'.54—dc22

                                        2008053399

First Edition: June 2009

Printed in the United States of America

0 9 8 7 6 5 4 3 2 1

For Georgia, Rudy, and Isabel

ACKNOWLEDGMENTS

The chicken on the ladder in chapter ten, "Ergot," is from my friend Paul Mavrides.

A draft version of chapter eleven, "Hieronymus Bosch's Apprentice," appeared in *Flurb* No. 4, September 2007.

In chapter seventeen, "The Maelstrom," I've appropriated some phrases from Edgar Allan Poe's masterpiece, *The Narrative of Arthur Gordon Pym of Nantucket*, and from his shorter tale, "A Descent into the Maelström." Thanks, Eddy!

CONTENTS

Hylozoism (from the Greek *hyle,* matter, and *zoe,* life) is the doctrine that all matter is instrinsically alive. Under hylozoism, every object is claimed to have some degree or sense of life.

—David Skrbina, *Panpsychism in the West*

HYLOZOIC

CHAPTER 1

AFTER EVERYTHING WOKE UP

Jayjay awoke beside Thuy; comfortably he molded himself against her. Early sunlight filtered in through the redwoods. The newlyweds were in sleeping bags on the forest floor beneath a tree. They'd teleported here to install their home. It was the first of May.

A big blue Steller's jay perched on a jiggly thin branch overhead, cocking his head. Jayjay teeped stealthily into the bird's mind. He savored the gentle jouncing of the branch, the minute adjustments of the jay's strong claws, the breeze in his comfortable plumage; he chirped contentedly, *Chook-chook-chook-chook,* then inhaled through the nostrils of his fine black beak, relishing the smells of fruit and flesh, studying the promising scraps on the ground, assessing the large creatures beside the mound of goods; but now, *Kwaawk kwaawk kwaawk,* one of the big animals moved her limbs. The jay released the branch, glided free, and flapped to the next tree. *Kwaawk kwaawk.*

"Kwaawk," echoed Thuy. "That's his name."

"All the others have that name, too?" said Jayjay.

"Yeah, but each of them says it differently." Thuy turned to face Jayjay, giving him a kiss. "I can't believe we own this piece of land. What does that even mean? We handed over our money so that a record somewhere says, 'Property of Jorge Jimenez and Thuy Nguyen.' But there's so many plants and animals already living here, and if you count the other silps too—it's an empire."

"I hope they don't resent us."

"Those nice smooth rocks by the stream like us fine," said Thuy. "Teep into them. See how eager they are to be in our foundation walls? They like the idea of being mortared together, and of rising above the ground. Beating gravity is a big deal for a rock!"

"You're *my* big deal," said Jayjay, teeping Thuy teeping him teeping her. The first few times that they'd telepathically mirrored each other, they'd felt themselves tobogganing toward the point-attractor of a cerebral seizure. Fortunately, you could always shut off your telepathy. With practice, Jayjay and Thuy had learned to skate around the singular zones, enjoying the bright, ragged layers of feedback—well, Jayjay enjoyed this more than Thuy. Not too long ago, he'd been addicted to merging with the planetary mind called the Big Pig. He liked head trips.

After a little more mind play, Thuy gently pushed Jayjay away. She was smiling, with her eyebrows optimistically arched. Her longish black hair hung loose, her pink lips were delicately curved. Hanging a few feet above her was a Stank shampoo ad. Thuy and Jayjay made their living as 'round-the-clock members of a reality show called *Founders*. But they'd learned to ignore the ad icons and—above all—the vast worldwide audience. If you were doing something really private, you could always turn off your teep. But fewer and fewer things seemed private enough to bother hiding.

"You really think we can teleport a whole house this far?" asked Thuy.

"Sure," said Jayjay. "Working alone, you and I can't teek much more than a couple of hundred kilograms at a time. But with a dozen of our friends pitching in, for sure we can move our little house here from San Francisco. We'll build the foundation today, and this evening—*alley-oop!*—we drop our cozy nest into place. Housewarming party!"

They'd already brought bags of sand and cement for the foundation, also a big flat pan for mixing the mortar, a mortar hoe to mix it with, plus a pair of mortarboards and trowels. Jayjay liked tools, and had managed to borrow these via the human mindweb. The silps in the tools were stoked about the coming job.

"It's gonna be hard moving all those stones for the foundation," grumbled Thuy. "It's so peaceful here in the woods. I feel like lying around and thinking up a beautiful scene for my new metanovel. Or teeping with animals. Isn't this supposed to be our honeymoon?"

"We can teleport the stones instead of carrying them. Teek 'em."

"That's work, too. When I reach out and remotely teleport a rock—I bet my brain wattage shoots up to a thousand."

"It isn't just your *brain* that does the teeking," said Jayjay. "We think with our whole bodies. Consciousness is everywhere."

"Whatever," said Thuy. "I'm just not ready to move hundreds of stones."

"Aw, come on, Thuy," said Jayjay. "When we were in high

school, you were always the goody-goody, not me. You're the ant and I'm the grasshopper. And the grasshopper's rarin' to go! Leap!"

"Put that stale rap away," said Thuy. "It's been a long time since I was an ant. I'm all grown up now. I'm every bit as wild a kiq as you." She rolled toward her knapsack and dug out some dried fruit. "It's too bad the rocks can't teleport themselves. Then we could just, like, teep out invitations and they'd all show up."

"Actually we're lucky that animals and plants and objects can't teleport," said Jayjay.

"I guess so," said Thuy. "Otherwise Kwaawk the bluejay would be eating these raisins instead of me. And if flames could teleport? They'd eat the whole world. I wonder if Gaia is actively preventing the lower orders from teleporting."

"I don't think it's Gaia's doing," said Jayjay. He'd been one of the first to figure out teleportation, and he liked to hold forth about it. "The ability to teleport is peculiar to the human mind. Rats and roaches are too carefree to fuzz out and teleport. Over the millennia, we humans have evolved toward thinking ourselves into spots where we're not. It's all about remorse, doubt, and fear. As for intelligent objects—sure the silps can talk, but they don't have our rich heritage of hang-ups: our regrets about the past, our unease about the present, our anxiety about the future. Humans are used to spreading themselves across a zillion worlds of downer what-ifs. That's why we can teleport."

"Depresso mongo," said Thuy. "Remorse, doubt, and fear? That's all you see in your life? How about gratitude for the things that worked out—like, ahem, marrying me! What about curiosity? What about hope for a sunny tomorrow? Happy what-ifs."

"Let's get back to the rocks," said Jayjay, in retreat. "Even though they can't teleport, they can tell us about their balance points. And whether they're a good match for their neighbors."

"I can just hear them," said Thuy. "Lay me now, mortar-forker!" She liked speaking extravagantly. It was a way of rebelling against her prim upbringing. "Trowel my crack!" She got to her feet to rummage deeper in her backpack, then pulled on her striped tights and a long-sleeved yellow T-shirt.

A great shaft of sun slanted into their woodsy glen, with gnats and dust motes hovering in the light. A friendly breeze caressed the newlyweds and stirred the needles on the trees. Kwaawk the blue jay squawked.

"Everything sees us," marveled Jayjay, putting on his baggy black pants and his green T-shirt. "Everything is alive. I like seeing inside Kwaawk's head. I think—if I wasn't a human—maybe I'd be a blue jay, or, no, I'd be a crow. They're so smart and tough."

"I'd be a dragon," said Thuy, filling her mouth full of nuts and chocolate. She continued her rap via teep. "Dragons are one thing my parents talked about that I really loved. The Vietnamese dragons aren't fat fire-breathers, you know. They're skinny crocodiles with snaky curves and fringed all over. Punk dragons. I'd be a dragon playing heavy rock and roll." Thuy paused to swallow her food. "I just noticed that a water spirit here doesn't like us. The silp in this stretch of the creek."

The mind within the narrow, burbling stream was what earlier generations would have called a genius loci, or "spirit of place." Far from being a superstition-spawned fantasy, the silp was quite real. Silps were emergent intelligences based upon chaotic natural computations as enhanced by the ubiquitous memory storage available via the recently unfurled eighth dimension. Silps were everywhere now.

Jayjay wasn't quite sure how to address the unfriendly spirit of the stream. But Thuy plowed right ahead.

"Hi Gloob," she said, eating another handful of gorp. "What if my husband and I build you a tiny little dam? You'll get a nice waterfall at the downstream edge, with some brook trout in the pool. We can bathe there."

"Gloob?" said Jayjay, smiling at Thuy. "Husband? You're like Eve in Eden. Naming the creatures."

"Gloob really *is* his name," said Thuy. "You just have to listen. Like this." She teeped him a mental maneuver she'd invented for converting a silp's self-image to an English name.

Jayjay listened inwardly to the crabby spirit of the stream, and, yes, Thuy was right, his name was Gloob. Gloob overlaid an image upon his eddies and lines of flow, the visage of a stern old man with trembling cheeks and curly beard. He didn't like the idea of a dam.

The friendly rocks at the stream's edge had names too: Clack, Bonk, Rollie, and Harvey. And the redwood overhead— her name was Grew. Unlike Gloob, Grew was happy to have Jayjay and Thuy as neighbors. Mammals were good for fertilizing her roots.

"But don't burrow!" cautioned Grew.

Intrigued by his newly learned ability to name the silps, Jayjay teeped into the aethereal chorus of atoms that made up his body. Each of his ten octillion atomic silps had its own distinct timbre. If he'd had the patience, he could have started converting the timbres into names to be stored in his lazy eight memory. But there were still practical limits to the sizes of mental feats that a person could do. An octillion steps was at the very edge of what you could expect to carry out in your head, even if you were as obsessive as Thuy's young friend Chu.

Teeping a bit higher up the great chain of being, Jayjay perceived the names of his organs and muscles. Larry Liver. Ben Bone. They'd still be talking after he died. At least for a while.

Gloob's scowling ropy face kept hovering in his mind's eye.

Jayjay walked over and took a pee near the stream, not right into it, but close enough to show Gloob who was boss. The little crests of the stream's riffles writhed. On the telepathic plane, Gloob was gibbering in fury. Jayjay pinched shut the channel connecting him to the angry silp. Bye, Gloob. That was one of the things that made lazy eight telepathy bearable. You could firewall things out.

"I say we build our foundation right here," Thuy said, scratching lines in the dirt with a shovel. She was telepathically comparing her marks to the dimensions of the two-room wooden cottage that she and Jayjay had put together in San Francisco.

Jayjay picked up a shovel of his own. "Perfect spot," he told Thuy. "It's flat, the light's good, and it's not too close to—to the stream. We'll scrape out little trenches for the cement mudsills."

Teeping into the Gaian overmind, Jayjay and Thuy viewed Earth's gravitational field as wiggly orange lines growing out of the ground. Helpful Gaia marked off equal elevation points on the lines, making it easy to see when the ditches were level and true.

"I'll mix the mortar!" said Thuy when the digging was done. "You get the stones."

Jayjay teeped one of stones he'd noticed before: Harvey. Harvey was the size and shape of a flattened cantaloupe. It would have been easy enough to walk over and pick him up. But Jayjay wanted to show off.

Teleportation was a head trick you played on yourself. You perfectly visualized two locations, got mixed up about which was which, then switched to being there instead of here.

When Jayjay had first discovered how to teleport—about six months ago—he'd quickly learned how to carry objects along. And recently he'd figured out that he could teleport things without having to move himself at all. This was telekinesis, called teek for short.

Teeking Harvey was a matter of merging into the rock's silpmind and coaxing it into a superposed quantum state in which the rock was both beside the stream and resting in the clearing. And then Jayjay asked the rock-mind, "Where are you?" precipitating a quantum collapse that put Harvey beside the foundation ditches they'd grubbed out.

Sitting in the clearing, staring at the spot where he was bringing the rock, Jayjay first saw a few twinkling dots in the air, then a ghost of the stone, and then the rock itself.

"Oho," said Harvey. His voice in Jayjay's head was orotund. "Not the kind of thing I'd do on my own. That fuzzy bit in the middle—how did we manage that?"

"You can watch me move your cousins," said Jayjay. "But you won't ever figure it out."

"Never mind," said Harvey. "I'll just sit here. It's good in the dirt." No guru could ever be as mellow and nonattached as a stone.

Over the next half hour, Jayjay lined up Rollie, Bonk, and Clack next to Harvey, along with another few hundred of their cousins from the edges of the stream. The rapid flipping between pure and superposed quantum states was making him queasy. He took a break, dropping to the ground next to Thuy.

Thuy had set up her big mortar pan in middle of where their living room would be. She'd carried some buckets of water from the creek and was rocking away with her mortar hoe— it was like a regular hoe except that it had two holes in the blade, the better to stir the water, sand, and cement.

"Remember, this is a special fast-drying waterproof mix," Thuy warned. "We better start spreading it around. Up and at 'em, grasshopper."

"I'm tired of teeking."

"So use your beautiful bod. I've got a bucket for scooping up mortar. I'm gonna mix a little more so there's enough for the whole first course of stones."

Stepping around the waiting stones, Jayjay lugged buckets of mortar by hand, laying down thick gouts of the gray cement. And then he and Thuy got on their knees and began setting the stones, using trowels and carrying little mounds of mortar on the flat square mortarboards.

The smooth stones were somewhat disk-shaped. Jayjay and Thuy set them upright on their thin edges, like rows of books. The stones helped out, teeping among themselves to decide who would fit best against whom. Some were smaller than others. Where necessary, Jayjay and Thuy mortared in extra stones to keep the top edge approximately level. All this took longer than expected, and the mortar was nearly dry by the time the base course was done.

"Now we can rest, huh?" said Thuy.

"Yeah," said Jayjay. "Let's eat those sandwiches I brought."

"Vibby," said Thuy. "Sorry I was rushing you with the mortar."

"Well, I'm the one who made us get up too early. You just wanted to lie in your sleeping bag and write." Jayjay hugged her. "Let's start over."

"I'd like that."

They ate their sandwiches, laid down, and made love. One flesh. Cozy as could be, they fell asleep for an hour. And then Thuy woke up.

"All our little friends are waiting for us," she said, nudging Jayjay. "And I'm not talking about the *Founders* audience."

Jayjay lay there, savoring Thuy's shape and sound and smell.

All around them, listening in, were the pullulating silps—in the pine needles, the sleeping bags, the dirt, and the currents of the air; in his hair, his muscles, and his molecules—silps without and within.

"I like having the big Gaia worldsoul," said Thuy. "But I get tired of all these tiny, pushy, minds."

"It's all good," said Jayjay. "Human minds used to be rare fireflies in the dark. But now everything is conscious—lit up. It's like day instead of night. Look over there—our foundation wall already has a silp of its own."

The mind in the low wall was something more than the minds of the individual rocks. She was reveling in her rectangularity. She was happy to know she would soon grow a little higher. Might she ask how soon would that be?

"Oh shut up," Thuy told the wall.

Jayjay and Thuy cuddled a bit more, while Thuy thought about her metanovel. And then it was back to work. Jayjay fetched a bucket of water from the creek. He was still blocking out Gloob's telepathy vibes, but he couldn't help notice that, by taking so many rocks, he'd made an ugly bare muddy spot.

Gloob's domain only extended about five meters in either direction, but other silps lived upstream and downstream: there was a separate silp for each little pool, cataract and bend. No point alienating these neighbors, too. In order to quickly search farther afield for building materials. Jayjay reached for mental contact with Gaia, the summit of the planet's hierarchy of minds.

He saw an Earth globe with jungle lips, canyon nostrils, ocean eyes, cloudy hair, and—floppy pig ears. The new Gaian mind had based her human interface upon the former orphidnet mind that had been called the Big Pig.

The round face winked, sneezed, and inhaled, creating a

wobbly vortex that drew Jayjay through the vasty caves of her nose holes into the interior of a virtual space demarcated by great smooth walls of living green tissue. It was like being a gnat inside a pitcher plant. Pale green pistils swung through the information matrix like snakes; each pistil's fuzzy triangular top formed a rudimentary face with two eyes and a snout.

"Aha," said a pistil, addressing Jayjay one-on-one. "It's you again."

As always, plugging into the global mind was getting Jayjay high. Gaia was brimming over with astute perceptions woven into crystalline truths mounded into white-light peaks and philosophical castles. Each time Jayjay came here, it required a distinct effort to stop himself from merging into Gaia for hours at a time. Those addicted to this style of ecstasy were known as pigheads.

Thuy hated it when Jayjay went mentally missing—last year she'd dropped him because of that. Nowadays he worked to manage his habit, not only to keep Thuy, but also in reaction to a hideous overdose experience he'd had three months ago. He'd merged into the overmind for six hours and it had literally seemed to last sixty years. He was still digging himself out from under the strata of false memories he'd accumulated during that session. Sometimes he felt like he was eighty years old.

Carefully keeping his focus, Jayjay told Gaia he was looking for flat rocks nearby. The triangular face bobbed gently, then spat out a glowing acorn. It was a locative hyperlink to the natural world.

Resisting the temptation to stay there enjoying the Gaian buzz, Jayjay dropped down to ordinary consciousness and mentally followed the acorn's link. He found himself in teep contact with a slate cliff beside a river in the very forest where he was building his home. The cliff's name was Herga. Thousands of jagged dark gray plates of slate lay at Herga's base. Not wanting to make another enemy, he asked the cliff if he might take some of her loose stones.

"I treasure every one of them," teeped Herga in a whispery tone. "But it's okay. I shed fresh slate every spring."

Physically still in the clearing with Thuy, Jayjay teeked one of the cliff's stones to lie by his feet. It was a rough-hewn little guy called Camber. Camber was proud to announce that he carried six trilobite fossils within himself; the trilobites piped up to agree. Camber also pointed out that his edges made up a jagged polygon of thirty-seven sides. He was perfectly amenable to being mortared into the foundation's sill course.

"Just so I feel a little breeze," he rasped.

Jayjay set Camber in place. Well and good.

And now it was nearly time for the giant blast of telekinesis needed to fetch the rest of the stones. But, wait, Jayjay's body was talking to him, asking for food. He ate a dark chocolate bar and, for good measure, he chewed up some roasted coffee beans.

"Are you bringing more rocks?" prodded Thuy.

Jayjay got to work, teeking a couple of hundred of Camber's relatives in the space of five minutes. Near the end of the teeking frenzy, the ground near the distant cliff starting looking oddly smooth—perhaps Jayjay was being too greedy, and the cliff's silp-mind Herga was teep-shielding her slates from him. Increasingly weary, working around the strange smooth patch for the last few stones, Jayjay momentarily lost track of what he was doing and almost mistook his own head for a rock, very nearly teeking it off his shoulders and across the clearing. *Ow.* He stopped. Enough rocks.

"You're wonderful!" exclaimed Thuy, looking at the pile of slate.

Although Jayjay felt like curling up in a ball and hugging himself, he squared his shoulders and smiled. He wanted to keep up appearances for his bride. He got busy laying the slates flat atop the base course of creek stones.

As before, the mortar was drying a little too fast. Thuy scolded it. The mortar said it would do what it could to slow down its crystallization. Silp-minds had some slight control over the qubits of their innate quantum computations.

Jayjay worked the masonry, staying in close telepathic contact with his trowel. As he neared the end of one wall, he noticed a piece of slate that needed to be rotated an inch so that the course would come out even. He stuck his trowel into the crack between the stones, twisting it and pushing on the slate with his hand. The trowel and the slate were giving him good, steady mental feedback.

But now all at once everything got confused. The trowel wriggled out of the crack and sprang to one side, stabbing a deep gash into the ball of Jayjay's thumb. Chanting a solemn dirge, his blood oozed forth, thick and dark. Dropping his stoic facade, Jayjay cried out in fear and pain.

"Oh, poor Jayjay!" exclaimed Thuy. She fetched a clean handkerchief to press against the wound.

Meanwhile, the trowel was apologizing to Jayjay. "He pushed me," teeped the trowel in a narrow, triangular voice. "He meddled."

"Who?" demanded Jayjay.

"Gloob. The silp from the stream."

"We'll worry about Gloob later," interrupted Thuy. "First let's teep into your tissues, Jayjay, and I'll help you heal."

Jayjay delved down into his thumb to see the frantic hugger-mugger of his platelets, phagocytes, and dermal cells—with Thuy's lithe mindweb avatar glowing to one side.

"I can play traffic cop," said Thuy. "Directing your nutrients and white blood cells to your wound. You can get a thousandfold improvement over just letting the cells and molecules bumble along. I learned about the technique because Nektar was helping Chu fix that underdeveloped spot in his brain tissue. You've noticed how he's more sociable now, haven't you?"

"I guess," said Jayjay distractedly. "Don't go goosing my cells too hard. I don't want to flip them into cancer-tumor mode."

"Don't worry," said Thuy. "All I'll be doing is herding them. Leave it to me."

"Fine," said Jayjay and tuned out, relaxing into the human-scale world. Thuy had one arm around him, and with the other she was pressing the handkerchief against his hand, with her eyes unfocused. He looked around, wanting to distract himself.

Their foundation wall was nearly done. The sun was in the west now, slowly turning gold. A good day's work. A fine first of May. The redwoods swayed and sighed, the creek chuckled. Jayjay was feeling a tingle at the base of his thumb.

Jayjay reopened his telepathic contact with the stream silp. They had to talk. Gloob was scowling and tense—ready for the worst. Like everyone else, Gloob had lazy eight omnividence, that is, the ability to see everything on Earth. Gloob well knew how nasty humans could be.

Jayjay felt a blip of empathy for the unhappy silp—and he decided to end the feud. As a human, it was up to him to exercise the higher emotions.

"I'm sorry I pissed so close to your bank," he told Gloob. "I'm sorry I took so many rocks. And Thuy and I don't really have to make a dam. Let's be friends."

Gloob gleamed and grew smooth. "Maybe. If you behave." The silp paused. "About that dam—do you really think I'd get trout?" He spoke not so much in words as in pictures.

"You bet," said Jayjay, telepathically pointing out some minnows just upstream.

"And—do you think you could dig a proper latrine?" added Gloob. "On the uphill side of Grew?"

"Sure," said Jayjay. "And our house will have a nanoseptic system, with nothing but compost and pure water coming out." Gloob made a cheerful gurgling sound. The war was over.

"Behold!" said Thuy, gently pulling away the handkerchief. Jayjay's wound was healed, a pink line in his skin.

"You're amazing, Thuy."

"Come on in and splash off!" called merry Gloob.

With light hearts, Thuy and Jayjay romped in the stream for a while. And then it was back to work.

It only took another half hour to finish smoothing out the foundation wall. The mortar set up as hard as stone.

"Let's teleport our love nest now!" exclaimed Thuy. "We've still got an hour till sunset."

"It'll definitely take a dozen of us to move so much mass at once," said Jayjay. "And it'll work best if we're all pushing from the same spot. What if we gather in Ond's driveway, right where we assembled the house. You, me, Ond, Jil, Bixie, Momotaro, Nektar, Kittie, Chu, Darlene, Craigor, and Sonic. You want to help round them up?"

"*You* round up Sonic," said Thuy. "He'll be spaced as usual, you'll have to go there in person. For the others, it'll be enough to teep them. Meanwhile, I'll get my dad. He wants to help—even though my mother's against it."

Thuy's voice always got tight and high when she talked about her mother. The two of them had never gotten along well, and now that Minh had been crippled by a stroke, things were even worse.

"It's like Mom thinks you're still the same bad boy you were in high school," Thuy continued. "I can't forgive her for not coming to our little ceremony at city hall. It would have been the one last nice thing we could have done together. And now she lies there dissing you and pissing the bed. I'm terrible not to feel sorry for her."

"Don't beat yourself up," said Jayjay with a shrug. "*My* mother showed up at our wedding stoned, cried her head off, and asked for money. Whatever. Life is about moving on. You and me, Thuy, we're the only family that matters now."

"Daddy will be heartbroken if I leave him out tonight. He gets so sad and lonely staying home nursing Mom all the time. And she's always such a—"

"So go get your father already," interrupted Jayjay. "And, look Thuy, be patient with your mother today. Even if you don't want to do it for her—do it for you. You'll feel better about yourself."

"You're nice to give me good advice," said Thuy, hugging Jayjay's arm. "I'm glad to have someone who cares about my daily drama."

"I'm lucky to have you," said Jayjay, embracing her. "You make life worth living."

"We're married, Jayjay, we're really married. Do you feel old?"

"Ever since my pighead OD, I feel about eighty."

"Oh, stop that. I'm glad you've stopped tweaking on Gaia all the time."

They kissed and, just for a goof, Thuy teleported to her parents' house, right in the middle of the kiss. She grew translucent, then spectral, and dissolved in a cloud of twinkling dots. Jayjay ran his fingers through the air. Without his wife's lively presence, the teeming woods felt empty.

Or—maybe not. Two odd shapes were bumbling around in the high branches of Grew the redwood. A pair of stray paper kites? All the way out here? No, no, these things were moving on their own, undulating through the air. They were like large leather pillows, flat and fat, with slitty mouths and golden eyes.

Oddly, they were impervious to teep. Although Jayjay could see them with his eyes, he couldn't probe into them with his mind.

He made a series of wild guesses about what the beings were. The simplest hypothesis was that he was so tired from his wall-building that he was seeing things. Or perhaps Gloob the creek silp was putting these images into his mind?

But they really seemed to have some physicality to them. Might the shapes be woodland air current silps, bending the light so as to appear solid? Maybe the whole grove was conspiring to scare the settlers away?

The shapes were slowly spiraling down from the tree as if homing in on Jayjay, who was very conscious of being the only human within miles of here. As the forms drew closer, Jayjay began to see them as flying stingrays—with odd patterns of dots on their skins. Might they be hydrogen-filled sea creatures? Mutants?

Whatever they were, he didn't want to face them alone. With a quick effort of his will, he teleported to San Francisco.

CHAPTER 2

MOVING THE HOUSE

Jayjay landed in the Mission district, right outside the building where his friend Sonic rented a room. A quick scan of the neighborhood revealed no more flying manta rays. Already they seemed like a bad dream.

Sonic's crummy old building lacked a working door buzzer, so Jayjay just teeped within. He could see Sonic lying on his couch with his soft pet robot on his chest, his crammed room lit by a candle. Money was still a reality on postsingular Earth—and Sonic never had much of it. Jayjay made a quick attempt to teleport into Sonic's pad, but the apartment's air decohered Jayjay's vibe, not letting him form the crystal-clear realtime image of the place that he would have needed in order to hop in. Assuming that a person was on good terms with their local silps, the silps could block out telepathy, teleportation, or both.

"Hey," Jayjay messaged to Sonic. "Tell your silps to let me in." Sonic didn't seem to hear the message. His mind was elsewhere. Jayjay followed the strand of Sonic's attention to a pod of elephant seals bellowing in the surf off Año Nuevo north of Santa Cruz. The bulls were fighting for the right to mate, slashing away with their tusks, bloodying one another's necks and snouts. Each of the bull seals had a person's mind tracking it, each player was trying to help one particular behemoth come up with winning moves. It was an all-natural video game, a guided entertainment that Sonic had set up.

"Sonic!" repeated Jayjay, giving the message more force. "I want to come see you!"

Leaving his customers on their own for the nonce, Sonic opened his eyes and told his room to let Jayjay in.

"Whuff," said Jayjay, materializing in his old pal's lair, the worn wood floor crunchy with city grit. Boxes and boxes of junk lined the walls.

"Fuffo," answered Sonic. One of their jokey old greetings. The sounds of voices drifted in the open rear window, accompanied by the scent of garbage. Sonic looked run-down.

"You do remember about helping me move my house, right?" said Jayjay.

"I remember everything," said Sonic. "Every detail. It's paying attention that's hard." The people in the alley were arguing about whose turn it was to teek the garbage to the dump.

"I saw something creepy at our house site just now," said Jayjay. "These two shapes like stingrays flying down through the redwoods. Six feet across, easy."

"Did you talk to them?" asked Sonic.

"I was scared. Anyway, teeping with them didn't work. They weren't showing up in my teep at all."

"Maybe they weren't real," said Sonic, losing interest.

"Maybe," said Jayjay, shaking off the memory. "Let's not

mention them to Thuy. She's got enough to worry about. Let's talk about those elephant seals you were looking at. I've been hearing good things about the Sonic's Animal Animats tours."

"My biz," said Sonic, absently fondling his shoon, Edgar. "I steer my clients to the finest bestial doings. My customer base is the same newbs and goobs that went for my video game tutoring sessions. Back when video games mattered. Now everything's organic. Last week I embedded my clients into this epic war between red ants and black ants. It was hill versus hill. Those ants are frikkin' pitiless." Sonic rubbed his greasy face and yawned. "I'm making the nut. Only thing is, I'm online too much. I don't think I ate today yet."

"I'll buy you a burrito," said Jayjay. "We've got the time."

"Okay," said Sonic. "But first let me finish out this game."

"How many times have I heard that?"

"I gotta bring the seal-sex safari to a climax for my customers," explained Sonic. "But first I give 'em a big scare. That's why I get return biz and good ratings. Sonic's Animal Animats always kicks it up a notch. Last week in the middle of our ant war, I helped the red ants bring in an anteater. Devastating. And for today's rush, I've got a great white shark offshore." Sonic paused and mimed huge biting motions. His pet shoon robot, Edgar, imitated him, flexing his little body into a fishlike form.

"Even as we speak, I'm helping the shark notice the abundant prey," Sonic told Jayjay. "*Beat* your tail, whitey. *Eat* them blubbery mofos."

Jayjay teeped along, watching a ghostly, scarred shark come arrowing in toward the bloodied elephant seal bulls. The players riding the seals saw the shark from far away; it was the size of a rowboat. They sent their bulls wallowing up onto the beach— just in the nick of time. Some female elephant seals had gathered around, drawn by the roaring and the gore. They were keyed up and primed to mate. Weary of battle, the bulls elected to share the cows. A pinniped orgy began.

"You're all winners!" Sonic messaged to his charges. "I gotta bail. Giant squid versus sperm whales tomorrow!"

And then he was focused on Jayjay, all there, his brown eyes warm. Good old Sonic.

"Taquería now," said Sonic.

"Sure," said Jayjay. "Hey, before we go—how about you splash off in the shower? That way you'll make better company."

"Listen to my old running buddy," said Sonic, shaking his head. "He's turned priss. Like you don't remember when you and me and Thuy and Kittie were the Big Pig Posse—sleeping in hallways and cars?"

This said, Sonic went to clean himself up, picking his way among his dusty piles of mementos, little Edgar dogging his steps. And then the two guys teleported to the nearby Taquería Aztlán, one of the best. The inside of the restaurant was teleport-blocked to prevent pilfering, but just outside the entrance, a steady flow of early dinner customers were popping in and out of visibility, the air crowded with the twinkling dots and spectral forms of people in the process of solidifying or melting away.

These heavily trafficked spots were a little freaky; like a speeded-up ghost movie. Jayjay bumped heavily into a woman as they arrived—but fortunately the laws of physics blocked them from materializing in the exact same spot. You didn't have to worry about ending up with, like, the head of a house-fly or the legs of an old man.

"You teep how eager this burrito is for me to eat it?" said Sonic after they'd gotten their food. Their dishes were exactly as they'd visualized them—telepathic ordering was more reliable than spoken words. "The cooks here, they've got a way with ingredients," continued Sonic. "Inca and Aztec shamans, no doubt." He glanced over at Jayjay. "Thanks for treating, by the way. *Founders* is paying you good?

"You watch the show?"

"Yeah," said Sonic. He paused, chewing his food. "I teep into Gaia every night. It's glowy to be talking to you face-to-face again. The star."

"People are curious about me and Thuy because we're the ones who unrolled the lazy eight dimension this winter. But you could you could be in the show if you wanted to. My colorful friend."

"Stank Grooming Products," read Sonic, staring into the space above Jayjay's head. "BigBox Home Furnishings. Huffin Psi Secure. So bogus. What if our whole planet is an ad for the creatures of the subdimensions? What if the subbies are displaying us to attract intergalactic UFOs?"

"Hate to say this, Sonic, but you sound spun."

"That's because I'm so heavy into the all-new overmind. Gaia is much vaster than the Big Pig ever was. And trippier. Even my silps get high: my body and my organs and my cells. But I have to be careful. If your atomic silps get stoned enough, your molecules fall apart. The atoms are, like, 'Screw this H-two-O hassle, we just wanna be two Hs and an O.' *Floop!*" Sonic let out a dark, resonant chuckle. "Ace Weston, remember him? I fell by his room last week and there was a pile of soot in his bed. Carbon and trace elements. The oxygen, hydrogen, and nitrogen had drifted away."

"Did you really see that?" demanded Jayjay. "Or dream it? I've never heard of anything like that."

"Take a look. I'm an open book."

Jayjay probed into Sonic's memories—and promptly got lost. Packrat that Sonic was, he'd saved all of the details of his Gaian visions. The ubiquitous lazy eight memory upgrade had no size limits at all. Finding something in Sonic's memory was hopeless; it was like combing the entire surface of the Earth.

"Black dust," repeated Sonic. "Didn't even stink." He finished his burrito, wiped his mouth, and pushed Jayjay out of his head. "I've got a memory stash like I'm ten thousand years old, huh? I'm on the nod every night. I love it."

"What if *your* molecules come apart, too?"

"Gaia will remember me, dog. Dig this—the good thief on the cross said, 'Lord, remember me when thou comest into thy kingdom,' and Jesus went, 'Verily I say unto you, today shalt thou be with me in paradise.' Meaning that heaven is a memory bank. Those whom Gaia loves are immortal." Sonic drained his bottle of beer. "So anyway, I'm ready to move your cabin. We're grouping at Ond's?"

"You sure you're together enough?"

"Yea verily," said Sonic. "Let's hop."

They landed on the patio behind Ond's new monster house, overlooking San Francisco from a hillside in Dolores Heights. The new mansion was squeezed in next to Ond's old mansion, where his ex-wife Nektar still lived. The building crew had erected the second home in a month, making the most of their ability to talk to the materials.

The hilltop was pleasantly gilded by the late afternoon sun. Jayjay could see the Golden Gate Bridge and a sliver of the fog-shrouded Pacific. At the far end of the patio, graceful Jil Zonder was skipping from side to side with her arms outstretched, her lustrous dark hair bobbing. She was leading a dance class for a dozen of the soft plastic shoon robots. They were cute little guys, almost like living cartoons.

Jil had built up a nice business marketing shoons: she bought slugs of piezoplastic, trained the lumps to act like helpful dwarves, and sold them. People used shoons as toys, pets, household servants, and specialized workers. The silps in the plastic cooperated without complaint. Not having undergone millennia of evolutionary struggle to survive, silps weren't especially ambitious.

"Moving day?" said Jil, pausing to smile at Jayjay. She seemed to be glowing with health and good humor, but with Jil you never quite knew. She had a lot of inner demons. Last winter she'd suffered a harrowing relapse into sudocoke addiction, and her marriage had broken up.

Jayjay had played a part in that breakup; he and this desirable older woman had shared a brief, passionate affair—quite the hit on the *Founders* show. But now Jil seemed clean and calm again, comfortably settled in with Ond—a well-known nanotech engineer who'd admired her for years. Ond had been more or less responsible for setting the singularity and its aftershocks in motion. But the public had forgiven him for it. Things were going good.

A knobby, raw-looking teenage boy appeared, moving in stroboscopic hops. Momotaro, Jil's son. Close behind him were his younger sister Bixie and, taking up the rear, Ond's fourteen-year-old son Chu, all three of them pulsing in and out of visibility. Their trajectories were like dashed lines with the end of each dash shading into invisibility.

"Teleport. Stutter. Tag!" yelled Momotaro in his cracking voice, melting away and reappearing between each utterance.

"We. Aren't. Allowed. To run," called Bixie, who resembled a smaller, more delicate Jil.

"Only. Hop. One. Meter," added Chu, as he strobed toward them, filling the air with the sparkle of materialization dots.

"They've been doing this all day," said Jil with a sigh. "I keep telling them to save their energy for moving Jayjay and Thuy's cabin, but—"

"We. Never. Listen!" whooped Bixie.

Just then Chu managed to thump Momotaro in the middle of the back. "You're it!"

"Shoon war!" cried Momotaro, diving onto Jil's phalanx of robots, who began working him over like puppies worrying an older dog. Bixie cackled and joined him. Chu stood frowning to the side.

"Catch," said Bixie, tossing one of the shoons Chu's way. "Don't sulk."

Chu sidestepped the flying blob of struggling plastic, letting it plop onto the lawn and roll. "Momotaro is supposed to chase us now," he complained.

"Game over," said Momotaro, making a downward beep, an old-school video game sound.

"Cheer up, Chu," said Jil. "We're all going to Jayjay and Thuy's party in the woods soon. Say hi to Jayjay and Sonic, kids."

"I need a drink of water," said Chu in his flat voice. He turned and walked across the lawn to Nektar's house. Although he'd been working to heal his brain's defective empathy circuits, Chu still wasn't all that sociable, even compared to other fourteen-year-olds.

In the moment of silence they heard Nektar's voice rising in the front yard. Something about a tree.

"Live entertainment," said Sonic. "Let's go watch."

"It won't be interesting," said Jil in a disgusted tone. "Nektar picks dumb fights to get attention. The diva. I guess it's good for our show." Like the others, Jil got her cut of the *Founders* royalties. "Sooner or later Nektar will boss Ond right back into her bed."

"No way," said Jayjay, wanting to reassure Jil. "Ond's crazy about you."

"Enough about me," said Jil. "Let's pick on—Sonic! How come you never have a girlfriend or a boyfriend, Sonic?"

"Mostly I'm not really in my body," said Sonic. "And—"

"Sonic's a peeper!" yelled Momotaro. "Sonic watches Thuy and Jayjay doing it!"

Sonic smiled crookedly, unhappily. With so much telepathy, there were few real secrets anymore, but it was impolite to ferret out—and to publicly air—other people's intimate doings. "Little jerk," he said. "Would you like me to talk about who you peep?"

"Maaaabel?" crooned Bixie ever so softly before breaking into giggles.

"Shut up!" yelled Momotaro. "I'm sorry, Sonic! Never mind. Let's all go watch Ond and Nektar argue!"

Chu reemerged from Nektar's house, carrying a wool overshirt. "I'm ready for the woods."

The six of them walked through the narrow space between Nektar's and Ond's garages. Resting on blocks in front of the monster homes was the two-room cottage that Jayjay and Thuy had recently cobbled together. Seeing it, Jayjay felt a little rush of pride. The insulated, solar-celled roof had a generous overhang to shelter the projecting front porch; the wall's planks fit together as neatly as puzzle parts; the floors gleamed with parquet; the drains led to a nanoseptic tank beneath the floor; and they'd even built some custom furniture: a big bed and a wardrobe, a table and benches, two desks and a kitchen nook. The house's resident silp was pleasant and smart; Thuy called her Vrilla.

"Hi, Vrilla," teeped Jayjay. "It's almost time."

Beside the street, Ond and Nektar were standing toe-to-toe beneath a great spreading oak tree. Ond—a tall, tentative man with thinning blond hair—held a portable power saw and some kind of electrical outlet box. Nektar was wearing party clothes: a red silk skirt and jacket with black blouse, black tights and—as a concession to the fact they were heading for the wilderness—sensible black shoes.

"I'm telling you to give this tree some respect!" Nektar was telling Ond. "She's a hundred years old."

"I want to teach her to make electricity," said Ond quietly. Ond always sounded calm and reasonable—even when his actions seemed utterly bonkers. "Let me implant this special socket into the oak's side," he continued. "She'll heal."

"Fiddle, fiddle, fiddle," snapped Nektar, tossing her head so that her nanotinted blond ponytail flipped across her cheek, nicely framing a diamond in her ear. She had a flair for drama. "Enough is enough. The answer is no."

"Be reasonable, Nektar. This is my new business plan. Electric trees will be a boon to the human race."

"You and your boons," said Nektar. "First the nants, then the orphids, and now the silps. Has it occurred to you that people might be tired of everything changing every year?" Nektar turned to face the others. "Praise Gaia, it's time to go. I'm ready for a drink. Put your damned tools in the garage, Ond."

"Would you mind if I tested out my idea on one of *your* trees?" said Ond to Jayjay.

"Why bother?" said Jayjay. "I'm not even using electricity anymore. Communication is telepathic, computation is silp-based, we can ask our walls to heat or cool our rooms, and the ceiling glows when we need light. When I need to go somewhere I walk or I teleport, I don't even need an electric car."

"But teeking is hard work," said Ond. "Lots of people still use cars."

"With practice teeking gets easier," said Jayjay. "The power industry is on the way out."

"Things are changing too fast," muttered Ond.

"Now you see how it feels," said Nektar. "Put your toys away and let's go to the party, Ond."

Thuy and her father arrived, looking tense. They were carrying two large trays of Vietnamese appetizers made by Thuy's aunt under her mother's direction: damp rice-paper spring rolls, fried pork dumplings, fish balls, and a yellow-and-green gelatin mold with tiny shrimp and shreds of cabbage. Jayjay could hear old Minh's mumbled parting words echoing in Thuy's head. *"It's impossible to teleport a house!"* You could always count on Minh to be a bitch. Becoming disabled had only made her worse.

"Everyone here?" asked Thuy in a bright, brittle tone. She glanced around, counting heads. "Jayjay, Sonic, Jil, Momotaro, Bixie, Chu, Nektar, Ond, Thuy, and Khan. That's only ten."

"Craigor and Darlene said they'll be late," put in Jil. "Craigor said they'll make it to your housewarming, though."

"Craigor and Darlene won't help us move, but they're coming to the party?" exclaimed Thuy. "*That's* a big help. Look, we need twelve people right now. What about Kittie? Where's she?"

Nektar sighed. "Lureen Morales hired Kittie to paint a bedroom mural for her. That's Lureen's way of getting in her hooks. And Kittie's all starstruck, she's watched Lureen for years. It's disgusting. I'd like to teach that fat whore Lureen a lesson. *Oops,* here they come."

Ambling down the hill were Lureen Morales and Kittie Calhoun. Blowsy, busty Lureen was known for her long-running erotic reality show *Caliente*; in the pretelepathy days it had been a video blog. Over the years, Lureen had surgically changed her sex two or maybe three times.

"Hello, Nektar," sang out Lureen, sweetening her voice. She was wearing unbelievably tight jeans and a frilly white top. "When should we schedule that *lesson* you want to teach me? Tonight? Maybe Kittie can help. I'm *such* a slow learner."

Kittie guffawed. She was a good-humored, sturdy woman with paint on her sweat clothes and a brilliant blue tattoo on her neck. She'd been Nektar's girlfriend for the past few months, running a little business out of Nektar's garage, painting solar cells onto electric cars.

"All right now," interrupted Jayjay, eager for the move. "Let's all get inside our cabin and teleport it!" Jayjay and Thuy had already stowed their few possessions within Vrilla's rooms. Once they'd moved it to the clearing, they'd be all set.

Meanwhile, Momotaro, Bixie, and Chu ran inside and began bouncing on the newly made bed. Sonic joined them, big kid that he was. Jayjay, Thuy, Khan, Jil, and Ond squeezed onto the benches built into the corner by the dining table. The two trays of Vietnamese appetizers sat ready upon the table. Nektar, Kittie, and Lureen perched on stools around Thuy's desk on the other side of the main room.

Teeping together, the twelve became a temporary group mind, a twenty-four-legged organism. Jayjay made sure everyone was clearly focused on the foundation that he and Thuy had built in the woods. And then, on the count of three, they launched themselves thither, bearing the house and her contents along.

Teleporting involved cohering your wave function so intensely that you became, in effect, an exotic elementary particle. In terms of the quantum-mechanical approximation, you became a camel-humped wave function, simultaneously here and there.

But it was a little more complicated than that. Quantum mechanics was known to be only an approximation to the world's deeper rules. There were three new realms to take into account: the parallel spacetime of the Hibrane, the unexplored zone beyond the infinity of the lazy eight axis, and the subdimensional levels beneath the Planck length. While remaining quantum-mechanically orthodox, teleportation teased its practitioners with glimpses of the subdimensions.

As the shape of Jayjay's wave function shifted, he felt himself skimming across the surface of a hidden sea: the Planck frontier that separated ordinary reality from Subdee. Voracious, meddlesome subbies lived in the subdimensional sea. They'd once attacked Thuy by sending up harpoon-tipped tendrils. It was good practice to finish one's teleportation hops as quickly as possible.

But the mind force of the twelve teekers was barely adequate for the task of moving the house, and the passage was proceeding slower than Jayjay would have liked. And then, just when it seemed like they were ready to bloom up into the redwood glen—old Khan lost his focus.

Thuy's mother, Minh, was teeping him, she was having a hissy fit because they'd forgotten to bring along her special homemade ginger-plum dipping sauce. As the distracted Khan's mental grip weakened, the cabin teeped a yip of fear. They were sinking too close to the subbies' sea. Jayjay heard a noise like a wood chipper.

"Damn you, Mom," screamed Thuy. "Get away!"

Minh withdrew; Khan regained his focus; the house settled onto the foundation in the woods.

Amid relieved murmurs, the group unlinked.

"You must respect your mother, Thuy," said Khan. "It's not easy for her anymore."

"We're lucky we made it at all," said Jayjay, sticking up for his wife. He went over and looked out the door. Most of the porch had been gnawed away by the insatiable beings of the subdimensions.

"I'll teek for the sauce," said Khan, briefly closing his eyes. Two little pots appeared on the dining table. "So all is well. Thuy and Jayjay, I'm sorry about your porch."

"Main thing is we're here," said Thuy, giddy with relief. She hugged her father. "I'll apologize to Mom later. But let me enjoy this first, I've earned it. Isn't this spot beautiful? And our cabin likes it, too. Right, Vrilla?"

Running into the clearing, Thuy stretched her arms high overhead and twiddled her fingers, as if dancing with the trees. "That's pretty," said Jil. "The dance of the dryads. Like in a classical ballet." She jumped down from the doorway and joined in.

"Can we, um, start eating?" asked Momotaro, eyeing the appetizers.

"Very tasty," said Khan. "Do you know about Vietnamese food?"

"Sure," said Momotaro. "I love those soft spring rolls." He reached for one, and the rest of the crowd followed suit, quickly clearing the plates.

"That dipping sauce is to die for," said Sonic sardonically.

"Is there wine?" inquired Nektar.

"Hold on," said Lureen. "My treat." In a flash, she'd teeked in a case of champagne from her wine cellar. "Pop a few of these corks, would you, Kittie? I'll fetch some glasses, too. Come on, Thuy and Jil! Have a drink!"

"I'll get meat and fish from my restaurant," said Nektar, not to be outdone. "And some big salads. You do want to have a cookout, right, Jayjay?"

"Yeah," said Jayjay, out in the clearing now, arranging the leftover rocks in a fire ring. He'd already reassured himself that there were no flying stingrays to be seen.

"Scavenger hunt!" Ond told Bixie. "Bring Jayjay dry thin sticks and then some fatter ones. Dead but from a tree."

"I'll help," said Chu, who tended to hang as close to Bixie as she'd let him. It was obvious to everyone that Chu had a crush on the girl; she was only a year and a half younger than him. Bixie tolerated the fourteen-year-old's attentions, at least for now. Though odd and unworldly, Chu was smart and quite good-looking. He had big brown eyes, tidy features, pleasantly olive-colored skin, and shiny brown hair.

"Go get 'em, Chu," said Ond, smiling at his son. Inside the house, another cork bounced off the ceiling. The women were laughing uproariously.

In a matter of minutes, Bixie and Chu had assembled more than enough wood. Jayjay set about half of it alight, making sure to teep into the fire silp and beg it not to go out of control.

The fire crackled briskly, reveling in its consumption of wood, sending a thoughtful column of smoke into the growing dusk, blending with the wisps of fog in the high reaches of the redwoods. Steadily the air grew cooler. Slender Bixie moved closer to the fire, wrapping her arms around herself.

"Here," said Chu, handing her his wool overshirt.

"Frankenstein offers his coat to the meager orphan girl," said Momotaro. "Just kidding. Can we cook the meat now, Jayjay? Where's your grill?"

Jayjay teeped to BigBox Home Furnishings via one of the virtual ads that hovered overhead. Not that Jayjay generally liked buying new products—it was more Earth-friendly to borrow stuff via the Web. But in this case, it seemed like he might as well get a permanent grill for his homestead. It took only seconds to find the grill he'd visualized, to charge it to his account, and to teek it here, along with some lightweight plates and a picnic table.

The grill was simple: a heavy-duty wire rack with adjustable legs. Jayjay set it in place, and Nektar appeared from the house, bearing platters of raw steak, chicken, salmon, and pork medallions. Kittie followed, carrying a green salad, a bowl of strawberries, and a potato salad. The men gathered like flies.

"Dibs on a steak," said Momotaro.

"Chicken for me," said Ond.

"I'll have a pork medallion," Chu told Jayjay. "Don't let it touch anything else while it cooks."

"I would enjoy a piece of the fish," said Khan.

"One of each for me," said Sonic. "Surf and turf and sty and coop."

"You're hungry again after that burrito?" asked Jayjay, drinking from a bottle of champagne and passing it on.

"Aren't you?" said Sonic. "We just moved a frikkin' *house*! And it's getting dark and cold. Does your house have lights?"

"You can just ask the ceiling to glow. It has special paint. But right now, the dark is kind of cozy, don't you think? And look over there past the trees: a full moon is coming up. Anyway, we're omnivident, kiq. We can see with our minds."

"Like earthworms," said Sonic, waggling his head. "Sniffle snuff."

"You better fix that porch right now," Jil advised Thuy. "I don't want anyone to break their leg. And take it easy on that bubbly, Bixie and Momotaro. It's much stronger than you think."

"Let's fetch a piece of redwood trunk," said Thuy. "There's a fallen giant near here. Hey, Kittie and Nektar, can you pitch in?"

"That sounds a little too lumberjack for me," said Nektar. "Sawing logs in the dark? More up Lureen's alley. She's so butch."

"Sure I can help," said Lureen affably. "I had more sense than to dress all femmie. But the firelight through your skirt makes a nice effect, Nektar. Don't forget you're teaching me a lesson tonight."

"Oh, you're awful," said Nektar, finally giving Lureen a smile.

"Our clothes don't matter," interrupted Thuy. "We'll use our minds to teek a big block of steps right out of the log. Me, Lureen, Kittie, who else?"

"Oh, I'll help, too," said Nektar, not wanting to be a bad sport.

"And me," said Bixie. "Woman power! Let's stand around the fire like witches."

"Hand in hand!" said Jil, completing the thought. "We'll dance widdershins." She paused, checking Gaia's database. "That means counterclockwise."

The men were greedily hunkered around the picnic table eating fish and meat. The six women circled the fire, the yellow light flickering on their faces. Teeping as one, the women extracted an immense block from a fallen redwood nearby. A sharp crack sounded as the cellulose molecules broke their bonds with the main mass of the trunk. The women moved the block into place in front of the cottage. With a further round of sharp reports, they carved three pleasantly proportioned steps out of the block, adding the waste pieces to Jay-jay's woodpile. A hefty chunk slid loose and thudded to the ground.

"Is that a bear?" shrilled Lureen, breaking the trance. "A wild pig?" She leaned against Kittie, laughing. "Maybe we should go back home, honey. I can't stop thinking about your beautiful mural."

"Stick around," said Nektar. "It's our turn at the table. I'm really hungry now. Get away from the trough, boys."

"Just a second," said Jayjay, teek-flipping the meat and fish that sizzled on the grill. "It's not quite done. Have some more champagne."

"Getting back to what we were talking about before," said Ond to Jayjay, waving a chicken bone for emphasis. "You have a point about the whole power industry dying out. So what takes electricity's place—in terms of something to sell? I'd be glad for some ideas about that."

"Outsource your question to Gaia," suggested Sonic, running his meat-greasy fingers through his long hair.

"The pighead's universal solution," said Jayjay. He didn't want to talk about business at all. With Sonic here, and with the champagne warming his veins, he was feeling that old urge to merge into the global mind. Moonlight puddled the table, filtering in through the trees. Maybe in a minute he and Sonic could get high. His heart beat faster as he imagined the rush.

"Move!" yelled Thuy. "Up, up, up! Our turn!"

The men dispersed and the women took their places. Jayjay served them their grilled meats and fish fillets. He'd worked really hard lately, and Thuy was being just a little bit annoying. He deserved a break.

"*Yeah* you do," teeped Sonic, who was tuned right in on Jayjay's flow of thought. "I'm thinking we skulk over to that dark area by the stream."

"There's a nice flat rock we can lie on," said Jayjay.

But just then Craigor and Darlene showed up with Darlene's teenage sister Mabel.

"About time!" exclaimed Thuy. "Where were you when we were moving the house?"

Craigor shrugged. "Darlene was reading a metanovel; I was

fishing. Looks like the move went fine. You still eating? I brought a fresh cuttlefish." He presented Jayjay with a chicken-sized squidlike creature. "All gutted and ready to grill."

"I'll put it on," said Jayjay, wearily. "We've still got a little meat, too."

"How's my metanovel doing?" Thuy asked Darlene. Darlene was a kind of publisher, helping to distribute the data files of metanovels. She'd marketed Thuy's first effort, *Wheenk*.

"Great," said Darlene. "Metanovels are to novels as forty-foot totem poles are to the pocket-sized amulets that Native Americans made before they had steel axes. That's my new sales slogan."

"You could tighten the phrasing," said Thuy. "But the concept is good. Let me tell you about the sequel I'm working on."

"Do you like to surf?" Momotaro asked Mabel meanwhile. "I could take you out tomorrow."

"Maybe," responded the willowy teen. She regarded Momotaro, considering her options. "Is it easy?" She had a slightly detached demeanor, as if life were a show she was watching.

"Sure," said Momotaro. "The surfboards can think—and the surfers can teleport. It's a blast. Even little grommets like Bixie can ride the gnarliest spots."

"Well, okay," said Mabel. "I guess I'd like it."

"I might come, too," put in Thuy, overhearing them. "I could use a day off from thinking about the move."

Before Momotaro could answer, Kittie came orbiting into the range of the firelight, disheveled and grinning. "You will not believe who I was just talking to, Thuy!"

"To Lureen?" said Thuy, not all that interested.

"No, no," said Kittie. "To a stranger."

"In our woods?" said Jayjay uneasily. "Crap. I hope people aren't hopping here to harass us." He didn't want to get into the possibility that Kittie might have encountered a flying manta ray.

"It was Hieronymus Bosch," said Kittie, a thrill running through her voice. "I know it was really and truly him because he let me teep into his mind. I have so many ideas for my paintings now. I wish he would have stayed longer."

Jayjay did a quick, anxious scan of the woods. He wasn't seeing any strangers out there. Nektar and Lureen were sitting on a patch of moss sharing a bottle of champagne. More than likely Kittie was drunk. He peered into her bloodstream. Yes, definitely.

"Calm down, Kittie," said Thuy. "You're talking about— the medieval painter? What you really mean is that you saw, like, some Renaissance Faire type guy wearing a costume, right?"

"It was Bosch the great painter," insisted Kittie. "Or the Hibrane version of him. He calls himself Yeroon. I teeped him some of my work. It all happened so fast. And then he said he had to go home. He turned sideways and disappeared. Did I mention that he was thirty feet tall?"

"That would be a Hibraner, all right," said Jayjay. Everything was going nuts today. "Did you happen to see any flying manta rays?"

Kittie didn't even hear this. She was deep into her recollections of her big encounter with the Hibrane Bosch. "He liked my van painting of the woman and the squid," she said, smiling. "I teeped it to him. And he showed me how to paint heads running around on two legs. It was like meeting God."

"Ah, there you are," said Lureen, wobbling into the firelight. "Let's go, Kittie. Nektar's onboard. We're having a sleepover at my place."

"Fine," said Kittie, not quite so interested in Lureen as before. "Did you see Yeroon Bosch talking to me? A guy in a velvet hat, thirty feet tall?"

"You can tell us about it in bed."

And then they were gone.

"Let's make the fire huge," said Sonic, lugging over an armload of branches and scraps from the woodpile. The fire leapt up with a fierce exhalation of joy.

CHAPTER 3

JAYJAY AND THE BEANSTALK

The last guests stood around drinking and talking for a while, the trees whispering overhead, the full moon climbing into the sky, the brook babbling away. The party was down to the hard core: Sonic, Jayjay, Thuy, Craigor, and Darlene.

Thuy's hair was in messy pigtails, with stray wisps projecting on all sides. Lit by the moonlight, she looked inhumanly beautiful to Jayjay. He would have liked to get her into bed, but she was still talking about metanovels with Darlene. Craigor was passing around his bong.

Bored and bone-weary, Jayjay decided to slip away for the real high. He and Sonic made their way to the border of the moon-silvered stream and sat on the flat rock together, Sonic sipping at a bottle of champagne he'd brought along.

"Give us this day our daily rush," said Sonic. "On the nod as thou art in heaven. Ready?"

"Hold on," said Jayjay. It had been a while since he'd gone really deep into Gaia. He'd been a good boy. "I need to get myself together."

"So meanwhile let's game these swirls," said Sonic, looking down at the stream. For Sonic, all of reality was a video game. "We'll get into a linked pair of eddies and see how far we can make them go. Like a pair of backs running for a touchdown."

They played with the vortices for a while, Gloob joining in, subtly warping his flows to raise the level of the game. But then all of a sudden Gloob focused his turbulence on a particular spot by the opposite bank.

"Outsider!" teeped the stream silp. "Danger!"

As part of his ongoing telepathic connection with the hylozoic world, Jayjay had a low-level awareness of the wriggling and scuttling of the insects, protozoa, and bacteria in the damp mulch of vegetation along the stream's banks. Something was changing.

A tiny, horned creature—invisible only moments ago—was rapidly increasing his size, growing upward from a clump of moss. Writhing and settling into his new shape, this strange apparition on the dark bank became—how odd—a two-tined pitchfork balancing on his butt end. The pitchfork glowed a dusky shade of red.

The pitchfork's handle—or leg—flexed, and his two prongs vibrated, sending out a high, singing buzz that articulated into speech—a male hillbilly voice. "Jayjay," twanged the pitchfork. "Git high. I'll take you on the magic beanstalk. My name's Groovy."

The pitchfork gave off a strangely flavored teep signal that echoed his spoken words with an emotive sense he was offering something quite wonderful. "I can lead you clear to infinity."

"The silp in that weird forked stick is talking out loud!" exclaimed Sonic, who'd finished off the champagne. "That's not right, kiq. I say we throw the stick in the fire. See what he says then."

With an abrupt series of thumps the pitchfork hopped upstream, crashing through the underbrush. And then all was silent. The curious being had merged into the forest gloom, impossible to teep.

"He was a talking pitchfork named Groovy," said Jayjay. "Not a stick."

"Country cowfreak," said Sonic, giggling. "He told us to get high."

"Let's do that," said Jayjay. "Never mind the rest of it." Everything was too frikkin' weird today. Flying stingrays, a giant medieval painter, and now a talking pitchfork? He needed an out.

Jayjay and Sonic lay down, joined their minds, and spiraled up toward the piglike blue face of Gaia's interface.

"Hi, boys," said Gaia as they sank into her ultramarine funnels. "Ready for a really good time?"

The boys swooped and sang, savoring the sensual feel of raw thought—as enhanced by Gaian mind-tendrils.

Now and then Jayjay felt something pricking at him—prongs? Surely that weird pitchfork wasn't standing over him beside the stream? He didn't have the will to leave his trance and find out for sure. If anything, the pitchfork's prods were nudging him deeper.

At some point during the night's long, chaotic journey, Jayjay felt Thuy shaking him and walking him to their now pitiful-seeming honeymoon cabin. Waggish Gaia displayed a relevant archetype: The Groom Drunk on His Wedding Night. Not that Jayjay was truly drunk. In principle, he could snap out of his Gaia trip and be with Thuy right now.

But he didn't. That was the addiction thing at work. Once Jayjay got going on a run like this, he found it nearly impossible to stop. He collapsed onto the living room floor and lay motionless, knowing full well there'd be a stiff price to pay. But it was still night. Hours to go. And the flow of time was so deliciously slow. The Groom Drunk on His Wedding Night—what a hoot, what a blast.

"You're horrible," said Thuy, and went to bed.

Although Sonic was still lying on the rock by the stream, his virtual form hung nearby like a basking whale. "Yo," he called to Jayjay. "Let's go farther. Farther than anyone's ever been. Maybe all the weird critters we saw today are aliens. Maybe we can contact another lazy eight planet."

"Yaar."

Jayjay and Sonic labored in the unseen world, piling idea upon idea, energy upon energy, working their way high above the surface of the cartoony pig-eared icon that was Mother Earth. But they weren't getting all that far.

"Yee-haw!" hollered a voice. Groovy, the pitchfork, was in the mind space with them. Very aggressive with his tines, he pried at the base of their junk-pile observatory, toppling it to one side. Jayjay fell at some impossible angle, plunged through the very fabric of space—and slid toward wakefulness.

He was alone, lying on his back, hearing the wind in the trees. Or, no, that sounded more like shifting sand. Or like a cyclone? In any case, it was way past time to get in bed with Thuy. He stood up and opened his eyes.

He wasn't in his living room. He was in a—desert? For a moment he had a sense that he was standing upside down—like a fly on a ceiling. But that impression faded away. He was in a surrealist desert landscape of hazy pastels. The dry ochre ground bore elegant washboards of ripples from the steady wind. Swirls of lavender sand drifted overhead, with a bright, chalky spot betokening the presence of a white light somewhere far overhead.

Cactuslike plants were scattered across the parched plain, slowly moving his way, their roots like stealthy tentacles. Jayjay recalled Thuy's tale of her journey into the subdimensions—for this was surely where he now found himself. Thuy said the thorny plantlike subbies liked nothing better than to devour a traveler's flesh.

Jayjay looked at his hands and slowly flexed them. Every detail in place. He was really and truly awake—but in a nightmare world. He pawed the gritty air like a blind man, not quite believing that his cozy honeymoon cabin was gone. What had he done to deserve this?

"Let's climb a vine," said Groovy, suddenly at his side. The curious figure buzzed some mumbo jumbo and poked the ground with his tines. At that instant, a giant beanstalk appeared, so rapidly that it was hard to be sure if it had grown up from the ground or down from the sky. Be that as it may, it was solidly real, its stalk endlessly branching, and all of the branches draped with rustling heart-shaped leaves. The menacing subbies halted their approach and even began to drop back.

"Just come on and climb a ways along this beanstalk, son," said the garrulous pitchfork, thumping the heavy vine. "The stalk is a friend of mine, a native aktual name of Art Zed. Nothin' to be afraid of. You'll pick up some powers and you'll meet a couple of folks. Won't take long. And then you'll be back home with the frau."

Jayjay gazed at the gently swaying vine. It gave off a pleasant, musical hum. It stretched to infinity, an endless maze of branching paths. He'd wanted to get high, hadn't he? "All right," he said. "Let's go."

His hands and feet found ready purchase on the stalk; he climbed upward with ease. Groovy bucked along behind him like a caterpillar. Soon they'd reached the first fork.

"Right or left?" asked Jayjay.

"Listen to the beanstalk," said Groovy. "Follow his song."

The music seemed a bit louder to the right, a bit sweeter, so that's the branch that Jayjay took.

"Atta boy," called the pitchfork, close behind him. "And keep doubling your pace. Do it like a Zeno speed-up."

With the coming of lazy eight, scientists had begun discussing a theoretical trick for covering the endless axis of eighth dimensional memory in a finite amount of time—they called it a Zeno speed-up. In principle, you could search the first gigabyte of your lazy eight memory in a second, the next gigabyte in half a second, the next in a quarter of a second—and at the end of two seconds, you'd have searched your whole infinite spike of eighth dimensional memory, winnowing through alef-null gigabytes, *alef-null* being the mathematicians' word for the first level of infinity.

But in practice, each step of a search took a certain amount of energy, and there seemed to be fundamental limits to the speed at which you could do things. Normal people couldn't actually carry out Zeno speed-ups with their minds, let alone with their bodies. The nimblest human thought processes usually pooped out around ten octillion steps.

But right now, on this leafy beanstalk, a Zeno speed-up seemed physically possible. Jayjay was reaching each successive forking twice as quickly. Right, left, left, right, right, right, left, right . . . The beanstalk's sweet music was guiding him, and it was feeding him a strange, wonderful energy as well.

The farther he went, the bigger the leaves became. Or maybe he was shrinking? They were the size of houses, the size of stadiums, flipping past in a blur. Limbs working mechanically, following the song, not paying much attention to which forkings he took, Jayjay chanced a glance down toward the Subdee desert below. The flat expanse shimmered like a sheet of glass, and for an instant he could glimpse the contours of his cozy living room on the other side. If he turned his viewpoint upside down, it was as if he were crawling down a lacy root system, and peering up through his cabin floor.

Meanwhile the music of the beanstalk had segued into a voice, a man's murmur, so very similar to Jayjay's internal monologue that at first he mistook it for his own thoughts. But these weren't the kinds of thoughts he normally had.

"I'm a transfinite being," the vine was saying. "We call ourselves aktuals. I live in Alefville. Each of our tree branches has an endless number of jiggles. My apartment building has alef-one floors, and the town has alef-two streets. My full name is—"

An intense, skritchy sound filled Jayjay's ears. It was like hearing someone handwrite an endlessly long phrase in a fraction of a second. But, regarded in another way, it was really just a pair of syllables, a simple name that Jayjay could very easily say, a name which, come to think of it, the pitchfork had mentioned before.

"Art Zed?" said Jayjay.

"Yes. Before too long, you'll be visiting Alefville."

"Wow."

The pitchfork seized on Jayjay's moment of dreamy wonder to give him a cartoon poke in the butt—*yow!* He lost hold of the vine and skidded onto a heart-shaped leaf as big as a town.

"Hey, Jay," said the pitchfork. He bounced along on the viridian surface, coming to a stop, balancing on the butt of his handle. "This is far enough for today. Ten tridecillion branchings. You done good. I saw you drinking in that subdimensional glow off Art Zed. You slick, boy, you a, a—call it a zedhead."

Teeping down into his body, Jayjay did indeed sense something different. Even if he hadn't made it to the top of the beanstalk, the beanstalk's voice had done something to him. His thoughts were finer and more rapid than before. He felt great, euphoric. "Zedhead?" he echoed, laughing.

"Yeah, Jay. It means you can think longer and faster than other humans. You gonna be able to reprogram a hundred kilometers of atoms if you feel like it. Meanwhile I got some folks for you to meet. One of 'em is an old friend of yours. And the other one's gonna get you hot."

Jayjay had no idea what he was doing here, so far from home, and he didn't really trust the pitchfork. But he was feeling such well-being that it seemed like a beautiful dream. There was no rush to leave here, no rush at all.

Stray tendrils and flowers from the beanstalk drooped down over the leaf, making a space like a festooned ballroom, quite empty.

"They're comin' real soon," said the pitchfork. He rose up to his full height and set his tines to vibrating. Something like teep signals were beaming out from him—and immediately disappearing into another dimension. He was sending signals to the Hibrane.

Beside a fragrant bean blossom a gleaming line appeared and unfolded at impossible angles to form—a tidy harp.

"Oh, why did you make me do this stupid extra jump over here, Groovy?" She seemed fretful and disoriented. "I still have to unfurl lazy eight on the Lobrane and the Hibrane.

Well, I guess for this boy, what's his name, that's already happened, but, me, I'm just starting on my big time loop."

"This here's my girlfriend, Lovva," the pitchfork told Jayjay.

Oh wow. It was the same harp that Jayjay had played when he'd unfurled the eighth dimension some hundred days ago. He recognized her by her teep vibes. But unlike before, the painting on her soundbox was intact. It showed a pair of lovers beside a little blue demon playing a serenade on a golden harp of his own. The woman looked slightly Asian, with a delicacy to her features and a certain arch to her eyes. With a shock, Jayjay realized it was an image of Thuy. And the guy with her, could that be him? Beautiful. It was like seeing the solemn goddess of time bend around to bite her own toenail.

"Groovy, I don't approve," sang the harp. "I know what you're up to. You're planning to betray the Earth."

"I'm lost is all, Lovva," said the pitchfork, putting on an aggrieved tone. "It ain't my fault if I don't know where to find you."

"I'm on the other brane, Groovy," said Lovva. Ill-tempered though she was, her contralto voice rose and fell in smooth glissandos that set the pitchfork's tines to humming along. "I'm time-skimming. I already saw you there. You show up at the house of this painter who decorates me. I think his name is Hieronymus Bosch. Eventually I'm going to play the Lost Chord there. Apparently the harpist will be that young man who's with you right now."

For just a moment Jayjay felt like he could understand how and why the Hibrane Bosch had ended up in the woods by his cottage. But then the gears of logic dissolved into the milky glow of pleasure that was filling him here.

"This is our boy Jay," said the pitchfork. "I'll send him over to the Hibrane directly. He already met you on the Lobrane, so he's good to go. I called you here so's you could remind me where to send him. Also I felt like givin' you a nice funky strum."

"You're so crude," said the harp irritably.

"*You* the one who got lost. Needle in a frikkin' haystack."

"Don't always criticize me!" The harp's tone rose in a sharp crescendo. This was like listening to a married couple bickering—a spaced-out married couple who continually forgot what they were talking about. Speaking of spaced-out, Jayjay felt exceedingly high from the long rush of his ten tridecillion-leaf climb. None of this seemed serious, especially not the clownish pitchfork.

"Aw, I don't mean nothing," Groovy was telling the harp, leaning forward to give her strings a gentle flick. "Long as I can hear you, I'm happy."

"Sweet," said Lovva, dropping her ill humor and enjoying her mate's caresses. She sang a sweeping arpeggio. Looking down, Jayjay let his eye do a zedhead speed-up of 10,000,000,000,000,000,000,000,000,000,000,000,000,000,000 saccades, traversing the Art Zed beanstalk from the bottom to the leaf upon which he'd fetched up, not that he bothered to make note of the precise path. What mattered was that he was ten tridecillion levels down into the subdimensions. Forty-three zeroes. Far out.

"You on the beam now," said the pitchfork, watching his mind. "Eventually you'll get fully aktualized and hang with Art Zed. You'll end up coming to our world to help aktualize Lovva and me. It's all looped around."

Once again, Jayjay had the fleeting feeling of understanding the whole time-tangled pattern. "Will I remember this?" he asked.

"Some of it," said the pitchfork. "A little at a time. Okay, now, here comes our next mystery guest."

"Groovy, don't!" said the harp.

The pitchfork ignored her, setting himself to buzzing again. He was using his vibrations to make something. He was creating a physical object, one atom at a time—it was an ostrichlike bird, quite large, not yet brought to life. She lay limp as a butchered goose upon the leaf. But now an external burst of teep signals pulsed into her, whizzing down the lazy eight axis from infinity. The bird squawked, got to her feet, and raised her head. She was easily eight feet tall. Disturbingly, she had no eyes.

"Woe," sang the harp like a tragic chorus. "He's made a physical body for Pekka of Pengö to control! This creature will serve as Pekka's Earth-based agent."

"There's one of these things in the royal caves back home," said Groovy. "It's called a Pekklet."

The oversized bird came high-stepping across the leaf, her clawed toes sinking in with each stride. Her fuzzy, eyeless head swiveled, as if studying Jayjay via impalpable rays. Groovy twanged his tines in Jayjay's direction, and a reckless wave of enthusiasm swept over him.

"Yoo-hoo," yelled the besotted Jayjay, as if he had nothing to be afraid of. "Yoo-hoo!"

He drew out that last oo, putting some teep into it, throwing in a zedhead image of himself reflected ten tridecillion times in a pair of mirrors, making a different silly face in each reflection.

"Oh, yeah," said the pitchfork. "You do that gooood. You got her interested in you."

"Run, Jayjay!" shrilled the harp. "Pekka's the planetary mind of a world of ruthless colonizers."

But the warning was too late. Pekka's agent was already standing over him, probing his mind, her will unpleasantly strong, her two-toed claws deadly. She smelled musty. With a darting motion of her snakelike neck, she plucked off Jay-jay's sweat-stained shirt; with wet gasp, she swallowed it whole, working the bolus down her long neck.

The alien being let out a series of low, sweet clucks. Dande-lion fuzz sprouted from her head, growing fine tendrils that settled onto Jayjay and sank into his flesh. He had the distinct sense of hooks taking hold.

"You under her wing now, Jay," said the pitchfork, as if in sorrow. "Pekka's agent is knotting into you. Entangling your particle strings."

"You deliberately set him up!" repeated Lovva. "You're selling out his world! I knew this was coming, but I can hardly believe it. You're terrible, Groovy."

"I want me some glory," muttered the pitchfork. "Pekka promised that she'll have them Earthlings puttin' up statues of me."

"As if!" raged the harp. "A parasite like Pekka isn't going to keep her word."

"You think?" said the pitchfork, actually surprised. His voice took on a rare note of self doubt. "Wonder if I goofed."

"You are such a dumb hick."

"We know that Jayjay and his gang are gonna win out," said the pitchfork, regaining his cockiness. "Otherwise we wouldn't have seen them in our world. There's no harm in letting Pekka's birds take a shot. Everything's gonna come out in the wash."

"Maybe so," said Lovva. "Because I knew this was coming, I already teeped Glee. She became a Hrull pusher after we left, you know. She and her host Hrull are probably in the Lobrane already, relative to Jayjay's time." She studied him, reading his mind. "Yes, he saw the Hrull this morning. That's good. They can teach him about the reset rune." She heaved a tinkling sigh. "There's so much still to do before we go home and smash the aristos. And that's the only part I really care about."

"Worryin' don't help," said the pitchfork. "This tune's playin' itself."

And with that, the two of them dove off the edge of the leaf and disappeared, heading in opposite directions, leaving Jayjay to face the music.

His euphoria was gone, and his confusion was rising. He didn't really understand what Pekka was, nor what it meant for this Pekklet creature to be her agent.

The mental contact from the Pekklet was itchy, squawky, raw. Thanks to all the particle strings she'd knotted into Jayjay, she had an unbreakable connection to him—stronger than mere teep. The distant planetary mind behind the Pekklet was avidly pleased to have forged an unbreakable link with a humanoid from a lazy eight world. She had huge development plans.

Aching with regret, Jayjay backed away from the Pekklet, wanting to climb down the stalk. The giant bird followed his moves as if he were a juicy beetle. She chirped blindly at him, an almost cozy sound. Jayjay's sense of connection to her was physically palpable.

To draw the link yet tighter, the ungainly fowl began reshaping herself, tucking in a bit here, growing out a lump there—until she'd taken on the form of a statuesque woman, all curves and hollows, with ruffs of fancy feathers, but again with no eyes upon her blank face. The slinky shape embraced Jayjay, cooing words of love.

An exquisite sensation of erotic pleasure filled Jayjay's mind. And in that moment of sensual bliss, he agreed to do whatever the Pekklet wanted.

With a flap of her arms, the Pekklet flipped Jayjay off the edge of the leaf. He tumbled downward like a doomed giant, rushing past the vast tangles of the vines; he thudded onto the Subdee desert, and oozed through to his cabin floor. And now he was lying in the living room like before—but with the Pekklet controlling his mind.

His mouth dropped open and he made a tuneless hum. His penis was throbbing. An astronomical flow of information rushed through him and into the teeming night.

CHAPTER 4

THE MISSING GNARL

Having to fetch Jayjay from the stream bank to the house was annoying and depressing for Thuy. Some honeymoon. Once asleep, she dreamed of Jayjay as a zombie, a spider, a radioactive computer chip.

Just before dawn she woke, her mouth dry, her head pounding from the champagne. She sat upright in the lonely bed, listening. Raccoons clattered in the moonlit clearing, cleaning up the dinner's debris. The trees sighed; the stream burbled. But there was no sound of Jayjay's breathing in the living room, and when she teeped out for him, he wasn't there anymore.

She got a glass of water from the kitchen sink, surveying the empty room. The air was cool and calm. Jayjay must have gone back out soon after she'd walked him in. God*damn* him. Didn't he care about her at all? Was their marriage doomed?

If she wasn't careful, she was going to cry. To hell with that. She drank her water, peed, and went back to the bedroom. Just before she turned the light out, she noticed something outside her window: a forked branch leaning against the glass as if peeking in at her. Thuy teeped the thing, but got little reaction. Just a stick.

Suddenly she heard a noise. Running into the living room, she saw something small squirming on the floor. It was growing larger, like dough rising through a crack—oh my God, it was Jayjay! And then he was present again, sprawled on the floor, shirtless, shivering all over, with his eyes squeezed tight shut. He bucked his hips as if dreaming of sex. Thuy poked him, checking that he was real. It was so weird, the way he'd puffed up out of the floor. Had she really seen that? She couldn't seem to wake him. Never mind. At least he was here. Thuy buried herself under her covers and got a few more hours of sleep.

It was Sonic who woke her, wandering in from outside to blunder around the kitchen. He was rummaging for coffee, with his little Edgar shoon dogging his steps. Somewhere in the distance, harsh-voiced birds squawked.

"We're not moved in yet!" Thuy called to Sonic from her bed. "Nothing here for you. Go scavenge outside, bum." She felt strange—it was as if the subliminal hum of the atoms in her body had changed pitch.

"Tried that already," said Sonic. "The animals ate the left-overs, so I came inside for a hands-on food search. What a night. I shouldn't have slept so close to the stream. I feel like an old man. Look at our boy Jayjay. On the nod. Receiving truth. At one with the—"

"Oh, shut up," snapped Thuy, pulling on her T-shirt and tights. "You're a creep to have gotten him so high." She marched into the living room. "It was supposed to be our big romantic honeymoon night and now—oh God, look at that stain—I think he came in his pants while he was tripping. Prince Charming."

"I didn't get him high, Thuy. He did it himself. You've been around the block a few times, *chica*. You know how it works."

"You encouraged him, Sonic. You're—what do they call it?—an enabler. A lower companion."

"I'm a humble working stiff without a *Founders* paycheck," said Sonic. "An unpaid extra in the theater of life. Meanwhile I gotta lead my squid 'n' whale tour in half an hour. I can't believe you don't have coffee."

"Teek some in," suggested Thuy. "And fetch me a double latte while you're at it. It's the least you can do. Skeevy, slushed pighead that you are." Despite her strong words, she felt limp, as if her life were a tired script she was walking through.

Sonic walked to the door and stared out at the misty clearing. "Fogged in," he said. "I can barely see the trees. Jayjay and I got really high on Gaia. After you walked him in here, we made a kind of tower. It was vibby. Oh, and there was a talking pitchfork. He knocked down our tower and then I didn't see Jayjay anymore." Sonic paused, scanning through his eighth-dimensional memory bank. "That was about it," he said. "After that I was just asleep. I don't know what Jayjay got into." He sighed and rubbed his face. "Okay, yeah, I'll teek some coffee."

With a light rustle, three cups appeared on the kitchen counter: a double latte and two large black coffees, plus a container of cream. A moment later, three foil-wrapped breakfast burritos plopped down beside the drinks.

"Straight from Taquería Aztlán," said Sonic. "Enough for Jayjay, too. Dig in, Thuy."

"Not hungry," she said, taking a sip of her latte. She was wondering about something she'd overheard yesterday, remotely teeping into the conversation in the back yard at Ond's before they moved the house. "When you watch us have sex," she asked Sonic, "are you hot for me—or for Jayjay?"

"I like you two together," said Sonic with a shrug. "It's like you're my parents, only not disgusting. But if you really mind, I'll—"

"Oh, no *problem,*" said Thuy, gazing up at the BigBox ad near the ceiling. "There's so many watchers anyway."

"That crotch stain is pretty rude," said Sonic, studying his friend.

Thuy shook her head sadly. Everything seemed dull and gray. "You mentioned a pitchfork," she said. "Last night when I woke up, I saw a forked branch leaning against my bedroom window. And now it's gone."

"Yeah, it was a two-tined pitchfork like the peasants wave at Dracula's castle," said Sonic, remembering. "I glimpsed the pitchfork behind your house this morning too, as a matter of fact. He balances and hops on his handle like it's a leg. He's flexible. He was talking out loud to Jayjay by the stream right before our trip; he vibrates his prongs. He's got this hillbilly accent. He came along on our big trip."

"A stick?" said Thuy, nonplussed.

"More than a stick," said Sonic. "I bet he's an alien from another world. Wow. Why don't I feel more excited? Need more coffee. The pitchfork's name is Groovy."

"This is big news," said Thuy in an equally flat tone. "What's wrong with us today? Empty and numb."

"Oh, and did Jayjay tell you about the flying manta rays he thought he saw yesterday afternoon? Or, wait, I wasn't supposed to tell you about that."

"Don't tease me, Sonic."

"All kinds of aliens are after your husband," said Sonic, managing a grin.

"I wonder if I made a mistake marrying him."

"Look, I can't do the whole kitchen-counter relationship discussion this morning. I'm leading a tour for Animal Animats in like three minutes." Sonic paused, studying Thuy. "Don't get so bummed out. You have a hangover, is all. Eat something. Jayjay loves you more than anything, okay? It was a vibby housewarming, Thuy. Everyone had a good time. I gotta go. Squid versus whale."

Thuy ended up eating her breakfast burrito after all. Alone in the cabin, she began wondering if she could hear the thuds of an alien pitchfork hopping around outside. Was Sonic putting her on?

She thought of checking with Vrilla. The cabin's silp confirmed that, yes, she'd seen the hopping pitchfork, too. "And Jayjay shrank way down inside one of my floorboards for a while," added Vrilla. "Into the subdimensions. And now something else is down there."

Meanwhile Jayjay slumbered on. Drinking her coffee, Thuy let her mind wander away from last night's disturbing events. When reality got too harsh, it was always comforting to think about her current metanovel. The new one would be about life in this new hylozoic world, and she was going to call it *Hive Mind*. Even in her presently discouraged state, thinking of the work made her smile. A bright spot in life's frikkin' vale o' tears, a small zone where she was fully in control.

Usually hive minds were presented as totalitarian and dull. But Thuy had decided that was backwards. A brain's hive of co-operating neurons was a lot more interesting than a trillion independent nerve cells. An ant colony was way vibbier than an ant. And if you thought about the history of art and the history of science—as opposed to the history of governments—you got a sense that the emergent mind of massed human society could be a creative and wonderful thing.

Maybe the problem with politics was that Earth's nations

weren't *enough* like hives. As it stood, democracies were controlled by tiny power elites who used the media to enforce
uniform thought. A telepathic human society might instead
be based upon each of its members being heard. Flexible, intricate compromises could supplant the blunt instrument of
majority rule. . . .

Thuy lost the thread of what she was thinking about.

"I feel stupid," she said out loud, and then tried it again, doing a hick accent. "Ah'm a-feelin' duuuumb. Might as well go
surfin'. Sunny Californee! *Cowabuuuunga.*" She warbled the
long *u* sound up and down, heartening herself by being silly.

In preparation for the surf outing, she rummaged around
the bedroom, gathering warm clothes. She was planning to
leave Jayjay on the floor so he'd wake up alone and wonder
where she'd gone.

But now, damnit, she could only find one of her pigtail fas-
teners. "Where's your sister?" she asked the fastener as she
wrapped it around a hank of hair on the left side of her head.

"Don't know," teeped the fastener, a loop of elastic with two
red balls. It sounded sullen. Even the silps were dumb today.

Thuy found the other fastener lurking under her bed. It was
actually trying to make itself invisible. Too lazy to hold her
hair. And when Thuy got on her knees to reach for it, the little
object rebounded from her fingernail and scooted deeper into
the shadows.

Thuy slid the bed away from the wall and captured the stupid
balky fastener, with the uncooperative bed digging its feet into
the floor. What a day. As Thuy stretched the elastic with one
hand and gathered a pigtail with the other, the fastener's balls
managed a tiny rolling motion that sent it springing free. With a
joyful clatter, the fastener skittered under her bed again.

"Goddamn you all!" yelled Thuy, roughly yanking the bed
to one side.

Right about then Jayjay roused himself.

"Hey. What are you doing?"

"Don't you be asking *me* questions," said Thuy, fastening her second pigtail. "Addict."

"I had such a weird trip," said Jayjay, sitting up and rubbing his face.

Ordinarily Thuy would have continued berating him, but today she wasn't up for it. Mechanically she folded a towel and stuffed it in a carry-sack. "I'm going out on the waves with those kids," was all she said. "Momotaro, Mabel, Chu, and Bixie."

"I'll tag along," said Jayjay. "Is that food on the counter for me?"

"Sonic brought it."

"Good old Sonic," said Jayjay. He got to his feet and poured cream into his coffee. "I lost track of him last night. There was this weird pitchfork named Groovy. I think he physically pushed me into the subdimensions."

"Vrilla told me," said Thuy, still unable to feel much surprise. "Anyway, I saw you oozing up from the floor. What were you doing down there?"

"I was in Subdee," said Jayjay. "I even saw those flesh-eating cactuses you talked about. But there was a giant beanstalk, too. The pitchfork took me partway up it, and we saw the magic harp that you brought back from the Hibrane. Her name is Lovva."

"Hell of a trip," said Thuy, not liking it. "Great way to spend the first night of your honeymoon. And I hear you saw flying manta rays yesterday, too. Tell me, Jayjay, are you going nuts?"

Jayjay stared down into his cup, his face stubbornly blank. "The coffee looks wrong."

Thuy leaned over to peer into the cup, wanting to stay right on top of Jayjay's doings. The cream was spreading as an orderly white ellipse. No tendrils, no eddies, no chaos. The bland vibe of the coffee's silp filled her with unaccountable despair.

"Everything's horrible," she said. "I'm hungover and you're strung out and it's gray outside—oh, Jayjay, are we gonna blow our chance to be happy?"

"I shouldn't have spaced out on you last night," admitted Jayjay. "Sometimes I get this stupid idea that I'm missing something. I always think that when I network into Gaia, I'll get more. I'm sorry I didn't stay around."

"Don't be sorry for me," said Thuy. "Be sorry for you." She made a gesture that included the forest, Vrilla, and herself. "This is where it's at. *This* is what you don't want to miss."

"Yes," said Jayjay, pulling himself together. "I'm here. I'm not crazy. Maybe I imagined the manta rays, but I'm pretty sure the pitchfork was real." He managed the reckless smile that Thuy loved. "I'm ready to surf with you, *phu nhân*. Let's hop!"

"Okay!" But now Thuy remembered her fight with her mother last night. "Oh gosh, you better go down to Ond's alone and I'll meet you there. I have to stop by—"

"—your house to apologize to Minh," said Jayjay, completing her thought. "Keep it light. Don't let the old dragon ruin your day. Tell her we have to catch a particular tide at, like, nine thirty, so you have to be with me in five minutes."

"Good idea," said Thuy. She liked it when Jayjay's thoughts meshed with hers. Their private little hive.

Whatever had been wrong with Thuy wore off quickly once she'd left the Yolla Bolly gloom. It was sunny in San Francisco, a beautiful second day of May. The trees bobbed enchantingly in the morning breeze. Her father, Khan, was in the family's kitchen eating noodle soup with his sister. He smiled when he saw Thuy.

"Congratulations on the party. A real housewarming."

"Thuy?" croaked her mother from the bedroom. Thuy squared her shoulders and marched in there. Now that she'd left misty Yolla Bolly, her emotions were bouncing back.

Minh's lips were trembling, preparing for speech. She made a feeble gesture with the hand that wasn't a paralyzed claw.

"I'm sorry for being mad at you yesterday, Mom," said Thuy.

"Always mad at me," said Minh. It was annoying how Minh never accepted apologies. Instead she just used them as starting points for further attacks. It crossed Thuy's mind that she herself had been doing the same thing to Jayjay.

"Your husband very drunk last night," put in Minh, following Thuy's thoughts. "More than drunk. I teep him lying on the ground this morning."

"I wish you wouldn't spy on us."

"I worry about you," said Minh. "I miss my daughter sometimes."

"Oh, Mom." Thuy squeezed her mother's hand and kissed her cool, smooth cheek. Mom smelled bad. It wasn't her fault. It wasn't her fault.

"You want to stay for the day?" asked Minh.

"Oh—I can't!" said Thuy, standing up and starting to breathe again. "We're going surfing. And the tide is changing in five minutes."

"He told you to say that," said Minh. "That bad boy."

"Mom—" Thuy stopped herself before saying anything else. "Gotta run!"

She bid her father and aunt good-bye, then hopped to Ond's. Jil and Ond were in their kitchen having breakfast. Thuy got some coffee from them, and joined Jayjay, who was sitting on the patio. The tree shadows were lively and complex. And the cream in the San Francisco coffee swirled the way it was supposed to.

By now Thuy's emotions were fully up to speed again. That stain on Jayjay's pants was really bugging her. Her anger budded and bloomed.

"The reason you're an addict is that you're scared of emotions," she told him, drawing him aside. "Every time you're about to feel something, you want to run away."

"Oh give me a break," snapped Jayjay. "I worked my butt off yesterday. Moving the house, grilling the food, and putting up with your crazy parents. They're the reason you're so uptight."

"Oh, now you're making remarks about my family? My father is a wonderful man."

"So move back in with him," said Jayjay, faking a nonchalant tone. But Thuy could teep the sadness and self-doubt in his mind. Her volatile emotions flip-flopped, and suddenly she threw her arms around him.

"Oh, Jayjay, I do love you. It's just talk. I get carried away. We can work things out, can't we?"

"I hope so, Thuy. You're all I want in this world."

"Let's have fun surfing today. I'm glad you came."

"You and me," said Jayjay. "Let's go online and find some boards and wetsuits."

Thuy and Jayjay tuned out of the visual world and into the mindweb. They drifted upward into the virtual sky, seeing the city as a grid of glowing personalities.

"Hey," called Thuy to the world at large. "It's Thuy and Jayjay from *Founders*. We need to borrow surfboards and wetsuits for today."

With everyone and everything linked together, people's attitudes about possessions had changed. Given that you always knew where your stuff was, you didn't have to worry about getting it back after lending it. And you didn't have to lend to just anyone. The mindweb had a rating system in place; and if someone got a rep for trashing things, they were blocked from further borrowing until they made good on whatever damage they'd done.

Within seconds of Thuy's request, a few points of light flared up on the colorful map of San Francisco. People were eager to lend to celebs. In a just a few moments a well-off woman had equipped them with some smart boards and psipunk wetsuits that she and her boyfriend had barely used.

After teeking the goods to Ond's patio, Thuy and Jayjay undressed and pulled on their suits. In a few minutes they'd be teleporting directly to the Potato Patch break. The piezoplastic suits were like flexible display screens. Thuy's synched in with her mind flow to show a drifty pattern of hearts and ants.

"Whoah," said Momotaro, materializing on the patio, wearing a piezoplastic wetsuit as well. By way of miming his surprise at seeing Thuy and Jayjay, his suit showed an expanding ball of orange and yellow. "You sure you two aren't too old?"

"Jayjay's eighty," said Thuy cheerfully. The longer she was away from Yolla Bolly, the more like herself she felt. The liveliness of nature's computations made all the difference.

"Personally I'm glad Thuy and Jayjay are coming," said Bixie, walking out of the house, her suit showing fluffy clouds in a blue sky. "If it was just us four, it'd be—*eek*—a double date. Speaking of dates, where's Maaaabel, Momotaro?"

"Stop saying her name that way or I'll pound you." Spiked clubs and atomic cannons flitted across the surface of Momotaro's suit. Bixie replied with an image of smug pink armor.

"I'm ready," announced Chu, emerging from Nektar's house next door, a tidy white surfboard under his arm. His wetsuit was plain black.

"Here I am, too," announced Mabel, alighting on the patio, lithe and lovely in the morning sun. "I was trying to borrow a board and a suit, but nobody trusts me. Just because I've never borrowed anything here before."

"I'll get it for you," said Momotaro, and moments later the gear appeared.

Mabel changed clothes in the house—even though nobody had true privacy anymore, face-to-face nudity was still an issue. And then they were set. The six teleported to a spot on the seaward edge of the Potato Patch break—about a mile out to sea from the straits of the Golden Gate Bridge.

"Cold!" gasped Jayjay, paddling at Thuy's side. "I have an ice cream headache in my feet!"

The four others—the youngsters—had already propelled themselves to where the waves were actually breaking. The smart surfboards could pulse ripples along their bottoms to speed you up. But Thuy and Jayjay were in no rush to meet the waves. The Potato Patch breakers were ragged and intimidating.

"I love the ocean's salty taste," said Thuy, remembering her high school surf sessions. She squirted a little spout at Jayjay. "It was creepy how bland everything seemed at our house this morning."

"You stopped being bland as soon as we got to San Francisco," said Jayjay with a half smile. "Enter the dragon."

"Don't even," said Thuy, flipping her hair so the drops flew in his face. "I can't believe you were in the subdimensions last night. And what's up with that pitchfork? Where did the beanstalk lead to?"

"Supposedly it ran all the way out the lazy eight axis to infinity," said Jayjay. "The pitchfork and I climbed ten tridecillion steps up." His symmetrical features were smooth and sincere. "The beanstalk had a name: Art Zed. He taught me about thinking faster. The pitchfork said I'm a zedhead now. And then—I can't remember exactly. The pitchfork talked a lot. I told you the magic harp was there. She and the pitchfork are married. Lovva and Groovy. And there was . . . a tall bird." Jayjay fell silent for a moment, worrying. "I think something bad happened then. Oh, never mind. I just want to be here now. With you."

"We'll try for a wave," said Thuy, glad to change the subject. "See the big water bumps wallowing under us? Wave embryos. They're coming in from both the north and the south because of the tide pouring into the bay. The intersection of flows is what makes the Potato Patch so gnarly. *Cowabuuu-unga*. Did you ever actually hear anyone say that?"

"You know I've never been surfing before, Thuy. If I do catch a wave, I'm totally not standing up." Jayjay's suit displayed a cautious turtle-shell pattern.

"Follow me," said Thuy. "And listen to your surfboard."

She paddled ahead. Her surfboard's name was Everooze. Everooze was eager to help her carve some curl. He was teeping into the environment, watching the ocean's undulations. And his sensitive skin was in tune with the subtle flows of the water around them. Everooze suggested that if Thuy were to angle off to the right about thirty meters and wait there, she'd be able to catch a gigundo swell that was just now rolling in from the horizon. "Visualize, realize, actualize," added the surfboard.

Thuy passed the advice to Jayjay and they lay waiting at the spot that Everooze had picked. She kept her eyes on the ocean, watching for signs of the promised wave, not wanting to rely entirely upon telepathy.

Off to the left, Mabel had caught a ride. Although she was too self-conscious to whoop, her teep image was a giant grin. Momotaro was surfing at her side. Closer to the shore, Bixie and

Chu were already paddling back toward them, having caught a breaker the minute they'd arrived.

Thuy was teeping a coolness between these two. It seemed Bixie was annoyed with Chu for having gone so far as to try and kiss her after their first ride. Poor Chu. Now he was feeling rejected and unlovable. But what did he expect? Bixie was a bit skeptical of boys in general, and not all that interested in Chu in particular.

Meanwhile—oh, oh—here came a wave with Thuy and Jayjay's names on it. This was almost literally true. For, like every other natural system, the wave had a resident silp, and the wave-silp knew that the two kiqqie surfers were awaiting her. In fact the wave was in teep contact with Thuy, helping to plan her launch.

"Now," said the wave-silp as she slid past. "Cowabunga."

Kicking hard, Thuy made it over the foamy lip and slid down the liquid precipice, first kneeling on the board and then standing up, with Everooze suggesting muscle moves to improve Thuy's balance. The wave, the board, and Thuy were thinking as one.

Teeping over her shoulder, Thuy observed that Jayjay had missed the wave. She rode the breaker another sixty meters before shooting back over the wave's lip. Everooze helped her paddle toward her husband.

The big wave had been the first of a set, so Thuy had to duck under two successive walls of water. When yet another wave loomed up, she stopped ducking and teleported straight to Jayjay, teeking Everooze along.

Something was wrong. Jayjay was lying on his back on the board, slightly twitching. A fit? The twitching amped up; he was shaking all over. His skin was covered with vibrating goose bumps, like a pond in a rainstorm. His wetsuit bulged at his crotch.

Thuy took hold of Jayjay's board; she cradled his head so the seawater wouldn't slop into his mouth. He was making an off-key droning sound and gently bucking his hips.

"Jayjay?"

No answer but his rhythmic hum. Peering into his mind, Thuy saw part of his vision: a symmetric, overripe woman dressed in feathers, her breasts and sex exposed. A girlfriend? A porn show? Her face was very strange—oh. She had no eyes. Just smooth skin.

Thuy delved into the Gaian mind for help; Gaia was right here watching, dragonflies haloing her face. "That's not a woman," said Gaia. "It's an alien projection who latched onto Jayjay last night. She's called a Pekklet. She's controlled by Pekka, the world-mind of a bird planet."

Slavishly obeying the feathered fantasy Pekklet, Jayjay was repeatedly spewing out a particular psychic pattern, an insanely intricate construct that resembled a gear-based Swiss watch with innumerable colored worms inside it, each worm twisted into a different knot. Jayjay was using his whole body to send this teek pulse to—how weird—each and every atom in the vicinity, his manic spray of femtohertz data fanning fifty kilometers out to sea, fifty kilometers inland, and a hundred kilometers deep into the Earth's crust.

"Can you set him free?" Thuy implored Gaia. "Can you block the Pekklet's teep?"

"It's not teep," said Gaia. "It's a quantum entanglement connection to the Pekklet's flesh body, hidden in the subdimensions of your cabin floor."

"What's all this for?" demanded Thuy.

"I'm not sure yet."

Jayjay's spell had passed; he was staring glassy-eyed into the sky.

All around them the ocean had turned tame. The water's

tiny ripples were gone, as were the big rollers—there was nothing left but smooth, medium-sized waves.

Stabbed by jealousy over her husband's susceptibility to the Pekklet's sexual teasing, Thuy gave his shoulder a rough shove. "You think she's sexy? An eyeless alien bird?"

"I can't help myself," said Jayjay despairingly. "She's knotted into me. I'm her puppet." He groaned and sat up on his board, taking in the scene.

The sea was like a sloshing bathtub—limp and listless, as ordinary and uninteresting as their woods had seemed this morning. The clouds in the sky were fatuous balloons. Even Thuy was starting to feel calm and neutral again.

"The atomic silps—they're not computing the natural world in depth," said Jayjay. "They're wasting their cycles on this weird quantum computation that I programmed into them just now. No more gnarl."

"Let's teleport back to Ond's," said Thuy. She signaled the four teenagers that they were leaving. And then they were on Ond's patio.

CHAPTER 5

ALIEN TULPAS

Jil and Kittie were drinking tea and nibbling at a bowl of strawberries. Jil was training her shoons and Kittie was studying a blook—a rhodopsin-doped sheet of plastic capable of displaying images from every corner of earth.

"Back so soon?" said Kittie, looking up. "Something's wrong!"

"Jayjay had a kind of seizure," said Thuy. "An alien mind took him over. He reprogrammed the ocean and—oh God, it's reached here, too. Look how stupidly those branches move, all of them rocking in unison. San Francisco's gone as dull as a drum machine. Can you feel it?"

Jil and Kittie exchanged a puzzled look.

"You and Jayjay are high on Gaia?" suggested Kittie after a pause. "Pighead style? You shouldn't let him drag you down,

Thuy. Last fall you said that you'd quit being a pighead for good."

"This is real," said Jayjay in a low, gloomy voice. "Something strange happened to me last night."

"You acted like a pighead," said Jil in a mock-sweet tone. "What's strange about that? Getting high is what you're all about."

"I'm trying to change," said Jayjay stiffly. "But that's not the point. Last night I climbed up past lazy eight and I learned to think ten tridecillion thoughts in a second or two. And now this alien agent called a Pekklet is using me to steal the Earth's gnarl. She's making me cast malware programs into our atoms. They're called runes."

Jil held up a lumpy strawberry, making a show of studying it. "This juicy little fella looks plenty gnarly to me." She bit into it and grinned.

"It's gnarly because it grew *before* the change," said Jayjay. "But the next crop of strawberries will look like—like simple cones."

"And last night I thought I saw Hieronymous Bosch," said Kittie, not taking her vision so seriously today. "What a party." She guffawed. "Hey, Jayjay, did the aliens—*examine* you? Is the Pekklet beautiful? Does she give you a—"

"It's not funny!" yelled Thuy, turning red. "It's horrible. Look! This is what it's about." She turned on the hose and let the water play onto the stones of the patio. The water traveled in a perfect parabolic arc to spread across the ground in a smooth, even pool. No droplets, no bubbles, no spray, no fun.

"I don't get what—" began Jil.

"Then look at *this*," said Jayjay, seizing Jil's empty teacup and throwing it down to smash. The cup broke into six equal-sized pieces that settled symmetrically onto the ground like the petals of a magnolia flower.

"The world is acting like a cheap-ass video game," said Thuy. "It's almost as if we've been eaten by nanomachines and turned into sims."

"Tell us again what happened to you, Jayjay," said Kittie slowly.

"While I was waiting for our wave, I heard squawking and chattering," said Jayjay. "The sound was coming from inside my head. I remembered the sound from last night—when I climbed a subdimensional beanstalk and the Pekklet locked onto me. I see visions of her as—a sexy woman in feathers."

"*Oooh-la-la,*" said Kittie.

"The Pekklet gives me little pieces of quantum computer code," continued Jayjay doggedly. "She calls them runes. And I've been teeking the runes onto atoms over and over."

"He's completely spun!" exclaimed Jil. "Slushed!"

"I teeped Jayjay while it was happening just now," said Thuy loyally. "He really was teeking little jolts to atom after atom. I think he reprogrammed the whole hundred kilometer cube of Earth's crust that's under San Francisco."

"I was like an orchestra conductor," said Jayjay, a little proud of his abilities. "Playing a pitch pipe for ten tridecillion musicians—one at a time."

"Ten—what?" said Kittie, grasping for something solid to understand.

"A big number," said Jayjay, taking comfort in the math. "You write ten tridecillion as a one followed by forty-three zeroes."

"Oh."

"And the squawky feather-woman Pekklet made you do this—why?" said Jil, really doubting him.

"Well—the Pekklet is working for an alien planetary mind called Pekka. And maybe Pekka wants Earth to be an old-school data center, like when they used to keep all those microchip boxes in one building. Maybe Pekka is skimming off Earth's gnarl to run, I don't know, a corporate market-prediction engine for the feather boa industry of the Magellanic Clouds!"

Neither Jil nor Kittie laughed.

"Can't you feel the difference?" Thuy asked the other women again. "Can't you feel that your gnarl is missing?"

Jil shrugged. The conversation had trailed off. The thing was, thanks to the gnarl reduction, they didn't have enough mental focus to be properly alarmed. It was like—everything's fucked, but so what?

"I'm just coming off a horrible catfight with Nektar and Lureen," said Kittie, willfully retreating into neighborhood gossip. "The three of us had sex together last night, but then this morning, I'm the odd woman out. They both think they're prettier than me. Old slags. I just hope Nektar lets me keep using her garage after what I said to her and Lureen. I went a little too far."

"I'm impressed you brought them together," said Jil, content with the conversation's familiar turn. "They used to hate each other."

"Isn't anyone worried about Pekka and the missing gnarl?" demanded Jayjay.

"Maybe we women are sick of you always trying to be the center of attention," snapped Thuy, turning away from the apocalypse, too. "What did you say to them, Kittie?"

"I called them rutting rhinos," said Kittie allowing herself a slight smile.

"*That* goes in my next metanovel," said Thuy.

"I hear you're calling it *Hive Mind*?" said Jil.

"Yeah," said Thuy. "I'm merging with society. I'm thinking

that instead of me writing *Hive Mind, Hive Mind* will write me."

"My best murals are like that," said Kittie. "They paint me." She was scrolling through images in her interactive blook. "I bet that's how it was for Hieronymus Bosch. I have his pictures here."

"Oh, before I forget, can you pick up that cup you broke, Jayjay?" said Jil. "I don't want the kids to cut themselves."

"All right," said Jayjay, squatting to pick up the shards. "Is it okay if I raid your kitchen? Maybe if I eat something, I can focus on what we have to do. This low gnarl is turning me into a pinhead."

"Fine," said Jil. "Ond's in there napping on a couch."

Like someone hiding from the day by pulling covers over her head, Thuy continued peering over Kittie's shoulder at the blook. The Bosch pictures glowed, rich and lovely. Kittie tapped and rubbed to zoom and pan. One of the paintings, *The Garden of Earthly Delights,* showed a frieze of naked people around a lake. In a corner, two lovers sat by a blue demon playing a harp.

"You didn't really see Bosch at our party, did you?" said Thuy. "You were drunk."

"I feel like I saw him," said Kittie. "A thirty-foot-tall Hibraner version of Bosch. Maybe he could have jumped here because of the way the branes' timelines are skewed. He lived in Holland around 1490, you know."

"I wonder what that was like?"

"Actually, I've been studying up on Bosch's life for years," said Kittie. "His homies were tripping their brains out from ergot poisoning, and torturing each other for being possessed. Bosch himself is hard to figure. Sometimes I think he didn't like sex—he makes it so cold and weird. Or maybe he *did* like sex, a lot, and he felt guilty."

Kittie tapped an illustration in the blook, zooming in on a detail, then continued talking. "Look at the phallus-and-vulva shapes on this pink—I guess you'd call it a marble palace."

"The magic harp's soundboard was painted just like this," said Thuy. "The Hibrane harp that unfurled the eighth dimension. Did I tell you that Jayjay saw the harp again last night?"

"Where?"

"On, uh, that subdimensional beanstalk he says he climbed."

"Some heavy shit's coming down," said Kittie, shaking her head. "I never really got a good look at that harp when she was here. The subbies had been gnawing on it. And then that Hibraner Azaroth stole it right back."

"Well, it belonged to his aunt," said Thuy. "Come to think of it, they were part Dutch. The harp came down through their family from way back." She regarded the chilly nudes in Kittie's blook. "Do you really think an old-master type painter would take a lowly gig like decorating a musical instrument?"

"Painters take all kinds of jobs," said Kittie, flipping to a new image. "There's a hair-thin line between painter and bum. Did I tell you that when I was with Bosch last night, I teeped him my portfolio? He said he liked the monster series I'm painting on vans. God, I wish he'd stayed. We could work together. Krazy Kittie and Howlin' Hieronymus Hell Hearses!"

"I like the way everything in his pictures is alive," said Thuy. "Check out the pottery jug with legs. And that hill in the background is a man on all fours. It's like Bosch saw hylozoism coming."

"This is my favorite Bosch triptych," said Kittie. "*The Temptation of Saint Anthony*. Saint Anthony's feelin' it. He looks just like Bosch. Yeroon is looking out at us and he's all, 'Ain't this some waaaald shit?' Maybe he was tempted to imagine weird stuff all the time, but he was scared the visions came from the Evil One."

"Do you guys have any kind of plan about how to fix the, ah, the missing gnarl?" interrupted Jil. While they'd been talking, Jil had been messing with her little plastic robots. "My shoons can't do much anymore."

"I wonder if anyone besides Jayjay is spreading alien runes," said Thuy, reluctantly getting back into crisis-management mode. Jayjay himself was in the kitchen, eating a turkey sandwich and drinking a bottle of beer, not a thought in his head. Thuy gave him a mental nudge.

"Maybe I should check with Gaia," he said, reappearing on the patio.

"If you check with Gaia, you'll just take off on another pighead run," sniped Jil.

"Don't you be riding him all the time," said Thuy, mustering some anger. "You're a snotty priss-pot, Jil. You're just sour because Jayjay broke up with you to marry me. And then your husband left you. And now you're stuck with a geeky old man."

"I'm the same age as Jil," said Ond, emerging from the house with his thinning blond hair and sloping shoulders.

"Oh, hi Ond," said Thuy awkwardly. "The aliens are invading and I'm freaking out."

"I was doing a deep meditation about electricity," said Ond. His phrase for taking a nap. "But now I'm teeping this apocalyptic scenario from you guys? An alien mind-master made Jayjay reprogram our matter? This is huge!"

"Ond will fix things now," said Jil confidently. "You'll see. He's not like Jayjay, who's ruining the world as fast as he can."

"Jil—" began Ond.

"Oh, Jil's right," said Jayjay flopping despondently into a patio chair. "I shouldn't contact Gaia."

"Jil's a bitch," said Thuy before she could stop herself. "Sorry, Ond."

"Don't curse at my mother," said Bixie, as she and the three other kids reappeared, returning early from their surf outing.

"You grown-ups should be making plans," scolded Mabel. "The surf is flat and everything's wrong. I teeped to find out what you're doing about it, and you're just picking on each other and talking about stupid old paintings? Why don't you call in the army and the air force?"

"That'd be square," said Kittie wickedly. "I'd rather be dead than square."

"What if things stay this way for good?" demanded Bixie. "I feel so—*ugh*. Like a shadow or a toon."

"Maybe we're better off without gnarl," said Chu, giving the girl a pointed look. "It hurts to feel."

"You're all crazy!" wailed Mabel.

"Look, if nobody else will, I'm gonna contact Gaia myself," said Thuy.

"Vintage pighead move," muttered Jil.

"By the way, Jil, I'm sorry I called you a *BITCH*!" said Thuy, punching the final word. Deep down, she'd never really forgiven Jil for sleeping with Jayjay. No gnarl deficit was gonna erase that.

Jil started to get up from her seat, but Ond got in between them.

Happy to have had the last word, Thuy closed her eyes and circled up toward the great blue face of Gaia. The transition was slower than usual, and it was hard to keep her focus. But then Gaia flipped down a curly tendril to catch hold of Thuy's psyche, pulling her to a fresh-smelling niche, vaguely chapel-like, with an elegant ultramarine figure sitting on a couch, an ocean-blue woman with wave-swell breasts and kelp for hair—a Gaian avatar.

"This invasion is dreadful," said Gaia right off. "Like parasitic vines strangling an oak. Like a plague riddling a cow's flesh with pus-filled buboes. I'm the cow. I'm the oak. I'm considering drastic action."

"How far has the problem spread?" asked Thuy.

"Just Yolla Bolly and San Francisco so far. Two cubes of my body, each of them a hundred kilometers on an edge. Thanks to your husband."

"You encouraged him," said Thuy.

"Well—he and Sonic were being interesting," said Gaia. "I boosted them to a higher level. And then the pitchfork got involved."

"What *is* that thing?" asked Thuy. "I saw him outside my house during the night."

"Yes," said Gaia. "The pitchfork is the partner of the magic harp. Groovy and Lovva. I've known about them for a few days. Basically, Groovy and Lovva are humanoids like you, but they can shift their shapes. They come from a lazy eight planet, too. Their minds are temporarily infinite, and that means they have direct matter control."

"These are completely different aliens from Pekka and her agent? And different from the flying manta rays—assuming those are real?"

"The mantas are real," said Gaia. "But they're hard to see. They camouflage themselves very well. I think they're enemies of Pekka, so that's all to the good."

"This is nuts," said Thuy. "Why did you let all these weird aliens come after my husband?"

"Well, Lovva the harp's been very nice to us—she unfurled my eighth dimension, after all. So I thought that whatever her husband, Groovy, did would be good, too. And there's something else. Your and Jayjay's timelines are somehow very deeply knotted with the timelines of Lovva and Groovy."

"Oh, great," said Thuy.

"It's not all bad," said Gaia. "I never knew that people could travel to lazy eight infinity via the subdimensions, and last night Jayjay got partway there. The problem is that when he and the pitchfork stopped, the pitchfork incarnated a Pekklet and, as you know, the Pekklet is puppeteering Jayjay."

"So find the Pekklet," said Thuy. "Kill her. I mean, she's living right inside one of our floorboards. Come to think of it, I can pull up the board and burn it."

"Rearranging a few molecules isn't going to change anything," said Gaia. "The Pekklet is ten tridecillion levels down into the subdimensions. It's as if she were deep undersea where no storms can reach."

"So dive in after her," insisted Thuy. "Find her!"

"But the beanstalk is gone now," said Gaia. "So there's no obvious path to the Pekklet."

"Can't you do a sweep of the subdimensions?"

"You don't understand about subdimensional space," said Gaia. "It's exponentially large. The level where the Pekklet's hiding isn't just bigger than our universe, it's bigger than ten to the power of our universe."

"I'm not a scientist."

"Let's just say that unless one of you manages to aktualize yourself and get an infinite mind, there's no hope of finding the Pekklet."

"So now what?" asked Thuy. "How do we fix my husband?"

"I foresee a struggle," said Gaia, flipping her seaweed hair. A school of tiny, metallic-blue fish quivered amid the stalks. "I'm a rich prize. I have a highly evolved ecosystem and an unfurled eighth dimension. And it seems that, across the galaxies, humanoids are quite rare and valuable. You're one of the very few types of beings who can teleport or teek."

"So the alien birds want us, huh?" said Thuy. "And the pitchfork is helping them out. I wonder if Mabel was right. Maybe the army *should* nuke Yolla Bolly."

"The filthy nukes are gone," said Gaia. "I disintegrated all of the atomic weapons on Lazy Eight Day when the silps awoke. Your so-called leaders are covering that up. They want to keep you scared of them. But I can perfectly well wipe out Yolla Bolly and San Francisco without nukes."

"What do you mean?" asked Thuy.

"I'm able to control my lava flows and to shift my tectonic plates. I can place volcanoes at will. Vaporizing the Yolla Bolly wilderness won't destroy the Pekklet, but it'll definitely disperse the atoms that Jayjay infected. I might even tip California into the sea."

"But explosions of that size . . ."

The womanly blue figure of Gaia laughed ruefully, now more like the sky than the sea. A series of jeweled beetles sprang into flight around her cloudy head. "The firestorms, smoke, and dust could well make some of the higher organisms extinct," she said, expressively softening her hands into tentacles. "But—species come and go. What I'm a little worried about is that—should a full cleansing require highly cataclysmic eruptions—I might break into chunks."

"That's unthinkable," said Thuy, choosing her words carefully. "Not just for us, Gaia, but for you. You have to preserve yourself. You're a beautiful warm-centered planet. You don't want to be a frozen asteroid belt."

"I'd rather end up that way than be the slave of alien parasites. Drastic measures, Thuy."

"Let's try some partial measures first. Maybe we can fix it with computer science."

"Aha," said Gaia, fixing Thuy with an intense, sky-blue stare. "You rise to the challenge. Very well then. I want you and Jayjay to return to your house in the woods. See what you can learn about the alien invaders whom you'll find there. I don't know enough about them yet. It's hard to read their minds."

"Are you talking about the flying stingrays?"

"No, I'm talking about things like ostrich birds. They're called Peng. Transmitted here from Pekka's world. Thanks to Jayjay."

"At our camp right now?" said Thuy uneasily. "I thought we were just talking about—an infection in our atoms. A quantum computation thing."

"Have you ever heard of matter waves, Thuy?"

"No. I'm not into physics."

"You humans have huge new memory storage, plus the help of the silps and me—and you're still picky about what you learn?" said Gaia impatiently. "You're like stones. Or artichokes."

"I'm writing a new metanovel," said Thuy, defensively. "*Hive Mind*. I want to explore the ebb and flow of shared identities. Conscious minds used to be like isolated fireflies in the night. And now the light is everywhere. Our world is hylozoic. But I don't have to tell you this, do I?"

"I can't believe how long this conversation is taking," said Gaia irritably. "Centuries of my time. Let's stick to what I wanted tell you about matter waves. Everything is wave and particle. Think of atoms focusing matter waves on a single spot to produce a physical object. It's like a bunch of lasers focusing light waves on a single spot to produce a tiny sun."

"You're talking about tulpas," exclaimed Thuy, dredging up another obscure word that she happened to know.

"You humans are like walking bagpipes," said Gaia wearily.

"You make squeals and imagine they're thoughts. What's a tulpa supposed to be?"

"You're the global hive mind, Gaia. Look up Tibetan mysticism." Thuy's favorite musician, Tawny Krush, had led her to this topic last year. "A tulpa's an idea that becomes real."

"Ah yes, I see now," said Gaia quickly. "Quite the elegant squeal, really. So, yes, when you go up to Yolla Bolly, you'll be dealing with Peng tulpas. In their own way, they're as solid as you."

"Hundreds of Peng?"

"Not hundreds," said Gaia, becoming a tangle of vines and leaves with bunny rabbits peeping out. "Not at all. Three Peng aliens in Yolla Bolly, and three here in San Francisco."

"Huge aliens?"

"No, no, the tulpas aren't much bigger than you. It takes so very much matter to generate them because the computation is a quadrillion-fold inefficient. They parasitize a hundred-kilometer cube of my substance to compute three puny bodies amounting to a cubic meter of louse-infested flesh! It's an outrage. I hate them."

"If there's only three aliens at our camp, then maybe Jayjay and I do have a chance," said Thuy. "Maybe we could kill them." But even as she said this, she wondered if it might not be better to make friends.

"No compromises," urged Gaia, noticing Thuy's thought of mercy. "I'd try to kill them myself, but I don't have that kind of finely tuned control. In any case, it's going to be tricky. They're not ordinary matter, after all."

"Maybe Jayjay can erase them by undoing what he did to all those atoms," suggested Thuy. "Like I said before. Computer science." Not that this was a field she'd ever taken much interest in.

"Go there and see," urged Gaia. "Meanwhile I'll be planning my volcanoes, just in case." Her image mutated into a dense swarm of gnats.

Thuy drew back into ordinary consciousness. She was slumped in her chair like any pighead on the nod. Jil gave her an unfriendly glance. Thuy did a remote teep check on Yolla Bolly. Although she could make out their empty cabin, the connection went sparkling and gauzy when she tried to see into the surrounding woods. The only way to size up the aliens was going to be face-to-face.

"I overheard you telling Gaia that we're going to Yolla Bolly," said Jayjay. "I'm ready."

"Look!" said Chu, sounding satisfied. "We have guns."

The men had been gathering weapons. A candy-cane striped bazooka lay on the patio beside two futuristic pistols: a smooth, blue raygun and a knotted shape of wires and crystals.

"We borrowed these from a place called Seven Wiggle Labs!" said Ond enthusiastically. "It's run by two vibby geeks who used to work with me at ExaExa."

"I'm a stonker," teeped the blue raygun with the triangular fins. He had a reedy tenor voice.

"I'll test it," yelled Momotaro and snatched up the stonker. With a hyperactive cackle, he fired at a yellow-cushioned chair. A wavery femtoray flowed from the muzzle and the cushions' color drained away. The chair glazed over with symmetric patterns of frost, let out a plaintive creak, and collapsed into cubes that broke into still smaller cubes that crumbled into dust.

"It's supposed to shatter jaggedly," complained the blue raygun via teep. "I don't like cubes."

"Jagged or not, that gun might slow down some aliens, huh, Thuy?" said Jayjay.

Momotaro danced across the yard, teeking stones into the air and disintegrating them in mid-flight. A couple of Jil's shoons skipped along in his wake.

"And look at this vibby bazooka," said Jayjay. "It's a gobble gun." The helical stripes of red and white were continually rotating around the outer surface of the bazooka's tube, always in the same place, yet appearing to crawl forward—like a barber pole.

"Be sure and hold me out to one side when you shoot me," advised the device in a solemn fat-man voice.

Meanwhile Thuy picked up the third weapon, a glittery pistol made of crystals and metal wrap. Its knobby grip was of entwined silver and copper strands. Its barrel was a wire-wrapped line of rhomboidal crystals, ranging in size from dice to ice cubes. It was like an extravagant piece of jewelry, an objet d'art. She could begin to see the allure of exotic weaponry.

"I'm the opposite of the stonker," the gun teeped in a sweet soprano whisper. "I'm a klusper. I overload atoms with information and they vibrate faster and faster, until the target gets all crispy and bursts into flame."

"I want to shoot at the aliens!" yelled Momotaro.

"Absolutely not," said Jil. With a lashing gesture of her mind, she teeked the stonker from Momotaro's grasp. It made an audible slap as it landed against her palm. "I think Thuy and Jayjay need to leave now," she added.

"I'll take the stonker," said Chu. "I'm going with them. Nobody wants me around here anyway."

"Don't be silly, Chu," said Ond. "I love you, Nektar loves you, and so does Jil and your new brother and sister."

"I want to see the aliens," said Chu. "Maybe they're like me. Maybe I can make friends."

"You'd have to ask your mother," said Ond.

"She's asleep at Lureen's," said Chu. "Let me go, and I'll be back by supper. Nektar doesn't have to know."

"It's okay with me," put in Thuy. "Chu was pretty much help on the expedition to the Hibrane."

"Oh—all right," said Ond with a shrug. "I'll keep researching the situation from here. Hop right back if there's any danger at all. I'll be watching you."

Chu looked at Bixie as if he'd like to say something tender but he couldn't spit it out.

And then the three of them were in the clearing in front of Thuy and Jayjay's cabin. Although it was almost noon, the air was clouded by a sullen mist rising up from the sodden forest floor. The branches of the redwoods rocked monotonously in the steady breeze. The stream's flow was utterly free of turbulence, the water's surface a regular pattern of glassy bumps.

"It's even deader than before," said Thuy. Her hands hung dangling at her side. The San Francisco infection was wearing off from her atoms, but she felt no joy.

Their little house looked cheap and dull, and the silp that animated the house was dumb and slow. How silly she'd been to be so excited about her honeymoon.

The harsh bird cries sounded again.

CHAPTER 6

THE PENG

Standing in the clearing with the newlyweds, Chu felt hollow and distracted. He couldn't stop thinking about Bixie. This morning in the ocean he'd reached out to touch her sweet face, and then he'd leaned forward to graze her downy cheek. She'd frowned and shoved him away. Why didn't Bixie like him? He'd been working so hard to heal his brain and change his demeanor. He was learning about empathy. He was more sociable than before. It was wrong to treat him like an unfeeling zombie. He heaved a wistful sigh.

Three nasty-smelling man-sized birds stalked into the woodsy clearing, moving with an urgent, stealthy gait, now and then hopping a few feet into the air and flapping their stubby wings.

They resembled grubby ostriches or rheas: long-necked dirty

brown mops on scaly stilts, anything but cute. The down-ward curve of their blunt beaks lent them a sour demeanor. They pecked bugs from the ground, squawking to each other as they came.

"Stop right there," Thuy called to the unsavory birds. "Where are you from?"

The biggest one cawed his harsh response, sending along a telepathic signal that made the sounds into words.

"We are Peng from planet Pengö. I am Suller, with my ill-tempered wife Gretta and our no-good son Kakar."

"Why do you insult us in front of the new slaves?" squawked Gretta, aiming a sharp peck at her husband's feathered body.

"We're invading your planet," volunteered Kakar. "I think that's cool. I want to watch you mate." Chu almost smiled at this. He liked rude kids.

"Are we supposed to shoot them?" he asked Thuy, teeping her on a private channel.

"Me first," said Thuy, who'd just made a snap decision not to negotiate. "You hang back, Chu. You've got your whole life ahead of you."

Holding her crystal-and-wire klusper in both hands, Thuy hit the alien fowl with brilliant yellow femtorays: first Suller, then Kakar, then Gretta.

Their striped brown feathers puffed into flame like oily rags; their legs collapsed, their flesh hissed and crackled, giving off the stench of burnt hair. As the inferno consumed the Peng, they threw back their heads in ecstasies of pain, shattering the air with spasmodic shrieks. Poor Kakar.

Chu noticed that the fire had set some of the low-hanging redwood limbs alight as well. The low-gnarl flames were shaped like symmetrical triangles.

Other than the slow crackling in the branches, all was still. The Peng smoke drifted away. But then—with a brief staticky flicker, the aliens were back in the clearing, as solid and stinky as before. Kakar pecked up a banana slug; Gretta fluffed out her mangy mop.

"Not nice," said Suller, strutting toward Thuy. "You need to learn some manners, my furry female friend. How about if I—"

Jayjay powered on the gobble gun. With a throaty whoosh, the tube punched a narrow round hole through the forest, a cylinder of devastation half a meter across and several hundred meters long. The pulped debris was being vacuumed into the gobble gun's tube, and a thick black coil of condensed matter oozed like excrement from the striped barrel's rear.

Already four or five redwoods across the stream had begun hugely to fall, the weakened trunks giving way with fusillades of sharp pops. Chu noted that the redwood silps were intrigued rather than upset. In their view, being a fungus-coated log was as interesting as being a leafy tree.

Jayjay twitched the big tube with precise motions, his face clenched in concentration, working to eliminate every parti-cle of the aliens without doing excessive damage to the woods. Chu was impressed by his poise. Once the gawky birds were wholly gone, Jayjay aimed the gobble gun upward to prune away the branches that Thuy had set alight. And then he switched it off.

Grew was saved, but in the distance other trees continued falling for a minute or two. Each splintering collapse seemed to set off another. Chu put himself into a hyperalert state, poised to teleport out of there in case the Peng retaliated.

As the crashing subsided, the air twinkled again and—the aliens recongealed yet again, firm and solid as ever. Their mood was calmly triumphant.

Deeply intrigued, Chu teeped into Thuy and Jayjay's minds, fishing for info about tulpas. Back on Ond's patio, he'd been preoccupied by his monitoring of Bixie's mood.

In short, the Peng were like holograms, but made of matter instead of light. The local atoms were skimping on the complexity of their physical interactions, and channeling their quantum computations into generating the Peng. The atoms were producing matter waves whose mutual interference patterns were solid Peng tulpas.

Teeping down into the atoms around him, Chu visualized the process in mathematical terms. He'd soaked up a ton of math in the last few years—he loved the stuff. He was seeing a Peng tulpa as being the sum of a Fourier series, like a chorus of sine waves piling up to form a spiky squiggle. As long as the local atoms kept pumping out the matter waves, the Fourier sum kept coming back. The computations generating these three grotty birds were distributed across the whole forest. It was going to be very hard indeed to rub them out.

Quietly, Chu stashed his stonker in his pants pocket. The gun was begging him to fire it, but there was no use. Meanwhile, Suller darted forward and whacked Jayjay's gobble gun with his beak, knocking the tube to the ground. Gretta did the same thing to Thuy's klusper. But, *whew,* that was the extent of the Peng payback.

As casually as ducks eating gingerbread, the two fowl pecked the guns apart and swallowed the pieces, raising their beaks high to work down the larger chunks. Meanwhile Kakar devoured the entire coiled worm of crushed matter that had emerged from the gobble gun's rear. The Peng tulpas were truly omnivorous, capable of eating anything at all. And their matter-hologram beaks were forceful as wrecking bars.

A pair of bluejays peered down from the upper branches of Grew. Kwaawk and his mate. The jays scolded and cawed, teeping their distrust of the alien birds. The tree was unhappy, too, complaining about how stiff and stereotyped her motions had

become. The local silps resented the mangy alien birds for siphoning off the richness of their inner lives.

"How did your world's furry beasts end up bigger than the
feathered ones?" wondered Gretta, twitchily looking from the
bluejays to the humans and back. Her teep voice came across
as shrill and penetrating. "Your natural order is cockeyed. I
suppose that humans evolved from rodents? Nasty, scuttling
things. In primitive times, rats ate our eggs."

"We're descended from apes," said Thuy sullenly. "Not
rats."

"Apes, rats—it's all the same," said Gretta airily. She had a fey
mannerism of abruptly darting her head. "On Pengö, there's
nothing but birds, fish, worms, and insects. Our ancestors elim-
inated the pesky furries many millennia ago. I suppose we'll do
the same thing here."

"Have you always had telepathy?" asked Thuy, forcing a
semblance of a smile.

Closely watching her, and managing to grasp that she was
worried inside, Chu felt a sudden desire to bring a true smile
to Thuy's lips. Thus was born his new crush, the second of his
life. Jayjay didn't notice, he was turned inward, trying to figure out how to undo the atomic changes he'd helped bring
about.

"At the dawn of history, a squealing bag visited us," said
Gretta in answer to Thuy's question. "A noise-sack from a different reality. The flying bag's sacred squawks unfurled our
eighth dimension. All of our objects awoke, and we came to
know Pekka, the mind of our planet. Pekka is a bit like your pig-
gish Gaia, I suppose." Gretta arched her neck, looking around
the grove. "It's interesting to be on a primitive planet where lazy
eight is new."

"Your planetary mind—Pekka," probed Thuy. "She's the

one who sent you? I heard she has a local agent here—hidden in the subdimensions? She looks like you, but bigger and with no eyes?"

"That would be the Pekklet, yes." Gretta clacked her beak, snapped up a beetle, and returned to the topic of her home world's glorious history. "The flying noise-bag was our first miracle, and the second great miracle was when Waheer and Pekka learned to project Peng souls as runes. Thanks to Waheer's daring and to Pekka's divine wisdom, the adventurous among us can travel to teeker worlds and wear the bodies that you call tulpas." Gretta clucked and flapped her stubby wings. "Tulpa, tulpa, tulpa."

"I can see that we have a lot to learn from you!" said Thuy in her sweetest tone. "I'm terribly sorry about the misunderstanding with the guns."

Chu admired Thuy's effrontery, physically expressed in the insolent curve of her neck. The only misunderstanding about the guns was that Thuy had thought they might work.

Of course, Thuy was a twenty-seven-year-old married woman—and Chu was only fourteen. But she was surprisingly attractive to him, not that he could imagine actually trying anything with a woman that age. But . . . maybe? He loved her high pigtails. And she didn't get all upset if you happened to stare, not even if you looked under her clothes. Not like Bixie.

Suller had begun berating Jayjay. "At first I was going to thank you for casting the pioneer runes that brought us here," rasped the big bird. Overlaid by telepathy, Suller's harsh caws reminded Chu of Mr. Big, the head gangster in a video game, *Gross Polluter,* that he'd played as a kid. "I'm prepared to cut you in on a very sweet cash deal," continued Suller. "But—instead of saying hello, you and your wife try to murder us? What kind of garbage is that? It's lucky that you're our runecaster. Otherwise—" Suller darted his head forward like a woodpecker, bringing the tip of his diamond-hard beak to within a millimeter of Jayjay's forehead.

Reading others' emotions had never been Chu's strong point, but Suller was particularly opaque, what with his alien mind and his glassy bird eyes. It was hard to tell if he was angry right now, or if he was just practicing for being angry later.

As for Jayjay, he barely even flinched, so intent was he upon the problem of how to undo the runes that he'd cast into the atoms of the Yolla Bolly woods.

Thuy laid a gentle hand on Suller's subtly banded brown feathers, soothing him with her calm, reasonable tone. "How is it that Jayjay became your runecaster? What makes him so special?"

"He's a zedhead. He can carry out ten tridecillion atomic tweaks in a couple of seconds. And, best of all, he got snared by Pekka's agent."

Gretta got in on the conversation, her teep signal shrill and gloating. "Jayjay saw Pekka's agent and he yelled, 'Yoo-hoo!'" She jiggled her head and let out a trill of mocking laughter. "The Pekklet hooked Jayjay—*zack*. Whenever Pekka needs him, he's there. Our pet runecaster. We're here to civilize another ratty teeker world."

Suller studied Jayjay. "You've made a good start, I'll grant you that. You cast the rune for my family here in Yolla Bolly, and you cast the rune for Blotz's family in, uh, San Francisco. Wish you'd checked with me on that one, Jayjay. I didn't want Blotz and his family to end up so far away."

"Blotz!" exclaimed Gretta. "You didn't tell me they were coming, Suller!"

Chu teeped back to his father in San Francisco to check that Ond was hearing all this. Ond was sitting by the window in a darkened room of their house. "Keep your distance from

Suller," advised Ond. "And guess what—those San Francisco aliens Suller is talking about? They're in our backyard."

Ond directed Chu's attention to the patio of their Dolores Heights mansion. A trio of gawky birds were out there talking to Jil and Kittie. The birds were pecking up some bread and oranges that Jil had set out for them, now and then pausing to admire the view. "Their names are Blotz, Noora, and Pookie," continued Ond. "A father, mother, daughter trio. They came to our house because they're looking for Jayjay. He's supposed to help them do something."

"The guns don't work against them," Chu told his father.

"Yeah, I saw," said Ond. "We'll have to try something else. But with San Francisco's gnarl being siphoned off, I can't think straight. As soon as these nosy Peng leave our yard, I'm moving down to Santa Cruz with Jil and Nektar and the kids. According to my calculations, when you leave a Peng zone, the effects wear off. I'll get back to you when I can. Be very careful, son."

"Hey!" teeped Gretta, interrupting Chu and Ond's conversation. "I see what you're seeing: Blotz and his tacky wife Noora and their silly little daughter Pookie. It's so disgusting the way Noora holds her tail feathers pooched out to the sides. Does she really think that everyone wants to see her filthy cloaca?"

"Blotz and Noora are a high-class pair of Peng," Suller heavily told his wife. "Just like us. Eventually we'll establish a solid chain of Peng ranches between here and San Francisco, sweetie. Then we'll be able to visit with the Blotzes; strutting from ranch to ranch, merging the matter music. I'm thinking Kakar might even get Pookie to lay him an egg. They'd be a fine match, so shut your beak, okay? Warm Worlds Realty is bringing the cream of Peng society, no doubt!"

"What a crock," quacked Kakar. "Floofy's the one I want,

not Pookie. But, nooo, you had to bring me here. Blotz and Noora are broke losers—just like you guys. That's why you four took these stupid jobs as land developers. The cream of Peng society are the ones who are gonna actually *pay* Warm Worlds to have a ranch on Earth—if this place turns out to be livable, which I doubt. I swear I saw a rat just now."

"Rat!" squawked Gretta, hopping several meters off the ground and staying there, curiously suspended in midair.

With abrupt fury, Suller pecked Kakar hard enough to draw blood. Screeching piteously, the younger Peng bird flexed his legs and leapt for the roof of Thuy and Jayjay's house, extending his rudimentary wings for balance. He hadn't jumped hard enough to cover the distance, but, like Gretta, he came to rest in midair. Apparently the Peng could make themselves weightless. Kakar fluttered his wings till he'd reached the roof. Safely perched, he railed at his parents.

"I hate you! I wish I'd never been hatched!"

"Ungrateful fledgling!" croaked Gretta, settling back to the forest floor. "We only came to this terrible place because you're such a wild dreamer! Going to the cliffs to be an artist with Floofy—what a mess. Ever since then, Floofy's parents have been threatening us!" Next she turned on her mate. "And now I learn you've brought *Noora*? I know all about your affair with her, Suller. No wonder you're disappointed that their ranch isn't next door." Her voice cracked; despondently she lowered her beak.

Suller cooed softly and smoothed Gretta's feathers with his bill. Up on the roof, Kakar was examining the wound in his side. Chu almost offered to help, but he could teep that the gouge was healing fast; restored by the massed computations of the Yolla Bolly Peng ranch.

"My family . . ." teeped Suller, turning back to the humans with a sigh. "Never satisfied. Listen up, Jayjay. I can make you an attractive proposition. I want for you to do a series of tele-portation hops, a hundred kilometers at a time. At each spot you land, the Pekklet will feed you a rune for a fresh family of Peng pioneers, and you'll cast the rune into the atoms of the new ranch. The way Warm Worlds figures it, there's room for fifteen thousand ranches on Earth's land surface—what an opportunity!"

"No," said Jayjay. "I won't do it."

"I'll see that you're very handsomely paid for your runecast-ing," continued Suller smoothly. "Presently we're in start-up mode, with only seven pioneer families committed to come here, but I'm sure we'll have a land rush down the road. If all goes well, you'll be the richest man on Earth."

"I'd rather die."

"You *will* help us," said Suller coldly. "One way or another."

"You're worried about losing the—gnarl?" Gretta asked Jay-jay. She'd recovered her aplomb. Cocking her head, she turned her attention to Chu. "This boy doesn't mind the missing gnarl."

"I do, too," insisted Chu, wanting to seem like the others. But there was something to what she said. He liked things to be predictable and orderly.

"You furries will be better off without so much emotion and self-will," Gretta told Jayjay. "Leave the drama to us. We'll be your legends, your mythic queens and kings."

Teeping Jayjay for his reaction, Chu was shocked to see the intensity of the man's unhappiness. Jayjay hated himself for having opened the gateway to the Peng, hated himself for being an addicted pighead, hated himself for making his wife sad.

Chu found it painful to know these feelings. In the old days, before he'd started healing his autism, he'd been unable to visualize other people's inner lives at all. Sure, it was good to understand other people better now—but sometimes empathy was a drag.

"Why do you need a runecaster at all?" Thuy asked the aliens, twining her arm around her husband's waist.

"I'll answer that one," teeped Kakar from the roof. "Tulpa programming happens to be one of my interests." He hopped down into the clearing and cawed his explanation. "Each pioneer rune codes a small Peng family—bodies, brains, memories, the works. The runecaster has to be a teeker so he can program the rune into atoms, and he has to be able to think very fast so that he can do the full ten tridecillion atoms that you—"

"Spare me the geekin' details," interrupted Thuy, which was annoying for Chu. Thuy continued, "What I'm asking is why the Peng don't frikkin' *teleport* here if they want to invade? Why make it so complicated?"

"Listen to her, Suller and Kakar," cackled Gretta. "They don't even know."

"Not many races can teleport and teek," said Kakar. He raised his wings and bowed in an ironic salute. "Humans are special."

"I've heard that all the teeker races are descended from rats," said Gretta, twitching her head to snap a moth from the air. Jayjay shuddered and let out a faint hum.

"Apes, Mom," said Kakar shortly. "Like Thuy said earlier. Apes are the furry things with four hands that climb in trees. Do you act so dopey on purpose? Would Dad be scared of a hen who's not as dumb as him? I don't understand how you two hatched a genius like me."

Gretta tightened her beak, not deigning to respond to her son's insolence. Another moth appeared in the air beside her, and she caught that one, too. "Yum."

"You're saying that only humanoids can teleport themselves?" asked Thuy, looking back and forth between her husband and the aliens. "Only humanoids can reach into atoms and reprogram them with their minds?"

"Apes, humanoids, whatever," said Suller. "I wouldn't want to be one. Teek and teleportation come out of this neurotic-type syndrome. Those three teeker emotions—what do they call them again, Kakar? I always forget."

"Remorse, doubt, and fear," said Kakar, scratching a steady stream of banana slugs from the dirt. "You can teep the pattern in Jayjay's head, he's already thought about it. Remorse about the past, doubt about the present, fear of the future. What if, what if, what if. The pusher crew on a Hrull mothership at the Pengö spaceport told me about it, too. Pushers have it rough."

"*Yeah* they do," said Suller darkly. "You Earthlings are lucky we got here before the Hrullwelt ships found you."

Chu was thrilled by the mention of a mothership. It would be great to be in a starship crew, visiting rough spaceports on alien worlds like Pengö and the Hrullwelt—whatever that was.

"Tell us about your home planet," he urged Suller.

"My voice is tired," said the tall alien bird. "I've been squawking too hard. All this hassle and stress. I'll show you a— a kind of movie."

A flow of images began in the humans' heads, richly enhanced by data links. It was an ad for Warm Worlds Realty, with headquarters at planet Pengö's south pole.

The first scene shows the Virgo Supercluster, which stretches two hundred million light-years, encompassing the M51 Group as well as the Milky Way's Local Group.

The M51 galaxies sparkle like diamonds on black velvet, and now one of them begins to grow; it's the beautifully symmetric Whirlpool Galaxy.

"We are not alone," croons a bird's voice in deep, textured tones.

The viewpoint zooms in on a particular planet whose temperate zones are a filigree of green and blue. There are no open seas or level plains on this world, only a global maze of water channels and verdant rock ridges. A heavy frosting of ice coats the polar caps.

"Our planet Pengö is ancient," says the voice-over. "Our once molten core has all but crystallized; our continents have shattered. And thus our world's surface is a labyrinth of sea and stone."

The view swoops into winding, interlinked fjords with twisted trees growing in every crack. Flocks of birds scythe through insect swarms and wheel above the crystal waters, diving for fish.

"Our planet's beauty reflects the perfection of Pekka, our planetary mind," says the narrator. "And one species above all enjoys the radiance of Pekka's full favor. The Peng."

The shores are lined with dwellings: domed structures of nested stones, each hut with a door, two windows, and a ventilation hole in the roof. Peng birds strut in and out of the homes, knees bending backward, fluffy brown bodies bobbing up and down. They stroll along the shoreline, chatting with each other, snapping bugs from the air, wading into the shallows for frogs and minnows.

The Peng can fly, but not in the usual kind of way. Thanks to pale blue, ticklike symbiotes known as flight lice, they can make themselves weightless. Hovering like feathered blimps, the Peng use their tiny wings to maneuver. Now and then a Peng floats up a tree or cliff to peck apart a parrot's nest or a swallow's mud-daubed home, devouring the eggs and the fledglings.

"We Peng have been the dominant species for hundreds of thousands of years," resumes the bass bird voice. "Our ecology has converged to a lasting equilibrium."

A sequence of display cases flashes by, exhibiting the surprisingly few species of life on Pengö: trees and flowering plants, frogs and fish, earthworms and beetles, some smaller birds, the Peng—and no mammals.

"We revel in the simple perfection of Pengö's biome," quacks the narrator. "In the intellectual sphere, a similar process of refinement has taken place, raising our arts and practical crafts to a level that might seem to rule out further improvement. But great originals still emerge: wild talents like Waheer, who flourished one thousand years ago."

The viewpoint flies back in time to a chalky cliff. The cliff is like a public art gallery; its surface is decorated with chicken scratches. Peng artists are at work, using their beaks to scar the white stone, floating and fluttering along the face of the cliff.

The artworks fall into four types: jittery ovals that shape the outlines of eggs, chevron patterns that model Peng feathers, arches that represent Peng homes, and images of a shaded ring with a pucker in the middle.

Responding to Chu's puzzlement, the built-in glossary explains that the puckered rings represent Peng cloacas, which are the multipurpose body vents that birds of both genders use for excretion and sex. Chu bares his teeth in a reflexive gesture of disgust.

Back in the mental movie, a single grungy Peng jitters about on the higher reaches of the cliff, frantically pecking fresh images into the stone. This is Waheer. He wears his feathers tinted an unnatural shade of orange, with a defiant red Mohawk streak down the middle. Kakar, who is watching the show with the humans, caws approvingly.

Waheer's artworks are unique. Rat-tatting like a woodpecker, he engraves skeins of stars, spiral galaxies, flaming suns, distant planets. He's a science fiction visionary.

"Waheer's drive for transcendence inspired Pekka to a wondrous discovery," intones the narrator: *"Peng can travel to ape worlds via Pengö's cloaca!"*

The orange-feathered Waheer cocks his head, as if harkening to a call. He glides away from his space murals and—in fast-forward—makes his way across miles of ridges, disheveled and dogged, sometimes walking, sometimes buzzing through the air like a blimp, heading ever farther south, beyond the temperate zones and into the polar wastes.

The pocked, shiny snowfields are lit by shimmering auroras, by crimson and yellow streamers that emanate from a luminous hole located precisely at planet Pengö's south pole. Haunting alien music thrills the air. Pekka, the planetary mind, is calling Waheer to the special place.

The fuming polar vent, known as Pengö's cloaca, is the senescent planet's last sign of active volcanism. The hole bores into the depths like a mine shaft. At the deeper levels, an orange glow tints its mist-shrouded walls, for liquid lava lies below.

Waheer stands at the tip of an ice-glazed promontory that projects almost to the center of the smoking vent. Above him, celestial lances of auroral energy flicker across the sky

There is much to be explained about this uncanny scene. A quick montage of diagrams shows three salient facts. Firstly, Waheer, as transcendent artist, has visualized an intricate representation of his mind and body, a runic pattern containing all of his behaviors and personality quirks. Secondly, Pekka has reached through the lazy eight link to locate a suitable colony world, a planet named Pepple, populated by teekers resembling skinny green humans with three eyes. Thirdly, Pekka has forged a tight link with a gifted Pepple queen, bedazzling her with a mental image of an idealized Pepplese king.

The music swells. With a hopeful flap of his little wings, Waheer springs forward and lets himself drop like a stone.

"Our first pioneer," says the narrator.

Chu sees a stylized image of Waheer landing in a glowing lagoon of lava, accompanied by an X-ray skeleton flash, a sharp sizzle and an olfactory whiff of sulfur and fried chicken. Waheer's ashes form a fractal pattern of greasy swirls. The lava heaves, Waheer's stains fold back on themselves—and a sheaf of beautiful abstract forms rises from Pengö's cloaca, modulating the auroral streamers with the subtle song of—Waheer's rune.

The rune signal rises heavenward and then, just beyond Pengö's atmosphere, it veers into the eighth dimension like a river going underground only to emerge within Queen Ulla's mind on Pepple, there to be runecast into the queen's royal estate. The viewers catch a final glimpse of Waheer's tulpa, working hard as a flying steed for the three-eyed nobles, carrying a fat duke along in pursuit of something like a fox.

"And he'd hoped to be a court artist," says the voice-over with a chuckle. "Pepple has not become the most popular of our colony worlds."

The narration resumes. "In the tradition of Waheer, Warm Worlds Realty continues spicing teeker worlds with the glorious savor of our finest citizens. We've made the process simple, painless, and fail-safe."

Purposeful cheeping fills the background. Stone fences appear around the crater at the south pole, along with domed Peng houses and a double-sized meeting hall.

"Warm Worlds Realty maintains fine facilities adjacent to Pengö's cloaca. We carefully screen the candidates for interplanetary travel. The rigorous Warm Worlds selection process ensures that, should you make the grade, you'll be among an elite cadre of partner pioneers. Warm Worlds requires that our partner pioneers place their full economic resources in trust, and you'll be invited to bring as many as four family members along on your unparalleled journey. To schedule a preliminary assessment of your qualifications, contact Hulda Pekkandottir at Warm Worlds Realty today!"

"Invaded by real-estate developers," messaged Thuy privately. "I can't frikkin' believe this. Fix it, Jayjay."

"I did cast that pioneer rune onto all the atoms around here," messaged Jayjay. "I can remember the exact list of atoms. But I'm not quite sure how to put the atoms back the way they were. We better pretend to cooperate until I figure it out."

"I hate being polite to the Peng," teeped Thuy. "It's worse than when I worked at Golden Lucky Restaurant Supply and my rancid boss was in love with me."

It still intrigued Chu that people could make their outsides look different than their insides. How many personality layers did Thuy have?

"Struck dumb?" squawked Gretta, abruptly craning over to peer into Chu's face. "Didn't you like the movie? Oh, I see. You three are sneaking secret messages to each other. Watch your manners, rat-people. Secrets are rude. And we tulpas have superpowers."

"You're parasites," said Jayjay, forgetting what he'd said about being cooperative.

Gretta cocked her head, staring at him provokingly. She snapped another moth from the air, then ate another, and another. A steady drone was drifting from Jayjay's mouth. He had goose bumps on his skin. The dusty-winged insects were appearing from thin air. "How do you feel, Jayjay?"

Jayjay held his hands to the sides of his head. "You—I—" he gasped, stretching out his arms toward Gretta. "Stop it."

"You're our runecaster," said Gretta, quite oblivious to his discomfort. "And that's that. When I want a moth, I teep Pekka a request to start you up—and if she's ready, she has the Pekklet set you to work making a moth tulpa. Sometimes I have to wait a few minutes before Pekka notices me. It's not like Pekka is watching us every second, you know. She's working with a lot of teeker worlds at once. And sometimes the Pekklet has to take a nap. Don't imagine you're all that anyone thinks about."

Chu was tracking the motions of Jayjay's psyche, trying to memorize the mental moves. Each time Jayjay made a moth, he was sending atom by atom signals into the hundred kilometer by hundred kilometer by hundred kilometer volume of the Peng ranch—the cube of Earth underfoot. He was using partial Zeno speed-ups to get it done so fast.

"Oh, by the way, Pekka," added Gretta. "Can you have Jayjay put our family's rune onto the bodies of himself and Thuy again? They seem to have worn off. And put us onto Chu's atoms, as well."

Against his will, Jayjay opened his mouth and chirped. Right away, Chu felt slow and dull again, like he'd felt in San Francisco.

"Oh that feels horrible," exclaimed Thuy. "Stop making Jayjay do things for you. You'll wear him out."

"Wait till he goes on the road for us!" said Kakar.

"Let's get Jayjay to make us a house now," proposed Suller.

"But not a gray rock dome!" cried Gretta. "I want something splendid and strange—an opulent fever dream that you'd only find on a savage ape planet."

"I assume you don't mean a shabby wooden box like theirs," said Suller, casting a snobby glance at Thuy and Jayjay's cottage. "We're the top development reps here. We need a landmark home."

"Outlandish, ostentatious, over the top," agreed Gretta.

"So—how about a dome made of this fancy local stuff they call pink marble," suggested Suller after a minute's mental research. He teeped some instructions to Pekka, and shortly thereafter Jayjay moaned. A tulpa block of fine-grained stone thudded to the ground beside Chu, its rosy polished surface patterned with streaks and crystals, as full of incident as fatty Italian lunchmeat.

"Hmm," said Gretta, running her beak along the marble. "Wonderfully smooth. But, please, for once not a dome. Thuy—you're an egg-layer, you must have some aesthetic sense. What shape house might we adopt?"

"Go to hell."

"Evisceration," said Suller, sweeping his coarse, two-toed foot through the air, the claws very close to Thuy's belly. "You know that word? Come on, woman. Give my wife an idea for a house."

"All right, fine," said Thuy, her voice tense and annoyed.

Chu peeped to see the image Thuy teeped the Peng. It was lifted from one of the old paintings that Kittie had been studying on Ond's patio: *The Garden of Earthly Delights* by that guy Hieronymus Bosch. The top part of that picture showed a pond with four rivers branching out, each river adorned by a strange structure.

The wacky Thuy had selected one of these for the Peng house design, a pink monstrosity resembling a sandcastle, a hollow stump, and a thistle plant, adorned with a pair of questionable towers, and crowned by an arched, tapering pod that poked through a hairy ball.

"I love it!" exclaimed Gretta. "So authentic. So grotesque. Demand it for me, Suller. Be masterful." Her husband responded with an affirmative caw.

"How do you teep the instructions to Pekka?" asked Thuy, fishing for information. "She's so far away."

"You wouldn't understand, " said Suller loftily. "You're not a bird."

"I think they're using the same lazy eight connection that we use locally," said Chu, who was observing Suller's moves. "I guess all the lazy eight worlds are connected via the point at infinity."

"That's right," said Kakar. "Pekka could actually teep Jayjay directly if she wanted to. But to have full control of him she needs a local agent. A Pekklet. Oh look, he's about to make our house now."

Focusing on Jayjay's mind, now, Chu saw an image of a barebreasted, blank-faced woman in a spangled showgirl outfit. She held a feather in one hand, and a stun-stick in the other. The Pekklet? She made as if to tickle Jayjay's privates with the feather; doggedly he waved her off.

"Lay off the sex thing," Jayjay teeped angrily. "If you want me to cast runes for you, just ask. You don't have to reach down into my crotch."

"*Thank* you," said Thuy.

The Pekklet's image switched to that of a giant, eyeless Peng bird—but with the stun-stick still in readiness. All business now, she chirped Jayjay the rune for the new mansion.

Not that the rune resembled the design Thuy had selected. The rune looked like a branching tree, with a quadrillion forks along each branch, and with shiny glass balls hanging on tips. Maybe there was a ball for each molecule in the projected design? It was an effort for Chu to contemplate the rune's full intricacy.

But it was catnip for Jayjay, he scarfed down the rune and set to casting it onto each and every atom within the Peng ranch's hundred-kilometer cube, merging it with the Peng rune that was already in place within the atoms.

Chu tagged along for a bit, but then Jayjay picked up speed and left him in the dust. Meanwhile the air above the stream began to shimmer. The Bosch palace was taking form: twenty meters tall, molded from pink marble, a shape like a rotten, hollow stump with platforms and spires.

The structure rested astride the stream, damming it. The water flowed into a gap in the upstream side, pooling within the stump and spilling from an arched window on the downstream side. The pink palace's ground floor thus contained a private lagoon, which was lit by horizontal glass cylinders that penetrated the stump's walls, and the tubes were alive with—rats? Whoops! Goaded by the Suller-Pekka-Pekklet command loop, Jayjay edited the construct, changing the rats to beetles. And then the Bosch birdhouse was done.

Jutting from the stony stump's near edge was a knobby shelf fungus, deeply concave and stuffed with straw. The nest. A slanting marble slab formed a patio beside the nest.

Two pink towers rose from the patio's far side; they resembled penises—one squat and flaccid, one proud and tall with a mushroom cap. A transparent emerald tube rose vertically between them, with a final slab of marble balanced atop, forming a lookout.

A translucent, tapering pod angled up from the nest to graze the lookout, with the pod's tip curling into a spiral decorated with a diamond-encrusted letter *P* for *Peng*.

Kakar floated into the air and flapped a few times to reach the nest. He crowed with pleasure from his new perch; Gretta and Suller quickly joined him.

The birds fluffed up their straw, paced out the dimensions

of their patio, checked the view from their lookout, then floated down to their enclosed lagoon, making it echo with cheerful caws.

Meanwhile Chu went over the data he'd gleaned, hoping to be of use, analyzing the mathematical physics. He had observed that although the runes faded from any matter that left the self-catalyzing computation of a Peng ranch, when fresh matter drifted into a ranch, it kept its integrity. But neither he nor Jayjay could see precisely how to restore the corrupted on-ranch atoms to their original pre-Peng states.

Jayjay lay on the ground, weary and drained. Chu watched as Thuy leaned over him, giving him a drink of water, with her pigtails sticking cutely into the air. Catching Chu's eye, she winked at him, letting him teep into her private thoughts.

Although Thuy was worried about Jayjay, she was inwardly laughing at the Peng for using this particular Bosch shape for their home. Not that, being birds, the Peng would readily perceive the symbolism of the two giant penises. Chu felt a tingle as he and Thuy shared the naughty joke.

Thuy wandered over to the stream to ask the resident silp, Gloob, how he felt about the dam, perhaps hoping to enlist the irascible being in the war against the Peng. Gloob was still sunk in low-gnarl torpor. But by the end of the day, some living, unprogrammed water should be flowing in—after all the Peng ranch only extended fifty kilometers upstream. And maybe then Gloob could help.

"Wouldn't you like a wonderful rookery like ours, Thuy?" called Gretta. "Send me another image by the same designer and Suller will make it up for you."

"Our cottage is fine the way she is," said Thuy, her smile disappearing. "We don't want to live in a Bosch house."

"Oh let's give our house a new wing," said Jayjay, playing a deeper game. "Help guide me again, Suller. Your runecaster at your service." Chu could sense that Jayjay's plan was to learn still more about runecasting—the better to destroy the Peng.

"I'll have to approve the new design," chirped Gretta, pleased. "And, yes, Suller can petition Pekka to craft a rune for it."

"How about a comfy villa like this?" said Jayjay, teeping the birds an image of Ond's new house in San Francisco.

"I don't *want* a fat McMansion hulking over our poor cabin!" wailed Thuy. She wasn't getting it about Jayjay's gambit. "We haven't yet spent one single night in bed together here!"

"The big addition will be noble," said Gretta, ignoring Thuy. "But the walls should be pink marble to match our palace. As for the roofing—I want something terrifically extravagant."

"Gold!" exclaimed Jayjay.

"Jerk!" screamed Thuy, stuck in a loop of low-gnarl reactivity. "You'll turn our whole world into dull tacky crap!" She stormed past the Peng's palace and headed down the stream.

"Come back here, you!" squawked Gretta.

Chu tasted of Jayjay's emotions: his remorse, his yearning for reconciliation with Thuy, his determination to play along with the Peng in hopes of figuring out how to kill them.

"I'll keep an eye on her," Chu told Jayjay, and ran after Thuy himself. Yes, he definitely had a crush on this woman. Jayjay could teep this, but he didn't take Chu as a serious romantic threat.

"Calm her down," Jayjay teeped privately. "And watch how I build the house. Maybe when you get back we'll kick some Peng tailfeather."

CHAPTER 7

THE HRULL

Thuy was already a few hundred meters down the stream. Chu tried to catch up on foot. But this proved harder than he'd expected.

Due to the loss of gnarl, the silps in the plants and rocks weren't sociable. Brambly thickets crowded one bank, and the other bank was steep and slippery. Chu was forced to pick his way along the sullen stream's uncooperative stones and sand bars. The stonker gun made an unwieldy bulge in his side pocket.

In one spot the stream was choked solid with sticks and fallen redwood logs.

"Don't bother us," chorused the chunks of debris.

As Chu scrambled up the mossy bank to get around the

deadfall, the dirt chuckled, and his foot slipped out from under him. He fell heavily into the water, bruising his knee.

"Serves you right," said the submerged rocks.

Nature wasn't a nurturing mother out here; the local silps were like hostile natives jeering an outsider.

Although Thuy was well ahead of him, she was aware that she was being followed. Chu could have just teleported to her then and there, but he wanted to impress her by overtaking her on his own.

The stream deepened, and he switched to walking on the tangled banks, forcing his way through stands of manzanita chaparral, the stiff branches like stern claws.

"Don't snap our twigs," said the branches. "Or we'll really mess you up."

Chu slogged on, temporarily focusing his teep powers on Jayjay back at the clearing. Directed by signals from Pekka, Jayjay was humming the new rune into every atom on the ranch. The rune for the new house was shaped like a dish of hollowed-out candy mints, with a trillion-legged chocolate ant within each hollow. The art of designing a rune for a particular purpose seemed utterly opaque.

Testing out the feel of runecasting, Chu copied the rune onto a carbon atom in a blackberry bush leaf. It was a little tricky getting the atom to accept the new code; you had to come at it from just the right orbital angle. Incredible to think of doing this ten tridecillion times in a row.

Snapping his attention back to his immediate surroundings, Chu realized he'd reached the edge of a ravine. Just a few meters ahead, the stream sprang out over a rocky lip, the water falling in a smooth arc that was a grotesquely simplified version of a normal cataract. It had been about eight hours since Jayjay had zapped the surrounding hundred kilometers, which wasn't quite enough time for living water from the outer world to have flowed in this far.

Thuy was brooding by a lusterless pool at the bottom of the cliff. She glanced up at Chu without much interest; she was preoccupied with the teep image of the ugly new mansion that Jayjay had just finished creating.

Still too proud to teleport, Chu began picking his way down the side wall of the gorge. The thick humus of leaves and sticks slid beneath his feet. The shrubs were dead, brittle, and eager to break.

And now a silp dug a branch into his cheek. Chu could feel the blood beginning to flow. That was enough. With a quick, irritated motion of his mind, he teleported to the woodsy bottom of the canyon.

"My hero," said Thuy in a sarcastic tone. "Save me, save me." She gestured for him to sit down beside her. "Come here and I'll help fix your cut."

The two of them focused on Chu's skin and blood cells, healing the gash. Mind tricks were harder than usual, what with everything taxed by the effort of maintaining the Peng.

"That dumb Jayjay," muttered Thuy. Her cheeks were pink, her strawy hair was in spikes, her eyes were moist.

"He only built the extra house to learn more about tulpas," Chu privately messaged to her. "He wants to get rid of the Peng. Come on, Thuy. You're stuck in a loop."

"If it weren't for Jayjay, the Peng wouldn't be here in the first place," she said sullenly.

"Jayjay knows that," teeped Chu. "He's thinking that every second. He'd give anything to undo the damage."

Thuy's expression softened. "That's—that's true, isn't it?" she said out loud. "Thanks for reminding me." She reached out and touched Chu's cheek. "You've come a long way, kid."

"I won't be a kid forever," said Chu. "I'll have girlfriends. If only Bixie wasn't so—"

"Bixie got mad at you for wanting to kiss her, huh?" said Thuy out loud, smiling at him. "You've never kissed a girl at all, have you?" She puckered her lips and make a smooching noise. "Once you get some practice, you'll know to move in fast. Before your prey can bolt." Lips still puckered, she regarded him through half-lidded eyes. Maybe she was playing this up for the audience watching her live on the *Founders* show. Maybe she was trying to get Jayjay's attention. Maybe—

Heart pounding, Chu bobbed his head forward to plant a kiss. Thuy was fast as a snake. Perhaps his lips grazed hers for a nanosecond, but then she was off to the side, tut-tutting him. "I'm a married woman, Chu! Nearly twice your age."

"Sorry."

"Oh, that's giving up too easy. If you really want to kiss a girl, you have to keep trying. Unless she's making it very clear that she wants you to stop. Ambiguity, Chu. Mixed signals." Again she was pouting her lips.

Chu lunged at Thuy, got his arms around her and—she wriggled loose and slapped his uninjured cheek. *Smack!* The sting brought tears to his eyes.

"Why—" he began. "I thought—"

"Just showing you the ropes," said Thuy. "If you're good, I'll give you a second lesson some time." She batted her eyelashes, then shook her head. "I'm pretty upset about our cottage. I can't see living there at all. And the Peng have invaded San Francisco, too. This could be the end of everything." She heaved a sigh.

As if it were the most natural thing in the world, Chu leaned in and kissed her. She let him. She opened her lips and they touched tongues. The inside of Thuy's mouth was a wonderful magic cave. She hugged Chu tight, pressing her lithe body against his.

"But that's really enough," said Thuy, taking hold of his shoulders and holding him out at arm's length. She was breathing fast. "I'm not myself. You go try all this on Bixie. Could be that none of us have much time left." Suddenly her eyes widened and she let out a scream.

Turning around, Chu saw a pair of smooth shapes hovering by the waterfall, leathery flying manta rays with gently undulating wings, each of them three meters across.

"Oh my God," said Thuy. "These are the creatures Jayjay was talking about before. I didn't believe him."

"I'm Wobble," teeped one of the mantas. He had pulsing leopard dots on his back. His virtual voice had a choked quality, like a man talking while swallowing bread. "And this is my daughter Duxy. We're Hrull. We came to help you against the Peng."

"You—you flew here?" asked Chu.

"We came in a mothership," said Wobble. "Duxy's mother, Lusky. My wife. You'll meet her later."

The weightless manta rays drifted toward Chu. They were like meat blankets, with toothless letter-slot mouths and flecked yellow eyes. He could feel a gentle breeze from the slow, graceful flapping of their fleshy wings. Slow pink spirals rotated upon Duxy's hide.

"I'm here," Chu's stonker gun reminded him.

Chu drew the blue raygun from his pants. "Stay back," he warned the Hrull. "I can freeze you into dust."

"*Ooo*, femtotech," teeped Duxy, her virtual voice like a gargling soprano's. "It's fluky how every primate world goes through the same stages. Put away the gun, Chu. We Hrull don't kill. Instead we fly and we hide. You don't have levitation, do you? We have little friends to help us do that. Flight lice." She crinkled the skin around her eyes. A smile. She teeped their attention to the oddly shining, pale blue creatures that dotted her hide—no more than two dozen of them, the size of fleas. The flight lice had no eyes; their legs were buried in the mantas' flesh.

"Like on the Peng!" said Thuy.

"Those filthy birds got the flight lice from us," said Duxy. "But don't be asking us for flight lice till we've got a good trade relationship. It took the Peng a thousand years of negotiating to get them. Finally we traded the lice for complete food chains of marine life to seed our thousand seas."

"Are you from a lazy eight world, too?" asked Chu.

"A flying wind-sack visited us a long time ago," said Wobble. "The bag had a skinny horn that played a sound that unfurled an extra dimension." The Peng had mentioned something like this, too. Chu visualized a flying scrotum blasting away with a dicklike horn. He found himself thinking about sex a lot these days.

"On top of lazy eight telepathy, we have teleportation, too," Thuy was saying. "We can hop from place to place. Can you do that?"

"We hire teekers like you to help us," said Duxy. "We call them pushers."

"One of our pushers got a teep message that the Peng were about to invade you," said Wobble. "That's how we found Earth, as a matter of fact. Our pusher got a nice reward for sharing her information. Not that—"

"Let's show him what Lusky looks like," interrupted Duxy. "Our spaceship, Chu. You'll like her."

Mentally following Wobble's teep pointer, Chu and Thuy

viewed an empty field of shale fragments at the base of a high, airy cliff. Or, wait, the field wasn't empty. As Chu watched, a truly enormous manta ray came into focus; she'd been lying camouflaged upon the scree.

The mothership manta was an acre of smooth leather, with a central hump the size of a barn. Her skin flashed fizzy purple and yellow circles. A visual greeting. Her sharp tail twitched.

"Hey there, Chu," came the monster's teep voice, deep and round as the echo from a cave. "You're a likely lad. Good luck in your battle against the Peng! Whether or not you win, I'd like you to join my crew. I happen to need a new pusher."

Wow. Chu liked the thought. Traveling across the galaxies in a Hrull mothership would be like old-school space opera. As a pusher, he'd be teleporting the ship across space to other planets. And, once he was gone, maybe certain people like Bixie and Thuy would start missing him.

"Kakar said it's a bad life being a Hrull pusher," warned Thuy, as if she cared. "What if being a pusher is horribly dull? What if the Hrull paralyze you and make you into a zombie? What if Lusky cuts out her pushers' brains and plugs them in like chips?"

Chu tried to peek into Lusky's body, but she had her innards blocked off from teep. He was thinking that, if he shipped out with Lusky, he'd be without human contact—and maybe that would be a relief. He was tired of people whipsawing him with their emotions.

"Don't listen to Thuy," said Lusky, dismissing Chu's fears. "Pushers adore their jobs. Later you can talk to a female pusher whom I have aboard: Glee." And then the great manta disguised herself again. The slate field looked empty.

Thuy and Chu pulled their attention back to the glen with the waterfall.

"See how good we are at camouflage?" said little Duxy, hovering beside them. "If the Peng knew there's already a Hrull mothership here, they'd be wak-wakkin' mad. We'll share all kinds of tricks with you, once Earth becomes the Hrullwelt's ally."

"In other words, you want to use our planet for slave labor," said Thuy. Chu had to admire the way she got to the point.

"We Hrull are intergalactic eco-activists; our mission is to defend indigenous teekers against the imperialist Peng," said Wobble. He swept his spiked tail in a circle, gesturing at their surroundings. "The Peng are siphoning off the complexity of these woods, right? Look how rigidly the branches sway. And I'm sure you realize that your thoughts are sadly stiff and stereotyped. If those filthy birds take over, humankind will de-evolve. You'll lose your culture, your science, and even your ability to teleport. The Peng don't care. But the Hrull do."

"Can you help us drive off the Peng?" asked Chu.

"We'll show you how to strip away the Peng ranch computations," said Duxy. "We have a special atomic reset rune." Duxy pushed a pattern at Chu, a spherical mandala with a glowing eye in the center and—good heavens—a quadrillion wiggly spikes projecting from the surface like rays from a sun. Avidly, Chu memorized it.

"How fast can you think?" asked Wobble. "To reset the whole ranch, you have to individually reprogram each of the ten tridecillion atoms."

"Oh, oh," teeped Chu. "I'm gonna need help. Hey, Jayjay, are you watching?" He kind of hoped the answer was no.

"I'm there in spirit," said Jayjay's voice in Chu's head. He didn't sound friendly. "See, I wasn't kidding about the flying manta rays. I'm not as out of it as you two think. I know what's going on." Obviously he'd witnessed the kiss.

"Look, Jayjay, we have to talk," began Thuy. "Chu and I were just—"

"We'll get into that later," said Jayjay darkly. "We gotta save the world, and meanwhile to hell with our marriage, right? Let me try that reset rune on—oh, whatever. How about that lame excuse for a waterfall."

"Will Pekka let you do that?" asked Thuy. "I don't want her to—"

"Pekka isn't watching me just now. She's headtripping someone on another world. And her friendly local slavemaster, the Pekklet, is asleep."

"I wish I could do something to help you," said Chu, feeling bad that Jayjay was mad at him.

"Stand aside, horn dog."

Flapping close to the cataract, Duxy displayed the reset rune again, and Jayjay instantly set to work, using his mental speed to cast the rune into each and every atom of the falling water.

The reset rune impacted upon the tame flow and—the cataract went apeshit, blossoming with forking rivulets, quivery drops and veils of mist.

Sadly it was only a few seconds before all the revivified atoms had fallen into the pool, and the waterfall was once again a bone-dull, predictable curve. Chu was finally beginning to appreciate the glory of natural gnarl. He'd been too cautious all these years, wanting everything lined up in tidy grids.

"I want my own personal chaos back," said Thuy. "Can you chirp me, too, Jayjay?"

"Like you're not irresponsible enough right now? Like I'm in a mood to do you favors when you've been kissing that little boy?" But then Jayjay relented. "Oh, all right, I'll do it. But we have to hurry. Pekka's gonna be checking back on me any minute."

Thuy stretched her arms toward her distant husband. "Zap me, darling! Make me weird!"

Under the effects of Jayjay's nimble ministrations, Thuy's flesh vibrated like kneaded dough. Meanwhile, Chu had a try at teeping the spiky reset rune into a few billion of his own atoms; he chose a group near the tip of his nose.

He had no problem in mentally handling the reset rune.

He found himself able to push it into three billion atoms in a row. But the effect of this limited effort was nil. To make a lasting impact on how Chu felt, he'd have to change the better part of his body's ten octillion atoms. Although easy for Jayjay, so large a task was just at the limits of an ordinary human's abilities.

"This feels so great," exulted Thuy, turning a pirouette. She was back to her lively old self.

"Can you do the reset rune on me, too, Jayjay?" said Chu.

"Kiss my ass," said Jayjay. "How about that?"

"Why not do the whole Yolla Bolly ranch!" exclaimed Thuy. "And then we'll do San Francisco!"

"I want to," said Jayjay. "Those Peng tulpas are like ice sculptures in a blast furnace, kept together by a zillion gnats with trowels and Slushy cones. All I have to do is make the atoms stop working for them. But I don't want Pekka and her Pekklet to catch me. The Pekklet says she can paralyze me with her stun-stick. Maybe I better wait till the start of the next break they take, so I'm sure I have more time. I'll clear Yolla Bolly and San Francisco and maybe then I'll kill myself so the Pekklet can't use me again. Everything'll be great. You can marry Chu."

"Oh, Jayjay," exclaimed Thuy. "Don't dramatize. Don't talk that way."

"Look, while I'm deciding, I gotta focus on making supper for the squawky birds," said Jayjay. "They're watching, even if Pekka and the Pekklet aren't. See you in a minute." Jayjay tuned out.

"He's mad at us," said Chu.

"You noticed," said Thuy and let out a desperate laugh. "At least I'm gnarly again. I'm feeling—fey. Fa la la, we're doomed. When we go back there, I'll distract the Peng whenever Jayjay's ready to reset the ranch." Thuy turned a cartwheel and struck a pose, staring up at Wobble and Duxy.

"Teep this sound if you need us," said Wobble, emitting a skirling squeal. "The Hrull whistle. Our mission is to defend indigenous teekers against the imperialist Peng."

"You already said that line, Dad," said Duxy.

The flying rays exchanged a burble of laughter and flapped into the dark shadows of the woods, melting into invisibility.

"Sinister," said Thuy, shedding her air of giddiness. "What if they want to recruit, like, every family's firstborn child to be a pusher? Billions of galley slaves in their motherships. This is horrible."

"Let's go back to the clearing," said Chu. "We're the good guys. We're gonna win!"

"Ah, to be fourteen again," said Thuy.

The pink marble walls of the new house matched the fantastic Bosch pile of the Peng palace. Admiring the glitter of the new house's roof, the Peng had gotten Jayjay to add gold caps to their two penis towers. They'd also set a pink marble fire ring into the little patch of open space that remained in the clearing. Although the sun was still up, a goodly bonfire was blazing. The flames were dull and predictable, like colored paper tongues swaying back and forth.

Jayjay was busy by the fire, roasting a pig on a spit. He flashed a hard look at Chu and Thuy, and mouthed the words, "Still asleep." Meanwhile, the Peng were up on their second-floor patio, getting drunk on a keg of—wine? They'd pecked the top right off the barrel.

"Done sulking, Thuy?" cawed Gretta raucously. "You're just in time for our cockadoodle party."

"The word is *cocktail,* Mom," said Kakar. "Hey, Chu, we're drinking mead! Fermented honey. Runecaster Jayjay teleported it in with the pig. I'm feeling brilliant. Try some!"

"An excellent brew," said Suller, dipping his beak into the barrel and tipping back his head to savor the honey wine. "Possible slogan: Earth, the Flower World." He flapped one of his wings and hiccupped.

"Wait till you taste this roast meat," said Jayjay, cranking the spit. "Earth, the Swine World."

"Radiant nectar!" cooed Gretta, working a gulp of mead down her long neck. "I'm all shimmery inside."

"What fun," said Thuy, putting on her polite tone. Pekka wasn't watching and the Pekklet was still asleep.

Silently the three humans started an encrypted teep conference.

"I'm going for it now, after all," teeped Jayjay. "Who knows if I'll get another chance. You can stand guard, Chu."

"Are you sure that—" began Thuy.

"Worry about me," teeped Jayjay grimly. "Worry a lot."

"You and Chu work from our cottage," teeped Thuy, turning businesslike. "I'll distract the goony birds."

Just about then, Kakar got nosy about what the humans were privately conferring about. The young bird hopped off the patio and stalked over to wave his beak near Jayjay's head, as if sampling the vibrations.

Thuy smiled at Kakar and cut an energetic series of dance steps. The ostrichlike bird shuffled his feet, awkwardly following her rhythm. She drew him into a dance around the fire, with Gretta and Suller watching enthralled. The Peng didn't yet suspect that Thuy's matter had been freed. They were simply enjoying how lively she'd become. Kakar was dancing up a storm.

Jayjay and Chu made their way to the cabin behind the marble McMansion.

"Keep your hands off my wife," was the first thing Jayjay said when they were alone.

"I'm sorry, Jayjay. She was just trying to help me."

"You need help, all right." He was pacing around the room, distracted and overwrought. "So the flying manta rays are the Hrull? I couldn't teep a clear image of the one by the waterfall. She was camouflaged or something. Blending into the rocks. You think we can trust them?"

"What I think is that you better get started on the ranch right now," said Chu. He took a quick teep toward the Peng. It was dusk outside. Thuy had teleported the roast pig to the second-floor patio of the Peng's palace for the birds to feast upon, and she was up there dancing for them. The birds seemed very content.

But now Suller idly turned his head as if staring right at Jayjay and Chu, as if seeing through the house walls, as if seeing their plan. Mustering all of his mental force, Chu sent Suller a perfectly rendered image of himself and Jayjay—arguing about Thuy.

Displays of human emotion were of no interest to Suller. The drunk bird's focus twitched away. He dipped his beak back into the barrel.

"Start runecasting, Jayjay!" urged Chu.

"The Peng and the Hrull and the pitchfork," fretted Jayjay. "Three alien invasions at once. Why do I feel like we're totally fucked? Okay, here I go. Ten tridecillion copies of the reset rune."

"I wish I could be a runecaster, too," said Chu.

"You'd like a lot of things," said Jayjay. "But little boys don't always get what they want." He sighed despairingly. "Oh man, I truly don't want Pekka to hit me with that stun-stick."

But now, courageously, Jayjay started to hum, showers of bumps marching across his skin. He was using all of the component silps in his body, working multiple threads in parallel, moving concentrically outward from the cottage, the creek, and the clearing—ignoring the evanescent air and burrowing down into the ground. At this breakneck pace it would take less than two minutes for him to clear the Yolla Bolly ranch of Peng code.

Chu relished the fresh feel of life and energy in his body as Jayjay removed his Peng runes. The bonfire looked interesting again and the redwood, Grew, was swaying as chaotically as before. And now the sought-for effects of the atomic resets were taking hold: the tulpas were beginning to change.

Against the darkening sky, the Bosch house and the McMansion were crowned with pale coronas, like in an old picture of flickering Saint Elmo's fire on a ship's masts before a devastating electrical storm. The ruffled bodies of the Peng birds were growing smoother and more stylized. Sharp cusps formed at the ends of their beaks and claws; the birds' energies were draining off in wavery jets.

The Peng understood what was happening. But, slowed by the mead and by the ever-increasing disturbances in the Peng ranch's computation, it took them nearly a minute to launch their counterattack.

And by then Jayjay was protected by the reawakened silps of the trees, stones, and streams. When Suller tried to spit a klusper-style femtoray at Jayjay, a falling leaf diverted the ray's path long enough for Chu to shove Jayjay from the line of fire. When Gretta tried to run across the clearing to peck the two, a dead branch dropped from Grew to trip the Peng. As Suller fired another ray from his beak, the stream's flow undermined the Peng house's foundations to throw off his aim.

The Peng were getting smaller; they were dwindling to spiky globs. The Peng palace was melting away; and the marble Mc-Mansion had shrunk to a doghouse.

Chu sensed that Suller was about to teep to Pekka for help. The senior Peng had been too off balance to try before. But now he was readying his plea to send it out through the lazy eight link.

"Help us, Gaia!" cried Chu. "Jam Suller's teep!"

Gaia focused a blast of virtual noise on Suller and Gretta, scrambling their signals. But—oh, no!—off to the side, Kakar managed to teep out a crazed squawk.

On the instant, the rebellion was crushed. Pekka awoke the slumbering Pekklet, who used her quantum entanglement with Jayjay to slam him with a psychic stun-stick. Jayjay keeled over and crashed to the cottage floor like a toppling statue. He no longer had the power to think, let alone to move his limbs.

Thuy screamed and ran to him, kneeling at his side. Chu felt an unworthy twinge of jealousy.

An altered hum crooned from his Jayjay's mouth; his skin was still rough with bumps. He was vibrating at a femtohertz rate as before, but now he was restoring the runic computations that he'd just erased.

Out in the clearing, the atoms' matter waves were once again feeding energy into the spiky auras of Suller, Gretta, and Kakar. The Peng's bodies fluffed and fattened; their legs grew knobby and long. They squawked cheerful reassurances each to each. The outlandish form of the Peng palace humped itself back up, and the marble walls of the gold-roofed mansion grew into place, as dull as before.

Once again, Chu's body felt dim and slow. Should he and

Thuy teleport out of here, taking Jayjay along? Or stay to keep fighting the Peng?

The cabin door swung open and closed as if on its own. The air in the room wavered to reveal Duxy the alien manta ray. She'd snuck in here, only to drop her invisibility shield. Her elegant wings stretched from wall to wall, pulsing with pink spirals.

"Hrull!" squawked Gretta from afar. "Drill the Hrull with a klusper ray, Suller! And fry that crazy little boy!"

"Help me!" Duxy implored Chu. "Teek the two of us to Lusky's hideout before Suller kills us!"

Chu hesitated for a moment, wondering if Duxy were trying to stampede him. Why had she made herself visible here and now, if not to stir up trouble with the Peng?

A lemon-yellow femtoray bored a pencil-thick hole through the cabin door and out the wall on the other side.

"Ow," teeped the wall.

Wood smoke hung in the air. Luckily, Chu and Duxy had ducked the ray's path. But now Suller was preparing to send another bolt from his beak.

"Run!" Thuy urged Chu. "I'll stay here."

In a flash, Chu had teleported himself and Duxy to the field of slates where the mothership Hrull had lain. The great manta shape was nowhere to be seen. Instead, a much smaller Hrull was hovering above the stony wasteland: Duxy's father, Wobble, small like Duxy.

"What are you doing here alone, Dad?" teeped Duxy ingenuously. "Where's Mom? I wanted to get in her mouth to fly away from the Peng."

"On a pusher colony world, it's standard practice for an exploratory party to split up," said Wobble. "The monkey-men can turn violent in a flash. Duxy, you and I will flap west to the ocean. It's only a half hour's flight. We'll rest for a couple of days, sleeping in a cove and eating sea life."

"Yum!" said Duxy brightly.

"What about me?" said Chu.

"Ah," said Wobble. "You. You'll see quite soon."

With one of his sinister, gurgling laughs, Wobble flapped off with Duxy trailing him, the two of them shading into invisibility. As they left, something edged out from behind the bluff—and a shadow fell across the field. It was Lusky, vastly airborne, her mighty wings blotting out the red streaks and gold filigree of the dying evening sky.

With a gentle sighing sound, the big Hrull swept toward Chu, her mouth agape. Chu could have teleported away; he could have shot at the giant Hrull with his stonker gun. But stupidly he took off running across the slates, expecting to reach shelter by the cliff. He might have made it, but he tripped over a scarecrow figure lying on the ground: the fresh corpse of a skinny man or boy. Almost spitefully, the unused gun sprang from Chu's pocket and skittered far out of reach.

And then Lusky was upon him, huge and implacable. Chu teeped Thuy a last farewell.

"I'll love you forever."

CHAPTER 8

COMA NURSE

Jayjay lay on his side, his mouth downcurved in a death-mask grimace, his eyes like glass. Thuy rolled him onto his back so he'd be more comfortable; his head clunked against the floor. He'd wet his pants. She shuddered, thinking of her invalid mother.

The three Peng birds pushed into the cabin. Gretta ventured an exploratory peck at Jayjay's wrist, perhaps meaning to check his pulse, but digging deep enough to draw blood.

Thuy sprang at Gretta and slugged her, puffing dust from her shabby feathers.

Suller aimed his beak and sizzled a warning hole through the floor beside Thuy's feet. Holes in the cabin, holes in her heart, a hole in Jayjay's soul.

The Peng were squawking about wanting to move him

around the country opening more ranches, with Thuy acting as his nurse. Unbearable thought.

Just then Thuy heard Chu's voice in her head, bidding her farewell, saying that he loved her.

Reflexively she teleported toward the boy, guilty about leaving Jayjay's side so soon, but desperate for a chance to catch her breath.

Chu's call had come from the talus field by the cliff where the Hrull mother had been. The manta was airborne, a dark high diamond against the sunset sky all plowed in furrows of gold. A nude body lay on the vast waste of stones—oh no.

Thuy was trembling all over, her world was coming apart. First Mom, then Jayjay, now Chu—

She approached the inert figure. Male—but, no, he wasn't Chu. His skin was a yellowish shade of green, and the center of his forehead bore a third eye. A used-up pusher?

He smelled of sulfur, like some unappetizing vegetable. She took a step back, still studying him. His ribs stuck out; his elbows and knees were knobby lumps. Had the Hrull starved him?

Casting about, Thuy found the blue stonker gun. She tucked it into the waistband of her skirt, hiding the butt under her shirt. And then she teeped after the Hrull ship, wanting to contact Chu. But his access was blocked. Gone for good? Not likely. Chu would want to see her again, what with his big crush. That had been a sweet kiss.

For now, there was nothing to do but return to her disabled husband—still lying on the living room floor. The three Peng were so busy making plans that they'd barely noticed Thuy's brief absence. She stashed the stonker in the bedroom, then bent over Jayjay and removed his soiled trousers. She cleaned him up and teeked a box of adult diapers from a San Francisco drugstore where she had an account. Just like for her mother. How horrible.

Suddenly it crossed Thuy's mind that if she could teleport Jayjay somewhere far away from Yolla Bolly he might become her cheerful, healthy husband again. Of course! She poised herself for the jump, already growing translucent, but—

"We're not letting up on him now," cawed Gretta, reading Thuy's mind. "Don't forget that the Pekklet has full control of your husband's body. She'd sooner stop his heart than let him go free. So don't try any ratty little tricks."

"Okay," said Thuy, steeling herself. She'd wait them out. Sooner or later the Pekklet would sleep again.

"We need your man to open more Peng ranches," repeated Suller, his voice slurred from the mead. Pekka had reconstructed him exactly as he'd been just before the humans' failed attack. "You'll teleport Jayjay and nurse him for us, right?"

Thuy only nodded, waiting to see what came next.

"Eventually we'll open more California ranches, but the wife's got an attitude about that," continued Suller. "So first we hit the South. Lots of worms and beetles there, could be a draw. I've found a great spot to kick off our campaign. The Crown of Creation Worship Center in Killeville, Virginia."

"That's—that's a right-wing fundamentalist group," said Thuy, surprised at his choice. "They're idiots. They're against omnividence, telepathy, intelligence amplification, and the silps. They want to roll everything back."

"I've got a hunch they'll make good Peng partners," said Suller. "My family and I can't leave our ranch, seeing as how we're tulpas, but I picked a couple of human Realtors to help you, I happen to like their names. You four will make good money and we'll all be friends. Come on up to our patio and help us drink the rest of that mead."

Thuy begged off and laid Jayjay under a blanket on the couch. And then she started thinking about how to feed him. But something else was nagging her. It was her duty to tell Ond about his missing son. She put in an encrypted teep call.

"Chu did *what*?" said Ond distractedly. With so much going on, he hadn't noticed Chu's disappearance. He, Nektar, Kittie, Jil, and Jil's kids were out in the night together, looking for a place to stay in Santa Cruz—which lay south of the San Francisco Peng ranch.

Evidently the funky beach town was a madhouse of Bay Area refugees. Just now Ond was being threatened with a baseball bat by one of the always irascible Cruz locals. What with all the motels full, Ond's family had dared teleporting into a dark and empty beach house. But the owner had been teep-watching his property from a few blocks away, and had hopped in at the first sparkle of their teleportation dots, a weapon at the ready.

While Thuy watched from afar, Ond calmed the property owner by giving him some cash, and by promising him a cut of this evening's *Founders* royalties. Suddenly the owner was happy. He was hosting celebs. He wanted to seal the deal by smoking a joint.

"Just so I know you're good people," said the Cruzan, lighting up.

"Run that by me again, Thuy," teeped Ond, ignoring the landlord.

"I said Chu's joined the crew of a Hrull mothership," repeated Thuy. "A giant alien manta ray. She carries her passengers inside her body, and she conscripts humanoids to help her teleport. The Hrull call them pushers."

Ond began speed-scanning through Thuy's memories of her day, and she didn't have the heart to block him out. "What's that dead body I'm seeing?" he demanded, growing very agitated.

"I think that's the pusher who Chu's replacing," said Thuy. "So far as I know, Chu went of his own free will. He'll make his way back to us. I—I'm quite sure of that."

"He loves you?" exclaimed Ond, skipping from Chu's farewell words to the afternoon kiss. "And you led him on? He's a fragile boy, Thuy! How could you!"

"I was teaching him how to be with girls," said Thuy. Up till now, she'd been thinking of her flirtation with Chu as a harmless game, or even as a generous gesture. But now she began feeling ashamed.

"It's thanks to you he left on this crazy adventure," teeped Ond grimly. "And it's thanks to your husband the aliens are here at all." He paused, waving off the stoner landlord. "About Jayjay," he continued. "For the good of Earth, have you considered—"

"Killing him?" snapped Thuy.

Even as they talked, Thuy was teeking food into Jayjay's empty stomach: milk and apple sauce. Like stuffing a chicken. Jayjay seemed to sense the food appearing in his belly; the severe downward curve of his lips had lessened somewhat. It was doing Thuy good to be helping him.

"I could never hurt him," she teeped Ond. "We'll find another way. I'm thinking the Hrull can still help us. They're enemies of the Peng from way back. I know a special whistle for calling the Hrull. I bet Chu and the mothership are still around."

"I sure hope so," said Ond grimly. "Hop down to Cruz right now and give the whistle a try. It'll be better to do it outside the Peng's influence zone. Come on and bring Jayjay along. I can help you teek him if he's too heavy. Those Peng birds aren't watching you right now. They're passed-out drunk."

Sure enough, the three Peng were nestled in a fluffy heap on their mound of straw, gently snoring.

"I'd love to escape," said Thuy. "I feel so alone. But Pekka's local agent is hiding down in the subdimensions, watching Jayjay. The Pekklet. We have to wait for her to take a break again."

Ond was losing his focus. Some other refugees had just teleported into their newly rented house, an extended family of fourteen from the Mission district. Jil was in mother-hen mode, defending her two kids' beds. The house's owner reappeared to collect more money. And now Chu's mother, Nektar, tuned in on Thuy's bad news and began floridly freaking out.

"Get Jayjay into a quantum-mirrored room, and that should shield him from his link to the Pekklet," teeped Ond hurriedly. "The quantum mirrors work against quantum entanglement. I can get you into a room like that at Seven Wiggle Labs. I know the owners—Jayson and Stefan. Go there now! Then you can whistle for the Hrull and get Chu! You owe me that, Thuy. This is all your fault."

"You're not hearing me," said Thuy slowly. "The Pekklet might kill Jayjay with an instant stroke if I make a run for it while she's watching. For now I have to play along. We're off to Virginia to tulpify more Peng."

Nektar was shaking Ond by the shoulders, screaming at the top of her lungs. Ond cursed Thuy and broke the teep connection.

Thuy felt horrible now, and desperate for the presence of a friend. She didn't feel like dealing with Sonic, so she gave Kittie a call. A minute later Kittie was there in the flesh, solid and good-humored.

"I've been waiting to hear from you, girlfriend. What a hoot that you got those stupid birds to build themselves the house from *The Garden of Earthly Delights*. They're all drunk now, huh? Oh no, look at Jayjay. You need a hug, Thuy. I'll sleep here with you. We'll park Jayjay on the couch."

"Okay," said Thuy. "I could really use the company. But no sex."

"Perish the thought," said Kittie, undoing Thuy's pigtails and fluffing up her hair. "You're a married woman—who happens to be, ahem, a child molester."

"Oh God, you saw me kissing Chu, too?"

"All the *Founders* fans saw you. I checked the ratings half an hour ago, and that kiss is huge with our female demographic. And they're wild about Chu's good-bye to you. 'I'll love you forever.' So sweet. All the women are messaging that clip to each other."

"My life is a mess," said Thuy, bursting into tears. "I should have blocked my teep to keep that kiss off *Founders*. People are going to think I'm terrible. And Jayjay and I never even had a chance to make up."

"Cuddle time," said Kittie. The empty bed beckoned. The two women undressed and got under the covers. But—to the disappointment of *Founders* viewers everywhere—all they did was spoon together and fall asleep.

The next morning, Thuy woke to the sound of Jayjay humming and moaning. And suddenly the voices out in the clearing changed. The Peng had begun vocalizing like humans instead of squawking like birds.

Still on the couch, Jayjay relaxed again, and his goose bumps smoothed over. It was almost as if he were sleeping. But his diaper was soaked, and he wouldn't wake up. Trying not to focus on what she was doing, Thuy got to work changing him.

"Somehow I always imagined being married to a man would be like this," said Kittie, waking. "Oh, don't frown at me. Hey, look, the alien birds have turned into businesspersons!"

Although physically the Peng were still big ostrichlike birds, they were now wearing black pinstriped suits—thanks to Jayjay's latest runecast. Gretta had accessorized her outfit with gold earrings and a blue-on-blue polka-dot blouse. Suller and Kakar wore white shirts and red neckties. With his top pinfeathers slicked back, Suller looked like a gangster. And Kakar resembled a beaky grad student dressed for someone's wedding.

A pair of business-dressed humans arrived, bearing prominent teep-tags. They were a married couple, Chick Moon and Duckie Tarrington: "The top-earning team of real-estate professionals in the Bay area, specializing in spectacular statement homes." Chick was a pale gangly guy, like a Wild West yokel in expensive clothes. Humorless little Duckie was a tightly wound brunette, wearing so much makeup that her face had a plastic sheen.

"What would it take to earn your business today?" said Gretta, her newly tweaked voice an unctuous contralto. She cocked her head and fixed Duckie with a glittering eye. "Am I saying that right?"

"Oh, you sound fine," said Duckie, sizing up the regrown Bosch house—mighty odd in the morning sun. "But I'm not sure there's a good match. After all, you're alien invaders. If we were to partner with you, there'd be adverse legal exposure. What's more, you don't have title to any property, nor a bank account for paying fees." Her tone was flat and matter-of-fact.

"How about this!" said Kakar, floating into the air to fetch a heavy gold shingle from the roof of Thuy and Jayjay's marble mansion.

"I'm shiny!" teeped the shingle's silp as Kakar tossed it to the ground.

"Fool's gold," said Chick with a shake of his head. He gave the shingle a disparaging nudge with the tip of his tasseled black loafer. "I bet this tulpa stuff melts away if you take it off the Peng ranch. Duckie here didn't want to talk to you at all, but I said let's visit for the shits and giggles. I was expecting more of a freak show, to tell the truth. How come you're wearing suits? Are we supposed to think you're like humans?"

"Far from it," said Gretta huffily. "Compared to you, we're like gods."

"Sure you are," said Chick. "That's why there's a spot of white bird shit on the ground under your butt."

"We have our eye on a group of humans who are in fact likely to worship us," interrupted Suller before Gretta could escalate the argument. His voice was a dark tenor. "They're called the Crown of Creation."

"You know about them?" said Chick, recognizing the religion's name. "The Crownies. Hah. They're already upset that rocks and plants can talk. I don't exactly see them cottoning to alien birds."

"That's how much *you* know," said Gretta. "The Crownies will be eager to help us. We have a plan. All you and Duckie will need to do is to speak for us now and then."

"We're offering you two the opportunity to put sweat equity into the greatest land deal this planet's ever seen," added Suller, his voice hoarse and persuasive. He had a hint of an East Coast accent. "You just need to contribute some time on the road and, yes, put up with a little mud-slinging. Don't shake your head, Duckie! We're going to own your world. Get in on the ground floor!"

"Can you specify exactly what you'd want us to do?" asked Chick, after a long pause. He and Duckie were privately teeping together.

"Thuy!" cackled Gretta. "Are you decent? We're bringing the Realtors to see your husband!"

Soon it was a done deal.

Before setting out, Thuy teeked a wheelchair for Jayjay and

concealed her stonker gun inside a flap under the seat. And then she, Kittie, Jayjay, Chick, and Duckie hopped to the parking lot of the Crown of Creation Worship Center in Killeville, Virginia, leaving Suller and his family behind.

It was a hot hazy Sunday morning; the lot was full. Odd as it seemed, many people down South still drove SUVs, albeit retrofitted ones with solar cells and electric motors.

"I could really score some car-art gigs here," said Kittie, looking around. "Like, paint Good Ole Jesus gutting an eight-point buck. And paint the Rapture, with the Christians flying up and the sinners writhing in fire cracks. And, ah, the repentant Mary Magdalene in Mother Mary's tender arms."

In the wheelchair, Jayjay's head abruptly snapped back and his mouth flew open in a moan—as if he were having a fit. Showers of goose bumps marched across his skin.

"Here we go again," said Thuy with a sigh.

"What is it?" asked Chick the Realtor, alarmed.

"He's channeling Pekka," said Thuy. "He's making Killeville into a Peng ranch."

"Here," suggested Duckie, offering Thuy a lace-trimmed hankie. "Hold Jayjay's tongue so he doesn't bite it."

"Oh, he'll be fine," said Thuy, increasingly disgusted by her husband. "The Pekklet won't let him hurt himself. Just act like it's not a big deal. I don't want everyone staring at us."

Fat chance. Jayjay was moaning like a nut and pumping his hips. A pair of Crown of Creation parishioners approached: a rough-complexioned young woman with a ponytail, and a loose-eyed youth in a tan cotton suit.

"Hi!" said the woman, lacing her hands behind her back and pushing out her boobs. "We're Steve and Julie. Are you here for the eleven A.M. program? Donnie III does a powerful healing near the end."

"I bet he could do this fellow a world of good," said her partner, Steve, hunkering down to peer under the wheelchair. He was checking for weapons. A security agent. He could have just teeped under there instead of bending over—and then he might actually have found the stonker gun—but the fundamentalist Christians didn't approve of using mankind's new mental powers.

"We're glad we're in time," said Chick. "We came all this way to soak up a sermon."

"Not from around here?" said the ponytailed Julie. The skin on her cheeks was raw from scrubbing. "Are you from— from West Virginia?"

"Farther than that," said Kittie. "I'm a godless kiqqie artist from gay CA."

"I don't think that's funny," said Steven in the tan suit. Thuy noticed that he was clutching a zipped-up leather Bible. The Bible silp teeped Thuy that it was a pistol case.

Meanwhile, with a final ecstatic twitch of his pelvis, Jayjay had stopped moaning. The local gnarl had been successfully repurposed; Thuy could see a dullness to the clouds and a predictability in the motions of the trees.

"Oh!" cried Julie. "Look, Steve, look!"

Parading across the parking lot toward the hulking gray worship center were a hog-fat older man in clerical vestments, an old woman with a sprayed bubble hairdo, and a rangy younger man in vestments as well. Pekka had gotten Jayjay to mold the new Peng tulpas into the forms of the deceased first family of the Crown of Creation church. They were slightly larger than life size; their complexions were preternaturally clear and smooth.

"Dr. Macon!" exclaimed Duckie. "With his wife, Bonnie,

and their son Donnie Macon, Jr." The Realtor had done her research. Everything was going according to plan. "I thought— I thought they'd all passed on to their reward," she added disingenuously.

"A miracle," breathed Julie.

"Maybe so," said Steve, nervously toying with the zipper on his case.

Thuy and her party joined the crowd following the three disguised Peng into the worship center. It was a cavernous indoor arena, with Donnie Macon III standing upon a central dais before a robed choir. Donnie III was a lean, slit-eyed fellow, and he didn't look too happy to see his resurrected forebearers come swanning in.

Although Dr. Macon must have weighed well over three hundred pounds, he levitated, moving his body across the cavernous hall as nimbly as a character in a video game. As the tulpa of a full-fledged Peng, he'd been created with symbiotic flight lice in place. Fiercely grinning, he alighted upon the stage beside Donnie III. His wife, Bonnie, and his son Donnie Jr., flew to join him.

"We are blessed!" roared the Peng disguised as Dr. Macon. "We are blessed to revisit our home!" The beige-carpeted arena rocked with an avalanche of applause.

Thuy, Kittie, Chick, and Duckie were standing just inside the entrance, clustered around Jayjay in his wheelchair. Jayjay began humming again, enabling Dr. Macon to turn a Bible into a loaf of Wonder Bread, and a pitcher of water into grape-flavored sports drink. And then the fat tulpa sent a bouquet of plastic roses flying from his fingertips to alight upon Jayjay's lap.

"The Lord has called me from my rest to introduce the Sleeping Savior," bayed Dr. Macon. "Bring him up here so the folks can see, Sister Thuy."

Wearing a stiff, embarrassed grin, Thuy wheeled Jayjay up a ramp onto the stage. The all-white crowd was like a bag of bellowing marshmallows.

"The Savior has manifested Himself in the body of this ordinary, sinful man," exclaimed Dr. Macon. "He's a kiqqie and a Gaia-addict, yes, but the Almighty is using him to bring on the End Times. Gabriel's horn will push through the raging sea, and we will know salvation. It is your duty to help the Sleeping Savior actualize the Good Book's prophecies."

"Dr. Macon, Bonnie, and Donnie Jr. are alien invaders!" screamed the choirmaster just then. She was a charismatic woman with flowing red hair. "They're disguised Peng! The bird things we've been seeing in the news!"

"You'd do better to call us angels," said Donnie Jr. He was leaner and more polished than his father. A huge cheer went up when he spoke. He'd been a popular pastor before his death in a drunken car crash several years before. He leveled a minatory finger at the protesting woman.

A moan arose from Jayjay, and the woman's clothes were wreathed in fire. She rolled on the ground, screaming and trying to staunch the flames. Jayjay moaned again and she was doused in a gush of water.

"Do you still doubt us, Sister Vivian?" said Dr. Macon's wife, Bonnie, stepping forward to help the disheveled, but unharmed, redhead to her feet.

"Praise Donnie," croaked the choirmaster. "Praise the Sleeping Savior."

"God made Man and Woman as the Crown of Creation— just as they are," said old Bonnie, taking the microphone. Her huge hairdo made her face seem like a wizened patch of leather. "On a Peng ranch, this sacred order holds. On a Peng ranch, the sticks and stones aren't demonically possessed. On a Peng ranch, folks don't jack up their brains and intellectualize over every little thing." As she talked, her hands darted about like quick wrens.

"I warn you, some will set stones in the Sleeping Savior's path," intoned Donnie Jr., holding up his hands. "Satan's flying devilfish will seek to do Him bodily harm. We must see our Shepherd into His pasture."

"Yea, verily," added Dr. Macon. He flashed his appalling smile. "Lead us in a hymn, Sister Vivian: 'Onward, Christian Soldiers!'"

As the congregation raised their voices in muscular song, Thuy took the opportunity to trundle Jayjay down the aisle to rejoin Kittie, Chick, and Duckie.

"This is a nightmare," she murmured, all but blinded by a red haze of shame, and very aware of the merriment in her huge *Founders* audience.

"On to site number two," said Chick. "We're going for an optimal use of land, spacing the ranches ninety-five kilometers apart. I've picked out a nice location in the boonies—the hamlet of Yost, Virginia, to be precise. And after that we can step over to Charlottesville. Site three."

"The properties in Charlottesville have appreciated very handsomely in recent years," put in Duckie.

Materializing by the side of the road in Yost, Thuy saw fields, low mountains, and a feed wholesaler, closed for Sunday. A boarded-up gas station baked in the afternoon sun. She felt overwhelmed by the pointless vastness of the world. Was she supposed to hopscotch the whole planet opening ever more Peng ranches? Nothing, nothing, and more nothing.

Jayjay twitched and moaned.

"It's like we're bringing in Elvis's embalmed body to jump-start a mall," remarked Chick, drawing a stick of gum from his pocket. "Except I don't see no customers."

Small, teeped cries of protest were wafting in from the black-berry brambles, the poison ivy, the maple trees, the red dirt, the ants, the mosquitoes, and even the gray sheets of plywood covering the abandoned filling station's windows. The local hive mind. The ants had southern accents. Chorused beneath these more articulate plaints were the ten tridecillion tiny voices of the local atoms. None of them wanted to pay a gnarl tax to the Peng-producing matter waves. But they couldn't stop Jayjay.

He moaned for a few minutes, and the transformation was done. Everything was dull; the silps were still. Four Peng appeared in a pasture across the empty, cracked asphalt highway: ugly long-legged birds, craning their heads to gawk at the blank green hills and the placid cows.

"Let's move on," said Chick, rapidly chewing his gum.

"Scared of the Peng?" said Kittie, a little mockingly.

"Once you close with a client, you scram," said Duckie. "Before they start asking for changes."

"Good point," said Thuy. "I don't want these Yost Peng to ask for a palace like the Yolla Bolly Peng." She was feeling sorry for Jayjay again. He looked so wretched and pale. The horrid Pekklet was right there in his brain, knotted in by quantum entanglement.

Charlottesville was next. They landed upon the University of Virginia's lovely great lawn, with a well-proportioned rotunda at one end and columned arcades of brick student quarters running down the sides.

Although Thuy fully expected Jayjay to begin humming

again, he lay still. She could sense Pekka trying to kick-start her husband. But, for now, his only response was to slump farther back in his wheelchair. He was temporarily worn out.

"What a relief," said Kittie. "I hate having Jayjay cast runes onto me. They make me feel like I'm made of plastic."

"The runes seem to wear off when you leave a Peng ranch," said Thuy. "It takes a lot of atoms reinforcing each other to stay that dumb."

"Like a hall full of Crownies," said Kittie.

Just then a group of undergrads began pointing at them and yelling. Thanks to telepathy, the kids knew why Jayjay was here.

"Go home!" shouted a bearded boy. "Leave our town alone!"

"Alien stooges!" yelled a long-haired girl. "Traitors!"

Chick and Duckie hurried over to the students, intent on defusing them. The Realtors had plenty of experience with anti-development protestors.

Meanwhile, Thuy and Kittie bumped the wheelchair across the lawn to a mansion that had been retrofitted as an inn. They rented a nice pair of double rooms with a connecting door, the windows looking onto the verdant great lawn from the third floor. As in many dwellings, the inn's rooms had been cajoled into blocking teleportation. People had to buzz a clerk to get in through the inn's front door. The clerk helped them lug Jayjay in his wheelchair up the stairs, and for the moment they were safe.

While Kittie watched from a chair, Thuy laid Jayjay on one of their room's twin beds, fixed his diaper and mopped his face. He was really out of it. It wasn't just that Pekka was holding him paralyzed. He was utterly drained of energy; he'd sunken into deep slumber.

Thuy was tired, too. She lay down on the other bed, and

before she knew it, she'd napped for a couple of hours. She was awakened by Ond urgently teeping her to talk about Chu. By now he was frantic about his missing son. He was angrier with her than before. Biting back her own anger at the situation, Thuy said she'd try to find Chu soon. She closed the call and lay still, just breathing. It was early evening outside. Kittie was slouched in the chair; she looked like she'd been napping, too.

"Happy hour," said Duckie, opening the connecting door between the two rooms. The Realtors were working on a bucket of ice and a bottle of premium local bourbon.

"We jived those students pretty good," called Chick cheerfully. "I told them we're from Homeland Security, fighting the evil Hrull aliens. I signed them up as Hrull spotters and gave each of them a hundred bucks cash. Duckie told them it'd be a federal death rap to obstruct Jayjay because he's working for homeland defense!"

"We're problem solvers," said Duckie, gliding into Thuy's room, with two fresh highballs in hand.

"S'good," said Kittie, slurping.

"I've never had hard liquor," said Thuy, accepting her glass anyway. The bourbon had a festive smell and a jolly demeanor. It left a sharp bite in her throat and a warm glow in her gut.

Out on the great lawn, fifty Crown of Creation Church parishioners had bussed in to defend the Sleeping Savior. The Crownies were holding hands to form a human chain in front of the inn. It felt weird to have these be the people on Thuy's side.

Meanwhile, the bearded boy and the long-haired girl had gathered twenty or thirty like-minded companions. It turned out that—surprise!—they weren't buying the load of crap the Realtors had shoveled onto them.

"And the kid in front has a frikkin' noose!" exclaimed Thuy.

She was glad she still had the stonker gun hidden in the wheelchair's seat. She found herself wondering how many people she could kill before the power ran out. That's the kind of mood she was in.

A shouting match began beneath the streetlight outside the inn.

"What bullshit," said Chick, joining Thuy at the window, drink in hand. "The South is nowhere. What the fuck difference does it make if our clients siphon off some gnarl? *What* gnarl?"

"Don't be shallow," reproved Duckie. "Charlottesville has a rich history. President Thomas Jefferson himself designed the rotunda and the great lawn."

"BFD," said Chick. "I say we hop back to Yolla Bolly before these country-fried hippies string us up." He glanced over at Thuy. "Hubbie still on the blink?"

"He did a lot today," said Thuy shortly. She'd decided to make their break for freedom before they went back to the Yolla Bolly Peng ranch—no matter what. But for now she kept up a smile. "Maybe if Jayjay rests a little longer, he'll be ready to go again."

"Sounds like my husband," said Duckie with a snicker. "He rests a lot." The whiskey was hitting her. Thuy could practically see the cracks forming in her plastic face.

Chick shook Jayjay's foot. "Up and at 'em, runemaster! How about you teek a shot of bourbon into his stomach, Thuy? That'll put hair on his chest."

She ignored him. Teeping Jayjay on the bed just now, she'd discovered something wonderful. He was so drained and so deeply asleep that once again Pekka and the Pekklet had stopped watching him. Big Pekka was tending to the rest of her farflung empire, and the Pekklet was napping or maybe scratching around the subdimensions for food. They'd be checking back, of course, but right now Thuy had her shot.

She shooed Chick and Duckie from her room and slammed the door. Kittie grasped how things stood. "Let's teleport out of here fast," she proposed.

"Let's go out to the fire escape," said Thuy. "Remember that teleportation is blocked in here."

Jayjay stirred in his sleep, moving naturally for the first time since last night. The room picked up on this and responded.

"Don't let him reprogram us," teeped the creaky floorboards. "We don't want to be slaves."

"Maybe I should let those students hop in here," threatened the inn's faintly sour air. "We'd all be better off with Jayjay dead."

"Just give us two minutes," teeped Thuy, her mind seething with plans.

Down in front of the inn, someone fired a gun.

The motley crowd of students were confronting the Crown of Creation posse. Screams, thumps, and more gunshots in the dark. A fresh troop of Crownies arrived. An equal number of angry locals came teleporting to the lawn—and broke through the Sleeping Savior's defense line. Footsteps thudded on the porch; massed shoulders crashed against the inn's locked door.

Kittie and Thuy loaded Jayjay in his wheelchair and hurried down the third-floor hall to the window.

"You can have this," said Thuy, pulling the stonker gun from under the wheelchair.

"Awesome," said Kittie, taking it.

Downstairs the front door gave way with a sharp crack. Whoops and yelps sounded up the stairwell.

"Help me get him through the window," said Thuy. "Once we're outside I'll—"

"—call the Hrull?" said Kittie, reading her mind. "Are you sure that—"

"I figure they can escort us to San Francisco and I'll find that the quantum-mirrored room at Seven Wiggle," said Thuy. "And I have to try and get Chu back, too. And, to tell the truth, I'm—"

"—dying to see what it's like inside a Hrull," completed Kittie. "You're a wildwoman, Thuy. A star."

Footsteps were pounding up the inn's first flight of stairs.

"Hey!" called Duckie, peering after them from the door of her room. "Where do you think you're taking Jayjay?"

"Quack, quack," said Thuy, giving the unsmiling Realtor the finger.

And then Kittie and Thuy were on the black-painted iron grillwork of the fire escape with Jayjay at their feet. The night-gray trees watched warily—maples, chestnuts, and dogwoods.

"We're leaving," Thuy assured her surroundings. "Please block the students from teleporting right onto us. We only need a minute." And then she teeped the wiggly squeal of the Hrull whistle. For the moment there was no response.

The students had reached the second flight of stairs; the tops of their heads were coming into view.

"Back!" yelled Kittie. She leaned in through the window, stonker gun outstretched, and fired a wavery femtoray. The top steps of the stairs shuddered into ragged chunks that clattered down to the flight below.

The students paused, uncertain—and in that moment the fundamentalists boiled up after them. The hundred-handed mob wrestled itself to a standstill. Focusing her mind, Thuy teeped the Hrull whistle again.

And now, ah yes, something flickered in the dim sky. A blacker darkness covered the inn and the lawn. Lusky had been up there all along, waiting to become visible. An acre of wobbly flesh came gliding toward Thuy, the mouth a faintly glowing slit in the leading edge.

"Hrull!" wailed the student rebels and the Crownies, terrified in equal degrees.

"Not for me," Kittie told Thuy. "I'm teleporting to Cruz. Luck, babe. You want the gun?"

"Keep it. I doubt Lusky would let it aboard." Thuy smiled at her wise, jokey friend. "I'll love you forever."

"Just like Chu," said Kittie, kissing her. And then she grew ghostly and was gone in a confetti of bright dots.

CHAPTER 9

LIVE SEX

Sitting on the edge of the fire escape, Thuy stretched one arm toward Lusky, keeping her other arm wrapped around Jayjay's waist. She had to wonder if she were making a catastrophic error.

With a blast of warm, fishy air, the mothership manta ray's red-glowing mouth bumped against the metal fire escape. Thuy got to her feet, levered Jayjay over the lip, and followed him in.

"Hurry," teeped Lusky. "I'll camouflage myself and fly away."

Inside the manta, all was calm, with the space dimly lit by glowing traceries of magenta veins in Lusky's yellow flesh. The warm, damp cavity was smaller than Thuy had expected. She sat on the ridged floor with Jayjay stretched out beside her.

Although Lusky was teep-blocking herself from outside

viewers, Thuy could teep around the manta's interior quite well. She located Chu and a humanoid female lying nude on bunklike ledges toward the rear of the chamber. The alien woman had three eyes, her skin was chartreuse, and she smelled like Brussels sprouts.

A fleshy cone hung from the ceiling like a stalactite, shielding the dark tunnel of Lusky's throat. It was like a person's—what was the word?—uvula. The dull red uvula wobbled back and forth with the beating of the ray's massive wings.

"Hello, Thuy," teeped Chu. "I—I didn't think I'd see you again."

He sounded shy. Maybe he'd heard her imitating him when she said good-bye to Kittie. As usual, Thuy had been live on *Founders*—although, now, inside the Hrull, her teep to the outer world was blocked. But she'd be online again whenever Lusky opened her mouth. The ratings for this adventure would be huge.

"I'm glad you're okay," she told Chu. He really was very cute. "I thought you might be in outer space by now. Somewhere like the—Hrullwelt? Is that where this green woman is from?"

"Glee's from a planet called Pepple," said Chu. "She's a pusher for Lusky. Her boyfriend, Kenee, just died, I'm not sure why. I might replace him. But there's one part about being a pusher that I don't like."

Pepple—hadn't the Peng mentioned that place? But before getting into all that, Thuy needed to think about Jayjay. He was sleeping as deeply as before. She leaned over him, making him comfortable, teeping into his mental state. Thank God, still no Pekklet.

Suddenly the floor lurched and the sound of an explosion filtered in.

"The Crownies alerted your air force," teeped Lusky,

banking to the left. Her virtual voice came in pulses. She was flapping fast. "Even though the pilots can't see me or teep me, they're tracking my gravitational signature. Hang on tight while I try some moves. And get ready to push with Chu and Glee! We'll want to teleport out of here soon."

The manta heeled to the left, and did a loop. Breathing the warm soupy air as shallowly as possible, Thuy lay pressed against the membranous floor beside Jayjay, doing her best not to puke.

"I'm warning you right now that I'll spit out Jayjay the instant that the filthy Pekklet takes him over again," Lusky informed Thuy. "She'll set Jayjay to casting runes against me."

"Well, you can't just drop him from the sky!" said Thuy sharply. Maybe she could get away with being masterful. "I want you to ferry us to Seven Wiggle Labs in San Francisco, Lusky."

"We'll talk about all that after we hop," said Lusky noncommittally. "Right now I'm dodging jets."

"Look, we don't have to be inside you at all," snapped Thuy. "We can perfectly well teleport to California on our own."

"Except that your husband is too zonked to teleport himself," said Lusky. "At least for now. Also you're hoping for a nice ratings bump if you try and rescue Chu. Don't think you have secrets from me."

Thuy sighed and sat up. The damp heat was oppressive. It might have been more comfortable to strip down like Glee and Chu, but she didn't want to be teasing the boy. It might make her look bad.

The space inside the manta's mouth was like a low gothic chapel. In addition to the two pusher bunks by the throat, there were a pair of larger ledges near the front, perhaps for the absent Wobble and Duxy. Fleshy feeding tubes dangled in each niche. But the humanoid woman, Glee, looked emaciated.

"Glee just *looks* puny," said Chu, in tune with Thuy's thoughts. "She's her normal weight; she's tough, like beef jerky. Lusky feeds us as much as we like. She needs to keep her crew healthy."

"Kenee didn't look so healthy," said Thuy. "He looked dead."

"Kenee had a—a personality problem," teeped Glee, getting in on the conversation. She was using a teep voice that carried a lilting, throaty accent. "Not really Lusky's fault."

The thud of another explosion filtered through Lusky's flesh, and the great Hrull rocked heavily one side.

"Whoops!" teeped Lusky. "Time to push, guys! What if we skip California and go straight for the Hrullwelt?"

"Gaia needs us," protested Thuy. "Drop Jayjay and me in San Francisco like I said—and release Chu, too."

"Chu's my pusher now," said Lusky. "He wants to stay."

"I'm not so sure," said Chu. "I need to think about it a little more."

"So, fine, we'll go to SF," said Lusky equably. "Start charging my pusher cone. You help, too, Thuy. Just try it this once. Once you have the full pusher experience, you might want to stay on, too."

Chu and Glee focused their attention and began teeking at the ship, trying to move it with their minds. That's all that pushing was. Thuy joined in. But, for the moment, nothing happened. The manta ray was too heavy for three people to move all at once.

"Don't stop," urged Glee. "Nothing is wasted. Our teek goes into the pusher cone." She was referring to the fleshy uvula at the back of Lusky's mouth.

Drawing on her mental visualization tools, Thuy saw the quantum jiggles of their telekinetic waves as orange and purple bands that wrapped around the wobbly, dangling pusher cone.

Glee's three eyes were golden in her triangular green face. She had smallish breasts, wide hips, and a human-looking pubic mound. Thuy was ever so slightly jealous to see this alien female stretched out nude so close to Chu. Absurd to feel that way, but there it was. Maybe Thuy was a little jazzed to have a youthful admirer. Jayjay sure wasn't doing much to make her feel sexy.

As Glee, Chu, and Thuy continued teeking at Lusky's bulk, the pusher cone trembled and grew moist. Slime glistened on its surface; drops dripped to the floor.

"Hrull gel!" teeped Glee. The goo had an invigorating smell, like musk and cloves, a scent with a somehow purplish quality.

Galvanized by the odor, Glee stopped pushing and sat up. No matter, the teek accumulator was full—and now it discharged an illusionistic switcheroo of spacetime frames.

"All right," teeped Lusky. "We're over San Francisco. I'm going to circle in a holding pattern while you three enjoy your treat."

"Drop your teep block," Thuy told Lusky. "I want to see for myself."

"No," said Lusky. "I don't want those planes to find me again."

"Gel time!" messaged Glee. She was crouched beneath the pusher cone, scooping up slime from the puddle, smoothing the funky stuff onto the skin of her minimal breasts.

"What is it exactly?" Thuy asked uneasily.

"Health," teeped Glee, smiling over at her, showing her pearly teeth. She stretched out her glistening green hands. "Try some, Thuy and Chu. See how it feels to be a real pusher."

"The gel is a drug?" said Thuy, taking a careful step back. "From the Hrull mothership's body?"

"I haven't taken any yet," said Chu, standing at her side. "After each hop, Glee gets some. This is the part about being a pusher that I don't want. I don't like doing things that make me lose control."

"I'm with you," said Thuy. "I bet that gel is totally addictive."

"Gel is my bond to my pushers," said Lusky, not really contradicting her. "You'll love it."

The three-eyed Glee grinned at them, but for the moment made no move. Thuy poised herself to kick the wiry alien girl in the stomach if need be. And Chu took a fighting stance as well. Useless Jayjay continued lying limply on the floor.

A deep laugh gusted up from the manta's throat—and she sprung a surprise. Her great mouth puckered, forcing Thuy and Chu against the sulfurous green woman beneath the pusher cone.

Glee's slime-coated hand massaged Thuy's face, her slender fingers working the gel deep into the chambers of her nose.

Wow!

The gel was great! Thuy didn't feel zonked, not even high— just *really healthy*. All aches and weariness drained from her frame; the tension she'd been carrying in her shoulders was gone. She felt like she'd done yoga, taken a shower, and napped.

The mouth's walls opened back out.

"You see?" teeped Glee with a sunny smile. "The gel is good." She'd smeared it on Chu as well. "There's another effect, too," she continued, slyly winking her third eye. "It makes you feel like—you know."

Thuy knew. She was already feeling the tingle in her loins.

"Do you want to?" said Chu, looking at her with a sweet, tentative smile. "Please? I don't really know how, but—"

Thuy cast a quick glance at Jayjay. He was lying there with

his eyes closed. She was sick of being his coma nurse. He'd brought all this on himself, getting so high and yoo-hooing Pekka. She'd never felt so horny in her whole life.

But—Chu was an innocent kid. Fourteen. She thought back to her own self at fourteen, with her girlish dreams of dates and dances and the perfect kiss. The pumping and grinding of actual sex would have horrified her.

"No, Chu," said Thuy, fighting back her lust. "It wouldn't be good for you. You're not ready."

She was doing okay, she was taking the high road—but then Lusky teeped into her head and nudged her over the edge.

As if in a dream, Thuy undressed, laid down on Chu's bunk, and began passionately kissing him, her visual field overlaid with the pulsing networks of Lusky's veins. Glee sat off to the side on her own bunk, looking amused.

"Do it, Thuy," moaned Chu. "I love you."

With Chu urging her on and the gel throbbing in her cells, Thuy found herself unable to summon the will to stop.

They moved from kissing to fondling, and then to the real thing, Thuy on top, Chu on top—back and forth, in and out, the lovers riding volcanic waves of sweet sensation, kissing each other over and over again. Chu came once, twice, three times, and Thuy more times than that.

Perched upon the lovely boy, riding him down the stretch for one last orgasm, Thuy happened to glance toward her husband. Oh shit. Jayjay's eyes were wide open, fixed upon her, fascinated. But his limbs were paralyzed again. The Pekklet was back in charge. No teep block could keep the Pekklet out. Jayjay opened his mouth and began to moan and hum, gently twitching his hips. Goose bumps sprang into relief on his skin. In that instant he seemed utterly loathsome.

"I have to ditch him!" blared Lusky, angling toward the

ground. "Oh, why did I wait so long! I was busy watching you two! And, damnit, some more jets are coming."

The manta ray's mouth parts twitched, inching Jayjay forward so that she could spit him out. The great jaws opened to reveal the chockablock pastel homes of San Francisco blanketing the hills far below. It was nearly dusk here; the air was moist with fog. A plane roared past, trying to force Lusky down.

The wind and noise brought Thuy to her senses. It suddenly struck her that, with Lusky's mouth open, she and Chu were visible on *Founders* right now. And Chu's penis was still in her vagina.

Poor Jayjay was wedged against Lusky's lower jaw, with his head turned at an awkward angle. Thuy's heart flip-flopped.

"Don't," she screamed, pushing herself off Chu and scrambling after her pitiful husband. "You'll break his neck!"

But now Jayjay slid free and lurched across Lusky's lower lip, halfway out of her mouth, moaning a rune, beaming it into the flesh of the manta. Thuy grabbed his feet, dizzied by the downward view. They were at least two hundred meters above the ground.

"Let him drop!" teeped Lusky. "He's—"

Thuy heard a series of crunches and wet snaps, like a butcher's cleaver cutting up a chicken. Jayjay's rune had not only killed Lusky's flight lice, the rune was telling the atoms in Lusky's wings to opt out of their chemical bonds.

Chunks of flesh tore loose. The alien manta was coming apart. Lusky shuddered, twisted, and corkscrewed into a downward death spiral, the wind beating in through her slack, gaping jaws. A harrier jet whooshed past with a gloating waggle of its wings.

"Hop!" Thuy screamed to the others, then teleported herself and Jayjay to the pavement. Fortunately she had the presence of mind to adjust her velocity to match that of the ground.

Chu and Glee did the same; touching down lightly at her side. They'd landed at Sixteenth and Valencia streets in the Mission district. A block away, Lusky hit a row of shops like a bombed airliner, sending up a gusher of glowing orange Hrull blood.

Jayjay had sunk back into his coma, and the effects of the gel on Thuy were fading fast. She felt healthier than usual—but dead tired. And guilty as hell. Jayjay had only been unconscious for one day—and already she was cheating on him? What kind of wife was she? And what about little Chu? Awful.

Chu was nude and smelled of sex. "Oh, Thuy." His face twisted in distress. "I really just wanted to make out. And Jayjay saw us. And probably my parents. And Bixie." Abruptly his voice rose to a shrill cry. "Your gross *Founders* fans are slobbering all over us!"

"I'm going to salvage the leftover gel," teeped Glee, ignoring the drama, heading east down Valencia Street toward Lusky's shuddering bulk. "Come with me, Chu. I can get you out of here."

"Salvage?" said Chu, slowly processing the word. "You're addicted to that stuff, right, Glee?"

Glee looked back over her green shoulder at him, showing her small white teeth in a knowing smile. "So are you, a little bit. A real pusher now." Her teep voice was vaguely Eastern European.

"I can't stand it," said Chu softly. "I want to die."

"Don't worry," teeped Glee, taking a step back toward him. Her triangular green face looked sympathetic. "You will learn to control the lust. The first gel session catches pushers by surprise. Those Hrull—they are slimy." Glee made a sound like a squirrel's chirp. Her laughter. "You and Thuy were very erotic."

The alien woman's smirk aroused Thuy's protective instincts. "You keep your hands off him, Glee."

"Easily done," answered Glee. Her three eyes twinkled. "Not to be rude, but you Earthlings—you are too fat. And you smell like a Pepple animal that resembles a tapir or a pig."

"You smell like rotten broccoli," said Chu.

"So chastity between us is easy," teeped Glee. "Gel is enough. Come, Chu. We'll find Lusky's daughter Duxy and push to the Hrullwelt. I am glad to have you as a fellow worker."

"Duxy is small," said Chu hesitantly. "There's no way we could ever squeeze inside her."

"With Mother Lusky dead, Daughter Duxy begins to grow," responded Glee. "This is part of the Hrull life cycle."

"Okay then," said Chu, squaring his shoulders. "I'll come with you. I can't stay here anymore. Not now."

"Good boy."

"What about me?" clamored Thuy, feeling left out. "Aren't I hooked, too?"

"With luck you can kick this addiction," teeped Glee, not all that interested. "You will feel an ache and a fever. Unbearable. You may break down and whistle for the Hrull. To beg for gel. Perhaps the Hrull don't come, and then in a day or two you are well. For me, a cure would take longer."

"I see," said Thuy, feeling very alone. Once more she turned to Chu. "Don't go with them," she urged the boy. "Come on with me. We'll kick the gel together. We can live this down. It doesn't have to be the end of the world."

"Good-bye," said Chu, walking away, unwilling to look at her. "Good-bye, good-bye, good-bye."

Thuy watched Chu follow Glee a block down Valencia Street, then stand there, still naked, waiting while Glee rummaged within the broken whale-sized mass that had been

Lusky. The alien woman emerged with something cupped in her hands. More Hrull gel. Chu exchanged a last wave with Thuy, and then he and Glee disappeared beyond the manta's bulk.

Thuy was naked and alone, with the sun setting behind her, and Jayjay unconscious at her feet. She teeped down into her body, assessing her condition. Was something going on in her womb? No. That couldn't be happening. Absolutely not. She turned her attention to other things.

People were creeping out of their homes, and no doubt the local Peng would be coming soon. Where was Seven Wiggle Labs anyway? Thuy was going there whether or not Pekka and the frikkin' Pekklet were watching them. She'd just realized that—duh!—there was no way Pekka would kill Jayjay on purpose. At least for now, Jayjay was the go-to guy, the one and only channel from planet Pengö to Earth.

She could teep the Pekklet's presence within Jayjay's mind, so she went ahead and said something to her: "You can shove your chickenshit death threats up your cloaca, bitch."

No reaction; the Pekklet was watching and waiting—blank-faced, eyeless, unreadable.

In any case, judging from Jayjay's limp posture, he was once again too wiped to start moaning and runecasting at the Pekklet's behest. So Thuy had a little bit of time to work with.

She was definitely too ashamed to ask Ond for help, so she teeped Sonic instead. He picked up on her signal right away, and moments later he was at her side, grinning and shaking his head. He'd brought Thuy an XXL T-shirt with a logo for his Animal Animats virtual game company.

"Hot little scene with Chu, Thuy, even if we didn't get to

see the start. An online classic. A hundred million hits already."

"It wasn't my fault," said Thuy, not that anyone was likely to believe her. They'd all seen her riding Chu.

"Nothing's anyone's fault," said Sonic kindly. "The world's a metanovel that somebody else wrote. Poor Thuy. Upside: maybe you can use some of this gnarly drama in *Hive Mind*."

"Hive Mind," said Thuy disconsolately. Her peaceful old life as a metanovelist seemed very far away. She was a pariah, a laughingstock. Sadly she donned the ugly shirt. Her life was ripped to shreds.

"Intruder alert," said Sonic. "The San Francisco Peng are closing in: Blotz, Noora, and Pookie. They don't teleport, but they can float like blimps and run like motherfuckers. See them up the block?"

Three big birds were sprinting toward them, their legs flexing backward, their necks stretched out long and at an upward angle, their nasty beaks aimed directly at Thuy. She remembered that the Peng could shoot femtorays from their bills.

"Ond's patio," she said to Sonic for lack of a better thought.

The two of them hopped to Ond's backyard on Dolores Hill, with Jayjay-the-millstone in tow. As Thuy had expected and hoped, nobody was home.

"Do *you* know where to find Seven Wiggle Labs?" she asked Sonic. "And do you think they'll let us into their quantum-mirrored room? I'm scared to ask Ond. Why don't you ask him? And I'll check with Gaia."

Gaia showed Thuy the target location of Seven Wiggle Labs, but when she tried teeping the lab, the dorky owners didn't pick up. Meanwhile, Ond had bounced Sonic's teep contact as soon as he realized who the call was from.

Looking down at the city from Ond's patio, she saw the three Peng buzzing through the air toward them, their necks like hungry, implacable snakes. Blotz, Noora, and Pookie. Ugh.

"Let's hop to Seven Wiggle," she said. "Once we're there in person, maybe they'll let us in."

Seven Wiggle Labs was on the bay, near the burnt-out hulk of the former ExaExa building. It was built like a bunker, low and round with no windows, ringed by a row of chrome bollards. Whoever was inside the place still wasn't answering teep calls.

"Hey," called Thuy, leaning into the archaic intercom grill by the solid steel front door. "We have to use your quantum-mirrored room! It's important. We're Jayjay Jimenez and Thuy Nguyen." The door's dark porthole showed no signs of life.

Three dots appeared in the sky above the smooth crest of Potrero Hill: Blotz and his family, relentless in their pursuit. They wanted to kill Thuy and take custody of Jayjay.

She began kicking the door. It stayed closed. Desperately, she teeped Jil down in Santa Cruz. Jil knew all the techies. Yes, they'd quarreled yesterday, but—

"Hey," said Jil, not sounding at all friendly. "What do you want?"

"I have to get into Seven Wiggle Labs right this minute, Jil. Please help me. And, look, I'm sorry I yelled at you and I'm sorry I fucked Chu. I was wrong. I'm horrible. Forgive me. Remember how I helped you when you had those nanomachines in your head? I saved your life, Jil. Get us into Seven Wiggle. Do it for Jayjay."

"Like you care about him so much," said Jil tartly. But now she softened, picking up on Thuy's bewilderment and fear. "Oh, all right, if it's that bad I'll help. I haven't forgotten what you did for me. We women have to stick together."

A moment later the lab door swung open. Sonic, Thuy, and Jayjay made it inside just ahead of the Peng.

"Perimeter flash dome!" shouted the excited geek who'd ushered them in—a skinny guy with orange hair, bulging eyes, and high-water chino pants.

"Perimeter flash dome!" echoed his cohort, a fat, bearded guy in a black T-shirt and voluminous cutoff jeans. There were only the two of them in there, surrounded by pallets of un-formed plastic, rolls of wire, bins of crystals, and newly made weapons: kluspers, stonkers, gobble guns, and more.

A sizzling sound arose. Looking out through the door's thick round quartz window, Thuy saw a curtain of purple light, tethered to the chrome bollards and arching overhead like a circus tent.

"It works!" exulted the skinny guy, letting out a happy cackle. He glanced over at Thuy and Sonic. "I'm Stefan," he said. "Jil says you're good people, face-to-face." He stared out the window, assessing the light-curtain's strength. "Beautiful hack, Jayson! Femtotech on parade."

The bearded man came over to peer gloomily out the quartz porthole. "Those Peng—they're out there pecking and blasting their rays and they can't get in," he said softly. "That part's vibby, yeah. But now they'll cut our power lines and then, after our generators run down, they'll peck us to bits. We've got enough fuel for twenty minutes, max. I told you not to let these people in here, Stefan. But then sexy Jil Zonder gives you a call and—whee!—you throw our lives away."

"Jayjay knows a way to take down the Peng," said Thuy.

Jayson glared at Jayjay on the floor. "The mighty runecaster, eh? Too bad he's brain dead."

"He's fine," insisted Thuy. "It's just that he's totally ex-hausted. Also he's being pushed into a coma by a Subdee agent for the Peng's home world. The Pekklet. If the Pekklet gets Jay-jay to start moaning again, we're screwed. So let's get him into that quantum-mirrored room of yours really soon, okay? It's the only way to block the Pekklet's quantum entanglement with him."

"Not a problem," said Stefan brightly. The guy seemed to wear a perpetual grin. "Let's give it a try."

"Next time, Stefan, ask me before you let in refugees," grumbled Jayson. "I mean, like, in our next life. Assuming God hates me enough to reincarnate me as your business partner."

"Lighten up, kiq," said Sonic.

Jayson squinted at Sonic, then made a grimace that was almost a smile. "Hey, I know you! Sonic's Animal Animats. I took one of your tours—I was teeping a walrus stalking this cute polar bear cub. A rare moment of personal bliss."

"Today's mission is even more fun," said Sonic. "We're saving the world from alien invasion!"

"Take us to the quantum-mirrored room," repeated Thuy. She picked up Jayjay's feet and Sonic got hold of him under the arms.

"Lead them in, Stefan," said Jayson, drifting back to his desk. "I'll stay out here and monitor the power."

"Good deal for me," said Stefan happily. "I'll get to see what Jayjay's like when he wakes up. This is the same guy who unfurled the eighth dimension, kiq. He and Thuy are big stars on *Founders*. She just did a live porno scene, too, in case you didn't happen to—"

"Shit!" yelled Jayson. "They got our power lines!" He gestured in the air, tweaking a virtual console that only he could see. Beneath the floor a motor coughed into life.

Roused by the hubbub, Jayjay twitched his arms and opened his mouth as if to moan.

"Hurry, Stefan!" screamed Thuy.

Stefan hustled them into the quantum-mirrored room. The walls, floor, and ceiling were slick with iridescent square-root-of-NOT varnish. Multiple reflections bounced off the walls, sour-colored pastel images overlaying each other in endless regresses.

"This place is doubly shielded," he bragged. "We've got quantum-mirror varnish against quantum entanglement, and the walls themselves are tuned to block out teep. This is, like, the most private room on Earth."

Sure enough, the quantum mirrors worked. The Pekklet was barred from Jayjay's head. And now, finally, he woke all of the way up. He hauled himself to his feet, glaring at Thuy.

"Damn you!" were his first words. "How could you!"

Something in her rebelled. Obviously she should apologize. But she didn't feel like it. "It wasn't my fault," she repeated. "Those aliens smeared an aphrodisiac drug onto us. And Lusky pushed me. And meanwhile you were into your disgusting jerk-off Pekklet thing. The way you were watching us, it was almost like you were—"

"Shut up! This all started when you kissed that little boy in the woods. Nobody made you do that but yourself. Whore."

"So that's where we stand?" said Thuy, her emotions boiling up. "Junkie. Loser. Pervert."

"A match made in heaven," said Sonic, trying to lighten the mood. "Meet the honeymooners. Come on, guys, can't we all play on the same team?"

"Play the fuck what?" said Jayjay, staring off into the warped reflections of the quantum-mirrored walls. "Play the fuck why?"

"I don't know how much you remember, Jayjay," said Thuy, trying to control her voice. "Chu and I met this little alien manta ray, Duxy, in the woods, and she teeped you the atomic reset rune? And—"

"I hate Chu. Don't ever talk to me about him again."

"That's progress," said Sonic, glancing over at Stefan. "Don't you think? The *ever again* implies a future together, no?"

"Oh, Thuy," said Jayjay, collapsing into tears, a heartbroken ghost of his brash old self. This was much worse than seeing him angry.

She hugged him tight. He felt good in her arms. Privately they teeped back and forth for a minute, sorting things out, rekindling their dreams, making a plan.

"Jayjay and I are going to the Hibrane," Thuy then informed Sonic and Stefan.

"What?" said Sonic, truly surprised. "What does the Hibrane have to do with anything? That's a completely different parallel world."

"It's all about untangling the links between Pekklet and Jayjay's particle strings," said Thuy. "A higher-dimensional jump might help. Anyway, if Jayjay just stays here and keeps setting up Peng ranches, some mob is going to kill him."

"Okay, but I heard that the Hibraners tilted our brane's timeline away from theirs," said Sonic. "They did it so that our jump code won't work anymore. They were worried we'd bring nants over there."

"Yeah, yeah, but nobody from here has actually *tried* to jump to the Hibrane since the tilt," said Thuy. "Maybe it'll be okay. And if we end up in Subdee or something, we'll jump back. It's worth a try." She was sounding a lot more confident than she felt. But she had her own reason for wanting to get out of here: she'd utterly disgraced herself.

"What about us?" said Stefan, his constant smile beginning to fade. "I thought you said Jayjay was going to wipe out the Peng when he got into this room."

"Um—in case you haven't noticed, it's impossible to teek out from here," said Jayjay. "Otherwise, yeah, I could cast the reset rune all over San Francisco and Yolla Bolly. Can you just tell the walls to let my teep and teek go through?"

"Well, no," said Stefan. "Jayson and I kind of hypnotized the wall silps into this very stubborn state where they're totally unwilling to turn off the teep block, no matter who asks them. You'd pretty much need to knock a hole in the walls to get any teep in here. But of course that would—"

"—let the Pekklet's quantum entanglement back in," said Sonic.

"Maybe her connection to Jayjay is already broken for good," suggested Stefan.

"Jumping right out of the Lobrane sounds best," insisted Jayjay. "It's what Thuy wants."

Right about then the generator died and the perimeter flash dome failed.

"That's wrong!" screamed Jayson in the next room. "There's still a half liter of fuel!"

The Peng started woodpeckering the front door. Thuy heard the harsh screech of tearing steel.

"Outta here, Stefan," said Sonic. "Let's you, Jayson, and me teleport our asses down to Cruz. All the hip kiqqies went there yesterday."

"Hadn't thought of that," said Stefan, brightening. "Yeah! We can leave the lab!"

"What a concept," said Sonic, winking at Thuy. "Geeks."

The two exited the mirrored room, slamming the heavy door behind them before the Pekklet could start anything new. Out in the control room, Sonic had to yell at Jayson for a moment. Even now, the bearded techie wanted to argue. But then the three of them were gone.

The next sound was of the Peng in the control room,

squawking among each other. One of the voices was deeper than the others, bossier—that would be Blotz. Maybe the Peng were a little scared of Jayjay.

"Time for the Hibrane, Thuy," said Jayjay. "Do you still remember the code?"

"You mean the Knot?" said Thuy, not wanting to use the pattern's full name—which was Chu's Knot.

"Yeah, yeah," said Jayjay. "Show it to me fast."

As Thuy arranged the filigreed mental pattern for teeping, a first tentative tap sounded on the door, followed by a full-on blow. A bulge formed on the inside. Thuy's mind froze up. They weren't going to have enough time to put together their cross-brane jump. They were doomed.

A high, fearful, buzzing sounded outside the door.

"The pitchfork!" cried Jayjay.

The Peng cawed and screeched; they stopped pecking the door. By the sound of things, they were fruitlessly threatening the pitchfork. The pitchfork's drone grew still louder; the Peng's voices became fuzzed and weak. And now Thuy heard their footfalls running away.

There was a moment of silence, and then something very tiny wriggled up from the floor. It was—the pitchfork, tunneling in via the subdimensions.

"Yee-haw!" he said aloud as he grew to human scale. "I stirred up the lab's vibes so them Peng don't feel comfortable. I been feeling guilty about helping the Pekklet weave her particle strings into yours, Jay."

"He really talks like this?" said Thuy, somehow more surprised by the hillbilly accent than by anything else.

"Yeah," said Jayjay, smiling for the first time today. "Groovy the pitchfork. I kind of hate him, but he makes me laugh."

"Go away," Thuy told the pitchfork.

"I'm the onliest friend you got," said Groovy. "After we

hook up with the harp in the Hibrane, I'll aktualize you two. You gonna be like gods. And then Thuy here is gonna tear that Pekklet apart."

"I'm for that," said Thuy.

She gathered her wits and teeped Jayjay the details of Chu's Knot: a pattern that resembled an intricately woven twine bracelet.

"I see it," said Jayjay. "Now what?" He hadn't made the trip to the Hibrane before.

"Focus on the image," said Thuy softly. She felt happy and sure of herself. "Let go of your inner voice. Put yourself into the gaps between your thoughts."

Jayjay got into the groove—and they jumped into a higher dimension, with the pitchfork following in their wake.

CHAPTER 10

ERGOT

Jayjay and Thuy flew side-by-side, their arms outstretched like superheroes, the pitchfork keeping pace. They were skimming across a vast, rolling ocean: a Planck sea of subdimensional eddies.

Although Jayjay was upset about Thuy's unfaithfulness, his overall feeling was one of immense relief. The combination of the quantum-mirrored room and the jump out of the Lobrane seemed to have unknotted the ties to the Pekklet. For the first time in two days, he was free. Feeling like a pelican hugging a wave, he waggled his body closer to the glittering Planck frontier.

Some shapes, like lumpy plants, popped through the surface—Jayjay had seen similar beings near the beanstalk.

"Oh hell!" said Thuy. "The subbies. Don't let them touch

you. They'll try to drag you under." She gestured to fly higher.

The tuber-shaped subbies morphed into heron heads upon wiggly necks, with white-gloved cartoony bodies beneath the waves. The subbies knifed along, leaving wakes of quantum foam, tracking the travelers with hungry eyes.

"My first trip to the Hibrane went really fast," said Thuy, uneasy at these presences. "But on the way back I got lost. And the subbies tried to eat me."

"I can keep them mofos down," called Groovy, his vibrating prongs wreathed in glowing mauve. "Looky here." He swept close to the Planck sea and spat a spark. Restless as a spider, the crackling energy webbed the surface. On the instant, the subbies dropped from view.

"What *are* you, anyway?" Thuy asked the pitchfork.

"Might could say I'm a devil and the harp's a god. I like to strum her real goood." He drew out the last word with relish.

"Get real," said Thuy.

"Okay, then," buzzed Groovy. "Here's real: the harp and me are humanoids from a world like yours, but right now we're on a trip out past infinity, we're superpowered aliens, playin' with your world. Bringing you lazy eight and aktualization. Turnabout is fair play—you're gonna do the same for us pretty soon. After the maelstrom."

"If you're a humanoid, why do you look like a pitchfork?" challenged Jayjay, not even wanting to think about the rest of what the alien had said.

"Once you an aktual, you can look like anything you like," said the pitchfork. "A harp, a pitchfork, a crow, a bagpipe— but never mind all that. We gotta worry about crossing this here Planck sea. What with the two branes all catawampus, the jump's much farther than before. But you can do it, Jay. Use what I taught you on that beanstalk. Pull the wife along and I'll follow."

Jayjay took Thuy by the hand, visualizing the endless beanstalk. Feeling light and nimble, he revolved his vision of the great vine to aim its axis in the direction they flew. And now, as he imagined a Zeno-style scramble up the stalk, he and Thuy shot forward as if in a particle accelerator.

They touched down upon a stone street in a town with no lights or teep. The mild, damp air bore the smell of human waste. It felt like spring or early summer.

A gentle thump sounded at their side: the pitchfork. Somewhere nearby, men were roaring a slow, deep-voiced song. A full moon hung above the stair-stepped gables, the buildings oddly tall.

Suddenly it struck Jayjay that his lazy eight memory was gone—taking with it a lot of the new science he'd learned. But not all of it. Looking up past the walls to the panoply of stars, he recognized the constellations. He used the north star to find the points of the compass, noted that the moon was in the west, recalled that at this time of year the full moon sets an hour or two before dawn, and drew a conclusion.

"It's about four A.M." he told Thuy.

"There's no teep to check that," she said fretfully. "This place isn't right. Last time, the Hibrane was almost like our San Francisco, and they had lazy eight. This is some kind of primitive backwater with no silps, and our extra memory is missing. Everything's mute. How do people live this way?"

"We're free," said Jayjay relishing the bucolic air. Already he was learning to ignore the bad smells. "It's great here. No Peng, no voices in our heads, no *Founders* show." He paused. "I still can't believe you did that with Chu."

"I can't either," said Thuy, her voice close by his side. In this street of moonlit buildings, her face was a faint oval. "I wasn't in my right mind, Jayjay. What we've been through the last two days—it's insane."

Dogs barked in courtyards nearby, perhaps annoyed by Groovy's buzz. He was standing beside Jayjay, balancing on his handle, vibrating his prongs at an ultrasonic rate. Now he slid down a few octaves, sculpting his reverberant tones into a voice.

"I got a powerful hankerin' to find that harp," said the strange being. "I know it's gonna work out. We've done all this before. She's already been through most of it."

"She has?"

"The harp is manifesting as a time loop. That's why we're outta synch. Seems like a god and a devil would be able to show up on the same brane, same place, same time—but Lovva, she always takes a wrong turn."

"Once you finish with the harp, we still have to get the Peng off our planet," said Jayjay. "Don't forget. You owe us that much."

"Gimme, gimme, gimme," said Groovy dismissively. He went hopping off, his handle rapping smartly on the stones. Someone lit a lantern and swung open a casement, the window absurdly high above the ground.

A slow, draggy squeal issued from a faintly visible alley farther down the street. Horn-shod feet clattered on the stones. Shambling their way was a muddy hairy beast the size of a truck. A giant hog.

"Run, Thuy!" cried Jayjay. The cobblestones were broad and high-crowned, with gaping cracks between them. At his very first step, he caught his foot and fell.

The monstrous hog was coming closer, slow but steady, snuffling his way through the fetid night. And a red-faced man in a nightgown was yelling from the window. The man's speech was doubly incomprehensible: the voice was warped like a screwed audio clip, and the words weren't in any language Jay-jay knew.

"Don't worry," said Thuy, as Jayjay got to his feet. In the faint, jiggly light, he could see that she was smiling. "There's a six-to-one spacetime scale difference between the Lobrane and the Hibrane. It's like we're one foot tall here—but we're tough as steel, and faster than weasels. I'm gonna terrorize that pig."

She flanked around the moon-silvered swine and planted a volley of kicks upon his muddy hams. Bellowing like drunken molasses, the coarse beast bucked his way past Jayjay and up the street.

Gazing at the scolding man in the high window, Thuy shook her fist and threw a stone right through his wall. The man made a triangle gesture and slammed his shutters.

"We're fast, dense super-gnomes," gloated Thuy.

Giant soldiers appeared around a corner, bearing lanterns, singing and swaying, with motley hats of leather and wool. The pig careened into them, producing a slow-motion pileup.

At first the soldiers laughed. But then one them spotted Jay-jay and began shouting, his voice shaking the air. Slowly, terri-bly, the soldiers drew their swords. The blades looked twenty feet long.

"Let's take that alley where the pig came out," suggested Jayjay. "We need a safe place to rest." The emotions and the runecasting had totally worn him down.

As they turned the corner into the alley, a vista opened out. The town was on a low hill, and from here Jayjay had a view across the massed buildings, pale and crisp in the moonlight. He saw stepped roofs, a church spire topped by a triangle, a city wall with gates and towers, and beyond that a river and a flat landscape stretching to the north. The sky out there was a strange shade of red. With a start, Jayjay realized the glow was from a burning village.

Torches flickered in the alley: a sooty, bloodied gang of soldiers was making their way uphill, returning from a nighttime raid, armed with crossbows and halberds, dressed in woven tights with soft boots and light cloaks, bearing shields embossed with swans and toads.

Jayjay turned back, wanting to avoid the warriors, but the besotted soldiers on the main street had drawn even with the alley's mouth. The revelers roared a warning to the battle party—and now Jayjay and Thuy were trapped between two groups of armed, unfriendly men.

All eyes were fixed upon them. *"Duivels,"* rumbled the soldiers' voices, slow and guttural. *"Gnooms. Guelders!"* Blades flickered and footsteps scuffed as the men squeezed closer to see the strange dwarves they'd trapped.

Suddenly the pitchfork returned, briskly pushing his way through the gathering mob. The soldiers flinched back from the curious creature's wriggly touch.

"Found the harp!" he twanged. "She's locked snug in an attic; she sang to me through the walls. She's waiting for Jay to come play that Lost Chord before she goes home. She taught me the local lingo; what you might call Dutch. I can buzz it into your skulls. Then you'll know what these bad-asses are sayin' about you."

"Don't!" cried Jayjay. "You'll hard-boil our brains!"

"Right now let's get back to the main street," said Thuy. "With our speed advantage, it won't actually be that hard."

Jayjay led the way, being careful with his feet and swiveling his head from side to side lest he miss someone coming at him with a sword. He dodged around the first two soldiers he encountered, and gave a third one a hard shove in the shin, a man wearing leather pantaloons. The guy tipped over as easily as a bowling pin. He had a heavy blond mustache and a smooth blue cap pulled low over his round head. Misliking the soldier's stupid, implacable glare, Jayjay gave him an extra kick.

Once in the clear, Jayjay and Thuy trotted rapidly down the street, evasively weaving from side to side, easily outpacing their few pursuers. Jayjay had a bad moment of thinking he'd been struck by a crossbow bolt—but it was only Groovy tapping his shoulder.

They crossed a bridge over a little canal, cut down a side street to the right, took a left, and leaned against a house, catching their breath.

"Hold on now till I learn you Dutch," repeated Groovy.

"*You* hold on," said Thuy. "Where are we, anyway? And when?"

"Harp says this town goes by the name of 's-Hertogenbosch," responded the pitchfork. The modulated whine of his voice was making the dogs bark again. "We're in the Duchy of Brabant, and it's early on Saturday the twenty-fifth of June, 1496, anno domini. Here's your language lesson!" His hum rose to a furious buzz.

The intricate sound assaulted Jayjay, swarming into his head like hornets. His mind bubbled with words and idioms, with syllables and phonemes. He felt unaccustomed twitches in his tongue, fresh shades of feeling in his throat. In the dark beside him, Thuy groaned. And then, finally, the buzzing stopped. Jayjay felt earthier than before, lower and more irascible—he felt Dutch.

"*Joepie!*" said Groovy. "Means *yee-haw.* I'm off to fetch your pal." With that he stumped off. Jayjay couldn't think what "pal" the pitchfork was talking about now—all he knew was that he was nearing the end of his rope. Had Groovy really said 1496?

Once again a window overhead flew open and a burgher with a lantern leaned out to yell. Reckless with exhaustion, Jayjay answered the man on his own terms.

"Shit-eater!" he hollered in fluent Brabantian Middle Dutch. "Come out here and I'll shove that lantern down your gullet, you addle-pated, pig-faced son of a whore!"

To Jayjay's chagrin, the man clattered down the stairs of his house.

"He understood you!" said Thuy with a weak chuckle. "Let's scurry off. We're darling elves spreading good cheer."

Hastening down the lane that had led them here, they bumped into a one-legged man with a wooden crutch.

"Greetings, friend," said Jayjay in the local tongue. "Can we follow you home?"

"We're poor outcasts," added Thuy, also speaking Brabants Dutch.

"Unclean dwarves despised by the Almighty," said the one-legged man, sizing them up. "I'm Maarten. I'll show you to a haven for the likes of us. Carry my booty and we'll make better speed."

Jayjay took a cloth sack from Maarten's shoulder; it held scavenged garbage. The beggar led them through a narrow space between a hedge and wall, across a moonlit vegetable garden, through a squeaky gate, and down a sandy path that debouched into a cobbled courtyard.

A group of ill-favored figures were gathered around a low fire. A three-legged kettle of soup simmered on the coals. Some of the company lay stretched out asleep, others were sitting up. Jayjay placed Maarten's sack at the fire's edge. A legless man in a striped blouse showed his teeth and emptied the sack: a fish head, a bone, a soft cabbage, a stale half loaf of dark brown bread. He pitched the first three items into the kettle, gnawed a bit of the hard bread, and passed the loaf to his neighbor.

Maarten nodded toward a large stone building abutting the courtyard. "The monastery of the Brotherhood of Saint Anthony," he said. "The Antonites are charitable to us. You can rest by our fire as long as you like. I'll fetch you some wine."

Sitting down between Thuy and the legless man, Jayjay looked around the circle of figures. Some lacked limbs, others had twisted spines or egregious harelips, some stared into the flames with haunted eyes.

"I'm Hugo," said the legless man. He had short-cropped hair and large, dark eyes. "Sinner that I am, I suffer from a plague that consumes my flesh: Saint Anthony's fire. My limbs loosen and drop. Would you like to see my talisman?"

Not waiting for an answer, Hugo reached into his striped blouse and drew out a small bundle of white cloth. Carefully he flattened out the cloth on the courtyard stones, revealing a leathery, mummified foot with the ankle bone sticking out. "Mine," said Hugo, a catch in his voice. "As a boy I danced on a rope and chased the maids; now I beg in the marketplace."

"Ick," said Thuy, rather loudly. Hugo let it pass.

"Here," said Maarten, hobbling over with a large bowl of dark wine in one hand. "The Antonites gave us a cask tonight. One of our number is scheduled for surgery in the morn." He pointed across the courtyard at a puffy beggar hunkered by the small wine barrel. "Lubbert. His leg is quite putrescent, poor soul."

Taking the large bowl, Jayjay noticed that Maarten's skin was flushed and ulcerous and that he was missing several fingers. But, what the hell, Jayjay drank some of the wine, just to show he was one of the gang. It was a surprisingly good red, quite light, and smooth as silk. Maybe it would help him sleep. Thuy was already lying on her side, pillowing her cheek on her hands. She had the right idea.

"Do you want any wine?" he asked her.

"I'd better not," she said, looking up at him with an oddly fraught expression. She was so beautiful in the firelight. Suddenly, she dropped a bomb. "I think—I think I'm pregnant."

"What!"

"I noticed this afternoon. I teeped into my uterus."

"After Chu?"

"That doesn't mean it's his, Jayjay. You and I had sex the other day when we were building the foundation for our house."

"But wait!" said Jayjay, his emotions in a knot. "We wouldn't want to risk having to raise a kid like Chu."

"Well—" said Thuy, her voice going up an octave, suddenly close to tears. "If it *is* Chu's child, maybe I'd owe that to him. I stole Chu's innocence today. I raped him. And then I let him go off to die in a horrible alien manta ray with a three-eyed junkie."

"Thuy—"

"Oh, I can't think. I'm exhausted, and I'm still messed up from the Hrull gel. Strung out. I know it's crazy, but I keep feeling like I should whistle for the Hrull so I can get more. Not that they have any Hrull here, do they? I'm sorry I'm so horrible."

"Just go to sleep," said Jayjay, patting her cheek. "I love you no matter what. We'll figure out a way to stop the Peng and then we'll go back home to—"

"But wait!" exclaimed Thuy sitting bolt upright. She turned to Jayjay, her face working. "I just realized that I don't have that Knot code in my head anymore. I'd stored it in my lazy eight memory, and when we came over here, all that part of my memory went away. We might be stuck here forever!"

She really broke down then, and Jayjay rocked her to sleep in his arms, nursing his bowl of wine. Finally, she was sleeping on her side.

Jayjay meant to lie down next to her, but somehow he felt too wired. So many things to think about. The strange pitchfork, the endless beanstalk, the squawky Peng, his draining labors as runecaster, the near success of the reset rune, the raw memories of Thuy and Chu, the dizzy sensation of the pitchfork vibrating Dutch into his brain, this medieval beggars' banquet, Thuy's pregnancy—and now the possibility that they might be living here for good. He couldn't remember the Knot, either.

"More wine for the fretful dwarf," said Lubbert, limping across the courtyard, carrying the cask beneath one flabby arm. He had a round, woebegone face. His skin was crimson, peeling, spotted with pustules. He had but two remaining digits on each hand. A pair of lobster claws.

While Lubbert was filling Jayjay's huge bowl, his bad leg gave way, and he tumbled onto Hugo, who snarled at him like a rabid dog. Lubbert wallowed around until he could lean his back against Jayjay's. All the while he kept tight control of his cask.

Thuy kept right on sleeping. The other beggars drifted in and out of the firelight. Lubbert and Jayjay sat back-to-back, drinking their wine. Jayjay was somehow too tired to nod off. Or maybe he was too drunk. Or too hungry.

That stale half loaf of brown bread had made it around the circle nearly intact, and Jayjay started chewing on it, softening it by dipping it into the kettle's broth. Although the bread tasted moldy and fungal, Jayjay ate most of the loaf.

He had a few minutes of extreme mental clarity, analyzing why it was they'd ended up so far into the past. But then he began feeling—very strange. Trippy. Dosed. His fingers were tingling; he was seeing trails behind moving objects.

He was so wasted that he relaxed into the trip without even questioning it. Setting aside the wine bowl and the thoughts of math and physics, he stared at the fire like the other goners, savoring the patterns, mechanically gnawing on the bread, becoming more and more convinced that the fire was filled with intelligent silps even though he couldn't teep them. Nature was alive from the start, even without lazy eight.

The sun peeped over the misty horizon and a shaft of light hit Jayjay in the eyes. With the light came a flashback to the pre-Singularity days when he and Sonic had been using chemicals instead of the Net to get high. They'd had a brief fad for the vintage psychedelic LSD, and had learned that acid's organic precursor is ergot, a type of fungus that grows on rye grain in certain years.

With a growing sense of agitation, Jayjay recalled that ergot contains a witches' brew of other alkaloids besides lysergic acid, eldritch chemicals which act as poisons with cumulative effects.

Abruptly he began hallucinating a chicken standing on a ladder reciting ergot facts. The chicken—who was wearing an academic gown and a tiny mortarboard—said that the first kicker about ergot poisoning was that nobody in the Middle Ages had ever realized that the affliction, which they called St. Anthony's fire, was caused by the bad grain in their bread. They'd thought the syndrome was brought on by sinfulness; and that the hallucinations were a form of demonic possession.

The second kicker, continued the chicken, was that if you consumed ergot for months or years, you'd get a blistery red rash on your skin, and your fingers would drop off, and in due time you'd lose your limbs—like Maarten, Hugo, and Lubbert.

Jayjay thought to drop his crust.

Lobster Lubbert lay sprawled behind him, seemingly unconscious. Jayjay lay down, too, letting the rising sun play on his eyelids, goofing on the colored patterns spawned by the light.

He might have slept, but now Thuy let out a whine. Sly Lubbert had snaked his arm over to her; he was tugging at her clothes, wanting to fondle her unblemished bare skin.

Utterly knackered by the cumulative insults to his brain, Jayjay struggled to his feet—and kicked Lubbert in the ass. Weeping with chagrin, Lubbert reeled over to the fire and picked up a burning coal, using a rag to hold it. He lunged at Jayjay, meaning to brand him. The coal seemed to be talking to Jayjay, mesmerizing him with its whispery voice.

"Run!" Thuy yelled, prodding her husband into motion.

The two of them escaped down the same main street as last night, although now it was luminous in the misty dawn, shaded with a continuous range of pastel colors. Hooves and wooden wheels clattered on the cobbles, bringing wagonloads of goods to town: cheese and milk, turnips and cabbages, chickens and rabbits. Market day. Two sweaty men rolled a barrel of beer; a woman balanced a tower of linens on her head. Noticing the little Lobraners, a soldier yelled.

Rounding another corner, Thuy and Jayjay suddenly found themselves inside a large cloth sack—as if subjected to some weird mathematical procedure involving the inversion of transfinite space to the interior of a sphere. The sack's mouth pinched shut, someone lifted them with a grunt, and they thumped into a wheelbarrow. Jayjay and Thuy were squeezed into the sack spoon-style, with Thuy nestled into Jayjay's lap.

"Maybe I really should whistle for the Hrull," said Thuy. "I wonder if any of them can hear us over here?"

"Please don't do that," said Jayjay intensely.

"Are we ever going to be normal again?" said Thuy, her voice breaking.

"Quiet!" said a voice in English, as sternly if they were two cats in a bag. "I'm taking you to the harbor." For drowning?

Church bells chimed as they trundled through the market-place. A smith hammered an anvil. Geese honked, pigs squealed, children yelled, and everywhere people were talking Dutch, really quite a cozy tongue—almost like English.

The wheelbarrow bumped down a slope. Jayjay heard the slap of small waves and the hollow knocking of boats. With another grunt, their captor slung them into the ribbed bottom of a skiff. Jayjay's heartbeat rose to a crescendo.

The sack opened and a face peered in: a Hibrane youth with intelligent brown eyes on either side of a tomahawk nose. His long hair was tied into a topknot. He was smiling at them.

"Azaroth!" cried Jayjay, giddy with relief. "You ended up here, too? Can you help us get back to the Lobrane?"

Originally Azaroth had lived in the Hibrane equivalent of twenty-first century San Francisco. He'd been making regular trips to the Lobrane to poach cuttlefish, but then he'd gotten involved with Jayjay and Thuy's struggle to save Lobrane Earth from the rogue nanomachine nants. Thuy had stolen the magic harp from Azaroth's aunt and Jayjay had played a Lost Chord that solved the nant problem by converting all of Earth's natural processes into intelligent minds: the silps.

The last time they'd seen Azaroth was when the Hibraner had come to repossess the harp and take it home. Azaroth had been in a hurry, as his fellow Hibraners had just then been working to disrupt the hyperjump route from the Lobrane to the twenty-first century Hibrane. Apparently the disruption was now sending incoming traffic to the Hibrane's fifteenth century.

"You can come out of the sack now," said the Hibraner. "I'm glad to see you two. Maybe we can help each other."

They were in a harbor where several 's-Hertogenbosch canals converged. Most of the harbor was within the city wall, which marched right through the basin. The scene was alive with large and small boats, everything mirrored in the undulating water. A fish market sat on a dock against the city wall, complete with a crane lifting crates from a scow. Azaroth's boat was moored on the inner side of the harbor, beside the cobble streets and wooden homes.

"Good old Azaroth," said Thuy. "I was hoping it was you. Are we safe?"

"Nobody will bother you if you're with me," said Azaroth. Always the flashy dresser, he wore a puffy muslin blouse and striped red and white tights. "I've convinced them I'm from the Garden of Eden. They think it's a real place, somewhere in the Caribbean or South America. These people have such a strange view of the world."

"Garden of Eden!" said Jayjay. "Don't tell me that Hibraners believe the whole Christian storybook?"

"*These* guys do," said Azaroth, with a gesture at the town. "Here in the fifteenth century, heaven and hell are the main thing they care about. Facts to remember if you don't want to be burned at the stake: Hibrane Christianity was founded by Jude Christ, not Jesus Christ; He died nailed to a wooden triangle, not a cross; His symbol is the cuttlefish, not the lamb. Our Lord Jude was a cuttlefisherman like me!" Azaroth laughed. "I can't believe we're in the Lowlands of 1496. I love it!"

As he talked, he was unmooring his boat and laying out his fishing gear. A few passersby had stopped to stare and point at Thuy and Jayjay. Quickly Azaroth maneuvered his skiff away from the shore.

"I was thinking about the time-slip this morning," said Jayjay, standing in the boat, his head level with the gunwale. "It's because you guys bent the Lobrane's timeline away from the Hibrane's time. Look." He swept his hands up through the air, sketching a pair of imaginary timelines, keenly sensitive to the trails. The lines started out parallel, but then one line drooped over to the side like an ergot-stricken stalk of wheat. "If you jump from the tip of droopy timeline, your path hits the other line down low. Time travel."

"What year would we hit if we hopped back to the Lobrane?" wondered Azaroth.

"Hard to predict," said Jayjay. "Maybe we'd be in the twenty-first century like before. Or maybe in 1200 B.C. But could be we'll never find out, because—"

"Oh, relax, Jayjay," said Thuy. "You sound like Ond Lutter. Like a numberskull nerd. I'm sick of worrying. Let's just enjoy this for now. The last gasp of the Middle Ages."

"It's fun here," agreed Azaroth. "I live in a tavern that's a bathhouse and a brothel. The Muddy Eel. I've got a thing going with one of the women. Anja." He smiled as he said her name. "I tell everyone I rode back from the New World on Columbus's ships. They're only just now getting the word about his voyages. You guys can be my cousins: tiny, doll-perfect pygmies from the Garden of Eden. Practically angels." He bent his back, rowing across the harbor toward the city wall.

Jayjay stretched his arms and breathed in the cool air, trying to relax, ignoring the faint sewer smell. Unfortunately, the ergot was still in play. All the boats looked like faces. Even the canal looked like a face.

"I guess that hillbilly pitchfork sent you after us?" Thuy asked Azaroth.

"Groovy," said the Hibraner. "He's friends with the harp. Those two are—"

"Look out!" interrupted Jayjay, pointing at what he saw as

a huge demonic cat skull rising from the water, jaws wide-open, with a corpse-worm peeping from a monstrous hollow eye socket.

"That's just a water gate, Jayjay," said Azaroth calmly. "An arch with a portcullis, and a burgher taking tolls. We're going fishing. That's how I earn my keep. I catch these big coarse fish with hook and line. They look like cod. I hook a few eels, too. And sometimes I net herring."

"Why—why are you taking us fishing?" asked Jayjay, feeling desperately adrift. He still hadn't had a chance to tell Thuy about his ergot poisoning. Talking was so much more work than telepathy.

"Obviously you need a rest," said Azaroth, gliding up to the water gate. "And if the locals see us together, they might accept your arrival. They're all gossiping about you."

The pop-eyed, white-bristled guardian of the gate was indeed curious about the two little doll-people who'd been running around all night. He quizzed them for several minutes. They calmed him by answering in colloquial Brabantian Dutch, slowing down their voices to be readily comprehensible. The guard said the soldiers had been worried the dwarves might be demons or, worse, spies from Gelderland. But he was perfectly willing to believe they were Azaroth's Dutch-speaking pygmy cousins from the Garden of Eden in the New World—especially after Azaroth gave him a silver coin.

"What's Gelderland?" Thuy asked Azaroth as they paddled into the confluence of the two rivers that flanked the town.

"The province just north of here. Gelderland's been fighting the Duchy of Brabant for twenty years. Our team torched a Gelder village just last night."

Azaroth rowed them up the Dommel River, following along the outside of the town wall. From the boat, Jayjay could see the town as a triangle, squeezed between the two rivers and bounded on the third side by a canal. The town consisted of thatched wooden houses and brick monasteries, also a cathedral and half a dozen churches. Each spire was topped with a tip-down isosceles triangle to memorialize Jude Christ's death.

People were ambling toward the town along a dirt road by the river: peasant youths and maids; a bearded man in a red cape and a top hat; a woman dressed in motley and carrying juggler's rings; a peddler with pots and pans fastened all over his body; an unshaven bagpiper with his wind-sack slung slack across his back. The marketplace was visible at the town's crest: a triangular plaza alive with humans and livestock. The massed sound drifted down, like a single, intricately articulated voice.

"It's a special market," said Azaroth. "Not just the usual weekend thing. Tomorrow they have the big annual Procession of the Virgin Mary."

"Can we help you catch some fish?" Thuy asked him.

"Yeah," said Azaroth, gesturing at some simple wooden rods in the bottom of the boat. "Throw in a couple of lines while I row to my favorite spot."

Jayjay worked a worm onto one of Azaroth's hooks and tossed it in from the stern. After a bit, the foot traffic along the river died down. It was peaceful, peaceful here, and the water was clean.

The sky was milky white; it could rain today. The mild Brabant landscape spread before them, with rows of trees along the edges of green fields. The willows had been cropped to stumps, with long shoots on their pollarded crowns.

Just then Jayjay felt a brutal tug on his line, nearly yanking the rod from his grip. He and Thuy hauled in the line together, eventually landing a slimy brown fish with spikes, a monster the size of Jayjay's own body. The thing flopped across the deck toward him, its yellow eyes alight with malice. Feeling the ergot again, Jayjay screamed and ran to the bow. But Thuy stood her ground.

She got the hook out of the fish—Azaroth said it was a dogfish—and continued angling. For his part, Jayjay settled down on the folded cloth sack in the bow.

"Nap time!" said Thuy, smiling at him.

Soothed by the gentle rocking and the quiet conversation of Azaroth and Thuy, Jayjay dropped off. He had the sensation of literally melting into his dreams—as if his figure and the landscape around him were deliquescing into oozy globs. This was disturbing, but better than being awake.

His restless mind set to forming patterns. The blobs became glub-glubbing subaqueous silps. Jayjay himself was a live worm perched upon a fishing hook that was somehow Thuy, and her pigtails were the hook's barbs. Jayjay tugged off a pigtail and wielded it like a paintbrush, revising the appearance of the scene.

Was this composition marketable? Perhaps not. Jayjay rubbed out the dream image with his oily sleeve and started a fresh one, repeating this entire cycle 1,496 times.

A whoop from Azaroth woke him. He was feeling better now. While he'd been sleeping, Azaroth and Thuy had caught a whole basket of fish, including a thick and wriggly pair of eels. And now the Hibraner was hauling in his fishing line once more.

"A big one, Thuy! Fish of the day! Hand me that gaff to drag him in."

The fish flopped into the skiff, bleeding from his mouth, thumping the deck with his tail, twice the size of Jayjay or Thuy. He was so fat as to be nearly spherical. Azaroth produced a remarkably sharp knife and slit the fish's belly open. Another fish popped out, and a third fish from within that one, all of them disgorging snails, minnows, and worms. Azaroth added the catch to his basket.

Glancing farther up the river, Jayjay noticed three tall gallows standing in a plain beyond 's-Hertogenbosch. The gibbets dangled ragged bundles: skeletons with scraps of flesh. Crows were picking at them. And, there, gliding down behind the gallows field to land by the river's distant curve—was that a flying manta ray?

"Hey, Jayjay," said Thuy, calling him back. She looked fresh and happy as life itself, silhouetted against the bustling little town. "It's vibby being medieval, huh? Azaroth says he gave the magic harp to an artist for repainting. He wants Lovva to look good again before he takes her back to his aunt. And guess who the artist is!"

"Hieronymus Bosch," said Jayjay, lacking telepathy but reading the answer from her tone. Not that he cared that much.

"You're up to speed, kiq! Jeroen is what they call him here." She pronounced it in the Dutch way, like *Yeroon*. "I bet that Kittie really did see him at our housewarming. It's all beginning to fit."

"I was sort of dreaming about being a painter, just now," mused Jayjay. "The dream was too big. Whatever you do, Thuy, don't eat any of the brown bread here."

"I'm so hungry I could eat just about anything," said Thuy. "Azaroth didn't bring any food. Weren't you eating brown bread with the beggars last night?"

As they drifted back down the river toward town, Jayjay finally explained about ergotism and its disastrous effects.

"That's so weird?" said Thuy when he was done. "Trust you to find a new way to get high." Her voice trailed off sadly.

"It was an accident," muttered Jayjay. But both of them knew that if he hadn't been pounding the wine, he would have known better than to eat the moldy bread. "Tell me more about Bosch and the harp," he said, hoping to change the subject.

"Bosch is just some local guy looking for jobs," said Azaroth. "When I got here I asked around for a painter, and someone mentioned him. I don't know that he ever turned out to be a famous artist over here in the Hibrane."

"I hope we're not about to do something that ruins his life and blocks his career," fretted Jayjay. It seemed a risky business to be poking around in the past.

"Or maybe it's just that Azaroth's an artistic ignoramus," said Thuy. "Can you name *any* painters, Azaroth?"

"Um, sure," he said, followed by a long pause. "Well, okay, I can think of one. Thomas Kinkade. That's the name of a chain store on our Fisherman's Wharf. It has a snack bar. I used to sell Pharaoh cuttlefish there."

"Kinkade's Krispy Kuttles," said Thuy, pulling back her chin to make a doofus face. "Maybe Bosch is safe."

"I saw the harp's painting on my trip up the vine," said Jayjay, glad the focus had moved away from him. "I wonder if Bosch can make it exactly the same?"

"The painting was on the soundbox," said Azaroth, not grasping the force of the question. "The subbies gnawed it off while Thuy had it. But I remember it pretty well, and I explained it to Jeroen. It *better* match, or I'll have trouble with my aunt."

"Not to mention having a reality-shredding time paradox," said Jayjay. He made a gingerly attempt to visualize what might happen if they disturbed the closed temporal loop of the harp's earthly manifestation.

"Lovva's painting showed a little harpist with a pair of naked lovers," said Thuy.

"I know," said Jayjay softly. "The painting looked like you and me."

"I thought that, too," said Thuy. "And it was like a detail of Bosch's *Garden of Earthly Delights*."

"She even knows the titles of this Jeroen Bosch's paintings!" marveled Azaroth. They were near the water gate. "I'll take you to meet him now. And by the way, the harp is really eager to see Jayjay."

"Good deal," said Jayjay. "Maybe she can help us again. Lobrane Earth has blundered into a whole new apocalypse." He sighed. "And it's all my fault."

"I wouldn't know about any of that," said Azaroth, sculling through the water gate with a nod to the guard. "But for starters, maybe Jeroen will hire you as assistants. You're exotic midgets. He loves strange things."

CHAPTER 11

HIERONYMUS BOSCH'S APPRENTICE

Once inside the town wall, Azaroth swung the boat into a narrow, putrid canal that wended its way under round-arched bridges and past verdant backyards. Bosch's house wasn't far.

Azaroth moored his boat beside a tiny dinghy. He put a likely offering of fish into a small basket, tossed a cloth over the remainder in the boat, then led Jayjay and Thuy through a garden of turnips and carrots, past a cellar door, and up three steps into Jeroen Bosch's kitchen.

It was a large room, with the ceiling and three of the walls covered by smooth white plaster. The inner brick wall held a fireplace adorned with stone carvings of skinny dogs with needle teeth and bat wings. The dogs' long tails branched into curling ferns that held up a mantelpiece—upon which a freshly roasted chicken cooled.

The ceiling was painted with an elaborately twining squash vine adorned with birds and beasties peeping from behind each flower and leaf. Counters and cupboards lined the walls; the floor was dark-varnished planks; a sturdy wooden table sat beside a window.

Two women were at the table: a plump servant girl peeling turnips, and a lean, gray-haired woman wearing a white linen cap and a bright yellow silk dress. Her air of self-possession made it clear that she was Bosch's wife and the lady of house.

"Good day, Mevrouw Aleid," said Azaroth with a bow to her. "I have a fine fat cod for you, also a tasty eel." Thuy and Jayjay hid behind Azaroth, peeping out. He drew the dogfish from his basket and held it up. "As an extra, I've brought this fearsome fellow to model for your husband."

"That's very good of you, Azaroth," said Aleid, with a cool smile. "But we didn't know you'd be delivering fish. We've already cooked."

"Eat my catch tonight," suggested Azaroth. "Have the chicken cold tomorrow."

Just then Aleid's eyes picked out Jayjay and Thuy. Abruptly she made the sign of the triangle. "Get the knife, Kathelijn!"

The red-cheeked young maid sprang to her feet, ran to the hearth and snatched up a long, skinny blade. Aleid hastened to Kathelijn's side and turned, watching for a move from the strangers.

"These are just my cousins from the Garden of Eden," said Azaroth nudging them into the open. "Jayjay and Thuy. Fortunately they speak good Brabants."

"Pleased to meet you," said Thuy in her sweetest Dutch.

She even curtsied. Seeing this, Kathelijn lowered her knife and let out a shrill, nervous giggle.

"Perhaps Mijnheer Bosch would like to paint us," said Jayjay. "We could assist in the studio or about the house. Being new to your beautiful town, we're open for any position of service."

"We should welcome dwarves?" said Aleid, incredulous. "Creation's cast-offs?"

"We're not dwarves," said Jayjay firmly. "We're little people, clever and strong. If you permit . . ." He stepped forward, grabbed one of the chair's legs with both hands, and lifted it into the air. Although the chair was three times his height, relative to his dense Lobrane body it felt like balsa wood, with a net weight no greater than a normal chair.

But his uncanny feat of strength only frightened the women, especially as he was moving so fast. Aleid found a knife of her own. Jayjay clattered the chair to the floor and backed away.

"Are you baptized?" asked Aleid, tapping the flat of her blade against her palm.

"I am," said Jayjay, whose mother was a knee-jerk Catholic.

"Me, too," said Thuy, who'd had a brief Christian period in grade school, thanks to a born-again aunt.

"Has Jeroen finished painting my harp?" asked Azaroth, trying to turn the tide of the conversation.

"Go ask him yourself," said Aleid. "Be warned that he's in a bad mood. A beggar keeps playing his bagpipe right out front. Can you hear it?" Indeed, shrill, frantic squeals were filtering in. "We give the man a copper to go away, and he always comes back to get more. Show Jeroen the dogfish and the little people. They might very well amuse him."

"We admire your husband's paintings," said Jayjay.

"You're so cosmopolitan in the New World?" said Aleid, surprised. "I had no idea." She paused, reevaluating the situation. "Were my husband to want you to stay, you should know that you'd receive no pay. You would sleep in our cellar. It doesn't actually connect to the house, there's an entrance from the garden. It could be like your own apartment. And you could eat the scraps from our table—we don't happen to own a pig just now. I don't suppose you eat much." Clearly Aleid was an experienced negotiator.

"We eat as much a regular people," said Thuy. "In fact, we're hungry right now."

"But we don't eat brown bread," added Jayjay.

"Neither do we," said Aleid, undermining Jayjay's half-formed theory about how Bosch was getting his visions. "We eat white," she continued. "Brown bread is for laborers and beggars. Are you nobles?"

"In a way," said Thuy. "We're known far and wide in our homeland."

"Can I feed them some carrots?" Kathelijn asked Aleid, sweetening her voice. "They're cute. Like dolls."

Aleid nodded, and the maid gave each of them a raw June carrot, crunchy and sweet.

"How about a couple of chicken legs, too," said Thuy. "We've had a long trip."

Aleid raised her eyebrows, but gave Kathelijn the go-ahead. Jayjay and Thuy made short work of the big drumsticks. Relative to their dense Lobrane jaws, the meat was spongy and easy to wolf down. It tasted wonderful. The women laughed to see the midgets eat so heartily and so fast. Then Kathelijn handed them white bakery rolls the size of their heads, and they gobbled them down, provoking further expressions of wonder.

"Go see Jeroen," reiterated Aleid when the eating was done.

Jayjay and Thuy followed Azaroth up a staircase to a sunny studio in the front of the house, clambering from step to step. As it happened, the studio windows gave directly onto the big triangular marketplace and its articulated hubbub. The room sounded with a hundred conversations, with vendor's cries, with the scuff of shoes and the clack of hooves—all of this overlaid by the vile drone of an incompetently played bagpipe.

A cluttered worktable sat in the middle of the studio, and beyond that was Jeroen Bosch, standing before the window, brush in hand, the light falling over his shoulder onto a large, square oak panel.

"Aha!" he exclaimed, seeing them. "Azaroth brings fresh wonders." His face was lined and quizzical; his mouth and eyebrows flickered with the shadows of fleeting moods. His chin was stubbled. He looked to be in his mid-forties.

"These are my cousins, Jayjay and Thuy," said Azaroth. "They're from the Garden of Eden."

Bosch smiled, clearly doubting this.

"Your wife says they might stay here and work for you," added Azaroth.

"I wouldn't have time to train them," said Bosch, his gaze drifting back to his panel. "I'm very busy on my new work."

Azaroth changed the subject. "How goes the progress on my harp?" The instrument was nowhere to be seen.

Jayjay looked around the studio, fascinated. The worktable held seashells and eggshells, drawings of cripples, a bowl of gooseberries, a peacock feather in a cloudy glass jar, and a variety of dried gourds. Upon the wall hung a cow skull and a lute. A stuffed heron and a stuffed owl perched upon a shelf.

Two newly painted panels leaned against the wall, facing toward Jayjay and Thuy, mottled microcosms, brimming with incident and life. The panels were half the width of the big square that Bosch was working on, but the same height, four times as tall as the Lobraners. Thuy was avidly staring at them.

"I'm nearly done decorating the harp," said Jeroen. "But she's locked in the attic. She's too precious to uncover with so many people about." He made a gesture toward the bustling marketplace. "Conjurors, charlatans, jugglers."

"I can't see it?" said Azaroth, incredulous.

Rather than answering, the painter set down his brush and walked over to them, keeping an eye on Jayjay and Thuy. He accepted the dogfish from Azaroth, set it on his worktable and propped its mouth open with a porcupine quill. "Hello," he said to the dogfish, making his voice thin. "Do you bring a message from the King of Hell?"

Bosch was playing—seeking inspiration by enacting a little scene that he might paint. To ingratiate himself, Jayjay responded as if speaking for the fish, flopping his tongue to make his words soft and slimy. "The pitchfork wants to strum the harp," he said, nothing better popping into his head. He reached out with his hand and waggled the fish's gelatinous brown tail.

Bosch nodded, appreciating the mummery, and then the artist fell to studying the singular objects on his table, nudging them this way and that with the tip of his delicate, ochre-stained finger—as if composing a scene. "Do you feel that all things have souls?" he asked Jayjay, turning his eyes upon him, brown eyes with flecks of yellow and green.

"Where we come from, it's obvious that everything is alive," put in Thuy, speaking Dutch. She'd slowed her voice to Hibrane speed. "Nobody debates it. It's a fact of nature, not a heresy. We talk to our objects and they talk back. That shell there, it might be saying, 'I'm spiral, and my inside chambers are private. I used to have a slippery mollusk inside me, but then a dogfish ate her. The air is eddying inside my empty mouth; it's faster and thinner than water.'"

"Very plausible," said Bosch, still studying the Lobraners. "And your names are Thuy and—Jayjay?" He said the name like *Yayay*. "Why are you here?"

"To see the harp," said Jayjay, finally finding his voice. "The harp is alive."

"I know this," said Bosch softly. "Her name is Lovva. I'd very much like to keep her."

"If you kept her safe in your family, that would be fine," said Jayjay.

Azaroth sharply cleared his throat, wanting to argue. Jayjay turned and addressed him in rapid English. "That's how your aunt gets the harp in the first place! Think it through. The harp is supposed to stay here and pass through the generations so that your aunt inherits her."

"Um—maybe," said Azaroth, confused. "But if I leave it here and come home empty-handed my aunt will—"

"It has to happen this way," insisted Jayjay. "We're in your past, dog. We have to make sure all the same events take place."

"You don't know Aunt Gladax," said Azaroth, unhappily shaking his head.

Bosch was looking back and forth from one to the other as they talked English.

"Here's an upside," continued Jayjay urgently. "If you give Jeroen the harp, you can ask him for a favor. Ask him to hire Thuy and me. That way I get a chance to play the Lost Chord and unfurl lazy eight for the Hibrane! It's all preordained."

Azaroth glared at Jayjay for a moment, then looked over at Bosch. "You can keep the harp if you let my cousins stay with you," he said in Brabants Dutch. "They need a home. They're just as clever and strong as full-sized humans. They can help you in your studio and around the house."

"You truly grant me the harp?" said Bosch, his face lighting up, wrinkles wreathing his lively eyes. "That's wonderful."

"She belongs with you," said Azaroth, not liking this.

"I suppose I could make Jayjay an apprentice," said Bosch. "My brother Goossen's sons avoid my studio. They chafe at my slow pace." The bagpipe music droned on, just outside. "For certain jobs, it's essential to have someone nimble and young," he continued. "Like painting escutcheons on the columns in the cathedral. Or decorating a house's gables. Or surreptitiously re-painting a—" He squatted down, studying Jayjay, wearing an impish smile. "Would you be willing to desecrate an icon for me, boy?"

"I would."

"What about me?" said Thuy. "I'm the artistic one. I'm a writer."

"If you're in here, I'll always be thinking about your tiny slit," said Bosch shaking his head. "Forgive me. I'm a weak and sinful man."

"I'm staying anyway," said Thuy firmly. "I'm Jayjay's wedded wife."

"Oh, now they have the marriage sacrament in the Garden of Eden?" said Bosch. He cocked his head, staring at them. His green and brown eyes were amused. "Don't imagine you can gull me. Where are you really from?"

"California," said Jayjay after a pause. "Not Eden, but, yes, it's in the New World, so far west that it's very nearly the Spice Islands, which is approximately where my wife's parents were born."

"The world grows apace," said Bosch.

"We were married in City Hall," said Thuy. "In California, that's just as good as church."

"Well, I suppose you can sleep here, too. But you'll have to busy yourself elsewhere during the days. Two gnomes underfoot is too much."

"She can spend the days with me," said Azaroth. "She'll help with my fishing and I'll show her around town."

"Fine," said Thuy. She was still studying the tall paintings leaned against the walls. "These panels—they're the wings of *The Temptation of Saint Anthony*!"

"Indeed that's the theme of my triptych," said Bosch. "Very perceptive of you to read the iconography."

"I recognized the panels, too," lied Jayjay. Thuy and Bosch just laughed at him, neither one believing him.

"Is your husband at least good with his hands?" Bosch asked Thuy.

"I guess so," said Thuy. "But, really, I might be the better one for you to—"

"Let's go, Thuy," interrupted Azaroth. "We'll take the rest of my catch to the fish market. And I'll show you the tavern where I live. Lots of vibby types in town for the annual procession. Musicians, actors, acrobats."

"The Muddy Eel," said Bosch. "Alive with whores and music. Which reminds me—"

With no transition at all, he strode over to the room's window and began screaming Low Dutch imprecations at the unseen man who was playing the bagpipe. The music broke off, and a tenor voice called up, wheedling for alms. Bosch cursed again; the squealing resumed.

"Do you want me to get rid of him, Jeroen?" said Jayjay. "I'll show you how useful I can be."

"Let it be so."

Jayjay and Thuy descended the staircase hand-in-hand, hopping from one step to the next, both of them very excited. It was a kick to be in Hieronymus Bosch's studio.

The ground floor front room was full of painting supplies: oak panels, pots of pigment, a workbench for mixing paints, cupboards of rolled-up drawings. Azaroth went into the kitchen to flirt with Kathelijn, the maid.

Peering out the front door, Jayjay and Thuy saw the pesky bagpiper at the base of the house's stone steps, red-faced and smelling of wine. Surprised to see the two tiny figures on the threshold of Bosch's dwelling, he broke off his musical assault. Wiping his ropy lips, he favored Jayjay with a sneer. But not for long.

Jayjay was on him like a sped-up goblin, pummeling him in the ribs. Too cowed to fight back, the bagpiper hurried away. Some of the bystanders booed, some cheered, and Bosch grinned from his window.

Jayjay bowed from the doorway and announced himself. "I am the new apprentice of Jeroen Bosch!" He took Thuy's hand. "And this is my wife. We offer you friendship; we require respect! Hurray for 's-Hertogenbosch!" Just to dispel any scent of the diabolic about the curious figures they cut, Jayjay slowly crossed himself.

"Triangle," hissed Thuy.

"Oops."

They made the correct sign in unison, touching left shoulder, right shoulder, navel, and left shoulder again. The people looked satisfied at this.

"I'll go upstairs now," said Jayjay as they went back into the house. "I'll see about meeting that harp and playing the Lost Chord. I'll ask her and the pitchfork how we can drive off the Peng. Maybe tomorrow we'll be back home."

"No big rush," said Thuy. "I like it here. Good to be away from all the crap. Hey Azaroth, are we riding to the Muddy Eel in your boat?"

"I'll row to the harbor and walk from there," said Azaroth,

still canoodling with Kathelijn in the kitchen. "If you like, you can ride on my shoulder like a Garden of Eden parrot."

"Be careful," said Jayjay, giving Thuy a kiss.

"Maybe it's all going to be okay?" said Thuy.

"I hope so."

"That was good work driving off the bagpiper," said Bosch when Jayjay rejoined him. "I shouldn't let him curdle my humors. I'm often guilty of the sin of anger. I myself play the pipes a bit, and to hear them mishandled that way—" His voice trailed off. He'd settled behind his painting once more; he was touching up the images of some tiny bas-reliefs depicted upon a temple pillar near Saint Anthony. "I fall into pride over my work," he continued, evidently in a confessional mood. "And I lust as well, though less so than in my youth."

"I don't see life that way," began Jayjay. "It's—" But then he broke off, silenced by Bosch's profoundly knowing eyes. Why not confess to a fault? "I guess you could say I'm too greedy for thrills," he allowed.

He was thinking of the ill-advised Gaia trip he'd taken when he should have been honeymooning with Thuy. Hell— he'd spent most of his life trying to get high, and yesterday he'd ended up paralyzed in a diaper while his wife had sex with another guy. And last night—this was the rich part—as soon as his paralysis had worn off, he'd gotten drunk with crippled beggars and had eaten a psychedelic that could make your fingers and legs drop off.

This was his actual life, the only life he had. He had a sudden sensation of standing on a ridge looking back at a valley devastated by years of strip-mining. His past.

"Drunkenness," said Bosch, divining Jayjay's thoughts. "You drink the world and end up with piss. The sin of gluttony."

"Well—you're a glutton for images," said Jayjay defensively. He gestured at the extravagant fantasies on the panels against the wall: the fish like ships in the sky, the burning cities, the devils and nudes and chimerical beasts.

"I don't take," said Bosch. "I make. You might pray for help, Jayjay. God's always watching."

"God? Where I come from, we have Gaia, a planetary mind. She's real. But—God like in the Bible? That's a barbaric myth."

"You're lost," murmured Jeroen, more interested in the images he was painting than in the desultory conversation. "You rail at the fog." He touched his dry, narrow tongue to his lips as he worked.

"Maybe God isn't what you think, Jeroen. Maybe God is— I don't know—a flicker at the bottom of the endless cracks between particles."

Bosch paused, brush poised in the air. "I freely agree that God is an unfathomable mystery. But the issue is that you regularly inebriate yourself. Nothing mysterious about that."

Uncanny how quickly the man cut to the core. Jayjay decided to talk about something else. "Nobody paints hell as well as you, Jeroen. Isn't it ironic how much more interesting hell is than heaven—or than ordinary life?"

"It's hard to imagine heaven," admitted Bosch. "But I'd say that ordinary life is no different than hell. My paintings show 's-Hertogenbosch and the country lanes. It's a matter of seeing what's really going on."

Jayjay walked around to Bosch's side and noticed an image of a dissected stingray. It gave him a turn.

"Are you working with the Hrull?" he blurted out. "Demonic aliens from another world?"

"Stupid people always ask if I'm possessed," said Bosch, mildly amused. "As if no sane and pious person could do something clever."

"Oh yeah?" challenged Jayjay blindly. This guy was getting on his nerves. "What were you doing at my party a few days ago?"

"We've never met before," said Bosch, beginning to be annoyed. "And I begin to regret that we met at all. If I look familiar, perhaps it's because you've seen one of my pictures. I paint myself into most of them. As a peddler, or a man standing on two ships, or a saint."

He pointed with the end of his brush at the kneeling figure in the middle of his panel. Saint Anthony was looking over his shoulder at Jayjay, his eyes calm and filled with self-knowledge.

In that moment Jayjay accepted that he was indeed a drunkard, an addict, a fool. His craving for excess had warped his life. He needed help. But—from God? What was God? Everything. Nothing. The white light. Saint Anthony's eyes.

"Help me," prayed Jayjay silently. "Please help me." He had no particular notion of what or whom he was praying to. It was enough to admit that business as usual had stopped working. He was losing his sanity—and his wife. His only hope was to surrender to something bigger than himself.

And now, in the wake of these thoughts, he felt a new sense of resolve. He could change. He really could.

Meanwhile Bosch continued painting. Perhaps the man was a genius, but certainly he was something of a prick. Jayjay didn't want to give him the satisfaction of knowing his advice had hit home.

"Can I see the harp?" asked Jayjay presently. "Now that the others are gone?"

"No."

"Um, my wife said you were supposed to decorate the harp

to look like your *Garden of Earthly Delights*. Is that what you did?"

"So you know that picture?" said Bosch. "I suppose you've been in the Brussels palace where it hangs?"

"I've—I've only seen copies of it," said Jayjay. "In California it's known as your great masterpiece."

"It was the youthful success that sent me down my path," said Bosch. "I painted the *Garden* fifteen years ago. I was thirty, near the start of my marriage. I thought I'd entered a paradise of love, but it proved more arid than I'd thought."

"You and your wife—you have no children?"

"Aleid had painful miscarriages and stillbirths," said Bosch. "Very sad. That part of our life is over." He paused, his face momentarily still. "I prefer to speak of my art. Perhaps this new triptych will be as highly regarded as my *Garden of Earthly Delights*. Or perhaps not. The important thing is that I'm still painting, still inventing, still in the game." Bosch chuckled. "How this new picture seethes. See the flying jug with the scythe? He farts his way through the air."

"Who's the triptych for?"

"It's a commission from the Brotherhood of Saint Anthony, here in town. In the left panel, the devil lifts Saint Anthony high into the sky, in the right panel he's besieged by lustful women, and in the middle he's surrounded by monsters conducting a black mass. I'm filling it with life: over one hundred and sixty humans, animals, and demons so far—and that's not counting the myriads of soldiers in the little armies. I've found a quick way to paint them. *Zack-zack-pip*."

"The Antonite brothers nurse the victims of Saint Anthony's fire," said Jayjay, homing in on a theory he'd formulated. "Do you know that condition is caused by a fungus in brown bread? I had an experience of it last night. I spent part of the night hallucinating in the Antonites' courtyard."

"And addling yourself with wine, I'm sure," said Bosch. "You should know that Saint Anthony's fire is caused by sin. The devil attacks a sinner like a wolf bringing down a lost wayfarer. Brown bread is no poison, it's the Lord's gift to the lower classes. The bread's essence is pure in and of itself."

"My point is that I want to know if you've been inspired by visions from the fungus in brown bread."

"Were your crippled drinking companions painting trip-tychs?" said Bosch, glaring at him. "And, pray tell, while you were with them, did you drink your own piss?"

This was leading nowhere. Jayjay let his mind stray back to the sense of calm he'd felt right after he prayed. There was no upside to arguing with the irascible, opinionated Bosch.

Studying the picture in progress, Jayjay let himself admire the old artist's facility at turning realistically rendered objects into bizarre beasts. Here was a jug that was a horse, a tree that was a man, a ship that was a headless duck. "Everything's alive," he said, returning to their common ground.

"Yes," said Jeroen busy with his brush again. "I'd like to hear more about the living objects in your—California?"

"Very soon a similar change will come to 's-Hertogenbosch," said Jayjay. "Everyone will be able to speak clearly with objects, just like they do back home. In fact, that's why I'm—" he broke off. He'd been about to reveal his plan to play the harp. But it would be better to approach her alone, lest Bosch raise some screwball objection.

After working a bit longer, Jeroen ran out of red paint. He took Jayjay downstairs and demonstrated how to mix ground pigments with oil and beeswax. And then, unexpectedly, he gave Jayjay a painting lesson.

"Here," said Bosch setting out a rectangle of wood, a brush, a palette, and five pots of paint: white, black, blue, yellow, red. "Today you learn to paint foliage. I have a particular model in mind. Wait."

The unshaven artist walked through the kitchen, greeted his wife in passing, proceeded into the back garden, and returned carrying an uprooted thistle plant, complete with purple flowers and downy seeds. He squashed the thistle down on itself, making a mound.

"You'll paint this until you can do it right," instructed Bosch. "I'll watch for a bit."

Jayjay experimented with mixing the colors to make shades of green, sketched in the vine, and added the leaves. The result was inchoate and soggy.

"At least you work fast," said Bosch. "Now let the light come down like snow."

Jayjay tried brightening the tops of his painted leaves and vines, but the wet oil paints slid and wobbled, further muddling the scene.

"Think ahead so you don't need layers," said Bosch. "See it before you paint." He produced a rag and rubbed all the paint off the wood. "Try again."

This time, Jayjay worked with a broader spectrum of shades. He enjoyed the alchemical way the colors changed as he blended the dabs of paint. His new leaves looked quite tolerable.

"Now for fantasy," said Jeroen. "See more than what's given. Let the shapes dance." He swept his sinewy hands through the air, limning sweet curves.

Jayjay tried extending the tendrils of the vine he'd drawn, and this went well enough, but when Bosch asked him to add seedpods and little birds, the thing turned into another brown pudding.

"I'll leave you to paint a third version alone," said Bosch, rubbing off the panel once more. He tossed the thistle plant into a corner. "Just dream this one. Let it be an Edenic thistle. I'll be in the attic, putting the finishing touches on my harp. I've painted two lovers on it, and until today I didn't know their faces." Aha.

Jayjay's third thistle turned out well. He liked painting. Somehow the work connected into him all the way down. When he pretended to be a scientist, he was always striving, always playing catch-up ball, trying to be a big brain. But painting was like physical play.

The clatter of cooking came from the kitchen, and good smells. Dill, onions, fennel. It was dusk. Outdoors the market could still be heard, but with more yelps, more music, and fewer sounds of animals. Party time.

Jayjay began thinking about Thuy, wanting to tell her of his new resolve. Was she really pregnant? Hopefully she'd be back soon. The Muddy Eel sounded sleazy.

Just as Jayjay was about to take his practice panel upstairs to show to Jeroen, a heavy knock sounded on the front door.

"Good evening, Mijnheer Vladeracken," said Kathelijn, admitting a sumptuously dressed fellow with a flushed, piggy face beneath a floppy velvet hat of a striking yellow hue.

"I've been chatting with Wim the vintner in the market," rumbled Vladeracken. "Strange rumors today. Someone saw a flying monster in the sky, a beast like a giant devilfish. There's talk that these might be the End Times. I've brought wine." He handed Kathelijn a half-empty jug, then glared down at Jayjay. "What's this smeary devil doing in here? I saw him preening on your front steps this afternoon with a smirking strumpet his size. They might well be Satan's emissaries."

"My new assistant," said Bosch, coming down the stairs.

"Cunning little imp, eh? His name is Jayjay. Jayjay, this is my neighbor Jan Vladeracken. Let's settle down in the kitchen."

Bosch, Vladeracken, Jayjay, and Aleid sat at the kitchen table while Kathelijn tended a kettle on the fire. She was stewing the fish and eel with spiced milk and turnips.

Vladeracken filled a pottery mug with his wine, and removed his gaudy beret. Bosch and Aleid took some wine as well, but Jayjay declined.

"I'm concerned about your altar painting, *John the Baptist*," said Vladeracken in a tendentious voice.

Bosch rolled his eyes and didn't answer. Aleid took up the slack.

"How do you mean?" she asked.

"As you very well remember, I commissioned this work from your husband when I was the dean of the Swan Brotherhood of Our Dear Lady."

"Really, Jan," said Aleid wearily. "Certainly we're proud that Jeroen's a member of the Swan Brotherhood, but this endless bickering is so—"

"This is more than bickering," said Vladeracken angrily. "It's an attack on my mortal soul."

Aleid said nothing, only shook her head. And for his part, Bosch jokingly peered at Vladeracken and made painting motions with his hand, as if he were depicting his neighbor upon an invisible panel in the air.

"Tell me the story," said Jayjay.

"No one cares but the ill-begotten dwarf," said Vladeracken. "Here's the tale, little man. I issued Jeroen the commission to paint John the Baptist for our brotherhood's altarpiece in the cathedral. Therefore it was my right to have myself depicted in the panel as the donor. Settled and done. My image lives in the Lord's house. God notices these things. It will be an incalculable benefit for me when I'm judged. Do you follow me, runt?"

"Yes, yes," said Jayjay, not liking the insults.

"You're impatient with Jan, too, eh? Well, listen to the twist. Victor van der Moelen, that walking piece of shit who's the new treasurer of the Swan Brotherhood—he says that I had no right to appear on the panel as the donor. For the painting was bought with the society's funds, not mine. I'm perfectly willing to reimburse the Brotherhood, but van der Moelen says that won't do. And now—"

Bosch twinkled and made rapid motions with his imaginary brush, as if erasing the imaginary portrait he'd just drawn.

"If you paint over me, I'll have your hide, Jeroen," bellowed Vladeracken. "I'll send my pigs into your garden. I'll bring bagpipers to your steps every day. I'll denounce you to the priests for saying objects are alive!"

"You have to go rest now, Jan," said Aleid, getting to her feet. "You don't want to miss the vigil tonight." Her chilly gaze skewered the meaty Vladeracken. "Go home to your wife."

"Forgive me," said Vladeracken, suddenly remembering himself. "My humors are addled. The hot sun in the marketplace. The rumors of the flying devilfish. Surely you understand."

"Out now," said Aleid.

The bully shuffled to the front door and left.

"I could paint over his image for you," suggested Jayjay to Jeroen.

"Exactly," said Bosch. "That's what I've spent the afternoon training you to do. Bury the pig-man beneath a Bosch thistle. You'll do it tonight, Jayjay, so that the painting is renewed for the Virgin's processional mass tomorrow. I'll be at the Swan Brotherhood building until dawn—our vigil starts the hour before midnight. This way, nobody can think the overpainter was me. Perhaps the emendation will be viewed as a miracle. The hand of the Virgin Herself."

"What a wonderful idea," said Aleid in a patient tone, humoring her husband. "But where's your wife, Jayjay? Our fish stew is ready."

Thuy was nowhere to be seen. Although she hadn't said for sure she'd be back for supper, Jayjay grew increasingly concerned. He wanted to run straight to the Muddy Eel to look for her, but Jeroen forbade this. The artist said Jayjay had much to do before tonight's commando overpainting raid.

Aleid stayed well out of the conversation; Jayjay had the impression she'd heard enough about the *John the Baptist* panel to last her a lifetime.

CHAPTER 12

PAINTING THE THISTLE

After supper, Jeroen had Jayjay help him prepare a little box with a brush, a small lantern, and six stoppered vials of paint, premixed to shades of yellow, rose, and green. Jeroen drew a floor plan of the Saint John's Cathedral, and then a detailed diagram of the Brotherhood's altar, and then two sketches of the targeted panel: one with the small kneeling figure of Vladeracken, the other with a fantastic, snaky, spiky plant in the donor's place. He wielded a wonderfully nimble pen, quite mesmerizing to watch.

Finally Jeroen was ready to leave for his all-night vigil. Unless Vladeracken were passed-out drunk, he'd be in attendance as well.

"I'm sure your wife will be here by the time you're back," Jeroen told Jayjay reassuringly. But then a sly, waggish look crossed his face. "Unless she's drunk or working as a prostitute."

"Oh, thanks so much," said Jayjay, flaring up. "Which deadly sin is it when you're a selfish, inconsiderate jerk?"

"Pride," said Bosch, far from abashed. If anything, he was enjoying Jayjay's reaction. "Kathelijn, run across the square and fetch Goossen's son Thonis. He'll be your guide, Jayjay. I'm leaving now. Truly, I'm sure your wife is doing fine." Was that a mocking flicker of his lizard tongue? He was gone.

Thonis proved to be a lively youth with a ready laugh, which rang out loudly as Jayjay explained his mission.

"My uncle's been talking about this for months," said Thonis. "He's a wonderful painter, but he's crazy. Nobody really cares about that panel except Jan Vladeracken and Uncle Jeroen. And maybe Victor van der Moelen. Van der Moelen is the duke's rent collector; he's the kind of man who looks at a newborn babe and sees a page of numbers."

"Vladeracken said van der Moelen is a walking piece of shit."

"Yeah? What does that make Jan? Never mind. The reason you're perfect for this job is because you're so small. They lock the church at midnight, you know. It's best if you go in there now, hide till after closing time, overpaint the panel, then climb out through one of the slits in the tower. I'll be waiting for you."

"How high above the ground is the slit?"

"Too high to jump," said Thonis. "Can you fly?"

"What are you talking about?"

"I heard you're miraculously strong. From the Garden of Eden."

"What if we bring a rope with a hook on it?"

"I know where to borrow one of those," said Thonis. "I

have a friend who's a chimney sweep. Come along; we'll get the rope on our way."

"Can we stop by the Muddy Eel?"

"The Muddy Eel, no, that's in the wrong direction. And we'd have to cross the marketplace to get there. The plan is that we sneak along the canal to the cathedral. Maybe you can visit the Eel after we're done. They'll be carousing till dawn." Thonis pranced slowly through a few steps of a jig. "Oh, before we leave, let me take a look at Uncle Jeroen's studio. I always like to see what he's been up to. What a mind he has, what a brush. If he didn't take so long to finish his paintings, I'd still be his apprentice."

Upstairs, Thonis studied the big square panel, and Jayjay looked out the window at the marketplace, hoping to spot Thuy. Some people were dancing, some were preparing banners and floats for the procession. Bonfires lit the wonderfully arcane and medieval scene. It saddened Jayjay to not be sharing this moment with Thuy.

Behind him, Thonis was chuckling over the images that Jeroen had painted onto the temple pillar beside Saint Anthony. "See this?" he said. "A monkey god, with a heathen kneeling and offering him a swan! That monkey looks exactly like Victor van der Moelen. And the heathen is my uncle Jeroen. He had to pay for a swan dinner for the Brotherhood last year, it made him mad, he said it wasn't his turn yet." Thonis's laughter redoubled. "Oh my soul, look at the hog-headed man in his silk robe. Alderman Vladeracken." Now Thonis gave Jayjay a sly grin. "And that gryllos-man with his legs coming right out of his head? That's you, Jayjay, with the paint still wet! Nobody's safe from Uncle Jeroen. He's been working on this triptych for a year. The Antonites are paying him, and he doesn't want to stop. It doesn't hurt that Aunt Aleid is rich."

"Are you a painter, too, Thonis?"

"In a small way. I paint murals on people's dining room walls. Flowers, God in the clouds, the triangulation of Jude Christ— the usual lot. You're a painter, too?"

"Today's my first day."

Thonis puffed out his lips and blew a stream of air. "Good luck making your plant look like one of Jeroen's!"

But somehow Jayjay felt confident. And then, just before they left Jeroen's studio, a faint, sweet song sounded through the ceiling. Thonis didn't seem to notice it. The harp was calling to Jayjay, only to him. Soon, Lovva, soon.

Thonis led Jayjay through the kitchen and into the garden. He paused for a quick peek into the cellar just to see where he and Thuy were supposed to sleep. A slanting door opened onto a gloomy low-ceilinged chamber with a straw-stuffed sack for a bed. It would do for a few days—provided Thuy shared it with him.

They boarded a small skiff and rowed along the canal's inky waters, making a brief stop while Thonis ran up through another dim garden to fetch a sooty rope and grappling hook. A bit more rowing, and then they debarked to creep through twisty lanes, emerging into a small square beside the cathedral. A party of legless beggars sat against the basilica wall, but there was no time to look at them.

With a whispered promise that he'd wait outside, Thonis shoved Jayjay in through the big church's wooden side door.

Although some pious souls were still in the house of worship, these pilgrims were gathered near the main altar, where an iconic black statue of the Virgin was on display. Encumbered by his box of paints and his sooty loop of rope, Jayjay lost no time in seeking out the smallest possible nook that could hide him. He settled in a dark recess beneath the altar of one of the side chapels nestled against the walls of the central nave.

He lay there quite motionless for the better part of three Hibrane hours, drifting in and out of sleep, catching up on his rest, thinking things over. Vladeracken's talk of a flying devilfish indicated that Jayjay had indeed seen a Hrull down by the river this afternoon. Was that a good thing or a bad? Hard to decide. Everything was so complicated.

The sexton was late in clearing out the pilgrims, and Jayjay wasn't the only one who was trying to find shelter here. He woke and listened each time another was rousted out and sent packing. But the sexton never thought of looking in Jayjay's hollow beneath the altar of the Bakers' Guild.

Finally all was calm. Jayjay crept out, feeling rested and reborn, as limber as an escaped sacrificial cuttlefish. Moonlight slanted in the cathedral windows, a sacristy lamp burnt above the main altar: God's eye.

Jeroen's diagrams were clear in his mind. Moving slowly in the gloom, he found his way to the niche that held the altar erected by the Swan Brotherhood of Our Dear Lady—but the entrance was blocked off by a bronze trellis. Without too much trouble, Jayjay slid his rope and his paint kit under the grating, and clambered over the top.

The altar was a hefty cabinet the height of a Hibrane man, with a smaller cabinet on top, and a statue of the Virgin atop that. Paint box in hand, Jayjay scaled the main cabinet and stood upon its upper edge. According to Jeroen, the *Saint John the Baptist* panel was on the inside of the left door of the upper cabinet.

Groping in the dark, Jayjay managed to open the door. The hinges squeaked unconscionably; he seemed to hear an answering scuff, although his heart was pounding so loud in his ears that he couldn't be sure. For several minutes he remained motionless, harking into the cathedral's tenebrous immensity, wondering how soon it would be safe to strike a flint, light his lantern, and get to work.

Was that a tapping sound nearby? He held his breath, still unsure if the noises were real. Yes, a definite thud, closer now. Jayjay lay flat on his stomach beside the upper cabinet, trying to prepare an explanation.

A tattoo of beats stitched across the stone floor, followed by final thump before the Brotherhood's altar. A low hum sounded, and a faint yellow glow illuminated the tines of—the pitchfork.

"Hey, boy," said the pitchfork softly. "Never fear, Groovy's here. You vandalizing them graven images?"

"Thank God it's you," said Jayjay.

"You're welcome! Let there be light." The pitchfork amped up his glow, refining it to a paler shade. No need to mess with flint and lantern.

"Beautiful," said Jayjay. "I'm about to paint a gnarly thistle onto this picture here."

Sure enough, there was *John the Baptist* on the inner panel of the upper cabinet's left door. The saint lay flopped down in a state of religious ecstasy. At his side was an awkward little kneeling image of Vladeracken. And on the saint's other side rested a symbolic cuttlefish with his tentacles demurely coiled.

"This is going to be fun," continued Jayjay, unstoppering his vials of paint.

"After this we go see Lovva, okay?" whined Groovy.

"Fine, but I want to look for my wife, too," whispered Jayjay. "She went off with Azaroth and never came back to Bosch's house. Do you know anything about her?"

"I visited with her in the Muddy Eel earlier on," said the pitchfork. "She was taking a bath with an acrobat, a whore, a magician and a fortune-teller. I expect they'll pass the evening in the tavern. Your missus is having fun."

"I guess that's fine," murmured Jayjay, not verbalizing his lingering sense of unease. After the scabrous scene with Chu, he felt terribly unsure about what Thuy was capable of doing. Not liking the look of the premixed green, he added a touch of rose to it. "How did you find me here, Groovy?"

"After seeing Thuy, I went by Bosch's place and heard you two jawin' about the big-ass paint raid. So I snuck in here, too. Did you hear any news about Lovva?"

"She sang a hello to me from Bosch's attic. Jeroen's at a prayer meeting till dawn. All we have to do is get into his attic without waking his wife. She's pretty handy with a knife." Jayjay paused, critically studying the paint blotches he'd just dabbed onto the panel.

"Looks like crap," opined the pitchfork.

"How do you even see, dung-prongs?"

"I'm all about vibes, boy. Sound, light, neutrinos, quantum wazoo, dark energy yinyang—listen up, I can help you paint good. You still remember about being a zedhead, right? What I showed you up on the beanstalk?"

"But I don't have lazy eight here."

"Look into yourself," said the pitchfork. "You wastin' what I taught you."

"All I know is that you made me Pekka's slave, you shit fork." Talking to Groovy, it was easy to fall into vulgarity.

"I'm sorry about Pekka, okay? I really did think she was gonna pay me off for shoppin' your world."

"What could Pekka possibly pay you? You're a god!"

"Well—" The pitchfork paused, as if embarrassed. "Like I keep tellin' you, back home I was a regular guy. We have a few

Peng on my planet, strictly under control, but Pekka knew to get in touch with me after I got aktualized. She said if I helped Warm Worlds Realty invade your world, she'd set you rubes to a-worshippin' me, bowin' down before statues of me and all."

"You wanted everyone on Earth to worship you? Statues of a pitchfork? Are you fucking nuts?"

"You were supposed to be makin' statues of me the way I am back home. Ronald 'Groovy' Blevins with green skin, three eyes, and sharp clothes. I'd relish the hell outta seein' big old icons of me. I mean, just take a look around this here church. Who wouldn't want to get the same ass-kissin' as that Jude Christ?"

"Where I come from, Christ is a great ethical teacher," said Jayjay. "Not some ego-tripping sleazebag who'd sell a planet into slavery."

"It all depends on your point of view, don't it?" said the pitchfork, his buzz sly and insinuating. "Anyhoo, when I asked that stuffed-shirt Suller in Yolla Bolly about Warm Worlds making good on their end of the deal, he told me I'd misunderstood Pekka's offer, or some shit like that. At least by then Lovva had called in the Hrull to teach you the reset rune."

"There's no end to your meddling!" exclaimed Jayjay, having trouble keeping down his voice.

"We doin' you favors right and left, Jay. You sure enough *should* be worshippin' my ass." As the pitchfork grew more confident and self-congratulatory, his buzz amplified. "What I wanted to say is that if you stop being a tight-ass and let your mind run top speed, you can let your paint do the thinkin' and that thistle will come out slick as snot."

Jayjay only nodded. It would be folly to maintain a steady stream of noisy chatter. Taking into account the pitchfork's advice, he looked into himself as he worked, picking up sympathetic vibrations from his fingers, the brush, and the paints.

In a way it wasn't all that clear where the boundary of his body really was.

Dialing his attention higher on the size scale, he felt a sense of union with the panel, the cathedral, and the culture of the town, as well. This wasn't lazy eight telepathy like back home; it was something more internal, more organic. Everything was an aspect of the divine One.

Jayjay painted slowly, making tiny brush strokes, pecking away until the image was quite acceptable: a floppy thistle with arching thorny stalks, translucent seed pods, and pair of raven-ously feeding birds. It was eldritch, outlandish, Boschian.

It was still dark outside, although it felt like he'd been work-ing for a full day. By Hibrane measures he'd been painting per-haps four hours.

"Lookin' good," said Groovy softly. "Let me bake that for you." The pitchfork leaned closer and added an infrared com-ponent to his glow. In a few minutes the fresh oil paint was dry and hard, as if had been in place for months or years.

Jayjay eased the cabinet door shut, stoppered his vials, wrapped up his palette, and wiped up the stray drops of paint with his sleeves. They were done. The pitchfork doused his tines' light.

Jayjay's back and shoulders were stiff and sore. He was see-ing his muscle pains as colors—not intellectually imagining this, but viscerally *feeling* washes of color in his brain. The sore muscle along the left side of his spine oozed a pale mala-chite green.

"I'm supposed to climb up the tower steps to a window and lower myself from there," he whispered into the dark as he clambered down off the altar. He slid his kit and his rope under the chapel gate and painfully scaled the gate while the pitchfork clattered his lean form through. The ache in Jayjay's right shoulder was a triangle of massicot yellow; his stiff legs were veined with ultramarine and ivory black.

Naturally the door to the tower was locked.

"Fuck this shit, Jay," hummed the pitchfork. "I'll open up the side door."

"Okay."

Groovy bent his handle, crouching low enough to feed one of his tines into the side door's keyhole. A brisk click and the door swung open.

Thonis was nowhere to be seen, but the beggars were still there.

"Greetings, Jayjay," said a small, dark-eyed form beside the door.

Thinking fast, Jayjay grabbed Groovy by the handle and rested the aktualized being on his shoulder, trying to minimize the strangeness of what the beggars saw.

"Hugo?" he essayed. "It's you?"

"We're shunning the Antonites' courtyard tonight. Lubbert died."

"I'm sorry to hear that."

"He was a good friend," said Hugo. "Too bad you two didn't get along. He bled to death after the amputation this morning." Hugo sighed. "And now I suppose he's in hell. Or, more likely, nowhere. My alms were good today because I'm sad. That always helps. Do you want some wine?"

"No, no. Did you happen to see a young guy waiting for me out here?"

"He left as soon as you went inside. Were you robbing the silver off the altars? Did you remember to empty the poor box, too?"

"Uh, no."

"Hold that door open for me, and I'll keep quiet about seeing you here."

"Good-bye," said Jayjay, as Hugo dragged himself into the cathedral.

"Farewell."

The full moon had sunk below the horizon. It was nearly dawn. Jayjay sank the paint kit in the canal, but kept the chimneysweep's rope and grapple. After a brief, intense argument, the pitchfork agreed to guide him to the Muddy Eel before they went to meet the harp.

As it turned out, the tavern wasn't far out of the way; it lay in a side street across the marketplace from Bosch's house. A few drab, bleary people were stumbling around the inn's public room. Jayjay saw no sign of Thuy but—oh shit, here came Jan Vladeracken, just emerging from the bathhouse behind the inn, fastening up his baggy silk pantaloons. Apparently he'd used the Swan Brotherhood's all-night vigil as a cover for visiting a prostitute while his wife slept.

"Bosch's devil!" exclaimed big Jan. "And he's carrying a rope and a pitchfork." The alderman didn't seem nearly so befuddled as at suppertime. Perhaps the vigil had done him some good, what little bit of it he'd actually attended.

Jayjay hurried out the door into the street; he wanted nothing to do with the alderman. But now Vladeracken noticed something else.

"Green paint!" roared the bully, running after him.

With his six-to-one speed-up factor, Jayjay should have been able to elude the big man. But he was tired and sore. And the oversized cobbles were so slick with piss and vomit that he had to carefully pick his way. Suddenly Vladeracken was upon him.

"Hands off!" buzzed Groovy. Lively as a magic cudgel, he

upended himself onto his prongs and whacked Vladeracken across the shins, making the man bellow in pain.

And then Jayjay and the pitchfork were down the street and across the triangular marketplace. Even now the space was peopled, both with drunks and with the pious, who were tending to the Virgin's processional pageantry.

"Your Thuy's sleeping in the basement," said the pitchfork, delicately feeling the air with his prongs. "I can hear her breathing, and the rustling of the straw bed."

"I'm so glad," sighed Jayjay, close to tears.

"So how do we get at the harp before Jeroen gets back?" asked Groovy, sizing up Bosch's house. "I can climb the wall like an inchworm, but you—"

"Carry up my hook and set it into the sill of that little attic window. And then I'll climb the rope."

"Yeah, boy."

Dawn was breaking with a sweet pink glow as Jayjay climbed the rope. A couple of bystanders saw him, but they didn't say anything. Jayjay pulled the rope up after him.

As he and the pitchfork pried open the attic window, Lovva sang a soft, rippling greeting. She looked the same as before: a gilded triangle with her front edge carved like a classical column, her crosspiece on top a shapely double curve, and her rear edge a hollow wooden soundbox. A scene was newly painted upon the soundbox, an image of two lovers listening to the music of a winged, pale blue demon playing a little harp shaped just like Lovva. The lovers resembled Jayjay and Thuy. Bosch had refined their faces before supper last night.

Haloed with a vermilion glow; Groovy skipped across the

floor to twine around the harp, passionately caressing her curious strings.

Downstairs Aleid cried out in her sleep.

Savoring the beauty of the harp's voice, Jayjay tiptoed across the attic floor. The harp was speaking to him, asking him to play the Lost Chord.

"Get off her," Jayjay told the pitchfork. "Time for me to do my thing."

Groovy thudded to one side. Downstairs, Bosch and his wife were arguing about whether they were being robbed.

Jayjay took his place behind the soundbox of the shoulder-high harp. He still knew the Lost Chord, yes, knew it in his muscles, nerves, and bones. Feeling like he had all the time in the world, he stretched out his arms and began to play.

The mellow notes blended like coats of runny paint, melding into gorgeous shades of sensation. That was the underpainting. And now Jayjay plucked a few extra notes as highlights, exactly here, precisely there. Space twitched, yawned, and awoke.

Jayjay lifted free his hands. He was done. Lovva continued playing on her own, sending the runes to every nook of the planet, unfurling the eighth dimension throughout this part of the Hibrane.

As of now, everyone on Hibrane Earth could see everything. And everything was alive.

CHAPTER 13

GLEE AND CHU

After Chu said good-bye to Thuy, he had to stand there while Glee rooted around inside Lusky's dead body, which was really gross of her. But he'd gotten to like the alien woman well enough that he waited for her.

Though Chu still didn't know anything about Glee's past, she seemed like a good-natured person who'd had bad luck. He'd noticed that she got pleasure out of whatever tiny variations of routine they experienced inside Lusky; she was always alert and commenting on things. He felt sorry for her for being hooked on the gel.

"Now I've got enough for a couple of days," said Glee, picking her way back through the rubble. She was wearing a sunny smile, holding up a scrap of Hrull skin in which she'd wrapped the gel she'd salvaged. "Want a taste?"

"That stuff's bad for you, Glee," said Chu, shaking his head. "Let's keep moving."

As they started off, Chu glanced back down the street for a last look at Thuy, still standing over the supine Jayjay, the sun low in the sky behind her. He waved farewell, and then the bulk of the dead Hrull was between them. Chu could hardly believe he and Thuy had been doing it a few minutes ago. He felt dizzy from that, and from the aftereffects of the gel.

Although Chu was keeping his teep anonymized so people couldn't readily spot him, he was still visible via the silps, especially if someone had a general idea where to look for him. Feeling paranoid, he double-checked to make sure he was logged out of the *Founders* show—and found that he and Thuy had been officially fired, at the behest of the corporate sponsors. All right. It would be fine with Chu to be out of the public eye. But, yeah, the money had been nice. Thanks to his *Founders* work, he had his own bank account.

In some ways he felt just as mature as Thuy. Had sex with her damaged him? For sure he was upset—and ashamed to have been seen. But, more than anything, he was surprised. He'd never realized sex would be so—what was the right phrase? Hashing his nonverbal memories into a key, Chu searched Gaia's word hoard for a match, finding: *Knobbly, exiguous, redolent, all-encompassing,* and *gnarly.*

That word again. Thuy and Jayjay were always going off about gnarl, but sometimes gnarly things weren't so wonderful. Particularly if they involved other people and if you were on the autism spectrum.

By way of checking the audience reaction to his sexual initiation, Chu peeped into a personal Gaia feed that he'd designed; it tracked all teep mentions of his name. A few of the comments were sympathetic or admiring; but many were mean and moralistic. The harshest were from people who seemed also to be lusting for him. Yuck.

In the real world, everyone that Chu and Glee passed on the street was staring at them: a three-eyed green alien and the underage boy from that *Founders* sex scene, both of them naked. Too much.

One of the stores in the block after Lusky had a pile of pants and shirts on a table on the sidewalk. Chu tried a pair of skinny purple jeans and a green T-shirt; the garments claimed they'd be perfect for him. Hylozoic Earth's intelligent objects tended to like being put to use. Chu teeped credit to the store's distracted owner, who was concerned about Glee's odor and the crashed Hrull next door.

Observing the purchase, Glee became very enthused about the little shop's clothes. Her excitement touched the once-blind heart of Chu. He told her he'd be happy to buy her anything she liked. After much deliberation—which just about drove the owner over the edge—Glee selected a flimsy summer shift of lilac gauze. The dress claimed that it went well with Glee's green skin—and convinced her to accessorize her look with a maroon cloche hat that the dress had befriended.

Having green skin wasn't unheard of in the Mission; people had been tinting themselves for several years now. And Glee's extreme skinniness could pass for a fanatical level of fitness. With her hat pulled down over her third eye, she looked almost normal, at least for this part of town. But she did have that sulfurous smell.

In the sunset-gilded street, a teleport flash-crowd had formed, with fresh ghostly forms appearing and solidifying every second. People were yelling surprisingly rude things. It was time to go. Chu was thinking that Glee might enjoy visiting some bigger stores. Hiding their trail by closing off incoming teep, Chu and Glee hopped to Union Square.

Even with the Peng siphoning off gnarl, San Francisco remained lively. Store lights gleamed in the dusk; the square buzzed with foot traffic. Glee looked around, taking it in, happy to be rubbing elbows.

Chu passed her his credit information, and she headed straight for Macy's, tightening her pores to keep the broccoli odor down. Chu himself relaxed on a bench in the square, trying to keep his anonymity. It wouldn't last long—soon someone's pattern-recognizing search routine would single him out, or Glee would charge a goody to his account and the sniffers would target Union Square, or some online agent would decrypt and trace the "I'm fine" text message that he'd just sent to his parents.

The clouds on the horizon were rimmed in dying shades of gold and lilac. How was Thuy doing? Routing his access through an encrypted channel, Chu teeped toward Seven Wiggle labs. Thuy and Jayjay had locked themselves into a quantum-mirrored teep-blocked room there. Sonic and the lab geeks yelled something about Thuy and Jayjay going to the Hibrane, and then they took off. The Peng arrived to peck at the inner room's door. Jayjay's weird pitchfork chased off the Peng for a minute, but then the pitchfork disappeared. The Peng came back and broke down the door to the inner room. It was empty. Maybe Thuy and Jayjay had made it to the Hibrane. Sensing Chu's telepathic gaze, squawky Blotz sent a mind-trace toward him. Chu broke the connection.

Certainly he shouldn't stay in San Francisco indefinitely. By way of further assessing his current situation, he tuned in on the national news stream—and found growing alarm over the crashed body of Lusky. A chorus of high-profile voices were shrilly denouncing the Hrull; loudest among them were the "resurrected" preachers of the Crown of Creation Church. And, paddling onto the tsunami of buzz, President Dick Too Dibbs had decided to give a national speech—starting right now!

The new president's popularity had been slipping ever since his inauguration day, which had also been Lazy Eight Day, when everything woke up. With the world gone hylozoic, the whole idea of governments based upon human power elites was seeming increasingly dumb.

"This week our planet has made contact with two alien races," intoned Dick Too Dibbs, speaking in his matter-of-fact Kentucky accent. "One is good, and one is evil. The Peng are personable birds who walk on two legs; the Hrull are depraved flying devilfish."

Dick Too Dibb's cousin Dick Dibbs had been president before him. The first president Dibbs had been convicted and executed for treason after unleashing the nants. Dick Too Dibbs claimed he'd learned from his cousin's mistakes, and during his first hundred days in office, he'd acted quite reasonable. But that was over now. At the behest of his party's fundamentalist supporters, he was throwing his support behind the Peng.

The president continued his speech, describing the Peng occupation of San Francisco and Yolla Bolly in glowing terms, depicting Suller and Blotz as problem-solving diplomats who'd come to make Earth a better world. He went so far as to hint that the Peng might be of divine origin. He didn't acknowledge the fact that they were now in charge of the Crown of Creation Church. Nor did he explicitly mention the phenomenon of gnarl reduction—he only made some vague remarks about the Peng having the potential to calm tensions worldwide.

It occurred to Chu that the majority of Americans wouldn't

even notice the missing gnarl. "Flat like me," he thought with a twinge. He truly had to learn to appreciate chaos, and to be as unpredictable as Jayjay and Thuy.

Just then, as a kind of gift from his subconscious, Chu thought of acting out the phrase *knuckle walkers,* which his mother, Nektar, often used when discussing the members of the Dibbs Homesteady Party. In the dusk, he began lumbering around his bench, bent over with his fists to the pavement, a caveman in synch with the voice of President Dick Too Dibbs.

"Ga hoink," he grunted. *"Yurk yurk!"*

Moving on to the Hrull, President Too Dibbs deplored the flying mantas as diabolic slavemasters. To pep up his presentation, he threw in a clip of today's Hrull-instigated sex act between the vile kiqqie Thuy Nguyen and her innocent victim, an autistic boy of fourteen.

This brought Chu up short. The fog of shame closed in. As if on cue, dots twinkled above his bench. A heavyset woman took solid form, teleporting in to confront him. She had short, glossy hair, a smooth face, and a dark mole on her chin.

"I've come to help," said the woman. "I'm bringing you in for abuse counseling."

Was she from the police? Who knew. With so many virtual agents winnowing the global data stream, anyone could have found him by now.

The woman wore a self-aiming, shoulder-mounted stun gun. The stun gun's nasty little silp claimed he'd shoot if Chu even thought about teleporting out. While Chu considered his options, the stocky woman slapped a quantum-mirrored "dunce cap" onto his head to block his teleporting ability—and handcuffed his wrists so that he couldn't tear the cap off.

Suddenly, Glee materialized, back from Macy's, happy in a strapless cream silk evening dress, and with a silk headband instead of a hat. She'd acquired some pricey gold earrings and a topaz ring as well. A real dent in Chu's bank account.

"Leave my friend alone," Glee teeped to the plump matron.

"Stay clear, ma'am," frowned the woman, her face curdling into lumps. She turned as if to threaten Glee with her stun gun—and in that instant, Glee's pusher-strength mind made an irritated gesture that sent the gun high above the Earth's atmosphere, closely followed by Chu's handcuffs and dunce cap.

Glee unfastened her headband and turned the glare of her golden third eye upon Chu's would-be abductor. "You. Leave. Now." This was the first time Glee had spoken aloud.

Utterly spooked, the coplike woman grew transparent and teleported away.

Before anything else could happen, Chu guided Glee on a second hop, this one to—randomly—Portland, Oregon.

They landed beside a fountain and a café. Glee readjusted her headband. "It is better here," she said, speaking slowly. She sounded like someone from Hungary, not that Chu knew much about the world other than what he'd seen in videos. "I am disliking the Peng as much as you," continued Glee in her warm, draggy voice. "At home we have Peng, too, but they live only in the aristos' castles."

"Hide us now, Gaia," said Chu aloud—and good old Gaia told the Portland silps not to pass on positional information about Chu and Glee's location. The lively Portland silps stood ready to help, unlike the Peng-drained silps of San Francisco or Yolla Bolly.

Glee and Chu were in a shopping district near the river, past dusk now, with laidback local grungers ambling down the shiny walkways, drifting in and out of warm-lit bars and cafés, chatting to each other in stores with fogged windows.

Teeping into the fine spring rain, Chu had a moment of illumination, seeing each and every tiny vibrating droplet. What beauty, what intricacy, what plenty. The native natural world was wonderful when the Peng weren't skimming off the gnarl. He'd had never really appreciated this before. He was growing all the time.

"More shopping now!" said Glee, still talking out loud. She was enjoying herself. "I want to buy raincoat." She found an olive and yellow-checked overshirt that went well with her green skin and her new cream dress. A moot point in any case, for Chu now realized that he shouldn't use his credit account in Portland, lest he once again alert the people searching for them.

"We can't charge anything," he told Glee. "And I don't have any cash. But we can ask the breezes' silps to angle most of the raindrops away from us. And we can teek away the last few drops that get through."

They moved down the street in a cone of dryness. Glee paused to examine a shop window with silp-inhabited pottery. "Each mug is brimming with a story," she observed.

"Sometimes Thuy sells her metanovels attached to mugs," said Chu. It made him happy to say her name.

"I wonder what happens to her now?" said Glee. "I don't find her in the mindweb."

"I think she and her husband went to the Hibrane with this pitchfork called Groovy," said Chu. "I teeped it while you were shopping at Macy's."

"Groovy the pitchfork?" Glee's voice rose. "Show me."

Chu found the sequence. Not only could the silps show you anything on Earth, their lazy eight memories allowed you to peer into the past.

"I know this person!" exclaimed Glee, studying the mental movie. "I recognize his thoughts. It's my Groovy, yes. Normally he looks like me or Kenee, but he's changed his form. Lovva was telling me about this when she guided us here. And she is now looking like a harp, yes?"

"How—how do you know this?"

"Groovy and Lovva come from my home planet. Pepple. They were my roommates."

"What?"

"More than roommates. Lovers. Especially Groovy. Lovva was prettier than me, but Groovy loved me more." Glee smiled, showing her little teeth. "I will be telling you details later. Now we enjoy the vibby Portland. Can we eat in restaurant?" Even with her skin tightened up, she still gave off a faint smell of decaying broccoli.

"Maybe we should eat in the street," suggested Chu. Thanks to the gel hangover, he didn't have an appetite at all. And restaurants bored him. His mind was racing with speculations about the pitchfork. "Come on and tell me about your past, Glee. Let's just share a candy bar or a slice of pizza. I bet we can panhandle enough money for that."

"No and no," said Glee. She teeped into the civic silp of Portland and found a recommendation for a pricy seafood place seven blocks uphill, Dez's Grotto. Although it went against Chu's normally cautious style, Glee convinced him to put off worrying about how they'd pay the bill.

They set off walking toward Dez's through the living veils of rain, Glee laughing and happy, focused on the moment. Each building interested her, and every person they passed. She was like a prisoner freed from jail. Nevertheless, just before they got to the restaurant, she ducked into an alley and pulled out her stash of Hrull gel. "So I have healthy appetite," she said, dabbing a bit on her neck. "You don't want?"

Once again Chu declined. He was in fact feeling a little—he guessed the expression was *junk sick*. Feverish and queasy, with his joints aching and a hammer-throb in his head. But he needed to tough this out. If he kept taking gel, he'd be a slave.

Dez's Grotto had dry seating under an awning out front. Chu and Glee got an outdoor table right away.

"What do you use to dye your skin?" the waitress asked Glee, clearly impressed. She was a fresh-faced, full-lipped young woman with her rain-wriggly hair in a bun.

"This is a gene tweak my people can do," said Glee. "I swallow sun like a plant."

"Wow," said the waitress, brushing mist from her round cheek. "That's, like, breatharian! I know a guy who talks about that. Where are you from?"

"She's from Budapest," put in Chu, inwardly surprised at how easily he could lie. "She's my aunt. She's hungry, but I'm not. I'm junk sick. Do you have some plain clear broth for me? With crackers?"

"Ooookay."

Meanwhile, Glee was teeping inside the restaurant, inspecting what the other customers had. "I want a bowl of those gray shells," she told the waitress. "And a platter like you gave that strong, loud man with the worm of hair upon his lip."

"That's our manager," said the waitress with a giggle. "I'll tell him you called him that. Okay, then, broth, clams, and sturgeon. Want a drink?"

"The bubbling glass that man drinks," said Glee. "I want."

"Our summer wheat brew."

"So tell me about life on Pepple," Chu urged Glee as the food began arriving. "And how you met the pitchfork. The silps are shielding us; people can't eavesdrop. Or teep me, if talking is too hard."

"You don't like my talk?" said Glee, almost coquettishly. She took a too large gulp of beer, gagged, shot foam from her nose, then bit into a clam.

"Don't eat the shells, Glee. Just the soft part inside."

"Pepple looks like Earth, but ten times so many people," said Glee, spitting out shell fragments. "We got our lazy eight a thousand years ago. They say it was brought to us by a dragon-headed woman with an electric guitar. She played powerful chords, and the extra dimension unfurled. Before lazy eight, we had even more machines than you. Now they've crumbled to rust. We get what we need from the plants and animals. My lovers and I grew our own house. Lovva, Groovy, Kenee, and me—we lived in a hollow tree with windows and beds, very pleasant. A four-way marriage, you might call it, not that we commoners have those kinds of ceremonies. We have no rights, not even any locks on the doors. For millennia the hereditary aristocrats have ruled—the aristos. One of them was stalking me. Count Foppiano. And that was the—"

But then the main course arrived. Chu sipped his broth, and Glee busied herself with her sturgeon fillet. After a bit, the waitress returned.

"Do you know about dessert?" she asked Glee.

"I will," said Glee. She teep-pointed inside the restaurant. "That brown cake your fuzzy-lip manager eats."

"Plain vanilla ice cream for me," said Chu. "No sauce, no cookies, just ice cream in a bowl."

"No problem," said the round-cheeked waitress, still study-ing Glee's skin with its blended shades of emerald, thalo green, and viridian. "Tomorrow I am definitely hopping to Hungary to check out your tweaks. Can you teep me a link?"

"Glee's data is secret for now," said Chu. "That's why we're shrouded in silent silps. We're hiding."

"And I bet that means you can't use credit," said the waitress, her voice turning acid. "And I'm not teeping any money in your pockets. And you said you're a junkie. Were you planning to skeeve off without paying? If you try that, the manager will kick your ass. The man with the worm of hair."

"Um," said Chu. "I wonder if we could give you Glee's earrings? And then maybe you yourself could pay for our meal?"

"I've been eyeing them, actually," said the waitress, holding out her hand. She weighed the heavy gold in her palm and teeped into the earrings' memory. "Purchased at Macy's today. Legit! You've got a deal." She sterilized the earrings with a pulse of teek, and put them on. "After-dinner drinks not included."

Over dessert, Chu prompted Glee to continue reminiscing. "You have Peng birds on your planet, too?"

"A thousand years ago, soon after lazy eight came to Pepple, the filthy Peng's god, Pekka, found favor with Queen Ulla the First. Ulla was a sorceress with a unique power of mind, enabling her to cast runes into vast numbers of atoms. Generation after generation, the line of Queen Ulla has been learning this skill from her, and they make a few Peng tulpas for each court. They use them as flying steeds on their estates—with no worries about their loss of gnarl. Fortunately for the common people, they live in castles far removed from our towns. We ordinary folk sing and sweat with no interference from the musty Peng birds. But the prowling aristos are a problem."

"And what about the pitchfork and the harp—you call them Groovy and Lovva? What did you guys do for a living?"

"We were performers. The Pepple art form is a blend of song, dance, and light. My mate Lovva, she teeped the music to match her songs. She chimed and twirled on stage and we three others supported her—me, Kenee, and Groovy. I shone lights from glowing rocks who were my pets, and Kenee collected money from the people who came in person or who teeped to see. Groovy knew the art of coaxing plants, so he trained fast-growing vines into stage sets for Lovva. The vines made mats of leafy coiled springs and towers like green dream clouds. Dear Groovy was clever with his hands, and very handsome, but greedy and a little dumb. He was always thinking he was made for bigger things." Glee paused, remembering, her eyes unfocused. "One summer night there came our last concert together. I think by now it was ten years ago. Something happened. A shining crow appeared; he circled Lovva and flapped his wing and suddenly there was a cyclone on our stage—a tornado coiling high into the sky. Lovva and Groovy were lifted into it."

"Where did they go?"

"I don't know. I myself had to leave my world that night, those ten years ago. Quite recently I had some teep with Lovva, and first she said she's been in your world for over five hundred years, and then she said it feels like only a few days. I don't understand. She used a special word: *aktualized.*" Glee shook her head and fell silent, brooding.

"How is it that they changed their shapes?"

"Lovva says that while you're aktualized you can look like whatever you want. She says you can mold matter by thinking endless thoughts."

"And the crow who brought the tornado?" said Chu, hopelessly confused. "Where did he come from?"

"According to Lovva, the crow came from your planet. I think maybe he was that man Jayjay whose wife you had sex with. And somehow he got aktualized, too." Glee sighed. "The aktuals don't pick you and me, do they, Chu? We only get to be pushers. I wish I could go back to Pepple. But the aristos would kill me. And I'm chained to the gel." As they talked, the rain had begun coming down harder. Chu was obsessively teeking away the drops that drifted under the awning, unable to stop focusing on the tiny details. "I'm very tired," said Glee. "Can we find a room?"

Checking the Portland city silp, Chu found a cheap hostel in a rough part of town—a good hiding place. He extracted twenty more dollars from their waitress for Glee's topaz ring, and they teleported to the hostel's dim lobby.

The clerk took their twenty without even looking at them. Once they were in their room, Glee rubbed on more gel and continued reminiscing.

"Kenee was more interested in politics than sex," she said softly in the dark, lying on the far side of the double bed. "And maybe more interested in Lovva than in me. The night after Groovy and Lovva left, Kenee was off at a demonstration against the nobles. My stalker, Count Foppiano, saw his chance. He teleported to my bed, wanting to rape me. I teeked off his head. I called for Kenee and he helped me feed Foppiano's body to the vorgs." A quick teep image of omnivorous lizards the size of dogs. "Of course someone saw us. With telepathy, only the ruling classes get away with crime. And for a commoner on Pepple, harming an aristocrat means death, always. I ran away with the Hrull that night, and Kenee came along—not that he was very good as a pusher."

"You teeked off the aristo's head?" interrupted Chu, disturbed by the mental image. "I've never heard of anyone doing that." He was lying on the flat bed beside Glee, not touching her.

"It's hard killing someone that way," said Glee. "People counter with their own teek, trying to hold their bodies together. But I'm strong. You're strong, too. You've got what it takes to be an intergalactic pusher. If you want."

Glee segued into spacey teep images of the Hrullwelt. It was a belt of water asteroids orbiting a central sun, a toroidal archipelago of sparkling globs. The whole system was an intergalactic trading hub. The Hrull had had lazy eight for much longer than Pepple, maybe a million years. Their legends said the great change had been ushered in by a flying bag attached to a squalling horn.

Chu watched images of the Hrull leaping from one giant glob to the next—moving goods among warehouses, meeting with traders, making transportation deals. Thanks to their flight lice, the Hrull could tweak their gravitational mass, steering themselves along optimal orbits among the planetoids.

Beings from all the galaxies flickered in and out of the Hrullwelt, some teleporting on their own, others riding aboard Hrull. The aliens brought in samples or whole shipments of goods, examined each others' offerings, arranged trades, and engaged pusher-powered Hrull motherships to transfer their cargoes from world to world.

Glee drifted into fantasies of Pushertown, a humanoid settlement amid the Hrullwelt planetoids, a verdant island with its own Edenic glob of sparkling sea. A few managed to retire to Pushertown, winding down their gel habits, chipping along on small doses cadged from young Hrull or from pushers still in the game. As Glee envisioned a peaceful twilight in Pushertown, her breathing grew regular and she fell asleep.

Chu himself lay awake for quite some time, muscles in agony, his head in a vise. He kept thinking about the little wad of gel that remained upon the windowsill. In connection with the gel, there was some noise he felt like shouting or teeping—but he didn't want to feed the obsession by trying to figure out what the precise sound was.

To take his attention off the drug, Chu focused on a mental puzzle: Was there any way to emulate Jayjay's ability to reprogram atoms so fast? It was easy for Jayjay of course. Being a zedhead, he could go into a speed-up and personally runecast a ranch's worth of ten tridecillion atoms. Jayjay had it made, he got everything. Not only did some alien pitchfork take him climbing on an infinite beanstalk, he also was married to sexy, fragrant Thuy—

He forced his thoughts back to the problem at hand. Maybe there was some subtle trick for spreading a rune across a Peng ranch without having to touch each of its ten tridecillion atoms. What if he could find a way to make the reset rune spread itself like a virus?

Chu figured he might be smart enough to find the trick. After all, he was the one who'd solved the encryption puzzle of hyperjumping to the Hibrane by designing Chu's Knot. It crossed his mind that he might contact Gaia for help with the viral rune problem, but he didn't really enjoy the trippy feel of the planetary mind.

Instead he turned to the room's ambient computation: the richly chaotic eddies in the air, the dancing dust motes, the quantum choir of atoms. Nature was a wondrous weave of quantum computations, and he was surrounded by intelligent friends.

Bascially, a rune was a quantum operator. With the silps amplifying his mind, Chu could see the space of quantum operators as a dreamy sea of filigreed billows. Certain of the operators formed something like an oyster bed, with interconnected siphons sucking in and spitting out. Others were like worms and nudibranchs crawling among the virtual shells, or like tiny crabs wriggling in the subdimensional mud. Chu drifted off to sleep, all the while exploring ways of hooking the operators together.

When he awoke, it was midmorning, the sky bright blue. He felt closer than ever to finding a way to make a rune spread across an entire Peng ranch. His dream visions were stored in his lazy eight memory. Another night or two like this, and he'd have the answer.

Glee was leaning on the windowsill, soaking up sun and watching the doings of the low-rent locals.

"Hey, you," she said over her shoulder, noticing Chu. "Almost time to go. I've used up my gel. I need to find Duxy now. You're in, right?"

Chu still felt achey and strung out. "I'll come see her," he heard himself say. "But I'm not sure I want to leave Earth."

Glee teeped the Hrull whistle—and Duxy teeped back. She was lying low with her father, Wobble, on the so-called Lost Coast of Northern California, a trackless stretch of beach between Eureka and Petrolia. Glee and Chu teleported there.

The Hrull were rested and plump; in fact Duxy had doubled her size. She said she'd been seining plankton, jellyfish, squid, and salmon from the sea. Of course, Duxy and Wobble knew that Lusky was dead. As Lusky's ex-mate, Wobble was particularly upset. For daughter Duxy, the death of Lusky was something more than an occasion to grieve: it was a metamorphic trigger for a stage of rapid growth. In a day or two, Duxy would be a mothership herself.

Glee convinced Duxy to test her burgeoning powers by coughing up a wad of gel. Glee smiled with relief as she rubbed some of the stuff onto her forehead—and right about then Chu lost control. He scooped up some gel and smeared it onto his pounding temples, onto his tight chest, onto his aching elbows—all the while teeping and singing the Hrull whistle, the very sound he'd been biting back yesterday. Duxy and Wobble giggled, but Chu didn't care. He'd never felt better in his life.

And then the two Hrull skimmed out across the waves, searching for their day's food. Duxy said they'd be back in a couple of hours. Chu and Glee perched on a boulder, gazing at the Pacific. The fog was far out to sea, letting the sun sparkle on the breakers.

Chu's rush of well-being was giving him an uneasy sense of enslavement. "I'm doomed," he told Glee.

"You can always kick the gel later on," said Glee. "Why not enjoy what we have right now? How about a swim? Or is the water too cold? I'm tough like a kelp plant, but for you—"

"Oh, I can tell my body how to stay warm," said Chu, glad for a distraction. "I'm tough, too."

So Glee and Chu waded in through the surf and swam, reveling in the sea's creatures and currents. Chu told his body to insulate him by keeping the blood out of his skin—and his body said, as politely as possible, that it knew perfectly well how to do that without a lot of stupid advice. After the first minute or two, Chu stopped feeling the cold.

Teeping down into the sea, he spotted a salmon. Glee saw it, too. She dove for the fish, but the telepathic salmon eluded her with a casual flick of his tail. With abrupt brutality, Glee teeked the fish's tiny brain right out of his skull. She clamped her teeth onto a fin and swam to the surface.

Back on shore, Chu and Glee built a cheerful campfire from driftwood, warming themselves and roasting the gutted salmon over the coals.

"Are you mad at us for killing you and eating you?" Chu teeped to the roast fish.

"I'm just the body," answered the meat. "The one you

chased is gone. Someone has to eat me, why not you? Everything flows."

The cooked salmon was crusty black on the outside, the inner flesh pink and succulent. Delicious. Glee took a little more Hrull gel, and Chu had some, too—why not?

It was such a beautiful day. The fog was creeping in again, spreading veils and tendrils across the sky: subtle, intricate shapes that rejoiced in the ocean airs. Chu and Glee nestled together against a friendly, sun-bleached log.

Chu began feeling horny again. He was getting used to Glee's rotten smell, and to her weird third eye. Maybe soon they'd be lovers?

"Us?" said Glee, reading Chu's mind. "How sweet of you to think that." Gently she rubbed his penis through his pants, staring at him as if trying to make up her mind. "I don't want," she said presently. The insinuating motions of her fingers stopped. "I don't want you living like me. You know how Kenee died? He overdosed. Most pushers go out that way. Hardly anyone manages to retire. Pushertown is a dream."

"Overdosed?" echoed Chu, flushed and confused.

"Pushers get extra gel rations when they find a fresh teeker world. And I am the one who found Earth—because Lovva teeped me where to find it. I got the reward, but Kenee was greedy. He rubbed the whole bonus stash into his skin. Fifteen minutes later he was dead." Glee sighed and shook her head. "Someday that may be me. It's no life for you, Chu. Go away while you can."

"Don't listen to her!" teeped Duxy, gliding down through the fog, her wingspan now grown to twenty feet. She settled on the stony beach, Wobble at her side. "I need you, Chu. You're strong. I can find you a better partner than Glee. Glee's nearly used up. We can kidnap that little girl you keep thinking about.

Bixie." Duxy's teep signal took on a slimy, leering quality. "I'll put gel on her and you'll teach her Thuy's moves." With his penis still stiff, Chu was almost tempted by the suggestion, but at the same time he was horrified. Bixie was too fine for this life.

"No," he said, drawing strength from the ubiquitous silps.

Duxy lunged at him, trying to swallow him whole—but she wasn't quite big enough yet. All she could fit into her mouth were Chu's head and shoulders. Undaunted, the manta tried to stun him with gel from the pusher cone at the back of her throat.

But before Duxy's dangling uvula could touch Chu's face, he'd teleported out of there. Where to? The Yolla Bolly Peng ranch. He figured it for a place where he'd have a chance of kicking the gel. The cantankerous Peng would fend off the Hrull with their femtorays.

"Come with me," Chu teeped to Glee in the fraction of a second before he left. "Save yourself."

"I can't change now," teeped Glee, the words tinged with hopelessness. "I'm in too deep. I've been doing this for ten years."

"But you heard Duxy," Chu teeped back. "She's ready to ditch you." Conversing at the speed of thought, they were squeezing a full conversation into the blink of an eye.

"One last payday and I'm out of this game," responded Glee.

"People in videos always get killed right after they say that."

"I'll miss you, kid." Glee's teep signal was weary, knowing, bittersweet.

CHAPTER 14

VIRAL RUNES

A nd then Chu was in Yolla Bolly. He found the Peng root-ing in the dirt near their strange pink house.

"Invader!" squalled Gretta.

"It's just Chu, Mom," teeped Kakar. "He's a good guy."

"You better not be planning another attack on us," teeped Suller in his usual bullying tone.

Once again, Chu attempted a lie—not only mouthing the words, but also forming the thoughts in the conscious part of his brain, practically believing the lie himself.

"I admire the Peng," he said. "You're awesome. I'll help you save our world from the Hrull." Surely the Peng were vain and desperate enough to believe him.

But no. Chu was going to need more practice. When it came to lying, the rest of the world had a big head start on him.

"He came here because he doesn't want the Hrull to make him a pusher," cawed Kakar. "He's hooked on the gel."

"Yes, I need your protection," admitted Chu.

"Maybe the boy is brilliant enough to be our new runecaster," mused Gretta.

"I'm the genius around here," bragged Kakar. "My girl-friend Floofy and I were the best new artists on Pengö."

"You should never have taken Floofy to the carving cliffs," chided Gretta once again. "She's too high caste for the likes of us. It brought trouble on our family, your running around with that chick."

"Thanks a lot, Mom," said Kakar. "Did it ever occur to you that Floofy saw something in me? And that she was grateful to me for helping her become an artist? With Floofy backing me, I had a chance of hitting the big time like Waheer. I covered half a cliff with my carvings. But then Dad had to murder us all, forcing us into that lava pit."

"We're the lead pioneers on a new planet," said Suller. "That's fame enough."

"We're ghosts on a monkey world. I hate it here."

"So, um, how is it that some people become zedheads?" interrupted Chu. "I'd need that skill for casting a pioneer rune onto a whole ranch of atoms." Or for casting—he thought privately to himself—the reset rune!

"It's all about digging down toward infinity through the subdimensions," said Kakar irritably. "There's some kind of transfinite beings at the very bottom. Under Subdee."

"I'd rather not go through Subdee," said Chu. Although he loved dreaming about odd worlds, his past trips across the Planck sea had given him a fear of the subbies. "There's got to be another way. Why don't you coach me about runecasting, Kakar?"

"Show him some runes, Kakar," urged Suller. "Tell him what the other runecasters do."

"A waste of time," said Kakar haughtily. "Ape-boy doesn't have the mental reach."

Chu came right back at him. "You're too birdbrained to know how smart I am."

"You wish," clucked Kakar.

The two of them were a well-matched pair of low-empathy know-it-alls. After a few more insults, they started working together, with Pekka's moth rune as their test case.

Kakar held the rune clearly on display in his mind. It was an outlandish pupa that resembled a spiky conch shell with smaller conch shells growing from each of its cusps—and still smaller shells upon those—down through ten or twenty levels. The shape was tinted a vast number of shades between pink and green.

By way of getting the feel of the moth rune, Chu programmed it onto a silicon atom in a pebble underfoot. As before, he had to push and twist to get the rune into the atomic silp's tiny mind, overlaying the rune upon the quantum computations already in place. After all, this Peng ranch atom had already been programmed with tulpa runes for the three Peng, the two buildings, and any number of moths and slugs that the Peng had eaten. Fortunately, runes had a linear quality, meaning that you could add them onto each other like color filters.

Chu programmed a few more atoms, improving his technique, and then he went into a modest speed-up, casting the moth rune into a few billion atoms in the pebble. The atomic silps began pumping out the right kinds of matter waves, but there weren't nearly enough of them to generate a visible tulpa. And by now Chu was too tired to do more.

"Wimp," sniped Kakar. "Lightweight."

"One-track tiny mind," responded Chu. "Let's not forget that you'll never ever learn to teleport or teek at all. You can't put the rune on even one atom, let alone three billion of them."

"At least I'm not a smelly ape."

Setting aside any hopes for the zedhead power of accelerating his mind to the ten tridecillion cycle rate, Chu returned to the alternate approach he'd considered last night. Why not create viral runes that could spread on their own? Delving into his lazy eight memory, he examined the hybrid quantum operators he'd dreamed up. They were writhing around like chimerical tropical centipedes—tufted, horned, color-splotched.

"Those thought forms are—you say vibby?" said Kakar, telepathically watching over Chu's shoulder.

"Thanks," said Chu. "I can show you how to make them. Here, you do this and this." He pulsed out the relevant motions of his mind, stitching together quantum computational operators and wrapping them into loops.

Kakar cooed to himself, as he built a new-style thought pattern of his own: a birdlike form with hairy feathers. The mindbird seized passing thoughts and turned them inside out. Including Kakar's next sentence. "Hit's a wine dink fo' rats. I mean—this is a new kind of art."

"You think so?" said Chu, flattered. "I'd call it math. I'm sorry I said you have a tiny mind."

"Well, I called you a few things, too. Let's just be friends. Do you think you can learn to canerust for us? I mean runecast."

"I don't feel so good right now," admitted Chu. The gel was wearing off. "Maybe I'll try again tomorrow."

"Lie down in our nest," said Kakar. "Stad will dand guard. You know what I mean. Dad. Violence is the one thing he's good for."

Chu dropped off to sleep amid tulpa pinfeathers. For the

first part of the night, the junk sickness blocked him from doing any meaningful dream work. His thoughts were frenzied
rats in a circular maze with a bowl of Hrull gel at the un-
reachable core. In the wee hours he snapped awake to find
himself frantically whistling. Shit. Leathery wings shadowed
the moon-pale fog. Suller began steadily firing femtorays.
Soon the citron-yellow beams had driven the mantas away.

Chu relaxed into the nest with a sense that he'd passed a
crisis. The aches and nausea were fading. He teeped to Grew
the redwood. Due to gnarl reduction, the tree's personality
was wan, but it was comforting to be in touch with the gentle
giant of the grove. The local silps were more than willing to
help Chu work toward becoming a runecaster. Everyone
wanted the Peng out of here.

Before dropping back to sleep, Chu hooked into his lazy
eight memories of the previous night's thoughts. He closed his
eyes and his work resumed.

He woke to passionate squawking. Suller and Gretta were arguing. Early morning sunbeams gilded the treetops. It was
good to be awake. With Chu's mind running so fast, his night
had lasted a terribly long time. A strange new shape—the fruit
of his labors—was floating in his head.

"Hey," teeped Kakar. The young bird was preening his rear
feathers, with his neck twisted around. "Ready to play? I'm
going nuts listening to my parents."

"Sure," said Chu, sitting up and telling his scalp to generate
a teep block. "First let me wash." He needed a minute alone.

He scrambled down from the Peng nest to splash in the dancing waters of the stream. Enough time had elapsed so that the

creek had refilled with living water from beyond the ranch's boundaries. The rune infection had an asymmetric quality. Matter that left a Peng ranch quickly went back to normal, whereas the stuff that came into an existing ranch remained in its natural, unprogrammed state.

Powered by the once again gnarly currents, Gloob had reemerged as his same cranky self. He was running tight eddies along the foundation of the Bosch house—undermining the improbable structure one grain of sand at a time.

Chu turned his attention to the snaky new form floating in his mind—he decided to call it Ouroboros after the legendary world-serpent who swallows his own tail. His Ouroboros operator was designed to transform ordinary runes into infectious, viral runes that might spread unaided from atom to atom. He was proud to have invented it with only the help of the local silps. He didn't like taking every problem to Gaia the way those stoner pigheads always did.

Heart pounding like a trip hammer, he stealthily brought the mandalic, quadrillion-spiked reset rune into his conscious mind—and fed it to his Ouroboros operator. The snake ate the rune and proceeded to swallow himself, starting at his tail. At the moment of evanescence, Ouroboros emitted a ghostly variation upon the reset rune, a moon to the original's sun.

"Come on, Chu!" squawked Kakar. "Why are you hiding down there?"

Hands shaking, Chu teeked the viralized reset rune into one of the oxygen atoms in the pool of water and—nothing happened. Shit. More thoughts from the dream work bubbled up.

Oh yeah, that's right, he'd already figured out that his Ouroboros operator wasn't going to work very well. The reset rune's quadrillion-spiked sun pattern made it particularly resistant to viralization. But maybe he could design a better version of the Ouroboros operator, and that would do the job.

A fountain of water shot up—Kakar diving into the pool.

"Are you runecasting?" demanded the alien bird, shaking drops from his feathers.

"Um—I was trying something out," said Chu, his thoughts racing. "I can show it to you."

It seemed okay to share this flawed Ouroboros because—yet more dream wisdom—*all* of the viral runes made by Ouroboros would have something wrong with them. Any Peng tulpas they produced would last at most a few days—if the viral runes even worked at all. Therefore—

"Stop blocking your teep," twittered Kakar. "If you hold out on us, Dad will come after you. We don't want that."

"Here," said Chu, baring the top layers of his mind. "I wanted to get this new hack ready without you guys breathing down my neck. I call it Ouroboros. Let's test it out."

In a way, spreading around more Peng runes might be a good idea. A taste of the dull life on a Peng ranch should shake the blind faith of the goobs backing Dick Too Dibbs and the Crown of Creation Church. And, given that the Ouroboros-built runes would decay rather quickly, no lasting damage would be done.

Settling down on the porch of Thuy and Jayjay's cabin, the youths resumed working with yesterday's spiky pink and green moth rune. Kakar watched as Chu fed the virtual moth pupa to Ouroboros. The snake ate the conch and then itself, generating a shimmery variant of the original moth rune.

"Wait, wait," clucked Kakar. "I don't get it. What did you just do?"

"You input a rune into my Ouroboros operator, and it made a viral version of the rune. Instead of having to teek your moth rune into ten tridecillion atoms, I only have to program the viral moth rune into one single atom and let it spread on its own. It stops spreading once it's covered the volume of a Peng ranch. And then it generates the moth tulpa."

"Oh," said Kakar, trying to keep his cool. "I see. Viral runes. Simple."

"Simple—except nobody ever thought of them before. You guys have been using runes for—how long? A thousand years?" Chu had the sense that he'd totally aced Kakar. Victory was sweet.

"I can hardly believe you're doing this for us," said the young Peng, studying Chu. "Is it a trick? Give me a demo. Put that doctored moth rune onto an atom and let's see what happens."

Chu teeked the viralized rune onto an iron atom in the dirt—and watched as the moth program spread with exponential speed from one atom to the next. Just as his dream calculations had promised, the cascade stopped after infecting the hundred-kilometer cube of ground beneath them. A moth fluttered up.

"Wow," said Kakar, snapping it from the air. He clacked his beak to assess the tulpa's savor. "Tastes fine. You're awesome, Chu."

"Make a Peng for us, boys!" cawed Suller, who'd been watching them from the nest. "Let Pekka feed you one of our customer's runes. We have an attractive single female pioneer waiting for a spot—name of Floofy. We can fit her onto our ranch."

"Floofy wants to come here?" warbled Kakar, his voice cracking with excitement. "She signed up with Warm Worlds?"

"She misses you, son. Pekka just told me. I'm more than glad to welcome the young hen. I want you to be happy."

"Damn you, Suller!" screeched Gretta. "Isn't one mistress enough?"

"Floofy is for Kakar, not me," trilled Suller, pleased to be taking the high road. "Open your ears and clamp your bill."

"Will Ouroboros work well enough, Chu?" said Kakar, his discordant voice wistful. "Can we bring Floofy here?"

"Sure," said Chu, starting to feel confident of his new trick—and also confident of his kicker—that the viral runes had an imperfect copying process that would inevitably make the tulpas decay.

"You have a secret," said Suller, eyeing him suspiciously. "It's about the reset rune, isn't it?"

"Unfortunately, my Ouroboros operator can't put the reset rune into an effective viral form," said Chu quite truthfully. He didn't mention that he hoped to do better very soon. "You guys don't have a thing to worry about. Give me the Floofy rune and I'll try making a tulpa of her."

"You might as well get the rune straight from the Pekklet," said Suller in a studiously casual tone. "She can send up some tendrils for quantum entanglement."

"No way," said Chu. "I saw what she did to Jayjay."

"I'll fetch the rune for you," said Kakar quickly. He closed his eyes, swaying and twitching his wings, soaking up the Floofy rune from afar. He passed Chu a copy of the rune and, while he was at it, appropriated a precise copy of the Ouroboros operator.

"Let's both try converting the rune so we can compare," suggested Chu, genuinely curious to see if his invention was going to work.

The Floofy rune was much more complicated than the moth rune. Chu saw a square wooden temple with a roof that curled up at the corners. Oily lamps burned within the sanctum, the flames bouncing glints of light from a quintillion shelves of gilded beetles. The rafters were painted orange with cloudy presences at the corners. Cascades of jewels dangled from the beams, strung onto threads by the sextillions, each gem etched with a glyph. In the shadow of the altar, a trio of shiny black frogs played instruments: a bone flute, a log drum, and a tendon-strung fiddle. The music sounded random and dissonant.

"That's Floofy to a T," burbled Kakar. "Wait till you meet her. She's elegant. Can Ouroboros handle a rune this big?"

"Of course," said Chu, although he had to wonder if this were true. "I'll race you."

He nudged Floofy's rune into his operator snake, then bent the overfed serpent around to swallow his tail. Ouroboros twitched, pulsed—and froze. The transformation process—which was running in Chu's own brain—had used up all the available in-skull memory.

Chu moved carefully to fix the hang. When meddling with your mind's computational architecture it was possible to do something utterly disastrous—such as terminating your autonomic life support systems. Slowly, safely, he redirected the Ouroboros computation into his higher-dimensional lazy eight memory.

With the extra memory resources in play, Ouroboros finished swallowing himself, leaving behind a shimmering, viralized version of the Floofy rune.

Kakar was already done, indeed he'd had time to start twisting his version of Ouroboros around, as if looking for a more effective configuration. This was disturbing. What if Kakar perfected rune viralization before Chu did? But surely that was unlikely. Chu felt he was smarter than the bird.

A cursory check showed that the youths' transformed versions of the Floofy rune matched. "Hurry up and make her now," urged Kakar, repeatedly clacking his beak. "All you have to do is zap one lousy atom!"

So Chu teeked his viralized Floofy rune onto a sulfur atom in a bluejay dropping on the ground. The rune rushed out across the Peng ranch, infecting each of the ten tridecillion neighboring atoms. And, lo, a new Peng tulpa appeared amid the trees. The ramshackle distributed construction had worked.

Floofy was skinnier and nimbler than the other Peng. She wore her feathers dyed purple and black. She pecked at the forest floor and at the redwood trunks, exclaiming over the grubs and ants. And then she walked forward, head bobbing on her *S*-curved neck, her teep communications allusive, outré, incomprehensible.

By way of greeting, she teeped Kakar an image of a jar of honey with an emerald dragonfly inside. The dragonfly's face looked like Kakar's.

Kakar ran toward Floofy, rhythmically twittering. He strutted back and forth, bucking his head and raking the ground with his muscular two-toed feet. With a quick tattoo of his beak, he embossed a little carving on a stone. Floofy watched with interest, her tail feathers slowly parting. Kakar crowed and leapt into the air; Floofy did the same. It was nice to see Kakar so happy. The lovebirds withdrew to the pool beneath the Bosch house for some serious billing and cooing.

"Well done!" Suller told Chu. "I'll bring in the Realtors now. I've been making plans with them."

"I'm not going on any worldwide tour like you wanted Jay-jay to do," said Chu.

"Not a problem," said Duckie Tarrington, materializing with her fellow Realtor, Chick Moon. "Now that anyone can be a runecaster, we'll train a special corps." Duckie's plastic face creased in an optimized smile. "It's very nice to meet you,

Chu. I've heard so much about you." Her earrings flashed with the motions of her head.

"Howdy," said Chick, shaking Chu's hand. He was dressed like a rancher tycoon, in a powder-blue denim business suit with gray piping around the lapels. "That Peng minister, Dr. Donnie Macon, he says his followers are rarin' to dial down the gnarl. Trust the dumb-ass fundies to help aliens invade." Chick let out a dry chuckle. "So how about this mumbo jumbo rune converter of yours, Chu—is it simple enough for a purple-assed baboon? Can you teach it to them Crownies?"

"We don't need to teach them all that," crowed Suller. "We'll transform the pioneer runes ourselves and pass the viralized runes directly to our new agents. All they'll have to do is teek one rune onto one atom per Peng ranch. What a breakthrough!"

Chu felt increasingly uneasy.

"Hey, Kakar!" called Gretta. "Get off that hen and come out here."

Kakar emerged from beneath the Bosch house, his tail feathers mussed. Floofy pranced after him, joking about hatching chicks. She teeped an image of a giant polka-dotted egg in a nest made of velvet-draped branches.

"Atta boy, Kakar!" said Suller. "Let's try our new system. Do you want to cast some viral runes for us, Chick?"

"Negatory," said Chick, waving them off. "I'm only here for my five percent. I'll teep Dr. Donnie for your helpers— hey, Donnie! Send us those two Crownies we met in your parking lot—the guy with the gun and the girl with the tits."

"Nasty, nasty mammals," muttered Gretta.

An avid man and a young woman with a bad complexion appeared.

"Welcome, Steve and Julie from the Crown of Creation Church," said Chick with a exaggerated bow. "You remember me—good ole Chick Moon. This fella behind me is Chu Lutter-Lundquist, a likely screwball who's discovered a method for bringing in more Peng."

Julie smiled, threw back her shoulders, and placed her hands on her hips, showing off her figure. "Hi, there." She gave Chu a thoughtful look, as if she recognized him. "It's a blessing to be here."

"These four raggedy-ass ostriches behind me are how the Peng look when they're not disguised," Chick told Julie, enjoying himself. "They're just the same as your Donnie Macon. I hope your faith is strong enough to handle the truth."

"Dr. Macon primed us for this revelation." Gamely hanging on to her smile, Julie shot a nervous glance at the alien birds. " 'We have seen through a glass darkly, but now we see the holy ones face to face.' "

"1 Corinthians 13:12," put in Steve, supplying the scriptural reference. He was juggling his leather-bound Bible, seemingly oblivious to the fact that everyone could teep the pistol within its hollowed-out core.

"Bless you, my son," said Suller, swallowing the Bible with two snaps of his beak. "Never fear, we've come to bring Earth into harmony with the precepts of your church. We'll put an end to people being smarter than they're meant to be. We'll chasten and humble the plants and stones. Man will be the measure of all things."

"I can't abide a shoe or a chair acting like it's smarter than me," allowed Steve.

"We're the answer to your prayers," chirped Gretta.

"Golly!" said Julie, finally taking a moment to look around the clearing, dappled by the noontime sun. "What unusual homes."

Chu watched as Kakar got to work teaching the viralized moth rune to the two newcomers—or trying to. Steve seemed hopeless; maybe shoes really *were* smarter than him. But before long, Julie had the moth rune in her head.

"What am I supposed to do with it?" she asked.

"You teek it onto an atom," said Kakar in his know-it-all tone.

"Are you *kidding*? I've never teeked anything at all. My faith teaches that lazy eight, teeking, and mind-amplification are wrong. And the Bible doesn't say anything at all about atoms. I'm not sure the Lord sanctions that particular theory."

"Fine," said Chu, feeling less and less eager to help Crownies spread Peng runes. "Who cares."

"Coach the girl," ordered Suller, aiming his beak at Chu. "And don't try to skulk off by teleporting. I can shoot faster than you can think."

Chu frowned and took Julie aside. Meanwhile, Steve sat sullenly on the sidelines, watching a basketball game in his head.

"Do you *want* to be stupid?" Chu asked Julie.

Julie glared at him. "Papa says the old ways are the best."

"But now you want to learn the new ways?" said Chu, not liking the inconsistency.

"Dr. Macon says it's my mission to bring in the Peng," said Julie. "They'll keep objects from being uppity. I can feel the new godliness in Killeville, and in this grove." Her round gray eyes studied Chu. "I know you're scoffing at me. Perhaps the Peng *are* aliens—but surely the Lord is using them as saints!"

"Forget your 'Lord,'" said Chu. "Worship Gaia. She's real. She wants us to bloom."

"This guy's a complete heathen!" exclaimed Steve, who'd started eavesdropping. "I recognize him now. I saw him fornicating on the *Founders* show."

"You watched that, Steve?" said Julie, a little flirtatiously. *"Oooo."*

"You watched it, too, Julie," said Chu, suddenly seeing this in her mind.

Julie blushed. "At least I'm not addicted to some alien drug," she rapped out. "You need to let the Savior into your life, Chu. I have a feeling that the End Times are—"

"Get to work!" cawed Suller, blackening a spot on the ground next to them.

Chu showed Julie how to teek a rune onto an atom. It was strange to meet someone like this. Living in California, Chu had imagined that everyone else was advancing right along—but it seemed large parts of the country were stubbornly in the dark.

While Julie struggled to teek, Kakar was fiddling with his copy of Ouroboros, pulling it apart and reknotting it in strange birdy ways that initially seemed random and ineffectual. But then Chu realized that Kakar's underlying strategy was incredibly efficient. He was leveraging his redesign by drawing upon the full power of Pekka, his home planet's mind.

Leaving Julie on her own for a minute, Chu reached out to Gaia. Her round, green face wasn't far.

"I'm already working on it," Gaia said before he could even start explaining. "I understand. If Kakar can make really good viral Peng runes, your race is doomed." Her voice was like a softly gurgling fountain.

"I should have come to you sooner, Gaia," said Chu, feeling a wash of relief. "Can you make a viral *reset rune*? Maybe you don't need to use an Ouroboros-style operator at all. Maybe that was a false path."

"Pekka has the edge on me," said Gaia. "Her birds are diligent and they honor their world. But my humans—my humans are stoners or loners. If I can't find this thing, it's your own fault."

Just then Julie finally produced a tulpa moth, and Suller ate the results. "Well done, Julie!" exclaimed the big bird. "We'll bring in your friends, train them, and send you out. Onward Christian soldiers! Let the saints come marching in!"

"I say we convert New York City today," proposed Duckie. "Plus L.A., Tokyo, Shanghai, Mumbai, and Dubai. The sooner we take the power centers, the better."

"Some fat real estate you're talking about," gloated Chick. "No more nickel-and-diming with, like, Yost, Virginia." He raised his voice again. "Whenever you're ready, Donnie!"

Four more Crown of Creation emissaries appeared, two men and two women, fresh-faced and eager to learn. Chu groaned inwardly at the thought of tutoring them. But just then he heard an odd squawk. Something was wrong with Floofy. Ghostly purple flames sprouted from her body, long lavender tongues stretched deep into the woods. Shit. The Peng rune error terms were amplifying even faster than expected. Those plumes were Taylor jets, the mathematical artifacts that appear when a Fourier series begins to diverge.

Floofy's squawk rose to a desperate screech—cut short when her neck pinched in two. For a moment her jet-wreathed head hung in midair, beak soundlessly twitching. Her legs turned translucent and shriveled away. Head and body dropped to the ground. Floofy was a flickering pile of feathers—and then she was nothing at all.

"Chu's fault!" shrilled Kakar. "His Ouroboros is no good! He knew it all along! But I can do better."

With horror, Chu realized that Kakar had finalized his new version of the viralization operator, complete with built-in error correction. Kakar was calling it Ouroboros 2.0. And as for Gaia's search—she was getting nowhere.

Pushing into Kakar's mind, Chu tried to snarf a copy of the alien's wriggly new operator. The thing was a wild knot involving a fractal regress of loops that were braids of loops that were braids of—never mind.

"You lose, Chu!" hooted Kakar, blocking off his teep before Chu could get more than a fragment of Ouroboros 2.0. "I rule!"

"Kill Chu!" cawed bloodthirsty Gretta, just like before.

Suller had claimed he could shoot faster than Chu could teleport—but he was wrong. In a flash, Chu was on the steps of the Santa Cruz beach house his family had rented. Towels dried on the porch railing, plastic furniture lay scattered around the sandy yard. It was early afternoon, warm and sunny. The whole gang was lolling on couches in the spacious living room, resting up from lunch.

Chu's mother, Nektar, was eating apricots with her girlfriend, Kittie. Bixie and Momotaro were talking to their surfboards, readying them for the Santa Cruz waves. Jil was fooling around with a shoon in the shape of a miniature Peng, trying to perfect its bobbing gait. Ond lay supine on a stuffed chintz sofa with his eyes closed.

Chu was ashamed to face them—but there was no place else to go. "So here I am," he said, walking in.

"Where's Thuy?" said Momotaro, in a falsely bright tone.

"Don't you dare tease him," cried Nektar. "After all he's been through. Poor Chu. Thank God you're safe, dear."

Bixie gave him a penetrating stare, seemingly on the point of saying something—but then she dropped her gaze.

"I'm not staying for long," said Chu quickly. "Hey, Dad? Did you see what I did with Ouroboros? I was trying to get the Peng to overplay their hand. But—"

"Type two error," said Ond, not opening his eyes to look at Chu. He was still embarrassed about that sex scene. "I'm monitoring the Yolla Bolly Peng ranch. Your Ouroboros idea was a clever approach, but it's backfiring horribly. Kakar is making viral runes with built-in error correction routines. It looks like they'll make for long-term tulpas. Julie just runecast a new Floofy for Kakar. Look at that bird dancing! Ha, ha. I kind of like him. He's your friend, isn't he, Chu? A true geek, just like us two."

As Chu focused on the Peng, the room around him grew vague, which was just as well, what with Momotaro smirking at him and Bixie avoiding his gaze.

The exultant Kakar was in overdrive; he was processing hundreds of pioneer runes and passing them to the Crownies. The new runes were so slick and compact that even that dull-witted guy, Steve, could handle them. Chu made another attempt to wrest a full copy of Ouroboros 2.0 from Kakar's mind, but the bird's teep-shield was stronger than before, and smart enough to flash Chu an image of a two-toed foot kicking dirt at him.

"Julie's hopping down the West Coast, laying a fresh Peng ranch at each stop," announced Ond. "Man, she's moving fast. She's in Napa! The others are doing China, the Persian Gulf, and India. And, oh no, one of them is in New York."

Steve the Crownie was standing in Times Square, preparing to channel all of Gotham's gnarl into the tulpas of a single party of Peng pioneers. Parasitizing the great city's mind was trivially simple. The Crownie tweaked a single atom in a chewed piece of gum on the sidewalk; the rune raced out across the boroughs— and the Big Apple was a gnarl-free ranch for a happy family of four Peng pioneers.

"I blew it," said Chu, feeling blank and scared.

The local silps had picked up on the spreading fear. The Santa Cruz breeze grew fitful, the waves fell apart, pelicans wheeled uneasily in the sky.

"That Crownie girl is in Sausalito now," exclaimed Jil. "She'll skip over San Francisco, zap San Jose, and head for here."

"Help us, Gaia!" cried Nektar. "Help Chu like Pekka helped Kakar!"

"Gaia's not getting anywhere," said Chu bitterly. "Our planet's dumber than theirs. What I'll have to do is find Jayjay or the pitchfork."

"I'm ready to set off volcanoes like nobody's ever seen," teeped Gaia, her voice low and angry. "I'll atomize my whole crust before I let those Peng win."

"Don't do that, Gaia," said Bixie. "Chu saved you before, and he'll save you again. Chu rules."

Chu felt an unfamiliar sensation around his mouth. He was smiling. "Thanks, Bixie. I—I've been worried that you might think I'm—"

"Never mind that stuff. I like you the same. You're my friend."

Something crashed against the roof. Oh wow, it was Duxy's snout. But, just now, Chu was so happy that even this seemed wonderful.

The young manta was bigger than the house. Her beating wings whirled the towels and the beach furniture into the street like confetti. "Chu," she skirled, making the cottage's timbers creak. "Come out and play!"

"Don't!" cried Nektar. "Let's teleport home to San Francisco so—"

"I can't go to a Peng zone," interrupted Chu. "The Peng want to kill me!"

"Chu's our hero," said Bixie, smiling and tossing her head. She stretched out her arms.

Chu ran across the room and hugged her. It was friendly hug, not a romantic one. Bixie didn't feel that way about him.

And maybe she never would. But suddenly that seemed okay. It was good to be friends.

As the house shook yet again, Chu marched onto the porch to face the manta. Duxy wasn't the only Hrull out there. Some of those whirling shapes in the sky were other giant mantas, diving into the streets of Santa Cruz. They were gathering as many pushers as possible before the Peng took over.

Duxy settled onto the yard, her open mouth level with the porch. She'd grown to her full adult size—two hundred feet from wingtip to wingtip.

"Leave us alone," cried Kittie, at Chu's side with that same old stonker gun in her hand.

"It's okay, Kittie," said Chu. "I want to go with her. I have a plan. But, Duxy, only take me, okay?"

The great manta teeped her assent. With his exceptional powers of concentration, Chu was a prize. Moments later, he was inside and they were airborne.

"Hi, Chu," said skinny Glee, lolling on her bunk, quite stoned. "Duxy has been bribing me to tag after you."

"Can you believe how my daughter's grown?" teeped Wobble the Hrull, wedged into a bunk like an oversized leather cushion. Chu could sense the aging Hrull's anxiety about his fate. Once Duxy found herself a husband, her dad would be out in the cold.

"Start charging the teeker cone!" commanded Duxy.

"I'll help push you," said Chu. "But don't put gel on me. I'm done with that crap for good."

"Gel, gel, gel," said Duxy impatiently. "That's all you pushers talk about. You're not getting gel before the jump anyway. This is the big one, mind you, all the way to the Hrullwelt. And if you and Glee can't push me to the Hrullwelt alone, I'll circle back and get that little girl that you're so—"

"We can do it!" cried Chu.

"Fine, then," said Duxy. "It's time. Your whole planet's going to be Peng ranches pretty soon. And then the Peng will start exterminating the mammals. They always do that if they can. And I'm teeping that your planetary mind wants to blow up her crust. It's all over here. A dead end. Push."

"Give me a just a second to catch my breath."

Using encrypted teep, Chu fed his old Knot code to Glee.

"What's this?" she privately teeped back.

"The key to a parallel world. The Hibrane."

"Wonderful," answered Glee. "I am very ready for something new."

Down below, the other Hrull continued scooping up locals from the beaches and the sidewalks of Santa Cruz. People were panicking and trampling each other; faint screams drifted up. A tiny blond figure appeared on the town wharf, stretching out her arms for calm. Julie the Crownie. Focusing on her, Chu saw her furrowing her brow, getting ready to—

"Push!" roared Duxy.

Chu and Glee pushed—but not in the direction the Hrull expected.

They shot out of space like a pinched pumpkin seed, skimming across the glassy Planck sea toward the Hibrane, searching for Jayjay, for the pitchfork—and for Thuy.

CHAPTER 15

THE MAGIC HARP

Azaroth's upstairs room at the Muddy Eel had a single window and no lock on the door. Rather than glass panes, the window had a wooden shutter. An earthenware chamber pot peeped from beneath the bedstead like a rude joke.

"Did you say they have baths here?" asked Thuy. She felt lank and oily. Yesterday she hadn't even had a chance to wash after that insane fuckathon with Chu. Oh God, oh God. And last night she'd slept on the ground with beggars.

"The bathhouse is in back," said Azaroth. He talked rapidly, out of consideration for the fact that Thuy's natural clock rate was six times as fast as his. "You just walk through the inn. It's good. They use a spring in the bathhouse instead of canal water. The bath should be lively with so many people in town for the big market. They call it a stew."

"Come with me," said Thuy.

"I need a nap. Things are so wild, you'll blend in. There's all sorts of freaks around. Just tell Vrouw Engst you're my guest. She's the landlady."

It was dark now, and the inn's public room was filled with festive fairgoers: merchants, peasants, craftspeople, musicians, conjurors, acrobats, soldiers, actors, and surely some pickpockets. A raw-boned woman with short brown hair stood vigilantly by the kitchen door: Vrouw Engst. Speaking slow Brabants Dutch, Thuy introduced herself, saying she was Azaroth's cousin. Showing no real surprise at her new guest's one-foot-height, Vrouw Engst gave her a handkerchief for a towel and directed her to the bath.

It was a low-ceilinged, echoing room, lit by tallow candles. The rectangular tub was made of four low stone walls lined with varnished wood. Springwater trickled from a split boulder into a kettle; another kettle sat warming on a wood-fired stove. Though a bit smoky, the air was wonderfully moist and warm. A rear door stood slightly ajar, giving onto a kitchen garden.

A cheerful party of four sat in the tub, picking at a platter of roast duck and turnips. They cheered at the sight of tiny Thuy, calling out for her to join the stew, their voices low and draggy.

"You're in town for the festival?" said the woman on the left, loosely perched upon the knee of a well-muscled young man. She had big cheeks, pale blue eyes and a chipped front tooth. Her pale boobs bobbled in the water. "I work here in the inn. My name's Anja. What a nice body you have for a dwarf."

"I'm normal-sized where I come from—the Garden of Eden in the New World. My name's Thuy Nguyen."

"You're a friend of Azaroth's? He's such a handsome man."

Thuy shed her grotty clothes, slipped into the big bath, and swam about, enjoying the feel of the clean, lukewarm water.

"Paddle over here, my child," said a bearded man wearing a top hat and nothing else. He had one arm around a lean white-haired woman. With his free hand he made a mystic pass in the air. "We'll feed you. I'm Luc and this is my wife Dora. I make things disappear and she tells people where to find them. I've never seen you at the other fairs, dear. What's your trade, exactly? Cut-purse?" His hand drifted over to the duck and he ate a bit of it, his Adam's apple working up and down.

"Maybe she's an acrobat," said the man holding Anja. He had an even growth of pale blond stubble upon his scalp, cheeks, and chin. "Menso's the name; tumbling's the game. Stand on my hand, little elf, I'll raise you high."

Wanting to be friendly, Thuy found a perch on Menso's palm. Smoothly, though grunting with the effort, he raised her a full arm's length over his head. Being made of Lobrane matter, Thuy was much heavier than he'd expected. She rose on her toes and did a shallow dive into the tub, enjoying the downward glide through the air. The four applauded.

"A thimble of wine, dear?" said the weathered Dora, her voice slow and cozy. "Settle in by me, and I'll tell your fortune." Her lower jaw came up almost to her nose; she had but four teeth.

Top-hatted Luc clapped his hands and produced a tiny earthenware plate, seemingly from thin air. He served Thuy a portion of the duck and turnips. Thuy sat on the tub's rim and dug into the food, turning down the offer of wine. It was mellow here. Even without telepathy, she could feel a pleasant vibe of consciousness from the undulating water, the flickering candles, the glowing coals in the stove. Suddenly she understood a remark Jayjay had made when talking about his visions last night. Everything was already alive, even without lazy eight. Everything on Earth had been alive since the beginning of time.

This uplifting train of thought was interrupted by Anja. "Are you staying with Azaroth?" asked the blond woman in a suspicious tone. "You're not a freelancer, are you?"

"My husband and I are putting up at a local painter's house," said Thuy primly. "Jeroen Bosch?"

"Him!" exclaimed Anja, and let out a coarse guffaw. "He's been here a few times. A slimy catch. He wanted me to empty my chamber pot onto him before sticking in his carrot."

"Maybe you should do that to me," said Menso, playing with Anja's breasts. "We could roll around like pigs." His penis had risen so that its tip poked through the water's surface.

"*Pfui!*" said Luc, tossing his top hat over it and making a pass with his hand. "Don't frighten our little maiden from Eden." He lifted the hat and a single red rose floated where the lewd display had been.

"She's no maiden," said Dora, eying Thuy. "She's with child."

"How do you know that?" cried Thuy.

"I'm a seer." Dora stared fixedly at the spots of light dancing on the water. "I see more. You'll go down through hell— and end up in heaven. And then—how auspicious—you'll give birth to a hero. And there's something about—a pitchfork?"

"That's me," twanged Groovy in the local Dutch dialect, slipping in through the crack in the back door. "Howdy, Thuy."

"Satan!" shrieked Anja, her pink face turning pale. She billowed out of Menso's lap and raised her hands to the heavens. "Forgive me dear Lord for my life of sin!"

"He's not a devil," Thuy reassured Anja. "He's just a—a low peasant who can change his form. A harmless conjuror like Luc."

"I'm not staying here," said Anja, retreating to the far end of the pool. "Let's go to your room, Menso."

"I'm in the shared dormitory," said the stubble-headed acrobat, sloshing after her. "Do you have a private room?"

"Yes," said Anja in a low tone. "But that costs a little extra. And you can't dirty it up."

"How long can I stay?"

"Oh, till midnight," she said, feeling Menso's biceps and kissing his bristly cheek. Raising her voice and glancing upward as they left the room, she added. "I'll walk in the procession tomorrow, dear Lord. That's got to count for something."

Groovy dipped his prongs into the bathwater, making the tub tingle with rapid vibrations. It felt good, but at the same time it was annoying.

"The pitchfork is the one who'll take you to heaven," said old Dora, her eyes still glazed. "Down, down, down."

"Right! I'm gonna call up a native aktual to make a whirlpool for her and her hubbie," said Groovy, whipping up a little eddie in the bath water. "Pull 'em all the way through. Same as Jayjay did for me back on Pepple. Only he was a crow, and he brought us a tornado."

"I think he's talking about paths into the subdimensions," said Thuy uneasily. "The world's basement. It's under everything that we see. I fell into it once. Things live down there. Subbies. First they looked like birds and jackals, and then they looked like cactuses."

"Demons of the underworld," intoned Luc. "To me they look like lizards and bats."

"They look like whatever you expect to see," said Groovy. "If you'd pushed on deeper, Thuy, you'd already be a zedhead runecaster. I'm fixin' to take you and Jay past infinity. For a little while you'll be aktuals."

"I don't want any more changes right now," said Thuy,

longing for the meditative medieval vibe she'd sensed when first entering the tub. "Leave me alone, Groovy."

"I'll go check on Jay," said the pitchfork, and hopped toward the rear door, his handle rapping on the floor.

"I hadn't realized you're such a powerful mage," Luc said to Thuy, clearly impressed. "*Multum in parvulo*. Great craft from this tiny one. Suppose we talk at length in the tavern."

Just then three grimy soldiers entered the bathhouse with a pair of giggling women. Spotting the pitchfork darting out the back door, one of the soldiers called, "Halt!" But by then Groovy was gone.

Nothing daunted, the women shucked their gowns and splashed into the tub, letting out prolonged shrieks. One of the soldiers looked familiar—a man in leather pants and jerkin, with a blond mustache and a tight blue hat pulled down to his eyes. He was the one whom Jayjay had knocked to the ground last night in that alley. Busy fumbling with his clothes, he hadn't yet registered Thuy's presence. The wiry, dark-skinned soldier who was at his side did notice Thuy, but he was more interested in the full-sized women in the water.

Moving fast, Thuy hopped out of the tub and ran around behind the soldiers, pulling on her clothes on the way to the dining room. She found an empty table and slipped into a chair.

Across the tavern, three actors were rehearsing tableaux of Bible scenes, smoothly moving through Adam and Eve, the Annunciation, and the Second Coming of Jude Christ. Beside them a lutist, a bagpiper, and a drummer were tuning up. By the kitchen door, a pair of jugglers were practicing with the inn's bowls and pitchers, ignoring Vrouw Engst's admonitions to stop. Thuy was happy to be in this buzzing medieval hive.

Azaroth appeared and, spotting Thuy, sat down with her. "Nice and clean?"

"I am," she said, grinning.

"Who was in the stew?" asked Azaroth, interested in the inn gossip. "Anja? She's the one I really like."

"She was there. But—"

Azaroth waved off the rest of the information. "I'll tell you a secret," he said. "If I were to stay on, I'd think about giving Anja a better life. I can see her as a mother, can't you? Of course Bosch's maid isn't bad either. Kathelijn. A guy could really settle down here."

Before Thuy could respond, Dora and Luc joined them. "This is my friend the fisherman," she said, introducing Azaroth. "These two are—"

"Mountebanks, charlatans, swindlers," said Luc showing his teeth through his trim black beard. "You never did tell us your profession, Thuy." He'd garbed himself in a red cape that made Thuy realize she'd seen him on the road into town that afternoon.

"I'm a metanovelist," she said, then paused, trying to think of a better word. After all, novels didn't really exist in Bosch's time, let alone metanovels that were a thousand times as long— or thick, or deep, or branched . . . "I tell tales," she amended. "Mostly about me. I'd like to preserve all my thoughts, if I could."

"God preserves our thoughts in any case," said Dora piously. "He knows what's done and what's to come. My second sight flows from Him, you understand, and not from the Evil One."

"Oh, spare us the crap," said Azaroth impatiently. "I'm hungry."

"Thank you, but we've already eaten," said Luc, as smoothly as if Azaroth had invited them to a meal. "But we've nowhere near drunk our fill. Perhaps we can gamble for the check?" He wiggled his long fingers. A pair of dice clacked to the table and came to rest showing two sixes. He crooked a finger and the dice hopped into his hand.

"You are in grave danger," said Dora, suddenly clutching Azaroth by the sleeve. "I see manacles around your wrists. And above your head—a noose. If you buy us wine, I can tell you more."

"You met these two in the bath, Thuy?" said Azaroth, looking annoyed. "Hey!" he yelled to Vrouw Engst. "Roast pork for me. And a beer! That's it."

The musicians had launched a squalling reel. A fat man and a thin woman began a squat-legged dance, kicking and jiggling around the room.

"Tell us more about that pitchfork, Thuy," said Luc, raising his voice. "You say he's a sorcerer who changes his form? And he's training you in the black arts?"

"Shut *up*!" said Thuy glancing around. "Better order them some wine, Azaroth." With a shrug, the big fisherman complied.

"I'm sure Thuy would rather hear about us, dear Luc, than to talk about herself," said Dora, as the pitchers arrived. "How about when they ran us out of Antwerp because you stopped time by pouring honey into the cathedral tower clock?"

"That was because you told the mayor that the Spaniards would invade on white horses," said Luc. "And when he saw it was brown ticks on a herd of sheep, he said you'd be flogged at vespers."

"Well, I wanted to impress the mayor so he'd save you from the butcher whom you'd struck blind," said Dora.

"How did Luc strike him blind?" asked Azaroth, his mouth full.

"A self-working spell," said Luc. "I told the butcher he was under a curse for having slaughtered a coal-black pig. And for a couple of days he believed me. We did what we liked."

"That pig was good eating," said Dora. "And the butcher's wife was screwing his apprentice three times a day. The wife's the one who hired Luc to blind her husband in the first place."

"She went after the apprentice because Dora told her that a young man's sperm would cure her backache," said Luc. "And, you know, it did."

"Honey in the gears," said Dora, with a witchy, gap-toothed cackle.

The tales ran on. After a while, Anja and Menso joined them, looking well spent. Azaroth was a little put out to see the two together, but Anja flirted with him until he cheered up. Menso began telling stories about acrobats he'd known, including, he claimed, a man who could play a bagpipe with his ass.

"Sounded just as good as these fellows," he concluded, nodding his spiky head toward the inn's musicians. And then he started gossiping about a flying demon that had been spotted near the river beyond the gallows field. A monstrous thing like a devilfish or a sea skate.

Thuy didn't say anything to this, but she felt quite sure he was talking about a Hrull. And how would a Hrull have managed to jump over here? Most likely Chu was riding inside it. She really hoped Chu didn't mix into things before she'd had a chance to finish making up with Jayjay. In fact, it'd be best to go back to Bosch's cellar right now.

Just then a Hibraner snatched her out of her chair, the soft, sausage-thick fingers wrapping around her torso and her arms. Her captor was a red-faced man wearing a floppy gold beret.

"This little whore can service me now!" he boomed in his draggy Hibraner voice.

With the inevitability of a molasses-slow nightmare, the man shoved Thuy's head and shoulders so far down inside his ballooning pantaloons that her face was about to touch his— *ugh!* She landed a swift punch to his gut, doubling him over.

As she leapt free, Azaroth stepped forward to smack the man on the side of the head, sending him sprawling onto the tavern's filthy floor.

"Oh, oh," said Luc, rising from his chair. "That's Alderman Vladeracken. And so we'll bid you good night. Thanks for the hospitality!" He and Dora hurried off, but not before Vladeracken had noticed them. Meanwhile, Azaroth set Thuy on his shoulder.

"You'll all pay for this," croaked the alderman, slowly sitting up. "I'm not a man to be trifled with."

Menso had taken a peacekeeping stance between the two men. "If you fight, you can't drink here," he pointed out.

"You come trifle with *me,* Alderman," said Anja, dangling her boobs in Vladeracken's face and helping him to his feet. "Show me what a roaring lion you are. Shall we start with a bath?"

"We can finish there, too, for all I care," said Vladeracken, puffing himself up. "Let everyone see how I skewer a quail." He turned away from Azaroth and Thuy as if they were invisible. "Wine, Vrouw Engst."

His face stiff, Azaroth walked Thuy across the triangular marketplace. Even at this late hour, many were about, twining flowers onto wagons and brushing paint onto billowing sheets. Passing around the side of Bosch's house, Thuy found her way into his cellar and bedded down on the straw. She'd expected Jayjay to be here, but he wasn't.

Another crazy day. Was she really pregnant? Without

telepathy and omnividence, there was no way to double-check. If only it could really be Jayjay's baby. What was it that con artist Dora had said? Thuy was to give birth to a hero? That sounded nice. She smiled to herself.

She slept for a while, but then she woke, piqued by a pinprick in her armpit. She sat up in the cellar's humid gloom, scratching herself. It was still the middle of the night. Given that time went so slowly here, it was going to be a long wait for dawn. Another little stab of pain, this time on the nape of her neck. And then her ankle. Fleas! Wasn't there some ill medieval thing about rats, fleas, and the black plague? Shit.

Thuy was ravenously hungry. Compared to the Hibraners, she had a metabolism like a shrew that eats half her body weight per day. Creeping out from the cellar, she saw that Bosch's kitchen window was open. Leaning a garden ladder against the moonlit wall, she managed a successful foray into the house, helping herself to the breast of that chicken they'd started on yesterday, also a jug of milk and a boiled turnip.

Sitting on the back stoop, she stared at the sinking moon, amusing herself by making shrew faces—baring her teeth, drawing back her lower jaw, chewing the air. It was sort of relaxing to be off the mindweb, alone, creating her own fun.

Then she began worrying. Would they ever get home? And where was Jayjay? Was he off getting wasted again? Had he left with the pitchfork? Was he hurt? Should she look for him? But she didn't have the heart to go out roaming the streets for a second night in a row. Again and again her mind returned to her possible pregnancy.

She did some yoga exercises and then, as the moon set and the dew settled, she returned to the cellar. The fleas welcomed her. As a distraction, she began going over her plans for her next metanovel, *Hive Mind*. The draft material she'd had in her lazy eight memory back home was gone, probably forever. But the main ideas were in her trusty meat-brain.

Hive Mind would be about mythologizing life in the post–lazy eight world. Even though Thuy's potential readers were living the hylozoic life, they weren't necessarily appreciating it in depth. Yes, yes, the visionary work of Thuy Nguyen would help the cognoscenti comprehend the contours of their strange new reality!

She figured she'd use herself and her friends for characters, just like she'd done in *Wheenk,* her first metanovel, which had sold a couple of thousand copies. *Hive Mind* would be a sequel. As for the story, well—the adventure she was embroiled in right now was certainly exciting enough. But did it have a happy ending?

Flea-bitten and preoccupied, she drifted into sleep. Her plans for the metanovel became a matter of customizing the individual letters of her words. The letters were living beings, each of them a distinct shade of pale blue—cobalt, manganese, royal, ultramarine—and Thuy was carpentering magic spells into the secret recesses of the letters' hollow legs. At the end of the long, hexed night, the zany, quacking, jumpy troop sang a phrase as one, enveloping the world in a bright flicker that—

She snapped from sleep and sat up gasping. The cellar door framed a blossoming plum tree against a trapezoid of ineffably lovely lilac-rose sky. The sound of the Lost Chord was echoing across the newly awakened land.

The first thing Thuy did was to teep inside her uterus—finding a tiny free-floating embryo, a hollow ball of a hundred and twenty-eight cells, not yet attached to her womb's wall. The embryo's vibe was vigorous and focused. Thuy peered deeper, locating the sex chromosome pair in one of the eager cells: XX. A girl. Wow. And, according to Dora, the baby would become a hero.

The next thing Thuy did was to teep a quick hello to Jayjay in the attic and find out where he'd been all night? Doctoring a painting for Bosch in the cathedral, fine. She didn't explicitly get into the pregnancy thing with him yet. If he was interested enough he'd pick up on it himself.

And the third thing she did—which could wait no longer—was to get those frikkin' fleas off her bod. Taking firm mental hold of the five main offenders, she teeked them into the garden, setting them down on a flat stone gilded by the rising sun.

Pioneer fleas in a new land! Each of the five had his or her own little personality—a Vince, an Elvira, a Bela, an Erzsebet, and a Nadja—not that they actually called themselves that. Unlike the uplifted critters and objects in the Lobrane, the new Hibrane minds weren't using words.

The difference stemmed from the fact that, in the Lobrane, Lazy Eight Day had been preceded by a nanomachine-based form of telepathy and mind-amplification. The nanomachine web had served as an incubator for a race of virtual interface agents—the so-called beezies—who'd migrated right into nature's silps, enriching them with language and a human-compatible interface.

The natural minds of the Hibrane were less verbal. Teeping into the placid consciousness of the flagstone upon whom the fleas jittered and jigged, Thuy picked up the rock's delight at the first rays of sun, his tingly sense of the morning moisture oozing within his fissures, and his calm reliance upon the gravitational pull of mother earth. His thought stream was made of feelings rather than words.

Beneath the rock were ants, always Thuy's favorites. Teeping them, she savored the way in which an ant colony had a silp mind that was greater than the sum of its parts. The ants had a queen, yes, but she wasn't a ruler. The doings of the colony emerged from the hive mind. It was odd that human societies weren't run in the same way.

Wondering about Hibrane Gaia—this world's planetary mind—Thuy sent up a tendril of consciousness. She found a vast being who was vibrant and warm, but, lacking a human-tailored interface, quite inscrutable.

As a last step before joining Jayjay, Thuy cast her attention into the house to see how things lay. Jeroen was delightedly communing with his shoes, his water jug, and even the light rays bouncing off his bedroom wall. Aleid was conducting a quick survey of the entire contents of her house—Jayjay's noises in the attic had set off her fears of burglars—and already she'd noticed the fresh chicken bones near Thuy's lair. For her part, Kathelijn, the maid, was dreamily staring across town through her wall, focusing on the handsome body of Azaroth, who was washing himself with a basin in his rented room. Noticing Thuy's spectral presence, Azaroth arranged to meet her and Jayjay in front of the city hall, which faced onto the marketplace. Things were coming to a head.

Thuy teleported herself to the attic. The pitchfork stood by the window and Jayjay fingered the strange, glowing strings of the harp.

"Thuy!" He rose and embraced her. He already knew about the embryo.

"I'm not teeking her away," she said defiantly. "She wants to grow."

"No problem!" exclaimed Jayjay. "What's part of you is

part of me." His face split in a goofy smile. "Anyway—I just checked her DNA—and she's my daughter."

"This is real touching," crooned the sarcastic pitchfork.

"Have we done enough for you now, Groovy?" said Jayjay, annoyed. "Are you going to help us get rid of the Peng?"

"And you have to help us get back home," added Thuy. "I lost that special Knot code that I showed you. And Jayjay forgot it, too. You remember it, right, Groovy?"

"We'll be on our way pretty soon," said the pitchfork confidently. "Don't forget I'm fixin' to aktualize you two. I gotta plan out our route."

"Take a very good look at me, you three," interrupted the harp. "Remember me."

They got one last view of the painting on the harp's flat belly: a teeming garden with the two lovers that were Thuy and Jayjay. The demon musician beside them was, Thuy now realized, Jeroen Bosch.

The harp's body grew rubbery. Her curved crosspiece stretched out, straightening its crook. The front wooden column broke free of the crosspiece and flopped down. The harp unkinked herself. Twang by twang, her strings snapped. The column and the crosspiece split, making rudimentary legs and arms.

The harp extruded a head, and rose to her feet. Spreading her arms, she wriggled and shook, becoming a slender green woman with three eyes.

"Lovva from planet Pepple," the figure said aloud. "It's time for the good part. Crushing the aristos. My aktualization is nearly done." She smelled sulfurous and vegetal—like Glee.

"Wait!" said Jayjay. "You have to stay here for over five hundred years! So Thuy can steal you from Azaroth's aunt. Otherwise there's a terrible paradox."

"I've already done that," answered Lovva. "I traveled around a harp-shaped loop of time. Follow me soon, Groovy. We'll make Pepple a free world." She teleported herself away, becoming translucent, then transparent, and disappearing with a final sprinkling of glowing dots.

There was a beat of silence and then a pinpoint appeared in midair. Rapidly it grew, like an image drawing closer. It was a green alien woman with three eyes; an earlier version of Lovva coming at them from infinity. Settling in, she regarded Thuy and Jayjay with no signs of recognition. "Where are we, Groovy?" she teeped. "How did you get here before me?"

"Our worldlines are twisted all the hell around," said the pitchfork. "You're just coming in from being aktualized off Pepple, right?"

"It was wonderful to go past infinity, no? But, Groovy—why do you look so strange?"

"It's a goof," said Groovy. "I'm devilish and you're angelic. We were laughin' about it up thar past infinity with Thuy and Jayjay. Don't you recall?"

"I suppose," said Lovva, distractedly. "I keep repeating to myself the little tune they taught me. I must use it to unfurl these worlds. Remind me what else."

"You turn yourself into a dang harp," exclaimed Groovy. "And you stay here for five and a half centuries. That part bothers me a little. The way I heard it, we only stay aktualized for a couple of days of Pepple time." He paused to absorb some convoluted thought that Lovva teeped to him. "Oh, that's right. You'll be time-skimming. Like a skipping stone."

Still wondering what Groovy meant about seeing her and Jayjay out past infinity, Thuy went ahead and coached Lovva as she transformed herself into a harp. The shapeshifting alien pressed her arms together and stretched them out to make the crosspiece. Her belly flattened; her head retreated into her neck. Her legs swung up and fused to make a fluted front column. Her toes connected with her fingers.

Buds formed along the median of her chest and belly, sending luminous tendrils up to the crosspiece, forming the strings. Her green skin glittered and turned gold. And now a copy of Bosch's painting on the soundbox began taking shape. Jayjay got in on this, guiding the harp as she transformed her skin into layers of oil paint.

When she was done, two pale lovers stood nude in a meadow that seethed with black lizards and tiny birds. Beside them was a pale blue demon fingering a tiny, gold harp that was shaped just like Lovva. The lizards wore little hats, flying fish drifted in the sky, the trunks of the trees had ears, and hints of moisture glistened on the lovers' thighs.

Right about then old Bosch appeared, climbing through a trapdoor in the attic's floor. He was in an exalted mental state of joy and terror. He carried a palette and a paintbrush.

"This is the end of the world?" he asked.

"Not the end, a new beginning," said Jayjay. "We've awakened the souls of every object. You've been right to see things as alive, Jeroen."

"We'll live on?" exclaimed the grizzled artist, looking out the attic window at the marketplace. "A land of wonder." The rising sun was slanting across the cobbles, illuminating the festive banners that trembled in the day's first breeze. "Everything sings. The cloths revel in their draping. Dear God." His face smoothed over as he bowed his head in a brief prayer.

Wondering what Jeroen saw when he prayed, Thuy reached into his mind and caught a glimpse of a blinding light at infinity—a triangular, unblinking eye. And then the artist's meditation was done.

"What's that devilish thing?" exclaimed Bosch, pointing to the pitchfork.

"I'm what you'd call an artist, too," said Groovy. "Back home on Pepple, I train vines into stage sets. Sorry I can't stay and chew the fat, but I've got to do some prep work."

"Wait," said Thuy. "Teep me Chu's Knot first. Don't strand us here."

"Oh don't get your panties in a twist," sneered the pitchfork. "I'll be back in the nick o' time." Forestalling further discussion, Groovy hyperjumped into the region between the branes. Rather then melting away as in an ordinary teleportation hop, the effect was, rather, as if he'd turned a corner in some wholly new direction. His body foreshortened, became a line, and was gone.

"I pray that you're not sorcerers," said Jeroen uneasily. "The leader of the mercenary troops garrisoned here, Duke Ongeluk, is quite vigilant on this score, as is my tiresome neighbor Jan Vladeracken. The Duke is close with Father Kreeft of Saint John's Cathedral, I might add. They make blood sport of hunting heretics."

"This has nothing to do with sin," said Thuy, suddenly thinking of what Anja had said about Jeroen asking her for dirty sex.

Spotting the thought, Jeroen glared at her. "We didn't do it. It was a jape. I was young, unmarried, heated by wine."

"I'm just thinking that—" began Thuy.

"Never mind!" said Bosch, raising his palette and brush. "In the night I had another idea for my painting on the harp. So this morning I thought that, even if the world is ending, I might as well add my final touch."

"*There's* an artist for you," said Jayjay admiringly.

"See the little harp the demon in the picture holds?" continued Bosch, bending close to Lovva's soundbox. "The little harp should bear a painting that's a copy of my painting on this big harp."

"Only think the changes," chimed the harp. "And I'll make my skin into the proper colors."

Bosch smiled and set his palette on the floor. "As if painting with my eyebeams? What power! Yes, let's begin."

"But I tell you to do this fast," added the harp. "I'm eager to begin my tasks. I have to go into a trance so as to time-skim through the centuries. And then I'll meet dear, stupid Groovy in Subdee, and tell him how to find me here."

Bosch passed his sinewy hand across his brow and fixed his keen eyes on Lovva's skin. As if formed by a skin rash, tiny pimples of fresh color emerged. Bosch's face split in a stark grin. He was loving this. He was creating an impossibly detailed visual regress.

Lovva's soundbox bore an image of a demon with a harp, but now the demon's harp bore an image of a smaller demon with a harp, and this tiny harp bore a yet smaller picture of a hellish harpist, and so on—iterating down to levels that the naked eye could barely see. By way of capping the series, Bosch set a tiny triangle of ivory white at the vanishing point. The eye of God.

The harp sang a farewell chord and her mind turned glacially slow—at least as seen from the outside. It was as if she'd gone into suspended animation. She was time-skimming now.

"Speaking of painting," said Jayjay, wanting to push himself forward a bit. "Last night went fine, Jeroen. I covered that donor portrait with a thistle like you said."

Right on cue, Alderman Vladeracken's hoarse voice billowed up from Bosch's front hall. Unfortunately, Kathelijn had let him in again. And it seemed he'd teeped what Jayjay had just said.

"Fiends! Demons! You're responsible, Bosch! Your little goblin defaced the very altar of our Lady!"

"I hate that disgusting pig," said Thuy. "He practically tried to rape me."

"I should kill him right now," said Jayjay, socking his fist into his palm. "It'd be easy. Split his head like a watermelon."

"No, no," said Thuy. "That would make things worse. Let's go outside. We'll meet up with Azaroth and wait for that hillbilly pitchfork to take us home."

"But we'll have to confront Jan on the stairs," said Jeroen. "Or—I suppose we could climb out the window."

"What about your wife?" asked Thuy.

"Jan won't bother Aleid," said Jeroen. "Everyone's scared of her. Her family is rich."

"Let's just teleport," said Jayjay. "I'll show you how, Jeroen. It means that we hop from spot to spot. I discovered the trick back in California. You focus on the precise image of where you want to be, you get mixed up about whether you're here or there, and then you decide you're there. It's easy."

CHAPTER 16

TO THE GIBBET!

The three hopped to the market, landing near where some guilds had lined up for the procession: butchers in their aprons, carpenters holding adzes, and bakers whitened by flour, each group with a garlanded wagon bearing a keg of beer. Monks and nuns jostled priests in fancy robes.

A band of strapping young clerics arrived, carrying a canopied litter with the dark little statue of the Virgin. Ahead of them strode a hard-faced priest with bloodshot eyes. He stared at Thuy and Jayjay, not liking what he saw.

"That's Father Kreeft," said Jeroen. "And God help us, here comes Duke Ongeluk as well."

A leathery man in floppy boots and a pale green cockade hat emerged from a sedan chair. He greeted Father Kreeft, familiarly patting the ecclesiastic's rigid shoulder. Kreeft whispered something in the Duke's ear, nodding his head toward Jeroen and the Lobraners.

Peasants were dispersing from a cockfight that had just broken up. The mind-amplified roosters had no interest in clawing each other to death. Next to them were some actors playing the Bible scene of the Woman Taken in Adultery. They were having a little trouble with their performance, as they kept tripping over each other's ribald thoughts and breaking into laughter.

On every side, the merchants continued gamely hawking their wares. The locals had waited all year for this festival and they were loath to let things go off track. Doing their best to ignore the voices in their heads, they glared at the newly sentient objects as if they could force them back into dumb silence. But the caps, potatoes, sheets, and baskets were awake for good.

Now here came Alderman Jan Vladeracken pushing through the crowd, braying like the barnyard animal that he was. He buttonholed Duke Ongeluk and pointed at Thuy and her companions.

"Arrest these evil gnomes and their sorcerer, Jeroen Bosch! We'll string up the owl and his newts as a festal offering. If you can accomplish this, I'll see that our town increases your troops' pay!" Vladeracken strode over to Father Kreeft and handed him a little purse that chuckled with its fatness. "We rely on your guidance in executing this sacred obligation, your grace."

"Follow me," Thuy said to Jayjay and Jeroen. "Azaroth will help us." She wormed through the stockinged legs of the crowd, minding the voices of the shoes. Jayjay was right beside her, and Jeroen close behind.

They found Azaroth gazing dreamily at the fire of a great open hearth set up before the city hall: a furnace melting iron in a stone tub. Three grimy smiths were about to forge a special new bell in honor of this year's pageant. The mold for the bell sat on the ground. Grimacing against the heat, a smelter was standing on the rim of the tub, using a pike to work loose a stone stopper so the dull-red metal could flow.

The flushed Vladeracken had kept pace better than Thuy had expected. He was almost upon them, hollering and using his teep to point them out. In his wake came Duke Ongeluk with a platoon of soldiers, and Father Kreeft with his priests.

The smelter atop the tub glanced distractedly toward Thuy, and just then his foot slipped. He teetered, flailing his arms—and tumbled into the lavalike metal, partly rising up, then falling down again. In his death agony, he let out a series of hideous, juicy, telepathy-enhanced screams. The silp of the molten iron sang a solemn, antiphonal response.

What put the crowd totally over the edge was that the charred bones and greasy bubbles continued the telepathic screaming long after the smelter's spark of life was gone. Judgment Day and the torments of the damned looked to be commencing right here, right now.

Peasants snatched up sticks to whip their backs; merchants rubbed mud and ashes on their faces. The soldiers, priests, and town sheriffs began seizing God's enemies—starting with the beggars, the jugglers, and the magicians.

Fast on their feet and nimble with their teleportation hops, Thuy, Jayjay, Azaroth, and Jeroen stayed one jump ahead of the death squads. Their flickering transformations made them look all the more like sinister sorcerers—but they were loath to wholly leave the marketplace. Jeroen in particular wanted to see what came next. And so they twinkled about the steps of the city hall, first on one side, then on the other.

Faster than could be believed, the town bailiffs trundled torture and execution equipment onto the city hall's stone

porch. There was no thought of magistrates—these were the
End Times! By way of placating the angry God, His enemies
were to be flogged, mutilated, and broken on the wheel, with
the beheadings and hangings still to come.

"Oh no," said Azaroth. "They've got Menso, Luc, and
Dora."

"And my beggar friends, too," said Jayjay. "Maarten and
Hugo."

"We have to help them!" cried Thuy. Focusing her mind,
she began teeping the prisoners the secrets of how to teleport.
Keen old Dora picked up the trick immediately. As a bald,
puffing monk bent over her with a pair of red-hot pincers, she
grew translucent, dissolved in a puff of sparkles, and relo-
cated to the river road outside of town.

"I don't understand," teeped Luc, distracted by the whips
lashing his bloodied back. With a massive effort of will, Thuy
bodily teeked the conjuror to the road where his wife waited.
At the same time, Jayjay was coaching Maarten and Hugo,
who were being laid out on wagon wheels, upon which their
bones were to be broken by hammers. Hugo got the hang of
teleportation first—and what a thrill for him to flee faster than
a man with legs! Maarten followed close behind.

Just then, Jeroen grunted and fell against Thuy—and the
sky seemed to collapse onto her head. As she later pieced it together, a stealthy group of soldiers had descended upon them,
cudgels rushing down. They'd cloaked their approach behind
a particularly large banner, their minds too dim and brutal to
give off much warning teep. Before Thuy and her friends even
saw the need to escape, they'd been laid out unconscious on
the uncaring cobbles.

She awoke groggily, her head throbbing with pain. The sunny market's crowds and mounds of goods had been replaced by stones and gloom. The air was waxy, hostile, oppressive. Thuy was in a huge, cold room with a ceiling that looked a thousand feet tall. She sat up, shackled with chains attached to a heavy band of iron around her waist.

"Are you okay?" Jayjay privately teeped to her. "This is Saint John's Cathedral. They've moved the executions in here." He was chained by her side, with Bosch beside him, and Azaroth next in line, the four of them tethered to a stone pillar. The air rang with hellish screams of agony.

"Let's hop out of here!" exclaimed Thuy. "Now!"

"I don't think we can," said Jayjay. "I'm so dizzy."

"The cathedral obeys Father Kreeft," added Bosch. "The dour stones block our view of the outer world; the air envelops us like a shroud. I tried just now to—teleport? No use."

From the altar came the worst scream yet, followed by a swish and a thud. Menso's blond-stubbled head was—how horrible—bouncing down the sanctum's low stone steps, followed by the river of his whole body's blood.

In a spasm of terror, Thuy clenched her stomach muscles. With a little creak, the metal of her waist band began giving way. Another push and she'd be able to jump free. Her sixfold strength advantage was enough to snap the Hibrane fetters. But—

"Careful," said Azaroth, calling Thuy's attention to the two soldiers with crossbows standing over them. One was fat, blond, and mustached, the other thin and olive-skinned—she'd seen these two in the Muddy Eel last night. Their crossbow bolts were steadily aimed at her and Jayjay's throats.

"I'll think of something," said Jayjay. "Just wait."

"No more waiting," interrupted the fat soldier, smirking at him. "It's your turn to die."

A hooded foursome of monks grabbed Jayjay's arms and legs, untethered him, and bore him up the aisle. A hangman's noose had been rigged above the freestanding pulpit—which was now a makeshift gibbet, with a hangman standing in the preacher's stead.

Step by step the monks mounted the pulpit stairs. Kicking and struggling, Jayjay sent his chains clattering to the floor—but he was unable to break free of the monks.

Thuy had to save him. But still the two crossbows were leveled at her throat.

"Do something!" she privately teeped to Azaroth and Jeroen. "Make them look away!"

Moving his shackled hands in unison, Bosch fished out his paintbrush and a painting rag. He used the brush to flip the rag into the air, tossing it with such mind-enhanced precision that it looked for all the world like a devilish ghost.

"Demon!" roared Azaroth.

Briefly the two distracted soldiers tracked the rag with their crossbows. Seizing the moment, Thuy burst her manacle, snatched the sword from the thin soldier's scabbard, and charged up the aisle.

The masked hangman had already shoved Jayjay off the pulpit. He was arcing toward the floor, with the slack of the rope about to run out and snap his neck. Springing high into the air, Thuy slashed the rope in two.

"Yes!" cried Jayjay, and hit the ground running. He and Thuy zigzagged pell-mell toward the cathedral door. Jayjay splintered it with a single kick.

Reaching the clean outer air, Thuy began shrilling the Hrull whistle with all her might. Growing doubly brave, Jayjay sallied back into the cathedral, meaning to fetch Azaroth and Jeroen.

For a long few moments, there was no sign of any alien manta ray.

"I got them!" yelled Jayjay, emerging from the church with Jeroen at his side. Just behind them was big Azaroth, walking backward, clashing a commandeered sword against the blades of the pursuing soldiers.

"Come with me, you three!" called Bosch. "We'll hop to my home! We'll barricade ourselves. The Swan Brotherhood will protect us. And surely the Antonites will—"

Just then the pitchfork reappeared. He took a stand between the four allies and their enemies. Leaning toward the soldiers and priests, Groovy vibrated a funky, subsonic rhythm that set their enemies to clutching their bellies and shitting their pants.

And now, blessedly, Duxy came gliding in to save them, homing in on the beacon of Bosch's upheld brush.

"Damnit," said Jayjay almost petulantly. "That brat Chu's in there. If—"

"Don't worry," said Thuy. "I won't cheat on you again. Forgive me. Just like I forgive you for being a stoner."

"I'm not a stoner anymore."

"Then we're all good," said Thuy, and gave Jayjay a kiss before he could start unraveling the logic.

"All aboard!" twanged Groovy. "Paradise Special takin' off!"

They piled into the manta's gaping maw: Thuy, Jayjay, the pitchfork and—after a thoughtful pause—Bosch. But Azaroth was hung up. The fat blond soldier had managed to disarm him. The stubborn, burly man had his arms around Azaroth's chest, and his knife was poised just short of their friend's throat.

Teeping out to see what she could do, Thuy found Azaroth in a curious state of elation. "This guy is nowhere," he teeped confidently. "I've locked up his arms with my teek. That knife's not moving till I say so."

"Come with us," urged Thuy. "You have to get back to your aunt."

"No thanks," responded Azaroth. "I'm gonna take over this town. I'll marry Anja, or maybe Kathelijn, and have a lot of kids."

"You can't do that," teeped Jayjay, listening in. "What about the time paradoxes?"

"I'll be my own ancestor," said Azaroth. "So what?" And now he spoke aloud, in Brabants, his voice booming and grave. "In the name of our Lord, release me!"

A sudden push from his mind sent the fat, mustached soldier sprawling onto the ground, with his knife buried to its hilt in the dirt.

"Behold, I cast off the unjust oppressor," shouted Azaroth, smoothly raising his arms. Turning toward Duxy and her passengers, he made the sign of the triangle. "I enjoin these demonic invaders to leave, taking along our native son Jeroen Bosch to bring back images of the unseen worlds!"

As Duxy obligingly lifted off, Azaroth favored the growing crowd with a lordly smile. "I, a humble fisherman, was called here by our Lord to save your town." He made the sign of the triangle once again. "We have nothing to fear in this new order of things. It is God's wish that everything has a soul. With me to lead you, all will be well."

Cheers drifted up as Duxy lumbered into the sky.

CHAPTER 17

THE MAELSTROM

By the end of the trip from Santa Cruz to 's-Hertogenbosch, Chu had known they'd end up someplace strange. For one thing, the crossing took much longer than expected. And then his teep and lazy eight memory had disappeared.

"What now?" cried Glee when this happened. "We are weak in the brain!"

"Um, it must be that we're approaching a Hibrane zone where lazy eight hasn't been unfurled," said Chu. "I guess we're heading into their past. That would be because the Hibraners bent our timeline." Quickly he checked that he still remembered his Knot code. Yeah, it was there in his neuronal memory, worn clean and smooth by mental fondling.

"Can't we aim toward future?" said Glee, clutching her narrow head and squinting her third eye.

Duxy seemed upset, too. She made wet gargling noises with her throat, and bucked her body as if wanting to change course.

"Let's keep going the same way," said Chu. "We want to end up with Thuy, Jayjay, and Groovy."

"Urgle," said Glee to Duxy, calming her down. She'd lived so long among the Hrull that she spoke their language.

Duxy continued across the Planck sea until finally, with a sense of rounding a cold, windy corner and entering a calm, sunny lane, they emerged into the Hibrane. They were hanging in the air above a triangular town in the crotch of two rivers. With no teep connections, it wasn't easy to know precisely where or when this was.

Duxy angled beyond the town and landed by a marshy river bend. Lazy eight or not, her flight lice still worked. Stepping out of the manta's mouth, Chu happened to catch a good look at one of the lice, on the manta's lip. The critter was like a tiny blue wart, deeply rooted in the alien's flesh.

Chu would have liked some flight lice for himself—not that the Hrull or the Peng were offering to share them. The Peng birds got by with only five flight lice apiece. Blue warts wouldn't be so bad—if you could float like a feather.

But never mind that. Their jump had brought them to a pure, unspoiled land. The air was gentle, the sun sweet. It looked to be a little before noon on a pleasant summer day. Duxy drank from the river with hearty slurps, then flopped bodily in. She and Wobble began catching fish. Sitting on the bank in the lush, waist-high grass, Chu and Glee enjoyed the scene.

A road ran parallel to the stream. The passers-by wore tights and jerkins, gowns and headdresses. Sheep bleated, oxen pulled wooden carts.

"These people are big and slow," observed Glee.

"Hibrane," said Chu, keeping it simple. "Space and time are six times bigger here."

A goose-faced girl with a basket of wriggly eels paused to stare at them. When Chu caught her eye and waved, she sketched a triangle in the air and hurried off. Maybe it was that Chu and Glee were one foot tall—or maybe it was the alien manta ray in the river. In this world, Duxy was still the equivalent of thirty feet across.

Letting his eye rove, Chu noticed a gallows field with putrid skeletons dangling. Corpses lay upon wagon wheels atop tall poles, their broken limbs wrapped around the spokes. The Middle Ages.

A shout sounded from the road and a heavy arrow buzzed past, splashing into the water and scraping one of Duxy's wings. The Hrull let out a strangled cry and floundered ashore, her little father in her wake. Skillfully she made her hide match the riverbank; bravely she kept her mouth open. As Wobble got inside her, another arrow flew past—or no, these were crossbow bolts. Two bowmen knelt by the edge of the road; a third soldier was striding through the grass.

Moving like hysterical speeded-up toons, Chu and Glee took shelter in the Hrull's mouth. Quickly she spiraled up above the farms. Peasants in the fields and barnyards pointed at them.

"Urg burkle," said Duxy with the back of her throat.

"Urgle," repeated Glee, pulling her voice down into her neck. "Arb urgle gubble goo baam."

They found a quiet place beneath the flowering trees of an apple orchard, and Duxy's skin took on the appearance of blossom-strewn grass. Everyone was hungry and cranky, but there wasn't any food nearby.

Duxy told Glee that she wanted the pushers to carry her away from this horrible world right away. Wobble agreed.

Chu told Glee to tell the Hrull they had to stay here until they'd found the others. Duxy spitefully told Glee that nobody was getting any gel until they were out of here.

"I don't give a shit about that gross stingray gel," Chu told Glee. "Tell Duxy I'm sick of her bossing us around."

"We have to reason with her, Chu," said Glee wearily. "I myself will need gel very soon."

"Why not kick the habit like I did?" said Chu coldly. "It wasn't all that hard."

"I'm not you," said Glee, glaring at him with her third eye. Her anger boiled over now, and she grabbed his arm with both hands, painfully twisting his skin.

"Let go!" whimpered Chu. Glee's grip seemed unbreakable. She was stronger than she looked.

"You help me with Duxy," hissed Glee. "Or else."

"Um—maybe I should find some food?" he suggested.

"Do that," said Glee, her eyes like three coals.

So Chu managed to steal a goose for them to eat. He found the fat fowl in a barnyard abutting their orchard. The farmer and his family could be seen haying in a distant field. Chu's Lobrane speed and strength stood him in good stead for capturing the quarrelsome goose, who was nearly as big as him. While he was at it, he bagged three eggs.

After they'd all eaten, Duxy relented and got Glee high. Chu was comfortable just staring into the sky. It was pleasant, lying beneath the blooming trees and watching the long day wane. Life without telepathy and lazy eight memory wasn't so bad. Like Jayjay and Thuy before him, Chu formed the thought that, even without lazy eight, the things around him were alive. It was just that he couldn't talk to them yet.

Be that as it may, without telepathy, finding his friends might be hard. Perhaps tomorrow, he and Glee could sneak into the town, which was in fact visible from here, a hive of stone. But for the moment neither of them had the energy. The last few days had been taxing. As night fell, they stretched out to rest on Duxy's resilient wing.

Duxy dozed off, and Chu could easily have fallen asleep, too, but Glee, energized by the gel, was in a talkative mood. She quizzed Chu about the Hibrane versus the Lobrane—seemingly the concept was unknown in Pepple. She told him more of her past, and about her travels across the stars. Over and over she returned to the topic of finding Groovy.

"Do you think he is really in this town?" she asked, staring at the moonlit spires and the lantern-hung walls. "Tell me everything you know."

"I've only seen him indirectly," said Chu. "I teeped him at a lab in San Francisco. He seemed hyper."

"This is Groovy! That's him!"

"And I picked up some information from Jayjay. Jayjay says Groovy sold out Earth to the Peng."

"Silly guy," she said, as if it were some harmless prank. "Maybe he doesn't understand the danger. Our aristos have never let our Peng get out of control. They—hush!" Her eyes widened and she pressed herself flat on Duxy's wing.

Now Chu heard the noises too: the jingle of an armed squad of men. A torch flickered at the far end of the apple orchard. For a crazy moment he thought the farmer had called in soldiers to root out the goose thief. But the soldiers weren't here to help the farmer. Far from it. They were here to burn down his house and his barn.

Terrible screams split the night and then, more terribly, broke off. The flames leapt up in an ecstasy of destruction. Duxy awoke, frightened and ready to flee. Glee grunted and gurgled in the Hrull tongue, convincing the big manta not to break cover.

"If we fly off wild in the dark, we maybe don't find this

town again," Glee said, once Duxy had settled down. "I am so sorry for those people on the farm."

"Me, too," said Chu, meaning it, and marveling that he'd learned to care about strangers. Life was painful and, in the same measure, sweet.

When the marauders had gone, he crept through the dark orchard to see if he could help the farmer and his family. But they didn't answer his low calls. Feeling like a wretched scavenger, he drank a crock of milk that he found in the sole remaining structure, a stone springhouse.

And then Glee wanted to talk a lot more. She was saying that maybe she really *was* ready to kick the gel. In the end, he didn't get properly to sleep until the moon was nearly down.

It was Duxy who woke them. "Eekle eekle!" she piped. Sitting up, Chu realized that once again he could read the Hrull's thoughts and understand her speech. "I hear Thuy whistling for me," she was saying. "But there are armed men where she is."

"Lazy eight!" exclaimed Chu, taking in the sharp sparkle of the ambient minds. "Jayjay must have played the harp. Hello, trees. Hello—" But now he teeped the body of the pathetic farmer in the lee of his ruined house, soot sifting across his young, snub face. "Yes, let's go," he resumed when he could. "This is a cruel place, Duxy. Glee and I will protect you while we're fetching Thuy. We have our teek back now. We can deflect any arrows they shoot."

Little Wobble was bumbling about in the apple trees, ineffectively trying to catch a magpie, shaking showers of petals to the ground.

"This reminds me of Pepple," said green Glee, the pale

petals spangling her hair. "People, plants, and animals. No right angles; no machines. Oh, that poor farm family. I wish I could go home, where I know what to expect."

"Maybe there's a way," said Chu. "We're gonna meet the others now." Perhaps he could already have teeped Thuy and Jayjay—but he felt shy. He'd wait to see them face-to-face.

They flapped over the medieval town and landed in a square before the cathedral door. Sure enough, Thuy and Jayjay were there, plus a Hibrane painter holding up his brush like a torch. And to Glee's great delight, Groovy the pitchfork was with them, too. Azaroth was waving a sword, not that the soldiers were putting up much of a fight. Groovy had done something to double most of them over.

As good as his word, Chu deflected the few laggardly crossbow bolts the troops managed to launch. Meanwhile, Thuy, Jayjay, the painter, and the pitchfork clambered into Duxy's mouth with them. Chu sat beside Glee on her bunk, and Groovy squeezed in beside Wobble. The pitchfork hadn't noticed Glee yet; he was focused on his plans for the coming jump.

Perhaps they could have squeezed Azaroth into Duxy's mouth, too, but he teeped that he was planning to stay in this town and start running the place. He teeked his final opponent onto his back and gestured theatrically, taking credit for Duxy's imminent departure.

Belly sagging, the laden Hrull lifted off. To make more room, she'd left her mouth ajar. The Hibrane painter—really too tall for this space—lay just inside her lips, peering out. His fingers twitched with the desire to draw the unfamiliar views of his land.

"That's Hieronymus Bosch," said Thuy, perched beside Jayjay on the bunk facing Chu and Glee. "The big artist? Can you even believe it? He just painted a picture onto the harp."

"I see the little horn dog has a new girlfriend," interrupted Jayjay, glaring at Chu.

"I'm sorry about what happened," said Chu. "It wasn't really my fault."

"That's what Thuy says, too," snapped Jayjay. "Hrull gel must be hot stuff."

"Oh, stop it now, Jayjay," said Thuy. "I'm pregnant with your daughter!"

"That's great!" said Chu, keeping his thoughts flat and shallow.

"No gel till we get back to Hrullwelt!" announced Duxy, expecting the pushers to start begging for their drug. "But it's fine if all of you come along. The more the merrier."

"The more pushers she bags, the more she gets paid, is what she means," said Thuy. "And, Chu, teep all of us your Knot, will you? Groovy's been keeping us here. Jayjay and I need to get back to where we started out."

Chu teeped around the Knot, which miffed the pitchfork just a little bit, as he'd wanted to be the go-to guy.

"Don't jump till I give you the say-so," rasped Groovy. "I figured out the best way to steer you home."

"Bossy as ever," said Glee.

"Hey, sweet thing!" sang out Groovy, finally seeing Glee. He writhed past Chu's knees to lean against the Pepple woman's side. "I was hopin' to find you. I knew that Lovva had steered you to Lobrane Earth." He touched her cheek with his tines.

"It's really you?" said Glee, running her green fingers along the pitchfork's twitching handle. "I like you better with a face."

"How'd you end up a pusher?"

"I had to leave Pepple in a big rush. It was the night after you and Lovva disappeared. For me, it's been ten long years."

"Thought you looked a little worn around the edges," said Groovy. "But, hey, that's no never mind. You're still my gal, aren't you? I can't be happy with just plain Lovva. Like tea without sugar. What do you say you come back home?"

"That's my biggest dream," said Glee, her three eyes glowing. But then her face clouded over. "Only—the aristos will execute me. You see, I killed Count Foppiano."

"That duke of earl who was always sniffin' around?" said Groovy with a chuckle. "Good job! Lovva and me are fixin' to disintegrate as many toffs as it takes to bring down the old order. We'll still be superpowered for a few hours after we get home. Hell, Glee, you come along with me and you'll be the godmother of the revolution!"

"I'd be sick for days and days, kicking the gel. But—maybe. You really don't mind that I've grown older than you?" She batted her third eye and gave Groovy a tremulous smile. "Perhaps Lovva will be glad for that. She was always jealous of my looks."

"You're still smart and nasty, right? That's what counts."

"We're ready to jump now," said Jayjay, growing impatient. "Were you going to suggest a route, Groovy?"

"Oh, I'm gonna help you big time," said the pitchfork. "By the time you get back to Yolla Bolly, you'll kick butt on those featherdusters no doubt."

"Well, I just hope you realize how tricky the navigation really is," fretted Jayjay. "If we blindly head out perpendicular to this brane's timeline, I bet we'll hit the Lobrane at, like, one thousand B.C."

"We'll piss into the wind for the whole trip," said Groovy confidently. "Fly against time's natural flow. I laid us down a waypoint to aim for." He teeped them an image of a whirlpool in the Planck sea.

Chu's skin prickled. He thought of cold water covering his

face and dragging him into the endless deep. "I don't like that," he said.

"A native aktual is the silp for this particular swirl," said Groovy. "Her name's Beth Gimel. She's in tight with Art Zed, the aktual who made the beanstalk for Jay. She's not gonna swallow you all the way down, Chu, you ain't on today's menu."

"But we are?" said Thuy.

"It's all part of the loony loop we ride," said Groovy. "You'll do us like we done you. Feller says, *mektoub*. It is written."

"What about you, Jeroen?" Jayjay asked the weathered artist. "Would you like us to set you down before we leave?"

"No, no, I want to experience it all," said Bosch. "The demonic pitchfork tells me we'll see heaven, hell, and the Almighty Himself."

"What you might call a figure of speech," buzzed Groovy. "Puttin' it in the man's own terms."

"I long to see the Last Things face-to-face," continued Bosch, tapping his upper lip with his dry, narrow tongue. "And if this be but sorcery and sham—why, that's a kind of secret wisdom, too. I'm glad to put my life into upheaval. As a youth I dreamed of being a penniless wanderer. My small success as a painter has imprisoned me for too long."

Each of them hoping for the best, they pushed—launching Duxy across the glistening Planck sea, her mouth stuffed with Chu, Thuy, Jayjay, Glee, Bosch, Groovy, and Wobble. Once they were en route, the pitchfork flew in front, leading the way.

This time, lazy eight was in effect for the whole trip, and the travelers stayed in close teep contact. In order to fight their way up the timestream, the humans and the Pepplese pushed without letup. Their massed motive force was even a bit more than required; the surplus teek energies swelled Duxie's pusher cone.

Drained by the steady effort, Chu grew numb and dreamy. To avoid sitting knee-to-knee with Jayjay, he'd lain down beside Bosch, the two of them staring out of Duxy's mouth as she skimmed across the Planck sea, following Groovy's lead.

Perhaps a half hour passed. A high range of light gray vapor had appeared on the horizon, occasionally flaring up in lofty streaks. Here and there, the surface below them seemed to boil, as if stirred by powerful eddies. And now a prodigious bubble shot up from the sea directly below Duxy, accompanied by a spout of spume.

"Stop pushing!" teeped the manta to her crew. "I want to turn aside."

"Not now," responded Groovy from up ahead. "We're just gettin' good."

"He's crazy!" teeped Duxy. "He'll kill us all!"

Worn and bewildered as they were, the crew ceased their efforts. Surely it would be all right to drift for a bit and catch their bearings. But, as it happened, their cessation of effort made no difference. A fierce wind was driving them toward the anomalous zone ahead. And when Duxy tried to fight the gale, its true force become apparent. Her wind-whipped wings fluttered like ineffectual rags.

And so they continued bowling along in Groovy's wake. As always, the interbrane air glowed, and a still brighter illumination rose from the roiled sea, casting uncanny highlights on the lean features of the weathered man at Chu's side. Teeping through Bosch's eyes, Chu tasted the treasure trove of tint and shape that the artist saw.

The thin air thrilled steadily with a high-pitched vibration. The ocean's surface was beginning to tilt, as if they were flying downhill. This made the gray band along the horizon loom that much higher, like a gigantic cataract rolling into the sea, ranging to both sides as far as Chu could see.

Crosswise currents had begun ripping the sea to clotted foam. Through the seething rents, Chu could glimpse a chaos of flitting beings: the subbies. Some looked like men with the heads of birds, some like fish with human legs, all of them racing along half-submerged, pacing the travelers.

"Look out for them," warned Thuy.

"We have to jump away from here!" teeped Duxy once again.

"Wait!" blasted Groovy. "We're almost there."

Bosch only stared—fascinated, fatalistic, slightly smiling. Perhaps for him it was as if he were already dead.

And now, directly ahead of them, the ocean surface curved very sharply down, disappearing into darkness. With an effort Chu understood. They were dots at the edge of a maelstrom that was hundreds of miles across.

Duxy let out an anguished squeal; she opened wide her mouth and spit out her passengers, forcing them forward with her cheeks. Bosch, Thuy, and Jayjay went first. Chu managed to hook his feet onto Duxy's jaw for a moment, but little Wobble tugged him loose and let him drop after the others. The Hrull may well have meant to keep Glee, but, beckoned on by the hovering pitchfork, she gathered the courage to leap out, too.

As Chu hit the Planck sea, his immediate fear was of an attack by the subbies. But—as a small blessing—these creatures were keeping clear of the currents at the whirlpool's verge. Looking around, he saw Bosch, Thuy, and Jayjay ahead of him, with Glee and the reckless pitchfork floating behind. Duxy hung above them, fighting the hurricane wind as Wobble nestled himself into her mouth.

"Hrullwelt's thataway!" called Groovy, pointing his tines. Lightened of her main load, and empowered by the energies stored in her teeker cone, the manta sped off like a thunderbolt.

With an abrupt lurch, Chu passed over the maelstrom's lip and rushed headlong into the abyss. He felt the sickening sweep of descent—but then the sense of falling ceased. Looking around, he saw that the rotational forces had taken over; he was circling around an immense funnel, unfathomable in depth, with glassy sides that spun with bewildering rapidity, bearing him along. It was a scene of terrible grandeur.

Round and round the six companions swept—not with any uniform movement—but in dizzying swings and jerks that sent them sometimes only a few hundred yards, sometimes several miles, and sometimes through a full circuit of the kingdom-sized whirl.

For the moment, they were too drained to think of fighting their way upward against the maelstrom's currents, or through the cyclone winds that filled its core. And so the six coasted on, roughly grouped.

Visible within the glowing walls were the innermost recesses of the subdimensional world, alive with forms that grew the more baroque the greater the depth beneath the Planck sea's proper surface.

The high, chiming sound within the immense spindle had taken on the quality of heraldic music. Chu formed a mental image of the whirlpool as the bell of an otherworldly trumpet whose mouthpiece lay in an infinitely distant land below. Gabriel's trump. And now, within his mind, the music segued into speech. The maelstrom's resident spirit was talking to him.

"I'm Beth Gimel. An aktual. Our world is filled with infinities of all sizes. In my fireplace, the burning sticks have alef-null branchings, but the subtler flames have alef-one forks. The wood and fire merges into alef-two eddies of smoke. Groovy asked me to reach through the subdimensions to make a path to infinity."

Chu shut out the bewildering farrago and shifted his focus to the subdimensional world behind the maelstrom walls. With Bosch at his side he saw: a flying fish with a village on her back, a sow in nun's garb, a demon with the screaming mouth of a cat, and a squalling King Bagpipe perched on a millstone with a flag. As a continuing benison, the subbies weren't attacking. The living force of the maelstrom was keeping them away.

"We have to go home, Jayjay," called Thuy. "Think of the baby."

"Which way is it, Groovy?" yelled Jayjay. He paddled over and grabbed the pitchfork's handle with his hands. "I'll break you in half, you bastard."

"We ain't done yet," said the pitchfork with a rough chortle. He executed a quick, vicious flip that catapulted Jayjay far out from the maelstrom's glassy slope. With snickersnack movements too quick to follow, he tossed Thuy and then Bosch in Jayjay's wake. Glee watched impassively, and Chu paddled away as quickly as he could—not that the pitchfork was coming after him.

The funnel of winds whirled Bosch, Thuy, and Jayjay toward the central axis; ever tinier, they plummeted into the profundities below. A momentary wobble in the wall gave Chu a glimpse of the full length of the tube. The funnel's inconceivably distant nether terminus was marked by a blazing triangle of white light.

Curling his twin tines, Groovy clawed the air in exultation, "Yee-haw! You ready, Glee honey?"

"I am."

"What about me?" called Chu over the unearthly music.

"Jayjay will be back directly."

Glee sat astride Groovy like a witch on a broom. He flattened his tines and formed them into a rudder. Propelling himself counter to the whirlpool's currents, the pitchfork carved a steep gyre up the maelstrom's slope, shooting high into the air. At the last instant, he shifted his shape back to Pepplese form; he became a lanky, green, three-eyed hillbilly.

And then Glee and Groovy were gone.

So now it was just Chu and the maelstrom. He drifted for an indeterminate period of time, ever deeper, mesmerized by the chiming song that sometimes segued into the voice of the maelstrom's aktual. Beth.

He was absorbing her notions about the alefs, which were transfinite numbers lying beyond simple infinity. Beyond the glassy walls Chu seemed to see a great white cuttlefish with alef-seven arms. Below it swayed a primeval sea cucumber, seining the currents with alef-eighteen fronds.

"We're in the subdimensional zone for true," said Beth Gimel. "With the reciprocals of alef-ninety, alef-billion, alef-alef-ten and more. Levels below levels, all the way down. The transfinite numbers are as quirky and individualistic as the finite integers. The march of alefs is an inexhaustible source of surprise. Yes, I know it's too much for you. But Thuy and Jay-jay understand."

As his helical descent continued, Chu's mind began feeling lighter than ever before, more agile. Perhaps he was a zedhead now, capable of teeking ten tridecillion atoms in a row. But what use was that, if he was stuck between the branes forever? Although he felt rested enough to attempt flying away, he had no idea which direction led home.

He recalled an incident from Thuy's metanovel, *Wheenk,*

about how she'd made her own way back from the interbrane. She'd reached out with her mind and found the warm pulse of the one who loved her: Jayjay.

But Chu had nobody who cared for him that way. His parents were fond of him, sure, but they were busy with their own lives and, truth be told, he was a bit of a burden. As for Bixie—probably they'd never be more than friends. He was a loner. He was doomed.

But all the while, the whirlpool was changing. The sides of the vast funnel became less steep, the gyrations of the whirl less violent. The bottom of the gulf rose and, for a wonder, the maelstrom flattened out. Beth Gimel was gone.

A moment passed. A last fat bubble burbled from the depths, bearing within it—a glistening crow. He cawed, rose into the air, and circled Chu. A subbie?

"Don't worry," teeped the apparition in a friendly tone. "It's me, Jayjay. I'm still in aktualized form."

"I'm totally lost," said Chu. "Please don't be mad at me anymore."

"No matter. Never mind. Jeroen and Thuy and I have done so many things since then. But we're not finished. You have to help us save Earth from the Peng. I want to spray that Hrull reset rune onto every atom of Earth. I'll finish the job I tried to do before. It'll be easy for me now. I can think endlessly fast."

"Endlessly fast," said Chu, almost able to smile. "I'm a zedhead, so Jayjay is an aktual. Always a step ahead."

The crow feathered his wings and hovered above Chu, watching him with bead-bright eyes. "There's one catch," he teeped. "With all the jumping around, I've forgotten the details of the reset rune. I probably could have gotten it from someone in Alefville, but I didn't think of that. And I'd rather not go back up there now. Do you remember it?"

"Um—no," said Chu looking into himself. "But maybe we could figure it out. When you say you can think endlessly fast—does that mean you can see the end of every search?"

"That's a good way to put it," said Jayjay. "Like, when I want to change my shape, I scan through all the possible ways to reprogram my atoms—and I find the best one."

"Everything is always easy for you," said Chu enviously

"Can you help me or not?" said Jayjay, with an impatient swoop at Chu's head. "Or would you rather stay here alone?"

Something sharp nicked Chu's leg. A fish holding an ax. With the maelstrom gone, the subbies were closing in. Quickly he lifted himself into the air. "I'm ready. I can help. Don't we have to wait for Thuy?"

"I'm hoping she's gonna meet me at the cabin. We left Alefville in a rush. Just follow me."

The two touched down by the cottage in Yolla Bolly, Jayjay in crow form, and Chu still wearing the purple pants and green T-shirt he'd bought on Valencia Street—two days ago? He wasn't the least bit wet. After all, the Planck sea wasn't really water.

CHAPTER 18

TRANSFINITE

The pink Peng McMansions were still in place, and the redwood branches were swaying like metronomes. Fortunately it was nighttime. Suller, Gretta, Kakar, and Floofy were asleep. Chu took a seat on the cottage's moonlit porch steps.

While Jayjay flapped around the clearing, checking things out, Chu teeped across the planet. The viral Peng runes had been a complete success. Squawky tulpas were everywhere, riding high, strutting and pecking, killing off the mammals one by one. In contrast, nature's gnarl-deprived silps were stereotyped, stiff, sullen. The clouds, the ocean, the air—everything was as fake and lame as a low-grade virtual reality.

As for the human mindweb, the U.S. teep broadcasts were limited to ads for the Homesteady party and religious broadcasts from the Crown of Creation Church. And the media situation was no better in other lands. Each nation's rulers had thrown in their lot with the triumphant Peng. Creativity didn't matter to the politicos. Docility and predictability were preferred.

Meanwhile, deep below the planet's surface, Gaia was fiercely stoking her volcanoes, preparing an apocalyptic rain of fire.

"We need to get that reset rune happening pronto," teeped Jayjay, alighting on Chu's shoulder, his crow claws prickly against the boy's skin.

"Should be easy," responded Chu. "As long as you're infinitely fast, you can just zap every atom on the planet with any old reset rune. And to find one of those—" His voice trailed off as he began crafting a plan.

Just then Thuy appeared on the cottage's porch, growing from a dot in the air, glowing with power, ending up with her usual shape, gently lit by the moon. "Hey! I'm glad you guys are here." She looked a little sweaty and upset. "That's you on Chu's shoulder, right, Jayjay? Stop looking like a crow. You don't want to get stuck that way."

Flexing his body like putty, Jayjay returned to his accustomed form, hopping from Chu's shoulder to stand on the porch. He looked upbeat and excited, like he'd been on a long vacation. Stepping forward, he gave Thuy a hug and a kiss.

"Safe at last," she said, brushing back a damp strand of hair that had come loose from her pigtails. "It was rough getting away from Alefville." Suddenly she noticed the silhouette of the Bosch house. "My God, those four Peng are still here? Why haven't you two cast the reset rune?"

"We, uh, don't happen to have a copy of it," said Jayjay. "But Chu's gonna help me search one out."

"Hurry! Our aktualization will wear off soon."

"It's probably best not to have viral runes at all," said Chu, still working out the details of how to orchestrate the search.

"Over time, they might interfere with matter's ongoing quantum computations."

In the nest, one of the Peng let out a sleepy chirp.

"Get to the frikkin' point," hissed Thuy. "This has to end."

"Okay, then," said Chu, feeling glad, after all, that he wasn't married to her. "I'll set Jayjay up for a flat-out search through the infinite space of all the possible runes." With rapid mental moves, he teeped his friend a crisp set of requirements for the type of quantum computation he should be searching for.

"I'm starting now," said Jayjay, even as he absorbed the specification. And then, after practically no time at all, he added, "I'm done." He was displaying a grid of the million best candidates he'd found.

"Wow," said Chu.

"Go ahead and pick one," said Jayjay. "And I'll blast it all over Earth."

"Let's do one more step first," said Chu, even though he knew this would irritate Thuy. "Simulate each of these million guys for infinitely many years, just to weed out any of them that might ever break down or turn rogue."

"Done again," said Jayjay, displaying the best behaved of the reset runes. Lest they lose the prize, Chu fixed a copy in his own mind.

As he did this, he heard a definite squawk from the dark nest. The Peng were awake.

"You waited too long!" cried Thuy. "Here they come!" Suller and Gretta were halfway across the clearing. A femtoray drilled through the gloom.

"Take this, shit-birds," said Jayjay. With a casual gesture of his aktualized mind, he put the reset rune into every atom on Earth. Just like that. The Peng were gone, all of them. Gaia and the silps sang with joy.

"We're done!" whooped Thuy. "A free world for our baby!"

But then, with a kind of sizzle, all the gnarl on the ranch was gone again. Suller and Gretta were just where they'd been before, with Kakar and Floofy climbing down from the nest behind them.

Wanting to use his zedhead power at least once, Chu warbled the reset rune onto the ten tridecillion atoms of Yolla Bolly. Though it was an effort for him, it worked—but not for long. After a single beat of calm, the Peng were back yet again.

"Let me do it," said Jayjay. "Less sweat for me." He reset the Yolla Bolly atoms, the Peng went away—and once more returned. Jayjay went into mental overdrive, pulsing the reset rune onto every single Yolla Bolly atom every single second. Suller, Gretta, Kakar, and Floofy became ghostly stop-action figures, ever so slowly continuing their ineluctable approach, growing closer with each reincarnation.

Teeping the outer world, Chu found that the problem was limited to the Yolla Bolly ranch. Everywhere else on Earth, the Peng were gone for good. Only on Jayjay and Thuy's settlement did the tulpas keep coming back. There was some ongoing contamination by viral Peng runes here.

"It's like I'm pumping up a leaky raft in a lake of piss," complained Jayjay. "Where's the leak, Chu?"

By cranking up his mind's speed, Chu could view the world as if in slow motion. Now Jayjay cleared the ranch, now the Peng came back. Dialing his mental clock cycle higher and higher, Chu became able to track the spread of the viral runes that kept creating Suller's family. The waves of contamination were spreading out from Thuy and Jayjay's house. The three went inside the cabin.

Focusing even harder, Chu perceived that the infection was coming from beneath a certain spot on the living room floor—oozing up from the endlessly vast spaces of the subdimensions.

Suddenly a beak thrust up from the planks. An ostrichlike

figure grew to ceiling height, undulated her neck and cooed just once, very softly. A little ruff of fuzz adorned the top of her eyeless head.

"The Pekklet!" screamed Thuy. "Look out, Jayjay!"

But already the Pekklet had shot out tendrils to quantum entangle with Jayjay's flesh, once again snaring his will. He tottered across the room and crumpled to the floor.

"No!" shrieked Thuy. "No, no, no!"

Her mouth grew larger with each yell; her jaws pushed forward into a disturbing, inhuman shape. She was shape-shifting her head into a weapon of attack. The lower part of her pert face morphed into a toothy, elongated snout—the jaws of a dragon. Blood-red talons sprouted from her fingertips.

The Pekklet opened her blunt beak, hissing a warning. She puffed a fresh tangle of controller tendrils toward Thuy—who countered with an adroit burst of flame. Roaring defiance, Thuy lunged forward and sank her talons into the bully-bird's blackened chest. Widening her jaws, she bit off the Pekklet's head—and the struggle was over.

In the end, the Pekklet was mere flesh and blood. Eager to help, Chu teeked every last one of the dead creature's atoms asunder, wiping out her quantum connections, destroying her stash of viral runes.

Thuy leaned over Jayjay, murmuring to him. Seeing her dragon jaws, he lifted his hands as if in fear—but, no, he was weakly laughing, still stunned, but definitely himself again. With a musical growl, Thuy restored her head and hands to their usual form.

Victory? Not quite. For while the three humans had been focused on the Pekklet agent, a stray viralized atom had given the Yolla Bolly tulpas one last chance. Suller was standing in the cabin door, beak leveled, ready to drill them with femtorays.

Jayjay prepared to teek the reset rune across the ranch for

once and for all. But he was going to take another couple of seconds to fully get it together. Someone had to buy the humans a tiny bit more time.

Not letting himself think too deeply about what he was doing, Chu ran straight toward Suller, coming in under the deadly beak. He tackled the musty fowl and knocked him onto the porch floor. The two rolled down the steps onto the dirt, wrestling. With a quick twitch of his stubby wings, bony Suller flipped Chu onto his back. He cocked his deadly beak and—

Kakar pushed in between them, talking very fast. "Let me take care of him, Dad. I've got a thing going with this geek."

But even as Kakar said this, the Peng were beginning to waver and droop. Taylor jets fanned from Suller, Gretta, Floofy, and Kakar. Jayjay had cast the reset rune one last time.

"I had a feeling you'd win, Chu," said Kakar, on the point of melting away. "It wouldn't have helped us if Dad had killed you. I'm glad I saved you. But, please, can you do the same for Floofy and me? Ask your friends to make meat bodies for us. We'll be pals. And we'll share our flight lice with you."

"Can we?" said Chu to the others. "I don't have so many friends, you know."

"Make more Peng?" said Jayjay. "Get real, Chu."

"Kakar's smart," said Chu. "And Floofy is weird. Basically they're artists. Please?"

"Oh—why not," said Thuy. "I can use them in *Hive Mind*. They're like a symbol for you and me, Jayjay."

So Thuy used the last pulse of her fading infinitistic powers to create meat bodies for Kakar and Floofy—drawing on her all-too-clear memories of the rune that had repeatedly brought the Peng family back to the ranch.

The two birds were exultant and grateful. "We're here for real," trilled Kakar, shaping the words with his larynx. "At last."

"Let's make a post-digital magpie nest," twittered Floofy. "We'll tangle old-tech scraps into a big hollow ball."

"Not here, you won't," said Jayjay. "It's our honeymoon time. We're gonna get it right. Go home, Chu, and take the birds with you."

Chu settled back into his father Ond's and mother Nektar's adjoining homes in San Francisco. Kittie steered Floofy to a trove of piezoplastic, and the Peng built a marvelously garish nest on Nektar's roof.

Nature worldwide was gnarly and lively and free of tulpas. And Gaia stopped muttering about volcanoes. Jayjay, Thuy, and Chu had saved the world once again.

On the national scene, Dick Too Dibbs apologized and, when that wasn't enough, stepped down from the presidency. The same pattern happened worldwide. The dinosaur era of oligarchic rule had reached an end. The few rulers who didn't have the sense to abdicate were forcibly evicted, or worse.

Via a rapid series of teep referendums, nation after nation adopted new constitutions. No more presidents, no more senates, no more parliaments. From now on, countries would rule themselves via realtime public consensus.

Something subtler than the blunt instrument of majority rule came into sway. Laws became dynamically tuned compromises, continually adapting to social change. The post-digital body politic was as homeostatic and self-healing as the body of a living animal. It was odd to think that for so many millennia, people had lived in societies that were like crude, awkward machines.

The public's disapproval of Thuy was forgotten in the

excitement about her biting off the Pekklet's head. Sure she'd had sex with Chu, but it hadn't really been her fault. And now she was pregnant with her husband's daughter, which tapped a deep well of sympathy. She was a regular on *Founders* again.

In a bloom of self-confidence, Thuy published her topical metanovel, *Hive Mind,* via Metotem Metabooks. The number of access permissions sold was decent, if not overwhelming. With endless amounts of unmediated real-life action to teep, it was hard to push metanovels.

Always one for productizing things, Ond started a company with Chu, called Lutter-Lundquist Flight Lice, Inc. They were breeding and selling flight lice, and, as a value-added feature, Ond devised a method by which you could tune your flight lice not only to make you weightless, but also to propel you in whatever direction you chose.

As more and more people acquired the ability to zip through the air, flying became quite the new sport. In a way, there was no real reason to fly, given that everyone could teleport—but people enjoyed having the classic dream come true. Lutter-Lundquist Flight Lice was doing very well.

The popularity of flight lice was also good for Kakar and Floofy—it made them seem like valuable resources instead of like prisoners of war from a failed invasion.

The two became regular comic relief characters on *Founders*. Kakar had some small success marketing the bas-relief sculptures he pecked out from stone, while Floofy got involved in fashion design—in the coming season, there would be flocks of runway models gotten up like two-toed alien rhea birds.

Chu still wondered about the details of Thuy's and Jayjay's adventures at the bottom of the maelstrom, but, after all they'd been through together, he didn't like to pester them. So he enlisted Bixie to help.

Bixie proposed that she and Chu should take the expectant

parents for a pleasure flight along the Lost Coast of Northern California.

"Tell us everything that happened while you and Jayjay were aktualized," said Bixie to Thuy once they were underway—with *Founders* sponsors' ads trailing in their wake like blimps.

"I'm kind of surprised nobody asked me about this before," said Thuy in a noncommittal tone.

"They're all scared of you!" said Bixie with an elfin smile.

"But not you, huh?" The summer air fluttered the loose gown that Thuy wore over her growing belly.

"Not me. Come on and tell us the dramatic details."

"I've been thinking I should save those for my third metanovel," said Thuy. "If I don't give everything away in advance, I might finally get some good sales numbers."

"Oh just go ahead, Thuy," urged Jayjay. "You've been complaining about having to write a third metanovel in the same series. You'd do better to get this out of the way and write about something completely different for your next one."

"Please?" put in Bixie. "Our viewers will love you."

"Oh—all right," said Thuy. "Why not. I'll teep it to you as I remember it." And with that she began.

So, okay, the alien pitchfork flings Jayjay, Jeroen Bosch, and me into the core of this endless whirlpool. We're falling down through the subdimensions. I'm Dorothy in the twister, Alice in the rabbit hole, a drifting blossom petal.

Near the end, I start seeing this converging forest of bright lines ahead, and the perspective kind of flips. So it's like I'm staring up through a grove of redwoods, with the trunks all angling toward a glowing cloud. And the lines are Earth's lazy eight memory axes, you understand, with teep signals flickering up and down like beads on wires—and all the lines meet at infinity, which is what's inside that cloud.

Ordinarily when we teep a signal off the router at infinity, it's a hairpin turn, a hiccup, a click of static—you zoom up, you zoom down, and you don't see squat. But now we're floating toward infinity like gnats on a summer breeze. I'm hearing this faint fractal hiss from the glowing haze, an intricate buzz as if every silp in the world is whispering to me at once.

We ooze out of the tip-ass pointy end of the endless vortex funnel and we're right in the middle of the bright cloud. I grab hold of the cloud stuff with both hands and rip a hole in it; it has a scrunchy texture like cotton candy. Jeroen is real excited, he's yelling that we're at God's throne, but that's not exactly what we find.

What's nestled inside the hole is infinity. It's not a point like some people say, and it's not a triangle like the way Jeroen likes to draw God. It looks like a smooth figure eight, a fancy crystal all full of reflections and bright-line curves. I can feel the heavy vibe of all the teep signals bouncing off it.

We three stare at the infinite eight for a little while, and its sound is percolating into our minds and bodies. It's like a magic amulet, it's teaching us how to think endless thoughts.

Jayjay laughs all of a sudden, and he counts through all the numbers from zero to the top. Every one of them. Out loud. And then turns around and counts all the way back down. It's impossible, but I hear it happen.

Jeroen isn't satisfied—he's still wanting to find a golden throne—so he starts clawing at the cloud, digging through to this open space on the other side. If I'd been the one to pop through first, we might have seen a Jack and the Beanstalk castle and a mountain range; and if it had been Jayjay, we probably would have seen a San Francisco–style sprawl.

But it's Jeroen who gets through the cloud first, and the scene crystallizes into showing us his particular way of looking at things—a sky-high Bosch-style triptych with a dog-pile of weird creatures on the clouds in front of the panels, freaky wrigglers jumping in and out of the paintings whenever they like. Jeroen is riding high, he's pointing his brush at the giant triptych—he's calling out commands and seeing things change.

While Jayjay and I are getting our bearings, a little beast comes writhing out after us through the hole we made in the cloud. She says she's Beth Gimel, the resident spirit of the maelstrom that funneled us here. We're seeing Beth as a striped badger with a corkscrew nose—like a Jabberwocky slithy tove.

She's all, "Welcome to Alefville!"

And I go, "This doesn't look like any kind of ville at all, it looks like worms crawling around a billboard."

And then Beth explains that because Alefville is an infinite dimensional space, we lower-type beings are always going to see it in terms of things we expect to see.

It hits me that Jeroen's giant triptych is a variation on his *Garden of Earthly Delights,* with an Eden on the left, a creepy scene of frantic humpers in middle, and Hell on the right. That's Jeroen's natural way of organizing things—from Eden to Earth to Hell. History running downhill.

"But really it's a map of what you have to do," says Beth Gimel, who's reading my mind. "That's Pengö on the left, see, and Pepple in the middle, and the Hrullwelt on the right."

I'm like, "What do you mean, *do?* Aren't we in heaven? Can't we relax?"

"No," says Beth, and then she starts talking about how we have to bring lazy eight to all three of those alien worlds, and how we then have to bring aktualization to Pepple.

Jayjay is into this, he's gloating over the knotty logic loops, but I'm finding it hard to focus, as my body feels double-jointed and, frankly, I'm worried about the baby. My hands keep folding around and turning inside out, for instance, and when I smile, I can feel the whole shape of my head deform.

Beth picks up on this, and she promises me the baby is going to be fine, because my essential core will go back to being the same, once the aktualization wears off, which is going to be sooner than we expect. She says she's sorry about listing all those tasks for us, but that, if we wave with it, we can have some fun.

Around then I notice that the air is filled with sweet music. No sooner do I wish I could play along, then—*whammo*—I'm holding a vibby electric guitar just like Tawny Krush has.

"You'll be the one to unfurl lazy eight for Pepple!" says Jayjay. "You'll be their mythic hero."

"But Pepple already *has* lazy eight," I point out.

"Yeah, yeah," says Jayjay. "But they got it from you. You'll be showing up there a thousand years ago."

So I'm, like, *oookay,* I can do that. And to make my manifestation the heavier and more memorable, I let my head get all long and toothy and dragon-shaped. Jeroen is scared of me now, and he makes the sign of the triangle. I puff a little fire at him just to hear him yell.

"Don't forget that one of you is supposed to unfurl Pengö and the Hrullwelt, too," says Beth. "On the left and the right. Only for those guys, it'll be a *million* years into the past instead of a thousand."

"I definitely don't want to help the Peng or the Hrull," I say, and Jayjay doesn't want to either. So that puts Bosch on the spot, not that he exactly understands what any of this is about. But Beth works with him for a minute, and he turns himself into a big, fat bagpipe, which totally cracks me up.

The Bosch bag poots off toward the giant triptych, blasting lazy eight into the left panel for Pengö—*sqwooonk!* And then he jets over to the right panel for the Hrullwelt—*sqwakooonk!*

"Go on now, Thuy," urges Beth, so I fly into that central panel, and, wow, I'm in their world for a minute, I'm a hovering dragon-headed woman with a magic guitar. I get that Lost Chord going on my strings, and as soon as they hear it, the Pepple people are wigging out.

When I land back at our little starting point by the hole in the cloud, Jayjay turns himself into a crow, and he flies into the Pepple panel where I've just been, but for him, it's only ten years ago. And instead of playing music or singing a song, he's beating his wings in this weird way that draws Beth Gimel along after him, with her curly snout stretching out forever to become a magic tornado.

The next thing I know, Jayjay and Beth have vacuumed Groovy and Lovva out of Pepple, and they're standing beside us, all green and smelly and three-eyed, and they have no frikkin' clue what's going on. It's nice to be paying them back this way—to have me and Jayjay and Jeroen be the ones with all the secrets, us coming on all sly and knowing and meaningful, while these goobs are trying to figure out what's up.

So we feed them their stories about how they're supposed to bring lazy eight and aktualization to Earth, and we send them on their way, into our past. I'm starting to feel confused, but Jayjay has it clear in his mind, and he says we're about done.

Jeroen flies for home at this point, making a detour through the Lobrane on his way, because he's curious to see what he calls "the land of the gnomes." And Jayjay flies back into the interbrane to fetch Chu. Me, I head for Yolla Bolly, and when I get there—like everyone already knows—I meet Chu and Jayjay, and we save the world.

Thuy fell silent. Her tale was told.

"It's all tangled up," protested Chu, who was brooding about the muddled chain of cause and effect. "It doesn't make enough sense."

"It's what it is," said Thuy. "And now that I've told you this end part, I'm really not gonna bother writing that third metanovel the way I planned. Everyone can teep in to hear what I just said. This part of my story's over right now, just as it is. I'm ready for something fresh. Like having our baby."

"Vibby," said Jayjay. "A new life!"